Colin Forbes writes a novel each year. For many years he has earned his living solely as a full-time writer. He lives well away from London in the countryside. An international bestseller, each book has been published worldwide. Colin Forbes is translated into thirty languages.

He has explored most of Western Europe, the East and West coasts of America, and has visited Africa and Asia. All the locations in his novels are described from personal experience.

Surveys have confirmed that his readership is divided almost equally between men and women.

COLIN FORBES

RHINOCEROS

POCKET
BOOKS
LONDON · SYDNEY · NEW YORK · TOKYO · SINGAPORE · TORONTO

First published in Great Britain by Simon & Schuster UK Ltd, 2000
This edition first published by Pocket Books, 2001
An imprint of Simon & Schuster UK Ltd
A Viacom Company

5 7 9 10 8 6

Simon & Schuster UK Ltd
Africa House
64-78 Kingsway
London WC2B 6AH

Simon & Schuster Australia
Sydney

A CIP catalogue record for this book is available
from the British Library

Typeset by Palimpsest Book Production Ltd,
Polmont, Stirlingshire
Printed and bound in Great Britain by
Cox & Wyman Ltd, Reading, Berkshire

Author's Note

All the characters portrayed are creatures of the author's imagination and bear no relationship to any living person. Equally, Berg Island is an invention and bears no relationship to any existing island.

For

IAN S. CHAPMAN

Prologue

The first strange event was when Bob Newman, foreign correspondent, arrived at Heathrow to meet the American guest. He showed his SIS folder to pass through the formalities. Standing by the carousel, he checked the photo sent from Washington. On the back was a written description.

Six feet one tall, weight 190 lbs, clean-shaven, thirty-five years old. Newman spotted Mark Wendover at once among the crowd waiting for their baggage. Coming up behind him, he laid a hand on his shoulder.

'Welcome, Mr Wendover . . .'

The American, built like a quarterback, reacted in a most unexpected way. As he swung swiftly round, Newman saw his right hand stiffen in the gesture of a potential karate chop. Newman spoke quickly.

'I'm Bob Newman, here to meet you. Didn't they tell you? We did send a message.'

'Great to see you. Thanks for coming. May I call you Bob?'

'Of course.'

'Then I'm Mark. Sorry if I startled you. Haven't had any sleep for over twenty hours.'

'Better watch the carousel . . .'

'You're right. And here comes my bag . . .'

They were in Newman's car, driving into London, sitting next to each other when Newman asked the question.

And if I startled you, he thought, you certainly startled me. You were on the verge of launching an attack. Why?

'We're not quite sure what your status is. Cord Dillon, the Deputy Director of the CIA, was in a rush when he phoned and a bit vague about you.'

'I'm vague myself about what to do next. I was with the CIA for five years. It was OK, but too much paperwork for my liking. I did fieldwork too,' he added quickly. 'Shot a saboteur in Denver once. Left the outfit – the Company as some of the oldsters still call it – and set up a private detective agency. That did well – I've left behind a staff of twenty.' He looked at Newman and grinned, but the grin did not extend to his cold blue eyes. 'But that isn't why I'm here.'

'I gather you're here because you have information about the recent suicide of Jason Schulz, top aide to the Secretary of State.'

'Except it wasn't suicide,' Wendover rapped back. 'It was cold-blooded murder, amateurishly disguised to look like suicide.'

Why, Newman was asking himself, don't I feel comfortable with this guy? And why am I sure he's nervous? The traffic had temporarily stopped the car and he looked straight at his passenger.

Wendover had corn-coloured hair, cut very short, a handsome strong face of the type which would appeal to a lot of women. His long nose was broken, which seemed to add to his good looks. He had a wide determined mouth and just enough jaw to suggest strength without aggression.

'If it was an amateurish-seeming job, why is it being called suicide?'

'That's the mystery. The FBI was hauled off the case. Its chief is raging – and mystified. Schulz was supposed to have driven to a park in Washington, walked into a copse, leaned against the trunk of a tree, taken out a gun and blown the side of his head off. He was a very important man in the State Department.'

'So what's wrong?' Newman prodded as the traffic moved again.

'First, Jason's wife swears her husband never owned a gun – and we believe her. The weapon, a Smith & Wesson revolver, had the serial number filed off. So, impossible to trace where it came from. Second, he was found slumped at the foot of the tree, still holding the gun. The trouble is, the way his fingers were clutching the gun didn't seem right. More like someone had placed his fingers there after he was shot. Third, no trace of his car in the park. They found it parked in his usual slot in an underground garage.'

'With all that evidence, who on earth called off the FBI?'

'We don't know. It's pretty mysterious.'

'We've booked you a room at the Ritz. If it's all right by you I'll call later and take you out to dinner. Would seven be too early?'

'Just give me time to take a shower. Seven is fine . . .'

The conversation lapsed until Newman was pulling up outside the Ritz. Before Wendover grabbed his bag he turned to Newman and asked the question.

'Jason Schulz died five days ago. I gather Cord sent me over because Tweed is worried. Right?'

'We can talk about that over dinner.'

He watched Wendover, carrying a heavy bag, leap up the steps to the hotel like a ten-year-old. That doesn't look to be a man who hasn't slept for twenty hours, he thought.

In time sequence the second event occurred earlier the same day. Newman's chief, Tweed, Deputy Director of the SIS, had driven down to East Sussex at the invitation

3

of an old friend, Lord Barford. He had taken Paula Grey, his assistant, with him.

It was late on a brilliant sunny afternoon as he drove between the open wrought-iron gates and into the Barford estate. Paula, seated beside Tweed, gazed at the spacious parkland. The ruler-straight drive extended across to a large, distant Elizabethan mansion. The sun had shone first after lunch and there were still traces of a heavy frost, islands of white on the beautiful lawn, which was an intense green.

'You've known Lord Barford for a long time, I gather?' she remarked.

'When I first joined the SIS he was in command of Special Branch. In those days we found them very cooperative. None of the bitter and stupid rivalry there is between the two outfits today. He's one of the old school. Very wealthy but he felt he had to serve his country. He's very shrewd.'

'Looks like quite a party,' she commented as they drew closer to the terrace running along the front of the mansion. An assortment of expensive cars were parked below the terrace. She counted a Porsche, four Mercedes, a Lamborghini, five Audis and two Rolls-Royces.

As they mounted the steps one of the massive double doors at the entrance opened. A tall man who had to be in his seventies came out with a warm smile. Despite being near the end of March, a bitter north wind blew along the terrace.

'Lord Barford,' Tweed whispered.

Their host had a long head with a beaked nose, lively grey eyes which, Paula thought, missed very little. Wearing a velvet smoking jacket, he advanced towards them.

'Welcome to Barford Manor. It's been too long, Tweed. Who is your delightful companion?'

'Meet Paula Grey, my right arm.'

'I'm pleased to meet you, Lord Barford,' she said as she

4

shook his extended hand. 'If you don't mind my saying so, it's Arctic on this terrace and you're not wearing a coat.'

'Used to it, my dear. I was once shooting bear in Finland when the temperature had gone off the thermometer. Come in, come in.'

He studied Paula, saw an attractive woman in her thirties with a mane of glossy black hair, fine-boned features and a stubborn chin. He went on talking as they entered a large hall and a butler took their coats.

'You must be remarkably efficient and self-controlled to work for this young tyrant.'

'Young?' Tweed laughed. 'Your eyesight must be going.'

Barford stared at Tweed. He saw a man of medium height and uncertain age, well-built without any sign of a paunch and wearing horn-rimmed glasses. He was the man you passed in the street without noticing him, a characteristic he had found useful in his profession.

They were ushered into a large drawing room, luxuriously furnished but with great taste. A number of people seated with drinks on sofas and armchairs turned to look at the new arrivals.

'Introductions,' Barford announced. 'I told you Tweed was coming,' he began. 'The attractive young lady he has brought for my delight is his personal assistant, Miss Paula Grey. Now, this is Lance, my eldest son.'

A forty-year-old, still clad in riding gear, dragged himself up slowly. His arrogant face was long and lean but without his father's grace. Clean-shaven, he spoke in an extreme upper-crust drawl as Paula smiled, extending her hand. He bent down, took hold of it, brushed his lips across her fingers, a greeting she disliked.

'Don't often see the likes of you round here, my dear. I suggest you spend a few days down here. Plenty of empty bedrooms.'

'Thank you, but we have to get back to London tonight.'

5

'And this is Aubrey,' Barford said quickly, glaring at Lance. 'A little younger, a little politer.'

Aubrey had already risen out of his chair and was smiling. The smile was warm, welcoming. From his suit he looked like a businessman and he shook Paula's hand, not holding it too long.

'And this is our guest, Lisa,' Barford said with enthusiasm. 'She has brains as well as looks.'

Tweed agreed as he followed Paula in shaking hands with a slim, very good-looking redhead who was gazing at Tweed intently with a quirky smile, her blue eyes seeming to look inside him. She exuded intelligence and her movements were swift and graceful.

'I've been looking forward to meeting you, Mr Tweed. Please come and join me on the couch.'

'That would be my pleasure . . .'

Other people were introduced. Several women were looking Paula up and down with an admiration verging on jealousy. Tweed sat down next to Lisa and they began talking as drinks were served. Paula tried to avoid Lance but he took her arm and led her to an empty couch.

'I hear,' Lisa began in her pleasant soft voice, 'that you have a difficult job. In a very special form of insurance. To do with covering rich people against kidnapping – and then negotiating their release on the rare occasions when they are kidnapped.'

'Something like that,' Tweed agreed, secretly thanking his host for using his cover. 'But what do you do? I detect just the faint trace of another accent.'

'You have a good ear. My father was German, my mother English.'

'So are you a linguist?'

'Up to a point.' Lisa hesitated, gazed at him. 'I do speak German, French, Spanish, Italian and Swedish. What do I do? I'm a confidante. Silly word,' she said apologetically. 'People come to me when they have a delicate problem.'

6

She lowered her voice. 'I've got one now. Better not discuss it here. If I could come to see you some time. Although I expect you're very busy.'

Tweed took a card from his wallet, handed it to her. She cleverly palmed it, looked round casually, slipped it inside her handbag. The card he had given her gave his name, followed by General & Cumbria Assurance, the cover name for the SIS, with its Park Crescent address and the phone number for outside callers.

She had been nervous, he sensed. She seemed to relax when she had taken his card. They chatted about various places in Europe they both knew. The blow fell very late in the evening. It was after dinner and Tweed had a shock when he checked the time as Barford approached him, whispered.

'There's an urgent phone call for you. From no less than Gavin Thunder, Minister of Armaments. Silly name. Found out where you were from Monica, your assistant at Park Crescent. You can take the call in the library . . .'

When he eventually returned, Tweed kept an amiable expression on his face. He beckoned to Paula, then turned to Lisa.

'Sorry, but I have to leave now.'

'That's all right.' Lisa smiled. 'I also must go back to my flat in London. My sister is guarding the dog. Or maybe it's the other way round!'

'Do come and see me . . .'

'Do you know how to get to Alfriston from here?' Tweed asked as they drove away.

'Yes. Head back to the A27. I once visited Alfriston for the day. It's very old, has a lot of character. I'll navigate.' Paula glanced at him. His expression was now grim. 'Is there a crisis?'

'Jeremy Mordaunt, under-secretary to the Minister of

Armaments, has been found shot dead. Gavin Thunder spoke to me himself. Arrogant type. I'm not sure why I agreed to his request.'

'Surely it's a police matter?'

'That's what I said. But after Thunder had rung off I called my friend, Superintendent Roy Buchanan at the Yard. He said the Minister had contacted him, told him he wanted me to investigate. Roy had checked with the Commissioner and Thunder had already called him, demanded that I investigate the suicide.'

'I don't like the sound of this. Smells of political overtones,' Paula suggested.

'That's what I think. And how does the Minister know that it is suicide? The body was only discovered about an hour ago. The local police called the MoA.'

'I suppose Thunder thought of you because you were once the youngest homicide superintendent at Scotland Yard, as it was called in those days.'

'Still doesn't make sense . . .'

They had left the Barford estate behind and joined the fast-moving traffic on the A27. The headlight beams of their car pierced the dark and when Paula checked her watch it was close to midnight.

'Where has the time gone?' Paula wondered.

'Well, we had a leisurely dinner before we returned to the drawing room and chatted some more. The signpost says Alfriston coming up, off to the left.'

'I was just going to warn you about the turn-off. We'll soon be in Alfriston. It has occurred to me why you did accept this weird, if not illegal assignment. You've had two calls from Cord Dillon about the suicide of Jason Schulz in Washington. So-called suicide, according to Cord, who even called you from a public phone outside Langley. Which suggests he doesn't trust his own outfit.'

'This mysterious Mark Wendover he's sent over has

8

probably arrived by now. Newman was going to meet his plane. We will know more after we meet Wendover.'

They had turned off the A27, were driving along an ill-lit road which was little more than a lane. Paula decided it was time to lighten the atmosphere.

'You really seemed to get on well with Lisa, chatting her up before and after dinner.'

'Very intelligent, strong-minded,' Tweed remarked, 'but there is something odd about her.'

While Tweed was still in East Sussex, Lisa had driven back to her flat in town. She covered long distances at speed in her sports coupé. The roof was closed, the heating turned full up. The moonlit night illuminated the beautiful countryside once she left the A27 behind, but outside the temperature had dropped below zero.

After slowing to descend the curving road on the north side of the Downs she pressed her foot down again. There was no other traffic at that hour and on either side spacious fields covered with a blanket of glistening frost spread out. It is still not quite the end of March, she thought. And I have contacted Tweed.

Lisa drove at a sedate pace on reaching London. The last thing she wanted was to be stopped by a police patrol car. Taking her usual precaution, she parked in a side street near her flat. The car was her getaway in an emergency.

As she walked quietly along the deserted street to her flat she turned suddenly to look back. No one was following her. Glancing up at her first-floor flat window, she saw the light was on behind the net curtains. Helga, her sister, had not bothered to close the heavier curtains, which bothered her. But she could hardly expect her sister to take the precautions she herself always took.

As Lisa paused, taking out her key, she looked up again and frowned. The glass in front of the lighted window was fractured. Vandals? A brick hurled up? Tiger, her Alsatian, would have torn the culprit to pieces had he been able to get at him.

Once inside the hall, she closed the door quietly, locked it, put on the chain. She was uneasy. Without putting on the hall light she crept up the stairs, avoiding the treads which creaked. What was the matter with her? My nerves are tingling. Must be fatigue.

Lisa had the key to her flat door in her hand. As usual, she inserted and turned it quietly. Ridiculous with Helga and Tiger inside. She called out once she had closed the door, not wishing to startle her sister. Then she realized there was an ominous silence – normally Tiger would have heard her, come rushing out barking with pleasure.

She pushed open the half-closed door to the living room, then froze. Helga was lying on her back under the window, legs twisted from when she had fallen, a red patch on her blouse over her heart. Beside her Tiger was equally motionless, a large hole where the right eye should have been.

'Oh, no! Oh, my God!' she whispered.

Lisa looked at the torn net curtain, at the two jagged holes in the glass, at the scratches made by Tiger's paws close to the holes. She felt faint, sat down on a nearby chair, a lump in her throat.

'Get a grip on yourself,' she snapped.

Half her mind was paralysed by the horror while the other half worked out what had happened. Like herself, Helga, the older sister, had red hair, was about the same height. The fatal shots had been fired from a window across the street. The gunman had seen Helga – maybe standing by the window after nightfall – had assumed it was Lisa. Tiger had charged at the window, clawing at the glass. The gunman had shot him to keep him quiet.

Lisa went down on her knees, crawled across in case the gunman was still across the street, felt Helga's pulse.

Nothing. Tiger also was dead. She crawled back, only stood up out of view of the window.

'Do something. React!'

That was what her employer would expect of her. Not to crumble in an emergency. There was nothing she could do to help poor Helga. She had to get out of this flat quickly. Alive. She had a vital mission. She was the Messenger. She had to reach Tweed in the morning. To warn him of the terrible danger. That was why she was here.

She slipped into the narrow hall, went into the bedroom, blotting out the memory of the bodies in the living room. She packed her things in a small case neatly but quickly. Then she rolled back the carpet, used a screwdriver to lever up the loose floorboard. With mild relief when she saw that the file of papers with vital data was in the cavity. Grabbing hold of it, she stood up, slid the file inside the outer zip-up compartment in her case. Bending down again, she replaced the floorboard, rolled the carpet back in place.

She couldn't go back into the living room, but before leaving she stood close to the door and whispered.

'I'm so sorry, Helga. So very sorry. But I couldn't ever have foreseen this would happen . . .'

Swallowing, Lisa left the flat, closed the door, locked it and made her way carefully down the stairs. She had already taken the small Beretta 6.35mm automatic from her handbag and tucked it down the side of her belt round her trouser suit. With her case in her left hand, front door key in her right, she slowly descended the stairs, again avoiding the creaky treads. She paused before opening the front door.

'Get on with it,' she snapped.

She opened the door suddenly, went out, closed it swiftly, ran down the steps. Reaching the street, she kept moving but looked up at the first-floor window opposite. No lights in the building anywhere. The window from

11

which the fatal shots had been fired, she felt sure, was half open. By the front railing was a notice board. FOR SALE.

Lisa hurried back to her car, seeing no one, and drove off, keeping an eye on her rear-view mirror. She was alone in the cold night.

Parking near Victoria Station, she walked until she saw a rank of phone boxes. She dialled 999, asked for the police. A sharp-voiced man answered her call. She reported the murder, gave the address, refused to identify herself, slammed down the phone, went back to her car.

'That's the best I can do for you, Helga,' Lisa said aloud to herself.

When renting the flat she had given one of her many false names, paying three months' rent in advance. Near Ebury Street she parked her car in a wide alley. Grabbing hold of her case, she walked back round the corner and into a small hotel which still had lights on. In the small reception hall, behind a counter, stood a fat woman with purple-rinsed hair, arms akimbo.

'What have we here at this hour?' the woman demanded.

'I'd like a room . . .'

'Bit late to be comin' in off the street.'

'How much per night for a room?' Lisa had her wallet stuffed with banknotes in her hand. 'I'm an airline stewardess and my flight was delayed.' The woman unfolded her arms, her eyes on the wallet. She named an extortionate amount. 'I'll pay now for three nights,' Lisa snapped.

The room on the first floor was poorly furnished but the bed linen was clean. After locking and bolting the door, Lisa would have given anything for a shower but she hadn't the strength. So far she had held up but she was thinking, *seeing* Helga's body on the floor, Tiger beside her.

She had never got on well with Helga, who treated her husband like a servant, but now she gave way. Sobbing, the tears rolling down her face, she kicked off her shoes.

12

'I couldn't have done any more,' she choked. 'They'd just have taken her away, held me for questioning. And I am the Messenger . . .' She flopped on the bed, shuddering and shaking with remorse. When she woke in the morning the pillow was soaked with her tears.

Tweed drove slowly into the ancient village of Alfriston. By his side Paula tensed. Like entering the Black Hole of Calcutta. A police car stopped them in the High Street. In places, she remembered, it was so narrow two cars couldn't pass each other. The only illumination was a distant lamp attached to a wall bracket. Old buildings of stone walled them in. Tweed lowered the window, explained briefly to a middle-aged uniformed policeman who he was.

'I'm Sergeant Pole,' the policeman introduced himself. He bent close as Tweed emerged from the car. 'We 'eard a superintendent would be down from London.' Tweed nodded, avoiding correcting the reference to his rank. 'S'pose I shouldn't say it,' Pole went on, 'but we have a problem. Chap called Bogle, Assistant Chief Constable, has turned up. Throwing his weight about . . .'

He stopped talking as a small burly man wearing a dark overcoat and a wide-brimmed hat appeared. He reminded Paula of a pig and his manners fitted his appearance.

'Who the blazes are you?' he demanded.

'This is Superintendent Tweed from London,' Pole said quickly.

'And this is my assistant, Paula Grey,' Tweed added. 'Could we go straight to the body? I presume no one has touched it?'

'Course not. Sir,' he added as an afterthought. 'Know my job. I'm Assistant Chief Constable Bogle – from the next county. They're all down with flu at Eastbourne, plus a nasty accident on the A27. Happens all the time.

13

Pole, don't just stand there. Lift the tape so they can get through. I'll lead the way . . .'

Passing the walls of a few unlit houses perched at the back of the uneven stone pavement, they arrived at a tiny square like a large alcove. In the square was a dress shop, then a notice illuminated by a dim lamp away from the street.

> Steps to
> the Church
> Tye and
> Clergy
> House

Bogle didn't bother to warn them as he went ahead holding a flashlight. Parallel to the street there were two concrete steps, down past a wrought-iron gate pushed back against the wall, then a sharp right-angled turn to the left with six more steps leading down into a weird concrete tunnel with an arched roof. Paula, clutching her fur collar close to her throat, had produced a powerful flashlight that guided Tweed underground. The old concrete tunnel was only a few feet wide and disappeared into the distance, where it ended at a moonlit archway.

'There he is,' growled Bogle. 'Damned queer places people choose to commit suicide.'

Despite the fact that the left-hand side of the head was blown away, Paula immediately recognized the late Jeremy Mordaunt. The body was slumped at right angles to the tunnel, seated on the floor, head sagged forward, blood down the front of his Armani suit, legs spread out across the passage. The visible back of his suit was smeared with concrete powder, the fingers of his left hand were tucked inside the firing mechanism of a .38 Smith & Wesson revolver.

'Open-and-shut case,' Bogle rasped. 'Clear matter of

suicide. He leant against the wall, pressed the gun against his head, pulled the trigger, went to kingdom come as he slid down the wall.'

'Really?' Tweed was crouched down, close to the body. 'No trace of powder burns on his hand.'

'But,' objected Paula, 'he was right-handed. I saw him at a cocktail party recently. He held his glass in his right hand, and when he smoked a cigarette he held it in his right hand.'

Mordaunt's passport, the old type with a black cover engraved with the gilt seal, was lying close to his slumped leg. It was open at the page which gave the holder's details. Tweed, still crouched, facing the corpse, pointed to the passport.

'Mr Bogle' he asked, without turning his head, 'who first suggested to you it was suicide?'

'Obvious, isn't it?'

'Is it? Who did you phone when you reported this tragedy?'

'London.'

'London covers a lot of people. *Who* in London did you call?'

'Well, I saw from his passport who he was. So I decided it was a diplomatic matter. I called the Ministry of Armaments.'

'Naturally,' Tweed agreed amiably, still not looking at Bogle which was beginning to disturb the policeman. 'Precisely who did you speak to?'

'Can't see that this is relevant. I spoke to the Minister, Gavin Thunder. Must admit I was a bit surprised when he answered the phone.'

'Yes, that was a bit odd. Almost as though he was expecting the call. And who first mentioned the word "suicide"?'

'Well.' Bogle shuffled his feet. 'It was him – the Minister. Said something like "Oh, my God. Jeremy has killed himself, poor devil. Keep this under wraps. No publicity. I'll

15

send someone in authority down immediately." Then he rang off.'

'And had you explained to the Minister what we see now?'

'There wasn't time. I've relayed to you the exact conversation I had with him before he slammed down the phone. I did tell him the body was inside an underground tunnel down here at Alfriston. Nothing more.' He looked away from Tweed, who was now staring at him. 'Hit the nail on the head, didn't he? Suicide.'

'When Miss Grey has just told you that Mordaunt was right-handed? Are you suggesting that a man using a heavy gun to kill himself holds the weapon in his right hand, then bends his arm across his face, somehow manages to aim the gun at the other side of his forehead, pulls the trigger, then transfers the weapon to his left hand?'

'The autopsy will settle the matter,' Bogle almost shouted.

'That reminds me. Any moment now an ambulance from London will arrive with Professor Charles Saafeld aboard to take the body to his laboratory. Our top pathologist, he will perform the autopsy. I phoned him before we came here.'

'Bloody hell!' Bogle stormed. 'I've called Eastbourne to send an ambulance. We *do* have pathologists from here . . .'

'Then perhaps,' Tweed suggested as he stood up, 'it would be an idea to get on your mobile and recall your ambulance. I see from the powder on the wall your scene-of-crime crew have already been here, checked the surroundings and probably taken their photographs.'

'Of course they have,' growled Bogle and stomped off, up the steps and out of sight.

'I think Saafeld and his ambulance have arrived,' Paula reported after a brief visit to the outside world. 'I'll show him the way.'

'If you would, please . . .'

An imposing figure appeared. For a man of his heavy

bulk, Saafeld ran nimbly down the steps. His round, plumpish complexion had a pinkish tinge and he exuded an air of authority. He peered at Tweed over his half-moon glasses, nodded, took in the surroundings with swift glances.

'Hello, Paula,' he said quietly.

'This place is like a tomb.' She clutched the collar of her fur coat more closely. 'It's freezing.'

'A tomb,' Saafeld repeated. 'Complete with a body.' He looked back at a youngish man with a camera who had followed him. 'Reg. Take pictures quickly.' He bent down, hands covered with latex gloves, pressed a delicate finger on Mordaunt's right hand. 'No rigor mortis yet, but we'd better hurry.'

'The local assistant chief constable swears it's suicide,' whispered Tweed, bending alongside the pathologist.

'Suicide, my hat. Just a first impression,' Saafeld warned. 'Don't like the way the fingers are holding the weapon. And if he was standing, back to the wall, he'd have toppled sideways when the bullet hit – not slithered down the wall. But it's early days.'

'Can I call you in the morning – this morning?'

'Try eight o'clock. I work through the night, as you know. I don't promise anything . . .'

Tweed borrowed Paula's flashlight. She followed him as he walked the full length of the tunnel. The floor was useless for give-away footprints. Emerging under the arch at the far end, he paused, took a deep breath. In the moonlight the view was entrancing. A wide stretch of grass, then a spired church, a gem. He swept the flashlight along a road immediately beyond the arch. Vague tracks of probably a dozen cars. Old houses stretched away to his left and right.

'He could have been brought here by car, tricked into entering the tunnel. It's as quiet as the grave.'

They retraced their journey through the eerie tunnel.

17

Reg had taken his pictures, was putting the camera inside a case.

'Reg,' Saafeld called out. 'Bring the stretcher. We'll get him out now. It will be the devil of a job manoeuvring him round and up those steps.' Tweed offered help. 'No, thanks – this is a two-man exercise . . .'

Tweed and Paula reached the small square to find Bogle waiting, standing by a car with an unpleasant sneer on his pinched face.

'I'm off. To write my report. A very full report covering all aspects of your intrusion.'

He jumped into the front passenger seat, snapped at the driver. The car took off, its tail lights receding swiftly. Tweed turned to speak to Sergeant Pole.

'You've been in this area a long time?'

'All my born days, sir.'

'Are there any important people round here? Maybe rich?'

'There's Lord Barford. Family's been here for generations.'

'Any more recent arrivals?'

'Well . . .' Pole considered carefully. 'There's a Mr Rondel, a foreigner. Arrived about two years ago. Very wealthy, I'd say. Travels abroad a lot. Had a big mansion built inside an old abandoned quarry up on the Downs. Place went up in no time. Imported German workers.'

'Can you describe this Rondel?'

'Only saw him once. Drove a red Bugatti along this street as though it was Le Mans. Only caught a glimpse of him. Blond hair, youngish. Has a helipad by the mansion. Arrives there by chopper.'

'Any idea where he flies to?'

'Girl who lives here worked as a stewardess once at Heathrow. Told me she'd seen him boarding a Gulfstream. Think that's what she called it. Private jet. Big job.'

'Any chance of our driving to his place from here? Now?'

'You could.' Pole sounded doubtful. 'When you meet the A27 after leaving Alfriston you turn left. If you're not careful you'll miss the turning to Eagle's Nest – that's what Rondel calls his palatial place. A short way along you come to a turning off left – just before you reach another one signposted Byway.'

'I remember that turning,' Paula interjected.

'One hell of a road . . . pardon me,' he said to Paula. 'Unmade, it twists and turns up over the Downs. Get to the top and the road levels out, then starts to go down. That's where Rondel's place is, way back to your left. Right inside the quarry.' He frowned as a car's headlights appeared, driving into the village, the lights on full beam. They flashed twice, then were doused. The car stopped, Bob Newman jumped out.

'Monica called me just as we'd finished dinner,' Newman explained as he drove along the A27 with Tweed beside him.

Behind them Paula was driving Tweed's car, thinking she should have been in front to guide them. Would Tweed spot the turn-off?

'Called me on my mobile,' Newman continued. 'I'd met Mark Wendover at Heathrow, parked him at the Ritz, took him for dinner to Santorini's.'

'Tell me later, we're coming to the turn-off. There are things you should know . . .'

Tweed talked non-stop, providing Newman with all the data about Lisa at Lord Barford's mansion, his arrival in Alfriston, what he had found there.

As he was talking, Newman's skill as a driver was tested to the limit as the track they had turned on to kept switching back and forth on itself in a series of bends.

19

Left, then right again, then left. All the time they were ascending rapidly, along a potholed track where many cavities had not been filled in.

Behind them Paula too drove with ease and skill, revelling in the warmth inside her car. Using a gloved hand, she cleared a hole in the steamed-up glass of her side window. The view she looked down on was staggering.

From the base of the Downs flatlands of frost-covered fields stretched away endlessly to the north. Then she saw a caterpillar of lights crawling westward, realized it was a local train which had to be returning to its depot. She felt the whole of England was spreading out before her.

Tweed was telling Newman he had found Lisa an extraordinary personality. He described her, emphasized her intelligence, voiced his puzzlement as to what her real role was and why she was so anxious to meet him again.

'Nearing the summit,' Newman warned. 'Didn't you tell me Pole said that the road levelled out, started to go down and Rondel's house was on the left?'

'He did,' Tweed confirmed.

They crested the rise suddenly. Newman slowed down and behind them Paula, gazing through her windscreen, almost gasped. On the other side of the Downs a vast panorama came into view. To east and west were vast slopes of rolling hills. A distance away to the south the sea, caught in the moonlight, glittered like an immense lake of mercury sweeping into the Channel. The road began to drop. They pulled up. Newman freewheeled a few more yards, stopped. He left the engine purring to keep the interior warm, jumped out after Tweed and joined Paula, who had already left her car.

'There it is,' said Newman. 'Weird-looking. Expensive.'

'Look at the name,' said Paula.

A large aluminium plate was engraved with the name in front of a high wire fence. *Eagle's Nest.* Two high wire gates barred the entrance to the curving drive beyond. At the far end of the drive it turned towards a very large white house built of stone. The architecture was surreal, like a collection of white blocks or cubes perched at different levels on top of each other. To one side rose a tall round tower. The entire edifice was located deep inside an old quarry, its steep sides overhanging the house.

'Look!' Paula called out. 'There's something emerging from the round tower.'

'I've seen it,' Tweed replied.

Somewhere behind them was the muffled sound of a machine. Paula glanced back – just in time to see the crouched figure of a rider on a motorcycle. The machine was steadily negotiating its way up a steep path which, she guessed, led to the top of the Down overlooking the house.

'That's Harry Butler,' Newman reassured her. 'He insisted on guarding my rear all the way from London . . .'

He stopped speaking as a slim mast, like a submarine's periscope, its top a tangle of wired dishes, continued elevating until it was about twenty feet above the rim of the Down. Paula nudged Tweed.

'Someone's coming along the drive at a rate of knots. Looks like an old woman carrying a rifle.'

The hurrying figure appeared with astonishing speed on the far side of the closed gates. She stopped, her weapon, actually a shotgun, aimed at them. Her voice was harsh.

'Who are you? Private property. Why are you here?'

'Which question would you like me to answer first?' Tweed enquired mildly.

She was wearing an old heavy dark coat. It almost reached her ankles and Paula wondered how she'd moved so fast in such a garment. She was hawk-nosed, bony-faced, in her sixties, a menacing figure.

'Stop pointing that thing at us,' Newman ordered.

21

'Shotguns can go off almost by themselves. Want to spend the rest of your life in prison for murder?'

'Can't frighten me,' she snarled, but she swivelled the gun to a port position and it fired harmlessly into the air.

'See what I mean,' Newman shouted at her. 'Who are you?'

'Mrs Grimwood. The . . . 'ousekeeper . . . if you must know.'

The shot had echoed a long distance in the cold night air, would have been heard inside the strange house. Tweed was ignoring the verbal confrontation, his eyes glued to the tall mast. Seconds after the shotgun went off the mast began to withdraw swiftly. It disappeared inside the tower, was gone.

'Private property,' Mrs Grimwood yelled.

It was becoming like the repetition of an old gramophone when the needle had got stuck. Tweed shrugged, wondering why Paula had slipped behind him earlier. The old crone opened up a fresh barrage.

'That girl with you – 'as a camera. I want the film.'

'No, I haven't,' Paula lied. 'Can't you recognize a pair of binoculars? Get your eyesight tested.' *Silly old cow*, she added to herself as Tweed went back towards the cars.

They stood staring at the sea for a few minutes. Now it was like a sheet of crystal, flat, motionless. Paula heard the muffled sound of Harry Butler's machine return slowly down the path from the Down.

'I've got a suggestion,' Newman said as he joined them. 'Harry's had a long tiring ride. I could squeeze his small motorcycle in my hatchback, let him drive your car, Tweed – then the three of us could drive back together and talk.'

'Good idea,' Tweed agreed. 'Get your photo?' he asked Paula.

'Photos. Half-hidden in the shadow beyond the house I saw a helipad – with a chopper on it. I got that as well as the mast. They certainly want to keep that thing – whatever it is – secret . . .'

They were driving back along the A27, heading for the distant turn-off towards Petworth. Newman was driving the hatchback with Tweed beside him and Paula in the rear. Behind them Butler was driving Tweed's car. Unsettled by their visit to *Eagle's Nest*, the atmosphere up on the Downs, they were silent for a few minutes. It was shortly after they had moved on to the A27 when Paula peered through the rear window.

'There's a helicopter flying fairly high up behind us. The odd thing is it looks as though it came from Lord Barford's estate. Has he got a chopper?'

'No idea,' Tweed replied, his eyes half closed.

'Bob, what did you think of Mark Wendover?' Paula went on.

'Calls himself a freelance, which struck me as odd. What is he like? Only a slight American accent. His mother was English. Has a first-class brain, really knows his stuff. And he doesn't miss much. He's convinced Jason Schulz was murdered, then it was mocked up to make it look like suicide.'

'Two fake suicides,' Tweed mused. 'Three and a half thousand miles apart. Both men in top government posts – so both had access to top secrets. What's the link? I've no idea, but as you know I don't believe in coincidence. Could the assassin be the same person?'

'Easily,' Newman replied. 'The deaths took place roughly five days apart. Plenty of time for someone to do the job in Washington, then catch a flight over here from Dulles Airport.'

While they were descending the switchback road towards

the A27 a quiet voice spoke by radio-telephone to the pilot of the chopper waiting by his machine.

'Follow two cars leaving Eagle's Nest. Report their route. They are probably heading for Park Crescent in London. Give regular reports of their position to Bronze . . .'

The owner of the same quiet voice then pressed fresh numbers.

'Listen to me carefully. And don't make mistakes or you know what will happen to you. A chopper pilot will tell you at regular intervals the location of the two cars. I'm sure their destination is Park Crescent. Bronze, move fast. Steal an unusual vehicle – the target is smart. You have his description. Tell Zero to kill Tweed.'

'That chopper is still with us,' Paula said as they reached the centre of London.

'Probably not the same one,' Newman told her. 'London has them flying all the time. And Tweed is fast asleep.'

'Perhaps we had better stop chattering.'

'You stop chattering,' Newman suggested. 'Park Crescent is very close.'

'Look what's coming towards us. At this hour. 3 a.m. I don't believe it.'

The vehicle moving towards them along an otherwise deserted street was an old-fashioned sightseeing bus with an open top. The notice above the driver's cabin seemed superfluous. NOT IN SERVICE. Paula crouched down to get a better look as it crawled towards them. A pre-Second World War museum piece but tourists loved them. She saw the driver staring straight down the road, cap perched at a jaunty angle. Then she saw movement at the top of the bus, a man in the front seat aiming a barrel-shaped object.

'Look out!' she yelled. 'Gunman aboard . . .'

Newman turned the car across the path of the oncoming bus. Two sharp reports split the silence. Bullets tore holes in a side window, missing Tweed, who was slumped in his seat. Two more holes appeared in the side window opposite as the bullets continued their vicious track. Newman braked as the car slammed into a wall.

'Are you all right?' Paula asked Tweed anxiously.

'Yes. So who phoned ahead from Alfriston? Or Barford Manor?'

1

Lisa woke for the fifth time and it was daylight. She had felt exhausted when she had flopped on the bed in her clothes. After sleeping an hour she had decided to explore her room. Not daring to switch on the light again, she had crept over to the curtained window, cautiously pulling aside one curtain. What she had seen gave her the horrors.

Outside the window was a fire escape leading down into the wide alley where she had parked her car. She could see the vehicle a few yards away below her. Anyone who had managed to follow her could have mounted the fire escape and climbed into her room. She no longer felt safe.

Checking the feeble catch that locked the window, Lisa risked turning on the light. Working quickly, she hauled three cheap wooden chairs to the window, turned them on their sides, scattered them. At least that way she might have a warning of danger.

She thought of taking a shower and a wave of fatigue swept over her. Before she flopped on the bed again she tucked her Beretta automatic under the damp pillow, fell asleep. It was seven in the morning when daylight, penetrating the flimsy curtains, woke her again. She decided to get up.

She thought once more of taking a shower in the tiny bathroom, then reluctantly dismissed the idea. If someone came up the fire escape she'd be helpless, caught in the shower. She washed quickly, brushed her mane of red hair, put on a little make-up, felt better. The phone rang.

She nearly jumped out of her skin but reacted quickly. Lifting the receiver, she said 'Yes' in a soft voice. It was the old besom who had stood behind the reception counter when she arrived.

'Thought I'd better warn you. Coupla men are on the way up to your room. Said they was police. Rude sods, they are . . .'

'Thank you.'

She realized the woman had warned her because she'd resented the way they'd spoken to her. And she had obviously had doubts whether they were police, so they weren't in uniform. As a precaution – and due to her weariness when she'd arrived – she had opened the lid of her case but had taken nothing out except her cosmetics bag. She ran into the bathroom, grabbed the bag, shoved it back into her case, closed the lid.

Lisa had the window open, had rested her case on a metal tread outside, lifted one leg over the sill, when she heard the hard rapping on the locked door to the corridor.

'Police. We know you're in there. Open up. Police . . .'

The voice was hard, demanding. The rapping resumed. She started down the fire escape, not hurrying for fear she'd have an accident. She heard the savage splintering of wood. They were breaking down the door.

Two men had rushed into the room. Both wore dark business suits. One was of medium height, fat, and his black eyebrows, matching his hair, met over the bridge of his boxer's nose. His companion was small, slim with Slavic cheekbones, ponytail hair, a cruel narrow face and sideburns. He held a large knife in his right hand. The order had been it should be a quick *quiet* job.

'Not in bathroom,' the small man reported.

'Panko, the bloody window.'

Eyebrows rushed across, peered out. As he did so Lisa, who had reached the bottom steps, looked up, saw him clearly, ran to her car. Eyebrows swore.

'She's got transport. I'll get the car, you go after her. Pick you up in the jalopy . . .'

Lisa kept her cool, carefully inserted her ignition key as Panko tore down the fire escape. She had the engine going as he reached the bottom, stood in the middle of the wide alley. Without hesitation she drove straight at him. He jumped aside, brandishing his knife, pressing himself against the wall.

Lisa pressed her foot down, but travelling across the cobbled surface of the alley slowed her down. In her rear-view mirror she could see a large blue Ford pause at the foot of the fire escape. The little man jumped aboard, then the Ford was coming after her.

'Those aren't detectives,' she said to herself. 'Not when one of them is waving an evil-looking knife about. Girl, you're in real trouble . . .'

She decided to head for Waterloo station, but soon ran into heavy commuter traffic. The real danger loomed when she was approaching the bridge crossing the Thames. An amber light, which she hoped the car ahead would beat, turned red, it stopped. She braked.

'Well, I'm surrounded by cars with people,' she comforted herself.

Glancing again in the mirror, her brief release from fear vanished. She clenched her teeth. The small man had left the stationary Ford six cars behind her and was wending his way between the traffic towards her. The car she was inside was an old model and there was no mechanism she could use to lock all the doors.

All Skinny had to do when he reached her was to open her door, then ram home his butcher's knife. She reached for her Beretta, jammed behind her belt under her coat.

29

Couldn't get to the damned thing. She alternately checked her mirror, gazed at the red light.

'*Green!*' she prayed. 'For Christ's sake, turn green . . .'

Skinny was coming closer and closer. The light obstinately remained at red. Skinny was now one car behind her, sidling forward fast. She still couldn't get her hand on the Beretta. In any case, that would be a disaster. If she did manage to shoot him it would be a police case, probably keeping her out of action for ages. Skinny was grinning now. Had his right hand under his windcheater.

'Oh, *please!*'

Skinny had now arrived at the rear of her car, his hand half outside the unzipped windcheater. She could see the triumph in his evil eyes, the look of devilish anticipation. The lights changed to amber, to green. The traffic surged forward and she surged with it. She had a glimpse of him caught up in the mêlée of traffic.

'Run the bastard down,' she said aloud between her teeth.

Lisa parked the car in an underground garage near the station. Carrying her case, she walked rapidly to Waterloo, confident she had lost them. The large concourse was a swirl of people, hurrying to work after leaving their trains, which suited her. You were easily lost in a crowd.

Spotting a row of phone booths, she went inside one that had empty booths on both sides. Her first call was to the car hire company. She told them where she'd parked the car, that she wouldn't need it again. *They'll be happy*, she thought as she prepared to make another call – she had paid for another two weeks' hire.

Taking out the card Tweed had given her from her handbag, she pressed numbers. A woman's voice answered. She spoke quickly.

'This is Lisa Trent. I need to speak to Mr Tweed. I met

him at a party. He told me to call him so we could meet urgently.'

'I'm sorry, but Mr Tweed is out of the office keeping an appointment. He may not be back for a while.'

'In that case could I speak to Paula Grey? I met her at the same time.'

'I am sorry about this. Miss Grey accompanied Mr Tweed to the same appointment. Could you give me a message?' Monica suggested.

'Not really. It is Mr Tweed I have to talk to. I'll call back later in the day. Please tell him I phoned because I know he'll want to see me . . .'

Lisa put down the phone and turned round, then froze. Eyebrows and Skinny were marching purposefully across the concourse. They were heading in her direction.

Monica was typing furiously on her word processor when Harry Butler came into the room, parked himself on the arm of a chair. He removed the scarf that had protected him from the bitter cold outside.

'Well, Monica, I've put the hatchback in for repair. Took it to a pal who won't be reporting to the police the bullet holes in the windows. Tweed didn't want that. My car was just too far behind them for me to spot the old bus – otherwise I'd have nabbed the killers. What are you typing?'

'Tweed's report on the so-called suicide of Jeremy Mordaunt.' She had removed her earpiece. 'He dictated it on to the recorder, said he can think more quickly using the machine. Want to hear his verdict?'

'Guess you'll tell me anyway.'

Butler was a short man with wide shoulders, a man of great physical strength. He had a round head and an expressionless face. Normally he used words frugally, as though they were money.

'Tweed has no doubt Mordaunt was murdered. He dismisses the idea that he committed suicide as ludicrous. Why does the phone always go when I'm explaining something?'

'General & Cumbria Assurance . . .' She began. 'Oh, it's you, Professor Saafeld. I'm afraid Tweed is out but he's anxious to have your report on the autopsy . . .'

'Is that Monica?' the abrupt voice asked. 'My report is now ready – several copies.'

'I'll send a courier over to collect them immediately.' She hesitated. 'Can you give me an inkling of your conclusion?'

'Cold-blooded murder. Not a shadow of a doubt. The report has technical data. That's what I'll say at the inquest.'

He broke the connection and Monica used the phone to send one of their couriers over to Saafeld's mansion in Holland Park. Then she printed out the report for Tweed, talking as she worked.

'Nobody can fault Tweed now. Saafeld said it was cold-blooded murder. He doesn't normally use such strong language.'

'Copies of the reports going to someone?'

'Yes. Gavin Thunder for one. He'll throw a fit.'

Harry stood up. 'I've been thinking about who ordered Tweed to be killed. Newman told me where Tweed had been. Have you a file on Lord Barford?'

'Yes. In the safe. Combination is 87, 24, 95. Why?'

'Just curious.'

Harry walked over to the large safe recently installed in a corner of the room. His nimble fingers operated the combination, swung open the heavy door. A number of metal drawers were stacked with top secret files. He checked the A-to-Bs, found Barford's file, closed the safe and resumed his perch on the chair arm.

'Lord Barford is one of the most distinguished men in Britain,' Monica protested.

'So was Maxwell. For a time.'

Monica was intrigued. She knew Butler never trusted or was impressed by anyone. Not until their integrity had been proved up to the hilt. He skimmed the file rapidly.

'Monica, could you take down these extracts as I call them out? Right. Here goes.'

Brigadier Bernard Barford. Served Gulf War as Officer in charge Communications. Awarded MC. Rumoured to later act as liaison with obtaining lucrative armament contacts with Middle Eastern and Asiatic countries. Indonesia was mentioned in the rumours, a state to which Britain has supplied large quantities of military hardware. Nothing was ever confirmed concerning these rumours. Before the Gulf War Barford was a colonel in the Signals Corps. He commutes from his manor to London City Airport by Sikorsky helicopter.

'That's it,' said Butler. 'Just extracts I find interesting. And why did the government create a Ministry of Armaments – taking it away from the Ministry of Defence?'

'Politicians trying to be crafty. It deflects criticisms of the arms trade from the Foreign Office. And all of that stuff about Barford is rumour.'

'Except the bit about his helicopter.'

'Why is that significant?'

'Because a chopper followed us all the way from the Downs.'

'But,' Monica objected, 'Paula said this weird man, Rondel, also has a helipad and a chopper was sitting on it.'

'I was in the following car. I got the impression the chopper lifted off from somewhere near the Barford estate.

Can't be sure,' he emphasized. 'And where have Tweed, Newman and Paula buzzed off to?'

'It was Tweed's idea – to go and call on Jeremy's widow, Mrs Mordaunt. She lives in Eaton Square. He wouldn't let me phone her to say they were coming.'

2

When Lisa saw Eyebrows and Skinny walking towards her inside Waterloo station she moved fast. Grabbing hold of her case, she waited a few seconds until a group of businessmen were passing her phone booth, then slipped out under the cover they provided. There was a large bookstall in the middle of the concourse. She hurried inside, wriggled her way past the crowd, emerged on the far side.

Pausing, she whipped a folded scarf out of her pocket, wrapped it round her head, concealing her red hair. Now she had to get rid of her blasted case, which was slowing her down. She handed in her case to an official. Now she could really move.

Her next stop was the Underground. She bought a ticket for the first place which came into her head after glancing at a route plan. Highgate. Glancing behind herself as she hurried towards the escalators she saw Eyebrows, pushing people out of his way, coming towards her.

'Oh, God!' she said under her breath. 'Will I never shake them off?'

She saw a uniformed station guard ahead. Running up to him, she spoke in a deliberately shaky voice.

'That dark-haired man just made an obscene proposition to me. I'm frightened.'

'I'll have a word . . .'

At the top of the escalator Lisa looked back. The guard

was saying something to her pursuer. Eyebrows punched him viciously in the stomach. The guard doubled up as she ran on to the escalator and down it. At the bottom she checked the signs for the right line and kept running. She could move much faster without the case.

There was a crowded train arriving when she reached the platform. She looked back. Skinny was coming towards her, grinning, one hand inside his windcheater. Was he always wearing that hideous grin? Behind him Eyebrows followed.

As passengers left the train, others pushed aboard. A crowded carriage, people standing up. She had no option. She stepped into the train, kept saying 'Excuse me' as she worked her way deeper into the coach. The doors closed, the train started moving.

She was still working her way through the crowd, smiling as she apologized. The train rumbled on, swaying round a curve. She grabbed a rail above her head to keep her balance. She was now opposite carriage doors.

'Would you like a seat, madam?' a man suggested, starting to get up.

'Thank you, but I'm not travelling far.'

The train stopped three times. Lisa wondered whether to get off. No, she was safer in a crowd. Gazing back down the crammed coach she saw Skinny was having more trouble than she had experienced. Passengers were protesting, holding him up. The train was in motion when she saw a uniformed ticket inspector asking Eyebrows for his ticket. He hadn't got one. Earlier he'd leapt over the station barrier with Skinny.

'Sorry, Inspector,' Eyebrows started politely. 'Here's the money for two tickets. My little friend is on his way to hospital.'

'There's a ten-pound fine . . .'

Eyebrows produced a twenty-pound note, shoved it into the inspector's hand. Skinny was on the move again, closing on her. Lisa realized the train was a lethal trap. He only had to wait until it reached the next station before he slid his knife into her and left the carriage.

She tensed her right leg. The train was pulling into Tottenham Court Road. She knew the area well. Skinny reached her as the doors opened. She lifted her leg, ground her hard shoe down his shin. He yelped. She was leaving the train as Eyebrows grabbed hold of Skinny, who couldn't move.

'Make way,' he called out, holding Skinny under the armpits. 'My friend has a bad leg.'

He was heaving Skinny out of the train when Lisa vanished up a flight of steps. She got on an escalator and just before stepping off at the top glanced back. Eyebrows and Skinny were staring up at her from the bottom.

It was a relief for her to get out into the cold fresh air. She half-ran up Tottenham Court Road, then down a side street, then into Bedford Square. Slowing down, she took in deep breaths of air. The square, enclosed with fine old houses, was empty as she made her way round the miniature park in the centre.

'I've had about as much as I can take,' Lisa said to herself.

She looked back to check again. Between the trees she saw the two men entering the square. Skinny was walking normally, seemed to have recovered from his injured leg. She had to find somewhere to hide. Where on earth could she go? She was confident that so far the thugs hadn't seen her since she'd left the Underground.

Then she noticed what she should have remembered. Each of the terraced mansions had a basement area with steps leading down to it beyond open railed gates. She looked back once more, saw they were still coming, dived down the metal treads into an open basement area.

Only then did she realize it was occupied. An old tramp,

holding a bottle of whisky, was seated in a corner. He tipped his cap to her.

'Like a nip of the good stuff, lady?' he suggested, lifting the bottle towards her.

His accent was Cockney. His face was lined with age but his eyes were bright with intelligence. She had to trust someone. She spoke slowly, making her voice tremble – not a difficult task.

'Two men are coming after me, trying to hurt me.'

She had avoided using the word 'kill' – too dramatic and she was desperate for him to believe her. He used the neck of the bottle to point to an alcove under the pavement.

'Get you under there, lady. They stores the rubbish bags there, but it's the only 'idin' place.'

Lisa crouched down, went under the pavement, sat with her back to a wall. There was a smell of decay that she was hardly aware of. She felt sure the two thugs would come this way.

'I do have my Beretta,' she said to herself. 'Don't show it. The tramp will be scared out of his wits. Like me . . .'

The heavy clump of feet walking along the pavement above came closer. She froze when they stopped above her head. The tramp lifted the bottle, swallowed, pulled his cap lower as though going to sleep.

'You down there. Seen a girl with red 'air comin' along 'ere?'

The tramp opened his eyes, pushed up his cap. Then he did what she had feared he would do after the reference to red hair. He looked across at her. She knew a curl of her hair had slipped below the scarf. They'd come down the steps and she had no escape route.

Tweed, with Paula and Newman, had mounted the steps to the stately old house in Eaton Square, part of a terrace, when the front door opened. A man wearing a suit which would have been fashionable thirty years earlier emerged. Peering at Tweed, he descended the steps, swinging his silver-topped cane, and walked away. Tweed still held the door open while he read the names and numbers on a plate screwed to the side wall, then walked inside.

'I'll do the talking,' he told Newman.

'So I'll be the silent partner.'

The trees in the park outside beyond the road were black stark skeletons. A raw wind blew round the square. Once inside the hall Tweed found the right number, pressed the bell. They heard a lock turned, a chain removed. The door opened.

'Yes?'

'I'm Tweed. These are my assistants, Paula Grey and Robert Newman. Are you Mrs Mordaunt?'

'Yes.'

She was a brunette, attractive up to a point, her coiffeured hair trimmed short. Wearing a black dress with a white lace collar, she had a long sharp nose, a full mouth, pencilled eyebrows and cold dark eyes. Tweed cleared his throat.

'I'm very sorry to trouble you but I'm here regarding the investigation into the tragic business of your husband's death. My condolences, although words are meaningless.'

'You'd better come in.'

She ushered them into a large drawing room with tall windows, tasteful and comfortable furnishings – sofas and armchairs covered with chintz, matched by long curtains draped to the floor. Several Sheraton antiques, an unfinished piece of embroidery draped over the back of a sofa.

'Please sit down.'

'Thank you. We won't be long.'

'That's good. I have to go out soon. Would you like a glass of sherry?' she asked in her cultured voice when they were seated in armchairs.

'Only if you will join us.'

Tweed had expected her to ask for identification but she had omitted to make the request. In grief you are not the same person. He had noticed a large bottle of sherry, half empty, on a coffee table, an ashtray beside it full of used stubs. Almost as though she had been waiting for them. A water glass with a little sherry in it was also perched on the table. They all detested sherry but Tweed thought it might help to relax her.

'How unsightly,' she remarked and removed the water glass. 'I'll get the right glasses.'

She went over to a large cupboard, opened it and exposed shelves of leather-bound books. She swore, slammed the doors shut. 'Hardly know what I'm doing.' She walked to the only other large cupboard by the wall, a contrast in style to the cupboard she had first opened. Pulling back the doors, she revealed a collection of expensive glassware. Selecting four sherry glasses, she brought them to the table. Paula glanced at Tweed. He was watching her closely.

'I'm feeling better now,' she said as she poured from the bottle. 'Now, how can I help you?' she asked after sitting down, crossing her legs and sipping her sherry.

'Do you know whether your husband was under any kind of pressure recently?' Tweed enquired.

'Pressure isn't the word for it.' As she spoke she seemed to be looking at something beyond Tweed's left shoulder. 'I have been worried. Very. That beast Gavin Thunder is a slave-driver. Jeremy had very little sleep for weeks on end. And I never knew when he'd arrive home.'

'Mrs Mordaunt.' Paula had leant towards her. 'We understand you had a pet name for your husband. What was it?'

'I beg your pardon?'

Tweed, annoyed at the interruption, began cleaning his glasses with a clean handkerchief. During an interrogation a diversion could ruin the whole process. Paula persisted.

40

'A pet name – used between you and maybe at times when you had close friends with you. Not unusual with couples who are married.'

'I don't want to talk about that.'

'So,' Tweed intervened firmly, 'perhaps he was depressed?'

'Yes, he was,' she replied eagerly. 'Very depressed.'

'Did Gavin Thunder ever visit you here?'

'I've never met that man. Don't want to. I'm sure that his demanding personality didn't help the situation at all.'

'A delicate question,' Tweed said carefully. 'It would have been understandable in such a situation if Jeremy drank quite a lot . . .'

'Emptied whisky bottle after whisky bottle.' She had been answering questions more quickly after Paula's one query. She looked at her wristwatch, encrusted with diamonds. 'I hope you don't mind, but is there much more? I have a car calling for me and an urgent appointment to keep.'

Tweed stood up and Paula and Newman joined him. Paula stared round the room and then at their hostess who was reaching for a sable coat flung over the back of a couch. Tweed thanked her for her time as she led the way to the front door, fumbling in her handbag, producing a ring of keys. Attempting to insert a key she swore again.

'All these damned keys. I never remember which is which.' As she inserted another key she spoke over her shoulder. 'I will just say goodbye . . .' She had opened the door and a limo was parked outside. A uniformed chauffeur was striding up and down the pavement. 'Joseph knows I am late . . .'

Her shoes click-clacked down the steps. She had left Tweed to close the front door. The chauffeur opened the rear door of the car, closed it, hurried to get behind the wheel. Paula noted the limo's plate number.

Tweed held the front door open. A tall woman in a fur

coat, beak-nosed, probably over seventy but with refined features, had begun to ascend the steps in a stately manner. Tweed opened the door wider.

'We've just been to see Mrs Mordaunt,' he explained. 'The lady you passed as you arrived and got into the limo.'

'I beg your pardon, young man.' Her manner was imperious. 'That was *not* Mrs Jeremy Mordaunt. A complete stranger.'

'Excuse me, are you sure?'

'Am I sure?' Her manner was indignant. 'I have been living here for over ten years. Don't you think I should recognize my neighbours by now?'

Having said which, she sailed into the building like a galleon about to open fire on the enemy.

3

'Tweed is dead.'

The man, known as Mr Blue to a very few top officers in certain security circles, relaxed while he spoke to the aggressive man at the other end of the line. He sat at the back of the Mayfair bar. It had a long counter running along the opposite side. He was the only customer and the notice displayed on his table bothered him not at all. *Use of mobile phones is forbidden.*

Arriving in the exclusive establishment, he had asked the barman for the most expensive brandy he could see. He had tipped the barman generously so he knew no complaint would be made.

Earlier, after placing his glass on the table, he had walked into the cloakroom at the rear. Alongside the entrance the words FIRE EXIT were prominently attached to the wall. Walking to the fire door he lifted the steel bar, pushed the door open, peered out. He was looking into a deserted mews. A few yards to his right it led into a busy street.

Satisfied that he had an escape route – a precaution he never neglected – he returned to the table, drank some brandy and made his call. His voice was prudently low. The voice at the other end challenged his statement rudely.

'How can you be certain he is dead?'

Mr Blue paused, lit a menthol cigarette. He took his

time answering. He had realized long ago that people swallowed everything he said if they had to extract information bit by bit.

'Two bullets hit the target, I was told. Tweed slumped down. The car apparently ran into a wall. No one left the car while it was visible to the two men who accomplished their task. If that isn't enough for you then there is nothing more to say.'

He rang off before the other man could react in his normal blustering manner.

Stop looking at me, for God's sake, Lisa said to herself, willing the tramp to transfer his gaze anywhere else.

It seemed to work. The tramp looked at his whisky bottle, capped it. He shifted his position so he was sitting more upright. He burped, then looked up at the railings along the pavement.

'Girl with red 'air?'

'That's what I said,' snarled Eyebrows. 'Stop repeating what I've just said and answer the question, you louse.'

'Girl with red 'air,' the tramp said again. 'I've three wimin down 'ere. Two brunettes and a blonde. Don't think you're going to share. Come down 'ere and I'll smash your face in with this.'

Demonstrating his threat, he took hold of the bottle by the neck. Grim-faced, he hoisted the bottle and waved it slowly backwards and forwards. He stood up, continuing to wave his weapon.

'I'll go down there and slice his gizzard, Barton,' a sinister voice said from above.

'Panko, you'll shut your cakehole. He's just an old drunk. We're wasting time. Get movin' now . . .'

With a sigh of relief, Lisa heard the clumping of feet walking away further along the pavement. And now she

44

knew their names. Barton, Panko. The second name sounded Balkan. She had noticed his strange accent when he'd spoken. The tramp pointed a finger at her.

'Stay where you are. I'll make sure the rubbish 'as gone.'

He was absent for longer than she'd expected. She wondered whether he'd gone off to find another suitable hidey-hole to doss down. Then he reappeared, staggering a little as he came down the steps.

'Rubbish 'as gone. Went up Gower Street. Best go other way. Sorry about the stink in there.'

'I'm so very grateful to you. Heaven knows what you've saved me from.'

She had emerged from the alcove, was standing up. She reached for her purse, uncertain whether he'd resent payment. He seemed to read her mind. From under his shabby coat he produced a wallet fat with banknotes, showed it to her.

'I'm all right. Works the dustcarts. Odd way to earn me livin' but the money's good. Off you go . . .'

She threw him a kiss, climbed the steps, checked to her left, saw no one and hurried in the other direction. In Tottenham Court Road she flagged down a cab.

'Reefers Wharf in the East End. You know it?'

'Don't often go down there. Course I know it. I did the knowledge . . .'

Less than an hour later she paid the fare, then started walking. She thought it wiser if the cabbie didn't know where she was going. It was market day. The wide street was littered with stalls, men crying out their wares. Wearing a camel-hair coat over her trouser suit she became a target.

'Oi! Lady, we're givin' it away. It's April Fool's Day and I'm the fool . . .'

She hurried on until she saw the sign above the ancient pub. The Hangman's Noose. She pushed open the door and several sellers from the market were seated, drinking beer. Behind the bar a man saw her, gestured for her to move to a quiet end of the bar.

'Herb,' she said, keeping her voice down, 'I need a room. I haven't slept properly for twenty-four hours. Thugs have chased me. I gave them the slip.'

'Room Three. It's at the back.' He reached under the bar, surreptitiously handed her a key. 'Up the stairs and straight down the corridor. You get more beautiful each day, but you look all in. Have you eaten?'

'No, I haven't.'

'Thought not. Would 'am and eggs do?'

'I'm salivating. But there's a problem. I've left my case in at Waterloo. I have the receipt . . .'

'Give me it. Bert will drive there in my car. Be back here in no time.' She handed him the receipt, which disappeared inside his apron pocket. 'Give me a buzz on the phone when you're ready for the food.'

'Thanks, Herb. I could do with a shower first.'

'Room Three has all mod. cons. Bert will be back with your case in a couple of hours.' He leaned forward, whispering. 'No messages from Rhinoceros, whoever he may be, wherever he may be.'

'He's abroad. A very powerful man. I've never seen him and I've no idea where he is. Or who he is.'

Newman and Paula followed Tweed into his office. Newman waved a warning finger at Monica, gestured towards Tweed who had taken off his coat and settled behind his desk.

'Don't talk to him. All the way back from Eaton Square he hasn't said a word.'

'I have to tell him something,' she protested. 'Professor Saafeld's report with copies are in that envelope on his desk. Plus his own report which I've typed.'

'Thank you, Monica,' Tweed said quietly and opened both envelopes. 'Now let me see what he says about the autopsy.'

'And, Paula,' Monica went on, 'that sealed yellow envelope on your desk is from Art Baldwin. It's the photos you took of Eagle's Nest on the Downs. Art insisted he had to be present when you opened it.'

'He's a boffin,' said Newman. 'Like all scientific types he has tunnel vision. Nothing exists outside his world.'

'Not yet,' Tweed ordered. 'I've almost finished both reports and you'd better know what they contain . . .'

Not for the first time Paula marvelled at Tweed's agile brain. Besides having total recall of conversations and a first-class memory, he was also a speed-reader. He pushed aside the reports, took off his glasses, cleaned them on a new handkerchief, perched them back on his nose.

'Saafeld's report is damning,' he began. 'An open-and-shut case of murder regarding Jeremy Mordaunt. Which links up with my own conclusions. Monica, take a copy of each report, put them in an envelope addressed "Personal, for attention Gavin Thunder", send them at once to the Ministry by courier.'

'The Minister will explode,' Paula commented. 'I gather he was so determined it should be suicide.'

'Can't be helped,' Tweed replied as Monica collected copies off his desk. 'Now, our visit to Eaton Square. Anyone suspect something was wrong when we were inside the drawing room?'

'I did,' Paula replied. 'She didn't know where the drinking glasses were kept. Went to the wrong cupboard. When we got there she'd been drinking vile sherry out of a water glass. Clearly, after she'd arrived she couldn't be bothered to look for the right glass so she grabbed one from the kitchen. On our way out she chose the wrong key to open the front door. Then the furnishings of the room didn't fit her personality.'

47

'Very good. What was that question you asked her about a pet name for Jeremy?'

'I thought I might throw her off balance – and I did. I'd given her the impression we knew the pet name. She couldn't answer me.'

'Then we meet the haughty lady who lives there and she confirms our suspicions – although we'd already spotted the so-called Mrs Mordaunt was a fake.'

'Why would someone send her to impersonate Mrs Mordaunt?'

'Presumably,' Tweed speculated, 'someone guessed I would think of visiting Mrs Mordaunt. So they replaced her with a woman who would give me all the right answers. Building up the idea that Jeremy had reasons to commit suicide.' He blinked. 'And that could be the same someone who arranged for me to be killed. No, it couldn't be the same person. If they thought I'd be dead the charade of creating a fake Mrs Mordaunt would be pointless. I'm missing something here.'

'So where is the real Mrs Mordaunt?'

'That mystery worries me a great deal. I think I'd better call Roy Buchanan and ask him to start a search for her. Now . . .'

He was on the phone when Harry Butler came in. In his large fist he held a folded sheet of paper. He sat down while Tweed spoke to Buchanan.

'What's that piece of paper you're holding?' asked Paula, as curious as a cat.

'Wait. Then you'll see.'

He handed the sheet to Tweed the moment he finished his call. Sitting upright, he spoke as Tweed opened the sheet.

'Remember that chopper that followed us back from Alfriston? It did look to me as if it had taken off from Lord Barford's estate.'

'How high would you say it was when you saw it?'

48

'At a guess, about a thousand feet.'

'Was it gaining height?' Tweed persisted.

'No, cruising along.'

'Then it could easily have been the chopper we saw grounded at Rondel's place.'

'If you'd read my report. Just extracts from the file we have on Lord Barford.'

Tweed, surprised that Harry should have thought of checking the file, read the short report twice. Then he leaned back and stared at the ceiling. He was frowning.

'That was clever of you, Harry,' he said eventually. 'You left out that, after leaving the Army, Bernard Barford was chief of Special Branch for a while.'

'Didn't seem relevant.'

'I agree. What is relevant is that he owns a Sikorsky helicopter, commutes to London in it. Must have a pilot – I know he's never flown a plane in his life.'

He looked at Paula. She told him Monica had typed the report. He transferred his gaze to Newman.

'That means,' Newman remarked, 'we don't know which chopper tailed us to London, doubtless reporting our whereabouts – so that gunman could be waiting for us.'

'I could get Art Baldwin up here,' Paula suggested. 'Then we can open his envelope of pics, the ones I took. He'll go mad if I open it before he's with us.'

'Heaven save us from boffins,' Newman snapped. 'Although I will admit Art is undoubtedly the best interpreter of photos in the country.'

Tweed nodded to Monica, who phoned for Baldwin to come up. Within a minute there was a gentle tapping on the door. Tweed called out, 'Come in.' The door opened and a small man whose face vaguely resembled a squirrel's crept in. He wore thick-lensed glasses. Paula smiled and waved for him to come over. As she was opening the large envelope, Art spoke in a squeaky voice.

49

'I've printed the photos you took in Sussex. Original size and various enlargements.' He took a folding magnifying glass from his pocket. 'Very intriguing. I have comments.'

Everyone in the office, except Monica, got up, gathered round Paula's desk. She spread out the prints. She had used the new camera, invented by the basement boffins. At night it took very clear pictures without needing a flash.

'The chopper in the background,' Newman said. 'Can we bring that up more clearly, please?'

Art unfolded the small boxlike magnifying glass, positioned it over the helipad area. Newman peered down at it, grunted. Then he straightened up and whistled before he spoke.

'That, ladies and gentlemen, is a Sikorsky.'

'So,' mused Paula, 'that chopper which followed us . . .' She broke off, remembering Baldwin was with them. She had been going to say 'the helicopter could have come from Rondel's place.'

'I'm also deeply interested in that mast with a complex dish at the top of it,' Tweed said.

'Fred,' Baldwin began, 'who, as you know, is an expert on communications systems, said that dish is something advanced, something entirely new.'

He placed the magnifier over the dish. Paula sensed that Art was nervous, wasn't going to say anything more. She looked at Tweed and realized he'd had the same reaction. Newman peered at the image and shook his head. It meant nothing to him.

'That was it?' asked Tweed.

'Fred did tell me to keep his other conclusions from you until he'd completed his researches,' Art replied.

'So what is he keeping secret? I need to know now,' demanded Tweed.

'He is wondering whether the dish is designed to operate laser beams of enormous power that can eliminate any signals from all the satellites orbiting the earth.'

50

'Tell Fred to continue his researches, to drop everything else and concentrate on that dish.'

'I will. Can I go now?' Art asked timidly.

Paula knew he was not comfortable with a crowd of people. He practically lived in the basement. Had his meals brought in from a local deli. She blinked at Tweed once.

'Of course you can go,' Tweed said breezily. 'And my thanks for the good work you've done.'

'Just doing my job,' Art mumbled and almost ran to the door.

Tweed walked over to the windows and gazed across at distant Regent's Park. He remained there for several minutes, his hands tucked into the pockets of his jacket. Paula put her index finger to her lips to stop anyone talking. When Tweed swung round he walked briskly to his desk, sat down, looked round the room.

'I checked the number plate of that limo which drove away from Eaton Square,' Newman reported. 'Through contacts I've got. It was hired from Malibu Motors in Mayfair. I called them, saying I was Special Branch. A Miss Leatherbrother, accompanied by a uniformed chauffeur, paid the deposit and an extra amount in banknotes. The chauffeur has returned the car.'

'A dead end,' Tweed commented. 'What I expected.'

'There was something I should have told you earlier,' Harry said. 'Probably not important, but when I biked up to the summit of the Down overlooking that weird house . . .'

'Eagle's Nest?' Paula prompted.

'That's it. At the summit, about twenty feet back from the edge of the quarry, were a lot of rabbit holes, or so I thought. Shoved my arm down one and couldn't touch the bottom. It's like a rift circling the Down about twenty feet from the edge. Unstable, I'd say.'

'I'm sure a man who could afford a house like that had the area properly surveyed,' Tweed replied dismissively.

51

'What I was going to say was I think my first instincts were right. This scenario which is unfolding mysteriously has to be something very big, very dangerous. With international implications. Don't ask me what it's about because I have no idea.'

The phone rang. Monica answered, put the caller on hold, told Paula an Aubrey Barford was wanting to have a word. Paula looked puzzled, shrugged, took the phone and in a cool voice asked how she could help. The call was brief and when she handed the phone back she shrugged again as she went back to her desk.

'For some reason Aubrey Barford has invited me to have lunch with him at Martino's. One o'clock. I accepted – maybe I'll get some information out of him. At least he's the nice one. Couldn't abide his brother, that stuck-up ponce Lance.'

'See whether he'll talk about his father's way of life these days,' Tweed suggested.

'I'll do that . . .'

The phone rang again. This time Monica pulled a wry face when she looked at Tweed.

'The Minister is on the line for you. Gavin Thunder. By now those reports on Jeremy's death will have reached him . . .'

'Tweed here . . .'

'Thank you so much for sending the reports. I have a favour to ask you. Could you meet me for a quick chat? I'm a member of Marlows, rather an unfashionable club in Pall Mall.'

'I'd like to bring my assistant, Paula Grey.'

'She would be most welcome. Marlows has no apartheid where women are concerned, thank heaven.'

'When would you like us to come?'

'You couldn't make it in about half an hour's time? Or is that an imposition?'

'Just a second.' Tweed checked his watch. There was

time to agree and Paula could still make her appointment at Martino's. 'Yes, we can be there.'

'I'll look forward to seeing you both. Thank you again . . .'

Paula lifted her eyes to the ceiling. 'I bet he nearly blasted your head off after getting the reports.'

'On the contrary, he was very polite, most cordial. We'll get a taxi.'

Monica was surfing the Internet when the most hellish screeching filled the room. She stared in disbelief at her screen, her hands clapped over her ears. She used her head to gesture for them to come and look.

The terrible noise was so violent they all had hands protecting their ears as they joined her. Paula frowned. She had never seen anything like it. Thick lines, like missiles aimed from different directions, were shooting non-stop all over the screen. Newman used one hand to click the mouse. Made no difference. He hastily re-covered his ear.

Paula had glanced at her watch the moment the Internet went crazy. The diabolical racket continued, the eye-boggling lines never stopped skidding across the screen. When the noise ceased and the screen returned to normal Paula checked her watch again.

'That glitch lasted for exactly sixty seconds,' she announced.

'Let's go,' Tweed suggested. 'This new technology hasn't settled down yet.'

'But I've never experienced anything like that before,' Monica protested. 'Something very strange has just happened,' she insisted. But they were on their way out.

4

It was 11.30 a.m. Lisa had eaten the breakfast Herb had brought to her room. Her body was tingling with the second shower she had enjoyed and she'd decided she would go out. She was dressed to merge with the area outside The Hangman's Noose. A shabby old pair of jeans, an ancient blouse, a windcheater that had seen better days and an old pair of shoes with metal rims. She slung a well-worn shoulder bag over her shoulder and her hair was covered with a ragged shawl.

Going downstairs into the bar she was looking forward to wandering round the market. She loved the atmosphere. As she headed towards the door Herb called out to her from behind the bar.

'Wait a tick, I'm comin' with you.' He turned to a formidable fat woman also behind the bar. 'Millie, dear. Look after the place. I fancies a breath of fresh air . . .'

They had just stepped into the street when the sun came out. Wandering among the market stalls Lisa revelled in the aroma of fresh fruit and vegetables. The cobbled street was littered with discarded cabbage leaves, and inhabitants of the old houses, attracted by the brilliant sunlight, leaned out of first-floor windows. Lisa stopped suddenly for a second, then resumed her slow walk.

'You've seen 'im,' said Herb.

'Yes.' She grabbed a pair of tinted glasses from her bag,

put them on. 'Delgado. What's he doing here? He's a long way from Bulgaria or wherever he comes from.'

'That's why I came with you.'

Delgado, holding a large brown paper bag in his left hand, was standing on the far pavement, his dark eyes sweeping the area slowly. A giant, over six feet tall, he had a body to match his height. His greasy black fringe needed trimming and below it was a vicious face. A large nose broken in several places loomed above a wide cruel mouth, an aggressive jaw. He wore a long dark coat that almost reached his ankles.

'And he's brought a small gang of thugs with 'im,' Herb remarked. 'All foreigners. There's one.'

A small, powerfully built man, wearing a dirty baseball cap back to front, had stopped at a stall, grabbed hold of a banana, was eating it. The stallholder asked him to pay for it. The small man turned round slowly, finished his banana, threw the skin in the other man's face, waited. The stallholder decided not to make an issue of it when he looked at the culprit closely.

'I saw Delgado grab a leg of lamb off a stall, shove it into that bag he's holding. When payment was demanded Delgado produced a knife from somewhere. Blade must have bin eight inches long. He didn't pay.'

'What's going on?' Lisa asked.

'They're scanning the area. 'Ad a good look at my pub. They check out alleys, anywhere they could 'ide. That squat thug pinched the cap off Bert.'

'When?'

'They first appeared a couple of hours ago, got out of cars, scanned this area quickly, then drove off. I sent Bert after them on his motorbike. They drove to the West End, parked, then checked out expensive restaurants, discotheques. You name it. Now they're back 'ere.'

'You think they're getting ready for a riot?'

'Not yet,' Herb told her. 'Not if I read the signs aright.

They're choosin' targets for somethin' later. Here come six more of the tykes. Foreigners again. Walkin' separate as though they don't know each other.'

Selecting an apple from a stall, Lisa asked how much. The stallholder grinned, shook his head. He exchanged banter with Herb, who explained as they continued walking while she munched the apple.

'That was because you was with me. See that villainous lot that's just arrived? They're passin' Delgado as though he didn't exist. That's deliberate. Ever seen that brute before?'

'Yes. Once in a bar in Brussels. He caught me looking at him and I think he's a man who remembers people. Shouldn't you have some protection, with Delgado's mob casing the area?'

'Got a shotgun under the bar. Illegal. But not if Delgado ever comes in, waving that knife about. We'd better get back so I can help out Millie.'

'Did Bert make a list of the targets here and in the West End that Delgado was interested in?'

'He did.'

'Could I have a copy?'

'Course you can. I'll borrow it off Bert now. Can't think why you want it but you keeps yourself to yourself. Then, you're a smart lady . . .'

Customers were filling up the pub but Lisa was able to go to the end of the bar by herself. She copied Bert's list, then used the phone to call Tweed again. The same nice woman answered, regretted that Tweed was out again, asked if he could call her.

'I'll try again later, thank you . . .'

Tweed and Paula went inside Marlows, an obscure club located on Pall Mall alongside more prestigious establishments. Tweed was asking the porter if Mr Gavin Thunder had arrived when a small well-dressed man in a grey suit appeared in the hall. Well-built, he couldn't have been more than five feet four inches tall, Paula estimated, and he exuded physical energy as he held out a hand, smiling.

'Welcome, Tweed. Too long since we last met. And this must be the hyper-efficient Miss Paula Grey. And an attractive lady, if I may say so.'

'Thank you,' replied Paula as she shook his firm, muscled hand. 'I don't know about hyper-efficient but I get by.'

'With flying colours, according to many who know you. Shall we adjourn to the library? Very quiet in there. I'll lead the way . . .'

He was just as she'd expected. In his forties, he had dark brown hair, a high forehead, a commanding nose, a strong mouth. He walked rapidly and had an aura of amiability that put people at their ease. His most striking feature were his eyes, intense blue eyes that looked straight at you.

They followed him into a room lined with bookcases from floor to ceiling. The room was deserted except for a waiter and Thunder sat them at a small table circled with comfortable arm chairs.

'Coffee for everyone?' he suggested and nodded to the waiter. He sat forward, hands clasped in his lap, looked from one guest to the other.

'Got your reports, Tweed, as I said on the phone. Read both of them.' He spoke rapidly, like a man with an agile brain. 'Doesn't seem to be any doubt about what happened to poor Jeremy Mordaunt. Murder.'

'I'm afraid it was,' agreed Tweed and fell silent.

'What worries me, frankly,' Thunder continued when he realized Tweed was not going to say any more, 'is the inquest. It will, of course, be held at Eastbourne. That might just keep most of the press away. The government can do without yet another scandal.'

He kept quiet as the waiter returned and served the coffee. He only resumed speaking when the door had closed . . .

'Incidentally, I'm Gavin. Have I your permission to call you Paula? Thank you. I get so fed up with being addressed as "Minister".' He smiled. 'I feel like looking round to make sure I'm not in church.'

Paula chuckled and Thunder waved both hands as much as to say what a world we live in. He stared at Tweed, his expression grave.

'May I ask you a personal question? If you don't want to reply I'll quite understand.' He leaned forward again. 'At the inquest will you be telling the coroner you are still pursuing your investigations and request an adjournment?'

'I'm going to do exactly that.'

'Thank you for answering – between the three of us only.'

'Am I then to assume,' Tweed began, his voice sharper, 'that I am still in charge of the investigation? That would be most unusual.'

'You are to assume that, yes. I know it's unusual – there are people who would call it irregular. But there could be political implications, now we know it was murder. You see, Jeremy was very bright technically.' He paused. 'I have again to ask you to keep this just between the three of us.' He paused. 'A couple of days before Jeremy travelled to Alfriston he discovered my office was bugged.'

'And you'd discussed confidential matters in that room?' asked Tweed.

'Heavens, yes, I had. Thought I was safe there. So Jeremy removed all the listening devices. I decided not to report it to anyone.'

'Why?'

'Because I was beginning to wonder who I *could* trust.'

'Even among Cabinet members?'

'If you don't mind, I'd sooner not answer that question.

59

But I've been doing all the talking. Have you something you'd like to ask me?'

'Yes, I have. Do you know why Jeremy Mordaunt travelled down to Alfriston? Who he was going to see?'

'I have absolutely no idea. I kept him on a loose rein – he was clever and wouldn't tell me certain things until he had the complete story. I have made enquiries.'

'What about?'

'Discreetly, about who lives in that part of the world. So far I have only come up with Lord Barford. But since he gave up the job as chief of the Special Branch hasn't he retired?'

'One would expect him to have done that.'

'Oh, there is something else.' Thunder checked his Rolex watch. 'I'll have to go shortly. A Cabinet meeting.' He looked at Paula and smiled. 'You wouldn't care to come and keep me company – to prevent me from being bored stiff?'

'I don't think they'd welcome me,' she said, returning his smile.

'Before we go,' Tweed said, 'what was the something else?'

'I'd appreciate it if you'd liaise with Chief Inspector Roy Buchanan about your investigations. It would go some way to regularizing the situation.'

'I was going to do that anyway.'

They left the library, Thunder collected his coat, and they walked into the street. As they did so a limo pulled up at the kerb. Thunder swore, apologized to Paula.

'I did tell them to send an ordinary car for me. All this pomp and circumstance is so idiotic. Now, thank you both so much for giving me your time. And I've enjoyed your company.' He whispered the rest as the chauffeur opened the door with a flourish. 'Which is more than I expect to do when I get back to Downing Street . . .'

'You have your lunch with Aubrey Barford,' Tweed

reminded her as the limo moved off. 'Is there time for us to walk up St James's Street before you get a taxi?'

'Yes, there is.' They began to stroll. 'Well, that surprised me. I expected him to rave.'

'He can, I've heard. If a subordinate isn't quick enough or forgets something. And Thunder is the right name for him when he's speaking in the House of Commons. A magnificent orator. I've heard gossip that there's a cabal of Ministers plotting to remove the present PM – so they can instal Thunder in his place.'

'What did you think of his story about Jeremy locating and then removing the bugs from his office?' queried Paula.

'Gavin Thunder has an ingenious brain.'

5

At about the time Tweed and Paula entered Marlows a helicopter landed at Heathrow. Two passengers emerged and parted company as the sun came out. Both were men of the same height and in their forties. Here the similarity ended.

The athletic man with blond hair that gleamed in the sunshine boarded the motorized passenger trolley which had driven out as the chopper was landing. He radiated wealth. Clad in an Armani suit, he wore Gucci shoes, a Chanel tie and carried an expensive brief-case.

Once aboard the executive jet and settled in his seat he heard the engines starting up. An attractive stewardess brought him a glass of champagne and he leaned back to enjoy himself. The pilot had earlier filed a flight plan for Schiphol Airport near Amsterdam.

The flight took less than an hour. Landing at Schiphol, the passenger left the machine and stepped into a waiting limo. It drove him to the best hotel in the city where he alighted while the chauffeur, who had collected his case which had been aboard the jet before he'd arrived, handed it to a porter.

He registered at the desk. Victor Rondel. Once alone in his suite he noted with satisfaction a bottle of champagne waiting in an ice bucket. He went into the bathroom, locked the door.

Removing the blond wig carefully, he exposed thick dark

hair. He checked the time. Have a sleep here first, he decided, then a good dinner downstairs. When it was nightfall he would leave the hotel and wander down a certain street Amsterdam was famous for. Beautiful girls, wearing very little, would be sitting in showcase windows. He would take his time selecting the one he preferred.

Earlier, back at Heathrow, the other passenger who had alighted from the helicopter strode across the field towards his terminal, carrying an ordinary case. He wore a beret and a dark overcoat as he stepped it out. When the passenger trolley returned from the jet he climbed aboard and was transported to the terminal. He showed his passport in the name of René Pinaud and was just in time to board his next flight.

It was a boring trip of about fifty minutes to his destination. Glancing now and then out of the window he saw nothing but a sea of cloud. He refused all refreshments. When the plane landed he was among the first off. After passing swiftly through the formalities he climbed inside a company car waiting for him. It drove him to the area for private planes and he boarded the twelve-passenger Gulfstream private jet. Its interior had been luxuriously refurbished and he sank with relief into a leather armchair. The male steward in a fresh white uniform approached him. He spoke in German.

'Would sir like something to drink?'

'Just a brandy,' the passenger replied in the same language. 'Also a bottle of mineral water. Flying dehydrates . . .'

When the steward returned, his passenger had removed the beret he had worn pulled down tightly over his head. He took out a mirror and combed his blond hair.

'Something to eat also, sir?' the steward enquired.

'Nothing, Hans. A meal will be waiting for me when we get there . . .'

He glanced out of the window and again saw nothing except a sea of cloud. Alone, he took out a special mobile phone – special because it had a device which made interception impossible and was safe to use in flight. He pressed a series of numbers. At the other end a voice said 'Yes?' in German.

'Rondel speaking. I'll land in about a half-hour. I have to say the situation is building up dangerously. They are assembling formidable—'

'I prefer you to wait until you have arrived . . .'

There was a click and Rondel realized the connection had been broken. The voice had been, as always, authoritative but without a trace of arrogance. It had spoken slowly and each word was exceptionally clear. It was the voice of a very remarkable brain.

The sun came out as they were crossing the coast and Rondel concentrated on gazing down at the rippling blue of the Baltic Sea. On the mainland he had a glimpse of Travemunde and then it was nothing but blue sea.

The Gulfstream was losing height and he stared down for a sight of the island. Berg Insel – or Mountain Island – was located well clear of all shipping routes, a private fastness. The plane lost more height and he caught his first glimpse. A sloping mountain peak reared up at its centre. On the southern side sheer granite cliffs fell into the Baltic – the harbour and runway were on the northern shore.

As the machine dropped even lower he saw at the summit of the mountain the lighthouse which always functioned as dusk fell, or when fog covered the island in daylight. A short distance below it he saw the tall stone chimney-like edifice that housed the most advanced scientific system in the world.

'I still can't reach the man I must see,' Lisa protested. 'I have called several times and he's always out.'

'Whoever it is, you must persist,' Herb advised.

They were were eating lunch in an isolated room behind the bar at The Hangman's Noose. Herb was doing his best to calm her down but without much success.

'I *have* persisted, damnit,' Lisa snapped, banging down her fork.

'Have you an address?' Herb enquired.

'Yes, I have.'

'Is he the sort of man you can just call on, then?'

'No, I don't think so. I should make an appointment.'

'Then do that when you can.'

'Don't you think I have tried time and again? Seeing Delgado prowling round was the last straw.' She had raised her voice. 'Something very violent is being planned . . .'

She stopped speaking. The door from the bar had opened and a man stood looking at them. Delgado. Lisa reached under her jacket, gripped the Beretta behind her belt. The giant walked in closer.

'Heard my name. What you two doing?'

'This is a private room,' Herb said.

'What you two doing?' repeated Delgado, coming closer.

Behind him Millie rushed into the room, dashed into the kitchen, came out with a large rolling pin in her hand. Her face was very red. She brandished the rolling pin.

'Get out. Get back to the other side of the bar. Then get back out of the pub before I smash your stupid skull in, you scum.'

She seemed larger than Lisa had thought her to be. The giant took a step back, then another as Millie followed him. She yelled at him at the top of her voice. He ran back through the door, leapt to the other side of the bar. Herb was on his feet, just behind Millie. Delgado glared at him.

'Your place will be first to go up in flames . . .'

Then he rushed to the outer door, knocking over a table as he passed it. Customers' beer was spilt over the floor and he was gone.

66

'Sorry, gentlemen,' Herb said calmly. ''Ad too much, he 'ad. What he knocked over was lager. More comin' up. On the 'ouse . . .'

He closed the door to the room, leaving Lisa inside. She picked up a phone and pressed numbers. She was breathing heavily and held her throat when the same woman answered and she asked for Tweed, giving her name.

'He's here now. Sorry you've had so much trouble . . .'

'Tweed here. Who is this?'

'Lisa. We met yesterday at Lord Barford's party. Do you remember me?'

'Of course I do. You wanted to come and see me about something.'

Herb had come into the room. He was carrying a pail and a cloth he'd used to clean up the spilt lager. He paused, unsure if she wanted privacy. She smiled at him, went on talking.

'If I could come at six o'clock? It will be dark then and might be safer.'

'Safer from what?'

'Mr Tweed, large organized gangs of refugeees are prowling the city, choosing the places which will be targets when they start devastating riots. I don't think they're ready yet but I can point out the targets they've chosen so far.'

'Are you sure about this?'

'I've seen them with my own eyes. It's a huge operation and, at the moment, covers London from the West End to the East End. Have you a few men, tough men, you could bring with you? Just in case.'

'I think we might handle that problem, but first, could you get here at, say, 5.30 p.m. so we can have a chat? You have the address.'

'I'll be there at 5.30 on the dot. Don't be surprised how I'm dressed.'

'I'll look forward to seeing you . . .'

Lisa thanked him, put down the phone, turned round to find Herb staring at her, still holding his pail and cloth. He shook his head.

'Goin' over the top a bit, aren't we? Large organized gangs. There weren't so many of them. And look how Delgado scarpered when Millie went for 'im.'

'Bert gave me a long list of places in the West End he saw them looking at. Delgado will need a lot of thugs to cause mayhem over such a large area. I'm sure he's got reinforcements that we haven't seen.'

'Who is this Tweed?'

'Someone I know. Don't on any account mention his name to anyone.'

'I'm just goin' to forget the whole thing. Wish I knew where you'd been when you were abroad for weeks.'

'I don't want to talk about it. I need more sleep. Ready for tonight.'

As Tweed was relaying to Paula, Newman and Butler in his office what Lisa had said, the door opened and Marler, a key member of his team, walked in.

Marler, in his late thirties, was impeccably dressed as usual. He wore a warm beige suit, gleaming white shirt, a Valentino tie and carried a military-style raincoat with large lapels. Hanging it up, he adopted his favourite position, standing in a corner while he lit a king-size cigarette.

'Sense an air of tension,' he drawled in his upper-crust voice. 'Bit of excitement?'

Tweed began again, tersely reporting every word Lisa had said. Then, for Marler's benefit, he recalled the events since the journey he had made with Paula to Alfriston, the aftermath when two shots were fired into their car.

'Tweed, you live a charmed life,' Marler commented. 'And Newman's hatchback is parked outside, as good as new. Is this Lisa Trent trustworthy?'

'Frankly, I'm not sure,' Tweed told him. 'Which is why I've asked her to get here at 5.30. I want to grill her. But we should be ready. Harry, Pete Nield has just about had his holiday. Could you contact him?'

'Spoke to him on the phone this morning before I came in. He's bored. I can get him here in half an hour.'

'Do it when we've finished.'

'We carry weapons?' Harry suggested.

'Nothing lethal. We don't want to start a shoot-out.'

'Tear-gas bombs then?'

'Oh, if you insist. But if we do go with Lisa, and I did say *if*, we're only observing.'

'Organized gangs,' commented Newman. 'Sounds far-fetched. I think Lisa exaggerates.'

'I don't,' objected Paula. 'You haven't seen her, talked to her. I have. She's very cool.'

'She was on the phone,' Tweed agreed. 'Although I detected an undercurrent of anxiety.'

'Bob,' Marler began, straightening up. 'Organized gangs. You know I have a lot of contacts in this country – as well as abroad. I've just got back from Brussels. A contact, who I've found reliable in the past, told me he'd heard large groups of so-called refugees were being trained in the remote Ardennes in military style, using live ammunition.'

'Belgium is in a mess,' Newman replied dismissively.

'Also,' Marler ploughed on, 'another contact who lives in that model village near Weymouth phoned me today. Said there were rumours more refugees in large numbers were being brought ashore secretly after dark. Thought I'd pop down there and have a shufti.'

'More rumours,' Newman commented. 'Soon we'll hear the Martians have landed.'

'I'm driving down to Dorset,' Marler said firmly. 'I'll call you, Tweed, if I find anything. And, for your information, Bob, this contact is also very reliable. Toodle pip . . .'

★　　★　　★

69

When Gavin Thunder's limo reached Trafalgar Square it ran into the normal traffic jam. The Minister, who had just made a call on his mobile, tapped on the closed window between himself and the chauffeur. The car was stationary as the chauffeur slid the window open.

'Carson,' the Minister told him, 'I'm getting out here. I fancy walking the rest of the way.'

'Very good, sir . . .'

Thunder walked back the way the car had come. In Pall Mall, as he approached Marlows, he saw a tall fat man strolling along the pavement. He caught up with him near the entrance to the club.

'Good timing,' he commented. 'Now let's get inside so you can tell me how things are progressing.'

Oscar Vernon wore a grey overcoat unbuttoned down the front. Underneath he wore a pale grey suit, a pink shirt, a grey bow tie. In his early fifties, he had a large head, a fat face with bulging grey eyes, a pudgy nose, thick lips and an aggressive jaw which would soon be double-chinned. Everything about Oscar was grey and fat. In his right, well-muscled hand he carried a malacca cane with a curious circular knob.

'You'd like a drink?' Thunder asked as they sat in the library.

'Always.' Oscar chuckled. 'Double Scotch.'

'I'll join you. I've just had a conversation when it was difficult to keep my temper.'

Thunder ordered the drinks, then stared at Oscar, looking him up and down. Oscar was beaming.

'Do you have to dress in such a noticeable manner?'

'Before you have asked. Before I have told you no one takes me seriously. They think I am the clown. If only they knew.'

Thunder remained silent until the waiter had served them and closed the door. Oscar lifted his glass, drank half the contents, beamed again. Thunder leaned close, kept his voice low, rasping.

'So how are things progressing?'

'Under my command . . .' He drank the rest of the whisky, looked at the glass, a hint which Thunder ignored, '. . . they progress. As always. Reinforcements continue to arrive. A rehearsal will take place tonight.'

'You'd better be damned careful. It's far too early yet for the real thing.'

'This I know. Discipline. I insist. Under my command . . .'

'Yes, I know. The reinforcements – where will you train and hide them?'

'On the Bodmin Moor on the Cornwall.'

'They'll be conspicious,' Thunder objected.

'No. Tourist buses I hire will take them there. I go there myself. I see the Jamaica Inn for the tourists. They go there. Then they are gone – on to the Bodmin Moor.'

'You seem to have thought it out,' Thunder conceded reluctantly. 'And now I must go.'

'You go?' Oscar beamed, showing his large teeth. 'There is something more. No?'

Thunder reached a gloved hand into his pocket. He handed his guest a thick white envelope stuffed with fifty-pound notes. £10,000. It was his habit to make Oscar ask for the money. It exerted a degree of control over the fat man. He wore gloves to avoid his fingerprints appearing on the money or the envelope. He left the library.

On his way out he met the waiter. He told him to take another double Scotch to his guest in the library. It would please Oscar. More important, it would prevent Oscar appearing before Thunder left the building. Oscar counted the money quickly. The Minister preferred not to be seen in Pall Mall again with Oscar Vernon, dressed as he was.

*   *   *

71

Paula arrived at Martino's in a side street off Piccadilly, handed her coat to the hat-check girl, and saw Aubrey seated at a table in a booth by the wall. He was drinking and a half-empty bottle of red wine stood on the table.

Oh, my God! she thought. I'm going to have trouble with this one.

Aubrey stood up. In doing so he nearly dragged off the tablecloth. He lurched forward to stop the bottle toppling over and grinned. He was reaching for her to kiss her but she eluded him by slipping into the booth and sitting facing him.

'Welcome to the banquet,' he greeted her, his speech slightly slurred. 'What are you drinking?' The waiter had arrived.

'No starter,' she said quickly. 'I'll have Dover sole off the bone with French beans. No potatoes. To drink I'd like still mineral water. No ice or lemon.'

'I'll have the same. And a bottle of bubbly. Make it Krug,' Aubrey demanded.

'That's not for me, I hope.'

'We . . . are . . . going . . . to . . . set . . . this town . . . alight.'

As he paused between each word his fingers marched slowly across the cloth, straightened by the waiter.

'Champers is for you,' he told her.

'I don't want any. So if it's just for me cancel the order.'

He shook his head, winced, refilled his wine glass, drank half of it. She crunched a roll, began buttering it. He grinned foolishly.

'How is the Brigadier?' she asked him.

'The fighting old Brig. Pater has St Vitus' Dance. Can't stay in one place for five minutes. Do . . . you . . . know.' He leant across the table confidentially. 'Tell you . . . secret. Strictly *entre nous* . . . he flies all over the ruddy place . . . Brussels, Paris, Berlin, Stockholm.' He paused to drink more wine. 'How does he know . . . that's what you're thinking.'

Paula had suddenly realized she had a golden opportunity to extract information without appearing to do so. She drank some water as Aubrey stared at her, his eyes glazed.

'I don't believe a word of it,' she said eventually. 'You're making it up.'

'Oh, so that's what you think. Well, beautiful Paula, I've often hidden in a big cupboard in Pater's study . . . listened in when he makes his phone calls. So . . . there. What do you think of that?'

She thought it showed he was a little sneak, eavesdropping on his father. She smiled as she replied.

'Really?'

'Yes. Really. Really . . . Really.'

He was mimicking the way she had pronounced the word. She tucked one hand under her chin.

'I can't imagine any of these calls are important.'

'Can't you? Don't know much, do you, Paula? These calls he makes are *secret*. So there!'

The meal arrived. Paula began eating as soon as the plate was put before her. Her host stared at his plate as though he didn't recognize its contents. He had another drink, then smirked at Paula.

'My father isn't . . . retired at all.'

'Good for him.'

'He's matriculating people . . .'

'Matriculating? Sorry, I don't understand, Aubrey.'

'Manip-ul-ating people.' He smirked again. 'You are one beautiful lady.'

As he spoke his right hand went under the table, grasped her knee. She grabbed hold of the hand, removed it forcibly, slammed down her knife and fork.

'If you touch me again I'm walking straight out of this

place.' Her voice was calm, icy calm. 'I thought you were the nice brother. My mistake. Now behave yourself. Eat something – leave the bottle alone.'

'My profuse apologies. I don't know what came over me. I like you.'

'Your meal is getting cold.'

'I suppose you think I'm drunk?'

'We won't talk about it.'

'Paula . . .' He leaned across the table. 'Is there someone else?'

'Mind your own business. You know something? I'm not enjoying this lunch at all. I've lost my appetite,' she continued in her cool tone. 'I'm going to leave now.'

'You can't do that.' His expression turned ugly. 'No one walks out on me. And the staff here know me.'

'I'm sure they do by now. Goodbye, Mr Barford.'

She got up and quickly left the table. Collecting her coat, she went out to find a taxi. It might not have been pleasant but she had extracted intriguing information.

6

Oscar Vernon strolled up St James's Street, malacca cane held under his armpit like a sergeant major's baton. He beamed at several women who stared at his clothes, not realizing they thought them bizarre. Turning along Piccadilly towards the Circus he checked the time, began to hurry.

He had arranged to make the call from phone box to phone box. The subordinate he was going to speak to would soon be waiting. Diving down into the Underground, he found an empty booth, made his call. At the other end, near Reefers Wharf, the phone was answered immediately.

'Who is this?' Oscar demanded.

'Delgado here. There's a queue waiting to use this phone . . .'

'So what! Listen very good to me. This night at ten o'clock you do the rehearsal. It's been agreed from high up. By me . . .'

'The men – and the women – will be outside targets.'

'They had better be. Now listen very good. They look, they see. But no violence. Only if they need to do it to go away. You hear me?'

'I do. I will tell . . .'

Delgado swore foully, slammed the phone back, pushed his way roughly past the queue. Oscar had again slammed the phone down on him. Bastard!

*   *   *

Tweed, when Paula had left him in a taxi, had walked all the way back to Park Crescent. Walking helped him to think and the sun was shining strongly, so much so that he felt its warmth on his face.

Entering his office, he found Newman reading a newspaper and Harry Butler, a cloth over his lap, reassembling a 7.65mm Walther automatic he had been cleaning. He handed his coat to Monica and sat behind his desk, took a new writing pad from a drawer and began doodling names. To his annoyance Monica broke into a verbal flood.

'You remember that very strange thing which happened on the Internet? While you were out I phoned as many of my contacts as I could reach. You are listening, I hope?'

Tweed grunted. Newman had closed his newspaper and listened to her as she went on.

'I wanted to find out if it was just a local breakdown. It wasn't. I called Birmingham, Manchester, then New York, San Francisco, Miami, New Orleans, Paris, Berlin, Oslo and even Prague. Every one of my contacts told me their systems had gone haywire at the same time ours did. That is, allowing for time differences. And they all described the same thing – the devilish screeching which deafened them, those missile-like lines shooting over their screens.'

'A glitch,' Tweed mumbled. 'Never did like the Internet.'

Monica was about to protest when Paula came in, her face flushed. She went to her desk, threw the loop of her shoulder bag over the back of her chair, sat down, her hands clenched.

'Enjoy your lunch with nice Aubrey?' Tweed enquired.

'Like hell I did!'

Tweed stopped doodling as she recalled every word of the lunch-time conversation, the state Aubrey was in, what he had told her. Tweed began adding names to his pad.

'I'm sorry you had such an unpleasant experience,' he told her.

'But I did get some strange information from him regarding his father's activities. And jolly active he seems to be. But what Lord Barford is doing I can't even guess. Let me see.'

She went over to his desk, stood behind him, stared down at the pad, at the names he'd written down well spaced from each other. Jason Schulz (dead), Jeremy Mordaunt (dead), Bogle, Lord Barford – Brussels, Paris, Berlin, Stockholm – Aubrey Barford, Gavin Thunder, Mark Wendover, fake Mrs Mordaunt, Rondel, Lisa.

'I was trying to link up one person with another,' Tweed explained. 'So far I've got exactly nowhere. No idea of what is going on, but something is.'

'That's why you've drawn large loops round each name,' Paula remarked. 'You've used this technique before. And the only loop with anything in it is Barford's – you've put in the city names I said Aubrey had overheard the Brigadier phoning.'

'All of which gets me nowhere.'

'Why put Lisa last?'

'Because at the moment she's my only hope that may lead us to what is happening. Assuming she *does* turn up at 5.30 this evening.'

'I'm sure she will.'

'Are you? We know nothing about her. She's a mystery woman.' He looked at Newman. 'And have you any idea why Mark Wendover hasn't arrived here?'

'Well, as you know, I had dinner with him last night. Then he asked me to join him again this morning for an early working breakfast. He went out somewhere soon afterwards.'

'A lot of use he is.' Tweed started cleaning his glasses. 'You had a so-called working breakfast with him. A long one?'

'Yes. Well over an hour.'

'And during that breakfast you told him everything you knew as regards our trip to Sussex – the visit Paula and I made to Lord Barford's, then the grim business in Alfriston?'

'Yes, I did.'

'I see.' He perched his glasses back on his nose. 'I just wonder. I really do.'

Early that same morning, Mark Wendover had a large breakfast with Newman, then immediately left the Ritz. He was wearing a white polo-neck sweater, blue jeans, trainers on his large feet and carried a trench coat over his arm. He was in a hurry to get the show on the road.

From a car-hire firm in Piccadilly he'd noticed when Newman had driven him from the airport the previous day he chose a cream Jaguar. His next port of call was Hatchards, the bookshop. He bought an Ordnance Survey map of East Sussex, studied it for at least two minutes, then hurried back to his car. He didn't need a map of London – from frequent visits he knew his way round the city as well as he knew Washington.

He was on the straight stretch to Petworth when a blonde in an Audi overtook him, waved a triumphant hand. 'Can't have that,' he decided. He increased speed, passed her, waved a hand. She soon realized she had no chance of repeating her earlier performance as the cream streak became like a toy car way ahead of her.

Later, when he turned off the A27 to Alfriston, he drove at a sedate pace. It was a glorious day, the sun shining out of a cloudless sky. When he parked the Jag on the outskirts of the village he threw his trench coat into the trunk.

His long strides soon took him into Alfriston and he walked into a pub which had just opened. In the country a pub was where you heard all the local gossip. Smiling at

78

the barman, he ordered a pint of mild, sat down by the bar on a stool.

'You're my first customer today,' the barman told him. 'Here on holiday, sir?'

'Yes and no. Alfriston looks like the sort of place where nothing ever happens.'

'Don't you believe it. We've just 'ad a murder here. Up the road. Last night.'

'I like a good murder,' Wendover said cheerfully. 'Read a lot of thrillers. A local, I suppose.'

'No, it wasn't. A high-rankin' civil servant, so I hear.'

'Lived round here, did he?'

'No. Never seen down 'ere before. So why does he come down 'ere to shoot himself in an underground tunnel, of all places.'

'That sounds more like suicide.'

'Tell you something.' The barman leaned across the counter. 'The police is baffled. Show you where it 'appened if you'd come outside with me.'

Mark had only sipped at his drink. He carried the glass out with him. The barman pointed up the narrow street to where police tapes were still in place. Two farmers wandered past them into the pub.

'More customers. Excuse me . . .'

Wendover waited until he was alone. Then he poured the rest of his drink down a drain. He was careful about drinking and driving. Taking the empty glass back inside, he thanked the barman, walked out and a short distance up the High Street and into another pub. Except for the barman the place was empty. He ordered another pint of mild. The barman was a short, plump jovial type.

'Nothing wrong with startin' early, I always say. Just so long as you're not driving.'

'It's got a lot of character, this village,' Wendover remarked. 'But I don't imagine anyone important lives here.'

79

'Well, if I may say so, sir, you'd be wrong there. A bare five miles away Lord Barford lives. Got a big estate. Family's lived here for generations in the mansion, Barford Manor.'

'He does? I thought the aristocracy was being taxed out of existence.'

'Got a point there, you 'ave. Had two surveyors in here recently. One 'ad been asked to inspect the place. He was tellin' his friend his lordship's in deep trouble. Risin' damp, dry rot. He said the whole roof has to be replaced, and half the windows. Cost his lordship over a million. He lives well but he hasn't got that sort of money. And he's got a helicopter and a ridin' stable. Often rides over the Downs, he does. Towards the Eagle's Nest.'

'What's that?' Wendover asked, then sipped at his pint.

'One of these crazy modern houses. Very big. A chap called Rondel owns it.'

'Sounds foreign. Barford and Rondel are friends, then?'

'Don't think so. Lord Barford spent a lot of time abroad in the Army. Don't think he's keen on foreigners. Can't blame 'im.'

Wendover was aware that a few minutes earlier someone had come in and stood close behind him. He made a point of not looking round. The newcomer spoke, his voice unpleasant, arrogant.

'Mind telling me what you're doing here?'

'Yes, I do.' Wendover turned round. A short man stared at him with a hostile expression. He wore a dark, ill-fitting suit. 'Who are you?'

'Bogle. Chief Constable.'

'Assistant Chief,' the barman said.

'Barrow,' the policeman snapped. 'You keep out of this. I'll have a lemonade.'

'Boogle?' Wendover enquired. 'Like a bugle soldiers blow at ceremonies?'

'Bogle,' the policeman repeated. 'B-o-g-l-e. Got it?'

Here we go, thought Wendover. Newman had relayed to him over dinner Tweed's encounter with this character. He turned his back, sipped more of his drink. A hand tapped his shoulder. Wendover put down his glass, swung round.

'I don't like people who touch me.'

'And I don't like people who ignore me. I'm investigating a murder. You've been going into pubs and asking questions I find suspicious. I'd like to see proof of your identity.'

'Would you? You're going to be disappointed. Unless you can charge me with some offence. Incidentally, your lemonade is getting cold.'

With this parting shot Wendover walked out into the street. He was on his way back to his car, which took him past the open door of the first pub he'd visited. A shout from inside stopped him. The barman came running out.

'I think maybe you dropped this when you took your wallet out of your back pocket to pay me.'

He handed Wendover a small notebook bound in blue leather. Opening it, Wendover saw the letters MoA engraved in gold on the inside of the front binding. Riffling through the pages he saw a series of coded numbers and words.

'Thank you,' he said to the barman. 'Without this I'd have been lost at work.'

Slipping the book into his pocket he hurried back to his car. He knew from his time at Langley with the CIA that MoA was an abbreviation for the Whitehall Ministry of Armaments. He surmised that Bogle had probably dropped the book while he had been putting on his gloves, presumably to make himself look more official. Now he wanted to get out of the village before Bogle discovered his loss.

He had also decided to drive straight back to Park

Crescent. It could be important to Tweed to hear about the information he had picked up.

Seattle, Washington State, Pacific Coast. The HQ of the World Liberation Front was located in an apartment overlooking Lake Washington. This location had been carefully chosen due to its upmarket situation. Successful, well-off Americans were happy to live in this area. No one – including the FBI – would dream that dangerous revolutionaries might be found here.

In the spacious ground-floor apartment at the end of a block with a view across a trim lawn down to the lake, a man sat in front of the Internet. His long greasy hair was coiled in a ponytail. On the back of a nearby chair hung the jacket of the expensive business suit he wore. Leaving the apartment – or returning to it – he always wore a hat with the ponytail tucked out of sight. His neighbours thought he was one of those whizz-kids, something in electronics.

It was the middle of the night when he checked the time, then clicked the mouse to a repeat program on fitness. This catered to insomniacs of both sexes who whiled away the dreary hours following the instructor, a big man who was all muscle and no fat. Standing on a platform, he faced a class of mixed sexes, demonstrating exercises.

Ponytail had a pad open in front of him, noted down every third word of the instructor, who spoke slowly. The moment the program was over he glanced at the words which had formed into a message. He picked up the phone and dialled an unlisted number in London.

'Oscar here,' a rough voice answered.

'You sound like a comedian,' Ponytail replied and connection had been verified.

'You have the business report?' Oscar enquired.

'With this takeover the minimum of pressure can be used. End of report . . .'

82

In his room above a little-used warehouse at Reefers Wharf Oscar Vernon sucked the end of his pen. The correct interpretation of the word 'pressure' was 'violence.'

'This, I thinks,' he said to himself, 'is what Brits call the escalation. London will have the rough night.'

7

Tweed came back into his office after having a good wash. He had just eaten the lunch Monica had brought in from the local deli. He looked annoyed.

'I wonder if we'll ever hear from that boy wonder, Mark Wendover. If he does turn up I'm going to give him a real grilling.'

'I've been surfing several American sites,' Monica began. 'There was a weird one on gardening – the woman commenting spent ages between naming each flower. Then there was one on keeping fit. That was weird, too – the instructor took so much time between giving fresh instructions. I had the feeling it was coded.'

'Surfing the net.' Tweed snorted. 'Sounds like playing in the waves down in Devon. As for coding . . .'

'Monica,' Paula interjected, 'was once a code-breaker in the Communications building further down the Crescent. Until you spotted her potential and moved her here.'

'I would like what I wrote down about the gymnastics to be examined by our chief code-breaker,' Monica persisted.

'I'll call and get Jacko over here,' Paula said, going to the phone.

'Don't mind me,' grumbled Tweed. 'I only work here.'

'He's on his way,' Paula said.

Tweed took out his pad with loops round names, studied

it. A few minutes later someone tapped on the door. A slim blonde girl of about thirty came in, wearing a fawn trouser suit which went well with her hair.

'I'm Jenny,' she announced. 'Jacko moved to another job in GCHQ about a month ago. I'm the chief code-breaker.'

She took the sheet of paper Monica handed her. Newman looked at her and she was aware of his interest.

'I've an idea this could be fairly simple,' she remarked.

'Doubt if it's a code at all,' Tweed commented.

Ten minutes later she handed a sheet from the pad to Tweed. He pursed his lips as he read it.

With this takeover the minimum of pressure can be used. End of report.

'It was every third word,' Jenny explained.

'Obviously some business corporation working a deal,' Tweed said sceptically. Paula was peering over his shoulder. 'You see, it means nothing,' he said to her.

'I wonder. When they had those riots in Washington I saw them on TV. One thug yelled at the camera "It's a takeover." He meant they were taking over Washington – or trying to.'

'Did he?' Tweed looked thoughtful, then decided. 'I think for this expedition with Lisa tonight we'll marshal our forces. Harry, phone Pete again. Tell him to get here at once. Pity Marler is down in Dorset.'

'If you need me again,' said Jenny, standing up, 'just call me.'

'We will. And thank you for what you've done.'

'It was a piece of cake . . .'

She had just left when the phone rang. Monica answered and informed Tweed that Mark Wendover was waiting downstairs.

'Send him up. I've a good mind to put him on the first plane back to the States.'

Paula looked with interest at the tall well-built man

86

when he entered. She liked the way he was dressed infor-
mally, the way he smiled as he accepted Tweed's suggestion to sit down.

'I have to inform you,' Tweed began grimly, 'that here
we work as a team. I haven't heard one damn' word from
you all day. Where have you been? Then I'll want to ask
you a lot of questions about your background.'

'I did try to phone Bob Newman before I left the Ritz.
But there was no reply.'

'I came straight here,' Newman told him.

'Well . . .' Mark looked back at Tweed. 'I drove to
Alfriston, got some information you might find interesting.
Can I tell you about my trip before you hang me from the
nearest tree?'

'Go ahead.'

Tweed's expression gradually changed to neutral as he
listened intently to Mark. The American explained in great
detail everything he'd experienced while in East Sussex.
He had total recall for every conversation that had taken
place. He concluded by producing the blue leather-bound
notebook.

'You've done a very good job,' Tweed said as he
examined the book. 'I don't want to hear about your
background. You know what I think happened with this
notebook? Bogle was there before Paula and I arrived. He
denied touching the body but I think he lied. He found it
in one of the late Jeremy Mordaunt's pockets and kept it.
MoA. Very interesting. Paula, could you get Jenny back
here for me, please?'

'Something wrong?' Jenny asked when she arrived back
in the office.

'Nothing. Since you left us this book has come into
my possession.' He handed it to her. 'Would you say
the entries are in code?'

'Could be,' she said, after glancing through the pages. 'I
would have to work on it before I'm sure. MoA.'

'Yes. Which means no one except yourself in Communications should see it. Can you ensure that?'

'I can. I have my own little office to work in. It has three locks on the door – two Banhams and one Chubb. And I do have a safe where I keep top secret material.'

'That's top secret.'

'I realize that. Who shall I report to if I solve it?'

'Myself or Paula. If neither of us is available, then Monica.'

'I'll get cracking – literally – on it right away. Could I have a thick envelope? Something I can carry the notebook in so no one sees it when I get back to Communications.'

Monica found one for her. Jenny put the book inside, sealed it. She gave Newman a brief wink. She had hardly glanced at Mark, but Paula felt sure she would recognize him if she saw the American again.

'This make take longer than the other problem,' she warned Tweed and left the room.

For several minutes Tweed explained to Mark the Lisa situation. He emphasized that he was very unsure about her, told him how he had met her.

'Lord Barford again,' Mark mused.

'Yes. And from what you've told me Bernard Barford is on the rocks financially. Something I didn't even suspect . . .'

The phone had rung. Monica called across to Tweed. 'Lisa is waiting downstairs now. Bang on time.'

'Ask her to come up.'

Lisa came into the room, wearing a grey raincoat. Monica had offered to take it but she shook her head, sitting down at Tweed's invitation. He started by introducing everyone in the room except Paula by their first names only.

'Now, before we decide to go anywhere with you, I need to know far more about you. Where do you live?'

'In a flat off Ebury Street. I'd sooner not give you the address. Two very tough-looking men stalked me but I gave them the slip,' Lisa explained.

'Who were they? Or who sent them, if someone did?'

'I've no idea. Absolutely no idea.'

'This is all very vague,' Tweed suggested. 'At Lord Barford's party you told me your job was that of a confidante. Can you elaborate?'

'I should have said I was a security consultant.' She was relaxing now, no longer sitting stiffly in her chair. 'I look after one of the most powerful men in the world. He told me to come and see you.'

'I'm surprised he knows I exist.'

'He has deep contacts all over the world. He knows who you really are.'

'And who am I?' asked Tweed.

'Deputy Director of the SIS. That insurance stuff on that plate by the front door is just cover. He knows very big trouble is planned for London. He sent me over to find out first which areas they're targeting – so I could tell you. They're the West End and the East End. Tonight.'

'Who are the troublemakers?'

'Your stupid government lets in too many so-called refugees. They don't realize that many have been trained in guerrilla warfare abroad. I'm pretty sure that tonight is a dress rehearsal for the main attack which will come later. They'll be testing out the reactions of your police force. I don't know when they'll strike, but I'm sure it will be after dark.' She lifted a hand to brush back her mane of red hair. 'How many men can you muster?'

'Probably, including myself, say six. Except for one who will arrive shortly, they are in this room. One of them,' he went on, not looking at Newman, 'has SAS training. The others are up to his standard. Paula is among the six. I wouldn't make the mistake of underestimating her.' Tweed raised an eyebrow, looking at Paula.

'We have met.' Lisa smiled. 'I think she could be dangerous.'

'Would you like a cup of coffee?' asked Monica belatedly. She had been fascinated by what Lisa was saying.

'I'd love one, thank you very much.'

'This very powerful man you mentioned. I'd be happier if I knew his name,' Tweed demanded.

'I have promised never to reveal that.'

'Couldn't be Rondel, could it?' he asked casually.

Lisa looked down at her lap.

'No, it couldn't be,' she said.

'You know . . .' Tweed began doodling faces on his pad. 'If I've no idea where I can contact you we simply can't work together.'

'He said you were not only very clever, but also very tough and never gave up. I'm not living at the flat off Ebury Street any more. I've moved to The Hangman's Noose. It's a pub in the East End near Reefers Wharf. You could always get me there or, if I'm out, speak to Herb, the owner.'

'Is he trustworthy?'

'He should be.'

'Why, if I might ask?' interjected Mark, who had kept silent while he watched her.

'Why?' She turned on him. 'Because at one time he served with bloody Military Intelligence.' She took a folded sheet from her shoulder bag, handed it to Tweed. 'That is a list of the probable targets tonight.'

Tweed read slowly through the typed list. He was careful not to show his anxiety. He looked straight at her.

'This covers a lot of territory. My guess is that Herb, with his Army experience, has helped build up this list.'

'You've hit the nail on the head.' She smiled. 'He also said you were very quick on the uptake.'

90

'Herb, you mean?'

'No, the man who sent me over here as the Messenger to warn you. You said there will be six of us . . .'

'Seven. Including yourself.'

'We'll need transport to move us from the West End to the East.'

'And we have loads of it,' said Harry Butler. 'In all makes and sizes.'

'I've worked out how we'll travel,' Tweed announced. 'Three cars. I'll drive Car One with Paula next to me. Newman will drive Car Two with Lisa and Mark as passengers. Car Three will be yours, Harry, taking Pete Nield with you, if he does ever get here.'

'He will,' Harry said. 'And mine will be the four-wheel drive. I've reinforced the ram at the front. Might come in useful.'

'Could I go to the bathroom?' Lisa asked as she finished her coffee. 'That was very good,' she added, turning round to look at Monica. 'Thank you.'

'I'll take you,' Paula volunteered. The two women left the room.

'Well, what do you think of her?' Tweed enquired, glancing round the office.

'She'll do,' said Butler. 'I've been watching her.'

'Resourceful, reliable.' Newman gave his verdict.

'I second Bob,' Mark agreed.

'I case you're interested in my opinion,' Monica began, 'I think she's the tops. And in a rough-house my bet is she'd give a good account of herself. Notice the steel rims on the toes of her shoes?'

'No, I didn't,' Newman admitted.

'That's because she'd covered the steel with thick polish.'

'Sounds as though she could be an asset in our car,'

Mark said to Newman. 'And I thought we'd have to look after her . . .'

'You may find she has to look after you,' Monica commented wickedly.

'Weapons,' said Harry.

'I'm taking my Smith & Wesson,' Newman remarked.

'Now listen.' Tweed raised his voice. '*There is to be no shooting on this expedition.* Only if your life is in danger or you fear serious injury. The police will be there.'

'When it's all over,' Newman replied cynically.

He had just spoken when Pete Nield came in. He gave Tweed a little salute.

'Sorry I'm so late. Saw an accident on my way here. A lady had a broken leg. As usual, no one knew what to do. I lifted her into the back of a car which was going to drive her to a hospital. Got a glass of water from a nearby house and got her to swallow a couple of painkillers. Always carry stuff like that with me.'

'Ruddy walking medicine chest, you are,' Harry snorted.

The two men often worked as a team, knew they could always rely on each other. The contrast between them was striking. Butler always wore a shabby windcheater, denims which had seen better days, a pullover ragged at the collar. Whereas Nield, slim and erect, was smartly dressed in a blue suit with shirt and tie.

Tweed began talking, bringing Nield up to date tersely with everything that had happened. Nield listened carefully, perched on the edge of Paula's desk. Tweed repeated his warning about the use of firearms, showed him Lisa's list of targets, which caused Nield to whistle softly.

'Going to try and level London to the ground, are they?'

'As I told you,' Tweed snapped, 'it's supposed to be a rehearsal for a major event later.'

'If you say so . . .'

He stopped speaking as the door opened and Lisa

entered with Paula behind her. Everyone stared. Carrying her heavy raincoat with capacious pockets Lisa wore a leather skirt ending way above her knees. For a top she was wearing a gaudy silk blouse which fitted her tightly. It was sleeveless. Newman stopped staring, looked anywhere except at her legs.

'Sorry to dress like a tart,' Lisa explained. 'But a major target is the huge discotheque in the West End. I need to merge with the atmosphere. When we leave the place I'll put on what's in my raincoat pockets. Rolled-up sweater, pair of jeans, old windcheater.' She smiled. 'I'm only showing you this outfit so you don't get a shock later.'

Saying which, she slipped on the raincoat. Then she checked her watch, looked at Tweed.

'Shouldn't we leave during the next half hour? It's got late suddenly.'

'Transport,' growled Harry, jumped up, left the room.

Tweed introduced Lisa to Pete Nield, who shook hands, smiled at her.

'Welcome to the war party.'

'I don't want to hear any more language like that,' Tweed told him. 'It's the wrong attitude.'

'You hope,' Newman said under his breath.

'That SAS team I wanted here from Hereford has arrived, I hope,' Gavin Thunder snapped at the aide who had replaced Jeremy Mordaunt.

'It's across the street, secreted in a building near what used to be Scotland Yard, sir. I hope you don't mind my saying this – but don't they come under the control of the MoD?'

'Yes, but I talked the Defence Minister into agreeing. I can talk him into anything. You've heard the rumours. Tonight that foreign scum we've let in has planned an inferno. We'll keep the SAS in reserve, see how it develops.'

'I hope, sir, the Cabinet will go along with you.'

'None of your damned business. But as you've raised the point, I talked the Cabinet into agreeing, albeit reluctantly. We may need to show our iron fist.'

'Which, I hear, sir, is your nickname inside the Cabinet. Iron Fist.'

8

Action this day.

The words went out on the Internet, from Ponytail at his base in the apartment on the shores of Lake Washington in Seattle. Went out to be decoded by 'chief executives' in London, Paris, Rome, Brussels, Berlin and Stockholm.

Even as they were deciphered, 'tourist' buses were moving in to the centre of each city. There were no convoys to attract the attention of the police. Single buses packed with men drove in from different directions, heading for their targets.

Ponytail then turned to operating on the home front. The same coded instruction went out to San Francisco, Chicago, New York, Los Angeles and New Orleans. In the States Greyhound buses had been hijacked at pre-arranged points in the countryside, their passengers herded into barns where they were trapped once the doors had been locked. All mobile phones had been confiscated. Waiting gangs of rough-looking men boarded the empty buses which then proceeded to their destinations.

And no one realized that these three words of the instruction had once been the favourite phrase of Winston Churchill, urging lethargic civil servants to do what he said immediately.

It was 10 p.m. in London. Tweed and his team had entered

95

the basement restaurant off Piccadilly in separate groups, had sat at three different tables. The only member absent was Harry Butler, which left Pete Nield by himself.

They had eaten a light dinner – without alcohol – when Harry ran down the stairs from outside, made a gesture for them to leave.

Lisa, wearing her sweater and jeans, dashed into the ladies', carrying her raincoat. Locked in a cubicle she swiftly changed into her 'tart's' outfit, emerged wearing the raincoat.

'Vorina's, the discotheque,' Harry told them and dashed out and up the steps into the street, followed by Pete Nield. The four-wheel drive was parked nearby and they jumped into it. Tweed had taken the precaution of paying his bill early while he drank coffee. The others had done the same.

Lisa appeared, her raincoat belted tightly, joined Newman and Mark. They dived into their car, Newman taking the wheel. Tweed and Paula led the convoy – he had parked his car ahead of the other two vehicles.

'Where the heck is this Vorina's?' Tweed asked.

'In a side street off Regent Street. I'll guide you . . .'

The moment they entered the side street Tweed saw Vorina's. It was impossible to miss with the glow of lights shining out through enormous plate-glass windows. Earlier, after consulting Harry, Paula had arranged with him to rush out in the afternoon and purchase three members' tickets. One ticket admitted three people.

'Only ninety quid for that lot,' he'd told her when he came back and distributed tickets.

'Ninety pounds!' she'd exclaimed. 'It must be a high-class place.'

'Decide for yourself when you see it,' he'd told her.

They parked in a wide alley with the four-wheel drive in front. A doorman in a blue uniform checked their tickets while Paula stared inside. Behind the windows attractive girls in various states of undress were dancing. When the door was opened a blast of sound hit them, the latest modern 'music'.

Crystal balls of lights were suspended from the ceiling of the vast room. They flashed on and off non-stop in wild colours. On a platform halfway down the left-hand side a group of five young men were armed with saxophones, guitars, and heaven knew what else. Huge amplifiers built up the deafening noise to incredible decibels. Couples sat at tables, drinking and trying to hear each other. At intervals down the right-hand side were booths where men were playing at undressing their girlfriends. A number of older men were urging younger girlfriends to drink more. Tweed could see no activity the police would regard as obscene. They were all people of various ages enjoying themselves. But he didn't like the hellish noise or the flashing lights. *C'est la vie*, as the French would say. Paula grasped his arm after looking back.

'Trouble.'

Lisa, who had gone ahead, ran back to them, heard what Paula had said.

'Big trouble,' she warned.

At the entrance door a giant had pushed his way in, followed by a troop of ugly-looking toughs wearing ragged camouflage jackets. The doorman demanded from Delgado his ticket. The giant grabbed the doorman with one hand round the throat, lifted him off the floor, slammed him against the wall. His victim collapsed. A bouncer appeared, tried to grab the giant by one arm. Delgado grasped his wrist, whirled him round and round, let go suddenly. The bouncer crashed against the wall, collapsed. The giant's toughs were rapidly infiltrating the restaurant.

They ran from table to table, jerking the cloths off them, spilling plates and food and drink on the floor. One man, using a can of spray paint, swiftly defaced a wall with his graffiti message. *Down With Monny*. Tweed detected a degree of illiteracy.

Panic broke out. Women were screaming. Men were holding on to their partners, trying to escort them out through a wild mob. One woman with a semi-backless dress was refusing to leave her table. Delgado came up behind her, shoved in his huge hand, tore the dress down to her seat. Butler appeared behind the giant, grabbed a handful of his hair, crashed his head down on to the table, then went elsewhere. Delgado straightened up, dazed, staggered round.

The five-man entertainment group had stopped playing, stood scared stiff on the platform. A tough jumped on the platform, a graffiti can in one hand. He grabbed hold of the saxophone, squirted liquid inside it. The youngster whose instrument it was protested. The tough reversed the instrument, holding it by the horn end. Using it as a club he hit the youngster a savage blow behind the legs. The lad collapsed off the platform. Mark had just hit a tough on the side of his neck. His target went down like a sack of coals.

'Time to leave,' Tweed decided.

'Easiest escape route,' Lisa pointed out, 'is along the wall by the booths . . .'

Tweed was waving his hand to warn the others to leave. Butler saw him, took out a whistle, blew a penetrating blast clearly heard above the screaming and shouting. All the booths were now empty and there was a clear passage past them. Close to the exit Paula glanced back, saw Delgado, fully recovered, also heading for the street. He rammed his way through the scared crowd, shoving people aside.

Butler was ahead of them as they emerged into the street with Nield close behind him. Lisa grasped Butler's arm before he could run to his vehicle.

'Wait a minute when you're behind the wheel. Delgado has some other devilry . . .'

They were in their cars, their engines running, when Tweed lowered his window, glowering as he looked back at what remained of Vorina's. Delgado was wielding a huge sledgehammer, probably conveniently left on the pavement earlier.

The sledgehammer crashed into the window of Vorina's. The glass, a large sheet, fell inwards, broke into pieces when it hit the floor. A girl, her expensive dress torn, ran out into the street. A tough grabbed her, hoisted her, threw her through the gaping hole. She landed inside on her back amid the shattered glass. Lisa, who had jumped out of Newman's car, ran up to Butler, then ran back to Tweed.

'Piccadilly Circus next.'

'I know. Get back inside your car . . .'

The four-wheel drive moved off, followed by Newman's car and Tweed bringing up the rear. In no time at all they were approaching Piccadilly Circus down Regent Street.

'That was horrible,' Paula said. 'I'm sure I saw one man with a broken neck. Who are these bastards?'

'I did notice,' Tweed told her, 'that a number were British, but a larger number were foreigners. Kosovars, Turks, I think I even spotted an Afghan. At least we now know what we're up against. The trick is to find the top man.'

'Lord! Look at this.'

Every car parked – or abandoned – in Regent Street that they passed had windows, windscreens smashed in. One large store had no glass left in its windows. Toughs were coming out holding armfuls of expensive suits. The looting had started.

Thanks to Butler being in the lead, they drove straight down Regent Street. When groups of toughs stood in the road he drove ruthlessly at them. They scattered swiftly. At the Circus was a fresh mob. Eros had already been defaced by sprays of graffiti. A crowd of 'revolutionaries' occupied the top level. Butler was driving part way round with his window open. A hulking man threw a brick, aimed at the four-wheel drive. Driving with one hand, Butler caught the brick with his other gloved hand. He stopped, hurled the brick back with all his strength. It struck the thrower on the jaw.

'Let's clear that lot,' Nield suggested. 'Drive once round Eros.'

Nield was holding his latest weapon, a long wide-barrelled metal tube. Butler sat well back. As he circled once round Eros, Nield aimed the barrel through the open window at the top level. He pressed the trigger. A jet of ice-cold water sprayed the crowd, soaking them. When Butler had completed his circle the men and women on Eros was drenched to the skin.

'Dampen their ardour,' Nield remarked as Butler headed out of the Circus.

Seated in the back of Newman's car with Mark in the passenger seat in front, Lisa, occupying the back, had pulled on her jeans, her sweater, her coat. She was glad Butler had turned his heater full on. Her mobile buzzed.

She listened, said they were on their way, warned Newman, took out a little notebook with the mobile numbers of Butler and Paula, gave them both the same message.

'Herb called me. A riot's breaking out near The Hangman's Noose. A big one. I told Herb we're coming . . .'

Leaving the West End, everything became quiet. Paula welcomed the peace, the lack of violent people. At one point Tweed overtook both Newman and Butler, putting himself at the head of the column while Paula, a map open on her lap, navigated.

Realizing it was time for a news bulletin, Tweed switched on the radio. The announcer was just beginning.

'Reports are coming in of serious riots in the centres of Paris and Berlin. A commentator said they had the appearance of being coordinated since they started at the same time in both capitals . . .'

Tweed switched off, his expression grim.

'And here too,' he said.

'What does it mean?' Paula asked.

'That it's international. Which worries me. Which means we *have* to locate the top man.'

'And I think Lisa knows who he is. Which would put her on the other side.'

'It's a mystery, one I'm determined to solve.'

They said no more until they were approaching the East End. Tweed slowed down, drove more cautiously. In his rear view mirror he saw that Butler and Newman were close behind them.

'We'll soon be at Reefers Wharf,' Paula remarked.

'I wonder why they call it that? I suppose it's on the edge of the river.'

'No, it isn't. I was asking Lisa about it when I took her to the bathroom. The end near The Hangman's Noose is a quarter of a mile at least from the Thames. Apparently it was once a real wharf. Barges and small freighters used it to unload. Then some property speculator had the idea that if he filled it in he'd have some valuable real estate. So now most of the warehouses are offices occupied by companies paying sky-high rents. We're very close now, I think.'

They turned a corner and the street where in daytime the market was held stretched about before them. In the distance Tweed could see, by the light of flames, The Hangman's Noose. Someone had hung from the sign board a real noose with the mask of a grotesque head inside it.

'If it was chaos in the West End this is anarchy,' Paula said grimly.

There seemed to be far more thugs than those they had left behind. When it closed, the stallholders' tables used in the market were folded up, stacked against the far wall. These had been dragged into the road, piled up, set alight. Tweed stopped in front of The Hangman's Noose. They got out as Newman's and Butler's vehicles arrived.

Lisa jumped out, ran along to Tweed and Paula, pointed to a stocky man emerging from the pub. All the windows were boarded up and Herb was carrying a heavy club.

'It's been hell,' he said, addressing Tweed. 'They've been attacking women as well as men.'

Lisa left them. A thug was battering a man with his club. He turned, grinned when he saw her. She stiffened the side of her hand, hit him with a karate chop. He sagged and she grabbed his club. A fire engine had arrived and men in helmets were preparing to deal with the bonfires dotted down the street, flaring up viciously. Tweed noticed groups of thugs were gathered along the opposite pavement, listening to a strange tall fat man in a pink shirt, waving a malacca cane.

Harry Butler saw a fireman bent over a hydrant, attaching a big hosepipe. Then he had difficulty turning on the water. A thug, holding a knife, came up behind him as the fireman removed his helmet, which was getting in his way.

'Look out!' shouted Butler, running forward.

The thug hit the fireman with a club in his other hand. The fireman fell down. The thug turned to face Butler who smashed him in the face with his fist. The thug dropped the knife, lost his club, dazed by the tremendous blow. Butler grabbed his long hair, rammed his head back against a brick wall with such force he thought he heard the skull crack.

Glancing round, he saw the army of thugs, divided into groups, advancing across the street. Further down the street Mark, Newman and Nield were grappling savagely with different opponents. Bending down, Butler checked the hose. It was firmly screwed to the hydrant. With his gloved hands he picked up the hose and it needed all his strength to twist the tap of the hydrant. Water gushed from the tip of the hose. Raising it, he directed its powerful flow at one advancing group, then another. The power of the jet was so great it knocked flat each thug he aimed at.

Thugs with knives were assaulting the firemen trying to get down off their vehicles, preventing them from intervening. Once he had flattened each group of thugs he could see, Butler switched the jet to the fires burning in the street.

Paula, on her own, was stalking the fat man in a pink shirt. His behaviour seemed very odd. Holding his malacca came in both hands, she suspected he was directing the onslaught. At the very least he was closely observing the effectiveness of the attack. He was facing away from her as she crept up behind him. She rammed her .32 Browning automatic into his back.

'This is a gun,' she yelled in a fierce voice. 'Shove off and don't come back.'

The fat man dropped his cane. Then Paula was knocked off balance as a thug collided into her. She swung round, hit the thug across the jaw with the muzzle of her gun. He staggered back, slid down a wall, lay still. When she was free to turn round to confront Pink Shirt the fat man had vanished. She couldn't see him anywhere. And his cane had vanished with him.

Tweed was running after Lisa, who was pursuing Delgado. Her raincoat flapped as Delgado disappeared round a corner. As she peered round the corner he struck at her with a club. It grazed the side of her head. She staggered back, fell. Delgado came back, raised his club to finish her off. Tweed grabbed hold of the Beretta, tucked in the back of her raincoat belt. He hauled it out, aimed it point-blank at the giant. Delgado changed his mind, disappeared round the corner. Tweed peered round cautiously, in time to see the giant vanish down an alley. He turned his attention to Lisa.

Her pulse was irregular, her eyes closed. He lifted her as Newman appeared. Appalled, he gazed down at Lisa. Tweed snapped at him.

'We've got to get her to the clinic. No help round here. So drive my car if we ever reach it.'

Newman went wild, using brute force to clear the route to the car. He opened the rear door and, gently, Tweed carried Lisa inside, sitting down with her head on his lap. The rear door was slammed shut, Newman got behind the wheel. The car took off like a rocket, Newman keeping one hand on the horn, blaring non-stop.

9

They had been waiting at the clinic for an hour. Newman sat on a chair against a wall in the gleaming white-walled corridor. Tweed was pacing up and down, couldn't keep still.

'Why are they taking so long?' growled Tweed.

'They have to give her a thorough examination, I expect,' said Newman. 'She's in a private ward?'

'All the wards are private here. Who were you calling on that wretched mobile?'

'Harry, so he knew where we were. He's on his way . . .'

He stopped speaking as Butler appeared, hurrying down the corridor. His face was damp with sweat and he had obviously moved after hearing from Newman.

'How is she?' he asked.

'We don't know yet.'

The consultant, Mr Master, a friend of Tweed's, appeared in the corridor accompanied by a tall horse-faced sister Tweed immediately took a dislike to. Master looked at all three visitors with a serious face.

'I have a problem, Tweed . . .'

'Damnit, how is she? That's what we want to know.'

'Of course. She has concussion at least. The odd thing is she's now conscious and desperately anxious to see you. It can only be for a few minutes. Oh, this is Sister Vandel who will be looking after her.'

'Mr Master, I don't agree with her seeing anyone now,' snapped Vandel.

'You told me that before. What do you think, Tweed? Seeing you might settle her, if she's still conscious.'

'Take me to her now,' Tweed said decisively.

Master led the way down the corridor, opened a door numbered 25. The room was spacious, airy, light. Lisa was lying in a bed under sheets and a blanket. Her head rested on a pillow and her eyes were closed. The right side of her head was covered with a large bandage. Tweed was shocked by her complexion. Normally she had a reasonably high colour but her face was ashen. Part of her red hair had been tied back with a ribbon to keep it clear of the bandage.

'You see,' said Sister Vandel, 'she's fallen unconscious again. This visit is pointless.'

Lisa opened her blue eyes, gazed at Tweed. She raised a limp hand, indicating she wanted him to come close to her. Tweed, upset, but not showing it, smiled, sat down on a chair next to the bed.

'You're going to be all right,' he said softly.

She smiled, raised the limp hand again, telling him she wanted him to take it. He took hold of it, squeezed the fingers tenderly. She feebly squeezed his in appreciation. She was opening and closing her mouth, clearly trying to say something.

'She mustn't talk,' commanded Vandel from the other side of the bed.

Tweed gave her a certain look, cold, fierce. It was a look Paula would have recognized, seen only at rare moments when he violently disapproved of a blunder. Vandel looked away, disconcerted.

Tweed bent closer to Lisa. The expression in her blue eyes seemed to communicate that she was desperate to tell him something. Her mouth opened again and he sensed she needed to speak clearly.

'Ham . . . Dan.' She made one final effort. 'Four S . . .'

Then she closed her eyes, letting go of Tweed's hand.

He stood up and Vandel came over to hurry him out of the room. Tweed told Master to send the bill to Park Crescent when Lisa was fully recovered and left the clinic. They were in the corridor, the door closed, when Tweed turned to Vandel as Master walked off.

'Sister, your patient is an important witness. There is a remote risk someone may try to get in here to attack her. I'm therefore posting a guard outside her room round the clock.'

'We do not allow . . .'

'Sister, look at this.' He produced the folder which identified him as Deputy Director SIS, opened it, held it under her nose. 'If you continue objecting I can always have a word with Mr Master.'

'That won't be necessary,' she said hastily.

'Harry,' Tweed called down the corridor, 'bring your chair up here. I want you to sit by this door to guard Lisa against any intruders,' he told him as Harry arrived, plonked his chair next to the door. 'The only people allowed inside are Mr Master, Sister Vandel here and any replacement she brings and introduces you to while she's off duty.'

'Clear enough,' said Harry, staring blankly at the sister.

'If she recovers,' Vandel snapped, 'she'll have to be taken to another room for a second X-ray.'

'Understood, but Mr Butler will accompany her. Another member of my staff will take over from Mr Butler in a few hours. I will work out a roster of guards. Meantime, Mr Butler is probably hungry and thirsty.'

'A big mug of tea with plenty of sugar and a bit of milk – and a sandwich, ham if you've got it, will do me,' Harry announced.

'We're not running a hotel for visitors,' Vandel rapped out.

'Then I'll have a word with Mr Master.'

'Oh, well, I'll see what I can do . . .'

She stormed off down the corridor, disappeared. Harry opened his windcheater a few inches, showed Tweed the butt of his Walther.

'No one except those you mentioned will get near her. That Vandal is the dragon of the clinic. There's always one.'

'Van*del*,' said Tweed.

'Vandal will do for me,' Harry decided.

'I'll send Pete Nield to relieve you as soon as I can,' Tweed assured Butler.

'No 'urry . . .'

On his way out Tweed met Master again. He stopped to thank the consultant for what he was doing.

'One thing bothered me. Sister Vandel said at one stage *if* she recovers. I think she was simply frightening me.'

'One can never be sure, but I'm confident the phrase should have been *when* she recovers.' He looked annoyed. 'I'll have a word or two with Vandel. We'll take good care of the patient . . .'

Outside in the night Tweed found Newman seated behind the wheel of his parked car. He explained as Tweed got in next to him.

'I decided to stay with the car. It's unlikely any of those thugs will get into this area but I wanted to protect the car. How is Lisa?' he asked, driving off.

'I'd say she's completely exhausted, needs a lot of sleep and quiet. I didn't think she looked all that fresh when we left Park Crescent.'

He took out his notebook, wrote down *Ham . . . Dan . . . 4 S*. Then he showed the page to Newman. 'Mean anything to you? Lisa had trouble saying anything but that's what she said to me.'

'Not a thing. Is it important?'

'Lisa thought it was – to make the effort she did make to say that to me.'

'You probably didn't hear her properly. In her state it's likely she was confused.'

'I don't think she was. Could be the key to this bizarre international situation.'

'Heard on the radio Paris, Berlin and Brussels experienced the same type of trouble. The wreckers are abroad.'

'And it's just occurred to me,' Tweed ruminated, 'those are three of the cities Lord Barford visited recently. If we can believe what Aubrey Barford told Paula in a drunken stupor. And I think we can.'

10

Marler had driven to Dorset, visited his contact, a retired manager in a security company, living in the model village of Abbotsbury, north-west of Weymouth. He'd suggested his contact might like to join him, but the manager had said sorry, he was no longer in shape.

'And those villains I saw ferried ashore last night were the toughest I've ever encountered . . .'

So, for several hours, Marler had sat in his car alone. He had driven off the road overlooking Chesil Beach up a steep track. He was now behind the wheel of his car, parked out of sight behind a clump of shrubbery. The height gave him a clear view over the seaway east of Weymouth, over Chesil and west towards Bridport. High-powered night glasses hung from a loop round his neck.

Chesil Beach was a quite unique phenomenon. Instead of sand, six miles or more of a great bank of pebbles extended from Weymouth westward. Marler knew the area, knew that near Weymouth the 'pebbles' were almost the size of small boulders, gradually diminishing in size as the bank stretched to the west where eventually they were truly pebbles in size. He also knew that fishermen, coming ashore in a fog, could tell where they were by checking the size of the pebbles.

It had been night for several hours and outside the air was a bitter cold. He was far enough back and above

Chesil to keep his heater on. He had eaten sandwiches purchased from a roadside café on his way down from London, and occasionally drunk mineral water from a litre bottle.

Marler, the most deadly marksman in Western Europe, was blessed with an infinite patience. It was ten o'clock, very dark, when he saw something blazing out at sea, east of Weymouth. He focused his glasses, saw a small fishing boat on fire. No sign of a crew.

'The decoy,' he said to himself. 'To keep coastguards away from this area. They're coming and someone is well organized.'

A few minutes later he swore. He had just spotted a launch, a large vessel, packed to the gunwales with men, heading for the end of Chesil Beach near what was known as the Swannery. Then he saw the fog rolling in from the sea, blotting out the launch. He waited.

A few minutes later an old tourist-type bus, what his father would have called a charabanc, appeared from the direction of Bridport. It stopped, performed a two-point turn until it faced the way it had come. The vehicle was then parked near a point where Marler estimated the launch would beach. It carried the legend *Topsy Tours*. The fog swallowed up the bus.

Marler lowered his window, put his hand out. A few minutes later he felt a breeze. He closed the window, sat up erect, holding his glasses. The fog swirled, evaporated. The bus came back into view, so did the large launch as its bow hit Chesil. He focused on it.

A big man clad in waders, an oilskin, a sou'wester hat came ashore, bent down, picked up a pebble with one hand. In the other he was holding something Marler couldn't identify. Then the big man climbed the steep bank, saw the bus. He returned to the launch, lifted a megaphone to his mouth, called out instructions in as quiet a voice as possible.

Marler couldn't hear what he said but he could see the big man helping to unload his cargo, grabbing men by the arm, shoving them up the bank towards the bus. Marler studied their strange faces, agreed with his contact that this was a right bunch of villains.

Most looked foreign, out of the Balkans. What impressed – and worried – Marler was the military way they filed one behind the other up to the bus, carrying floppy bags. He took out his mobile, pressed the numbers of the police HQ in Dorchester, numbers he'd earlier memorized from a directory in an isolated phone box.

'Police 'ere,' a bored voice said.

'I'm reporting that a gang of illegal refugees are being smuggled ashore at the Swannery end of Chesil Beach. Send patrol cars . . .'

'Might I have your particulars, sir?' the bored voice asked.

'You'll lose them if you don't move fast. Put me on to a senior officer now.'

'Hold on a minute, sir. Maybe the sergeant will have a word . . .'

'You'll lose them,' Marler fumed, but there was no one on the line.

He waited, watching a whole column leaving the launch, climbing aboard the bus. He counted twenty men. Once aboard their transport, the bus moved off towards Bridport. Marler saw the big man was still waiting at the edge of Chesil Beach. Then a second tourist bus appeared, performed the same two-point turn, parked so it was also facing Bridport. The fog had cleared off the water and Marler heard the muffled sound of engines. Two large outboards, crowded with men, were approaching the shore where the big man had flashed a torch twice.

'Can I help you, sir? Sergeant Haskins here. What seems to be the trouble?'

'The trouble is you have at this moment a very large gang

of illegal refugees being brought ashore at the Swannery end of Chesil Beach. They're being taken away towards Bridport in old tourist buses with the name *Topsy Tours*.'

'Did I hear you aright, sir? You did say "Topsy"?'

'Yes.'

'Funny name . . .'

'For God's sake, get patrol cars to intercept the buses. I said they're on their way towards Bridport . . .'

'I heard that, sir. Might I ask exactly where you're speaking from?'

'Send patrol cars or I'll report this lack of action to the Chief Constable . . .'

Marler had had enough. The motorized dinghies had emptied their passengers with astonishing speed. They had scrambled up the bank, were already aboard the second bus. The big man had returned to the launch, was already steering it out to sea where presumably a freighter was standing to until it could winch the launch aboard. Then the freighter might well return to its pick-up point to take aboard another assortment of talent and bring it back to Britain.

Marler had switched off his mobile, feeling it was hopeless. The only thing he could do was to track the buses to their destination. He manoeuvred his car back down the track on to the road leading to Bridport. He rammed his foot down to catch them up.

A few minutes later a patrol car came towards him. Heavens, they had reacted. Then he saw the car was flashing its lights, waving him down. He had reduced speed when he'd seen it was a patrol car and now he stopped. The patrol car swung over to the wrong side of the deserted road, parked its front bumper inches from Marler's. A very young policeman got out, arrived as he lowered his window. Marler sat very still.

'Pushin' it a bit, weren't we, sir?'

'It isn't a built-up area.'

A second, equally young policeman arrived, a portly man who had the look of a man conscious of his importance. He was holding something, bent down to peer in at Marler.

'I'd like you to switch off your engine.'

Marler did so. Then he sat with his arms folded and tried to look expressionless.

'Been drinkin', 'ave we, sir?'

'Yes, this. And only this.'

Marler reached down for the bottle of mineral water. He held it up for the portly policeman to get a good look.

'Would you object to being breathalysed? The alternative is to accompany us to the station.'

Marler took a deep breath, reached out, took the nozzle. He blew into it with all his strength. Portly took out the breathalyser, studied it. The meter registered nothing.

'Thank you, sir. You can proceed now, when we've moved our car.'

'May I suggest,' Marler said politely, 'that you get in touch urgently with your Dorchester HQ?'

'Good night, sir . . .'

It was 3 a.m. when Marler arrived back at Park Crescent. He wondered where the time had gone. He was also surprised to find everyone waiting for him in Tweed's office. Paula, Newman, Butler, Nield and Mark were drinking coffee. Marler accepted a cup gratefully from Monica.

'You've done a good job,' Tweed began. 'Thank you for calling me on your way back. You must have found the police down there frustrating.'

'I could have strangled them.'

'Don't worry. As soon as you went off the line I phoned

Roy Buchanan at the Yard, passed to him all your information. He's phoning the Chief Constable down there – has done – and called me back. They've sent up a helicopter to comb the area you mentioned in search of those two buses.'

'Doubt if they'll find them. From Bridport there are three or four different routes they could have taken.'

'I agree. If you can stand it I'll tell you what's been happening up here while you were down there . . .'

Marler listened, adopting his usual stance of leaning against a wall. After he'd drunk his coffee he lit a king-size.

'This is developing into an international conflagration. All over Europe and now it's started in the States.'

'We watched a bit on TV,' Monica interjected. 'The pics were frightful and Washington thinks there are other cities targeted. They're trying to guess which ones.'

'I have Keith Kent coming in any moment,' Tweed told her. 'You remember Keith, the brilliant analyst of movements of large sums of money, often secretly. It occurred to me all this is being financed by a fortune, a huge one. Thugs like to be paid for their dirty work. Never mind the slogans "Down With Capitalism". Then there's the transport to move them over long distances. What Marler has told us shows that is going on. So who is paying out these vast sums? And why?'

The phone rang. Monica told Tweed that Keith Kent had arrived and he asked her to tell him to come up right away.

'Poor devil,' commented Mark. 'It's the middle of the night.'

'He's an owl,' Tweed said. 'Works best through the early hours . . .'

Keith Kent walked in. Of medium height, he was slim and clad in an expensive business suit. In his late thirties, he was clean-shaven, had thick dark hair and grey eyes which concentrated on the person he was talking to. Tweed introduced him to Mark, then asked him who could be financing the carnage.

'My best bet,' Kent replied, sitting down, crossing his legs, 'is the Zurcher Kredit Bank.'

'What?' Tweed was taken aback. 'It's a Swiss bank.'

'Used to be. Thank you, Monica,' he said as she handed him a cup of coffee. 'I'll need this. I happen to have spent a lot of time scrutinizing that bank. I have a strange story to tell you.'

Going back to the late 1790s, Mayer Amschel Rothschild was establishing the banking business, which was to grow into a colossus, in the Frankfurt Judengasse.

The Judengasse was the ghetto Jews were confined to and operated from. Enter Salomon Frankenheim, in his teens. Not a Jew, he had studied the Jewish faith, their rituals, their way of life. He then applied to Mayer for a job. Mayer put him through his paces, realized Frankenheim was a mathematical genius, took him on.

Frankenheim learned every trick of the Rothschild technique of trading. He was not thirty when he left Rothschild, slipped out of the Judengasse, formed what was to become the Frankenheim Dynasty in Paris.

Time passed. Frankenheim married, produced three sons. After their father's death they were running Frankenheim banks in Paris, Vienna and Rome, all of which were prospering.

More time passed until after several generations 1925 arrived. All the Frankenheims were long-lived but by then the head of the dynasty, Joseph, had no sons. Who was to take over this highly successful, all-powerful and very secretive organization?

After so many generations history repeated itself. Joseph adopted a son, name and origin unrecorded, who proved

117

later to be a mathematical genius like the founder, Salomon. When he was old enough to take control, still a young man, he followed the policies that had made the Frankenheims so rich.

Then, recently, he obtained control of the Zurcher Kredit Bank and changed the name from Frankenheim. What had been for so long the Frankenheim Dynasty now became the Zurcher Kredit. The present head was only known to a few – as Rhinoceros.

'That was a lot for you to absorb,' Keith Kent commented and gratefully accepted another cup of coffee from Monica.

'Why "Rhinoceros"?' Tweed asked.

'Because one of the earlier Frankenheims liked going on safari in Africa. On one trip he shot a rhinoceros. The symbol of the Frankenheim banks then became the head of a rhinoceros, with an engraved plate of the animal outside every branch of the bank.'

'I don't understand this,' Tweed objected. 'How could he possibly take over a Swiss bank? The Swiss make a point that none of their banks can be controlled by anyone except a Swiss.'

'Rhinoceros was clever. He persuaded the Zurcher Kredit directors to invest larger and larger sums in valuable property outside Switzerland. They did not realize he was using his own lawyers – to put the properties secretly in companies he controlled – outside Switzerland. When he had eighty per cent of the capital he began selling the properties – at a profit, being Rhinoceros – and then he re-formed the Zurcher Kredit to replace his Frankenheim banks. In Hamburg, in Paris, Vienna, Rome, Berlin and also Brussels. He has branches in other major cities.'

'How did the Swiss react?' Tweed wondered.

'Rhinoceros treated the original Zurcher Kredit directors very generously. Made them all millionaires. Result? The directors used the remaining twenty per cent still in their bank to buy more properties abroad, properties which Rhinoceros suggested. This kept them inside Swiss banking law. In due course these remaining properties were sold and the proceeds absorbed by Zurcher Kredit, now totally controlled by Rhinoceros.'

'I find this intriguing,' commented Tweed. 'What I would like to know is who is Rhinoceros, where does he live, what is his nationality?'

'I don't know and I can't find out.'

The phone rang. Monica looked surprised as she indicated the call was for Tweed.

'It's a Mr Rondel.'

'Tweed here. I don't think I know you . . .'

'You don't. Not yet.' The voice was warm, buoyant. 'Is this a safe phone?'

'It is.'

'I do my homework. I know quite a lot about you. I'm not referring to that smokescreen you put up – a negotiator in an insurance company specializing in covering wealthy people against the contingency of their being kidnapped. You are the Deputy Director of the SIS.'

'If you say so.'

'Mr Tweed, I'd like us to meet. At a convenient – to you – destination on the Continent. At a time convenient to you.'

'Before I considered agreeing I'd have to know the subject you propose discussing.'

'Of course.' The voice chuckled. 'I can see why you hold the position you do. The subject is what steps we can take to prevent the collapse of the West. I refer to the recent riots aimed at destabilizing the present system. I want to

119

find out who is organizing them, who is paying a lot of money to finance this very dangerous onslaught on our way of life.'

'Can you give me a number where I can call you?'

'Ah!' Another chuckle. 'The trouble is, I travel about a lot. Sometimes I don't know where I shall be myself tomorrow! May I call you again soon?'

'Please do. And thank you for contacting me . . .'

Tweed put down his phone, looked at Keith Kent who was drinking a third cup of coffee.

'Ever heard of a man called Rondel?'

'No, I haven't.'

'Was that really him on the phone?' Paula asked.

'It was.'

'What did he sound like?'

'Able, quick-witted, humorous, very pleasant. I'd say he has a very strong personality.' He transferred his gaze back to Kent. 'You were telling us about Rhinoceros. How does he operate?'

'In great secrecy. He lives somewhere in a secluded base – its location unknown.'

'You mean like Howard Hughes, the American million-aire who stayed locked up and guarded away from the world. A hermit?'

'Not at all. He travels about a lot. Always using a pseudo-nym – a different one each time. He uses commercial flights a lot, sometimes travelling Club Class, sometimes Economy. Never First Class. I've picked up that much about his habits and no more.'

'Is Rhinoceros honest? I did ask you how he operates.'

'He operates just like the Frankenheims of long ago – as the Rothschilds sometimes did. He rarely gives a loan. Very rich people trust his bank. They deposit huge sums of money there, knowing it will be safe. He charges a stiff fee but they don't care. They pay for peace of mind. Is he honest? He's the most trustworthy banker

120

in the world. Which is why I'm staggered at what I've discovered.'

'Which is?'

'Huge amounts of laundered money, source unknown, are passing through the Zurcher Kredit. I can't believe it, but it is so.'

'Doesn't sound like the portrait of Rhinoceros you painted.'

'It goes against all his principles. Clever accountancy is covering up what's happening. I stumbled on it. That's all I know.'

'And as regards who is financing these worldwide riots?'

'Can't help you. I'll keep looking.'

'One more question. How much is the Zurcher Kredit worth?'

'Eighty billion dollars. More than Microsoft . . .'

11

'M. Bleu', as he was known to a small circle of French security, already responsible for the murders of Jason Schulz in Washington and Jeremy Mordaunt at Alfriston, fiddled with his motorcycle, perched by the kerb a short distance from the Elysée in Paris.

He gave the impression he was repairing his high-powered machine. Tall and slim, he appeared to be more heavily built, clad in black leather trousers and jacket, his crash helmet pulled well down over his head. From under his visor he kept glancing at the exit from the Elysée, official residence of the French President.

He was waiting for the appearance of Louis Lospin, chief aide to the Prime Minister and his most confidential adviser. Walking towards him was a Frenchman, a mechanic by trade. He stopped by the motorcyclist, offered to help.

'*Merde!*' Bleu snarled the insulting response.

The mechanic shrugged, resumed his stroll. You couldn't even offer to help some people. Behind him M. Bleu glanced up as a car emerged from the Elysée courtyard. He noted the number plate. It was Louis Lospin's car. He pulled his visor down further, straddled his machine which started as soon as he turned the key. He began to follow the car at a discreet distance.

Lospin's car followed the same route it had taken the previous day. When it eventually pulled up in front of an apartment building in the select district of Neuilly, the motorcyclist stopped, parked by the kerb, watched.

In his left hand he held a stopwatch. He was checking the exact time it took Lospin to emerge from his car, climb the steps to the front door. He also noticed the chauffeur who had driven the car moved off quickly, as he had done before. Lospin was taking out his key to open the front door when the car vanished at speed round a bend. The same routine as yesterday.

M. Bleu was infinitely thorough in his preparations, tracking his target day by day, looking for a pattern, a routine. It was only when he had discovered one, had checked the timing by his stopwatch, located an escape route, that he decided he could approach his victim, do what had to be done quickly, then vanish.

What he didn't know was that at Interpol, situated inside a fortress building in a city a long way from Paris, there was a file on M. Bleu. In his tiny office inside the building Pierre Marin was examining his copy of the file. The French embassies in Washington and London had wired data on their subject to Interpol.

Why? Because the French never stop worrying. They didn't know of any connection between Schulz and Mordaunt, but they suspected there was one. So did Marin. He had read the file very slowly three times, even though there was very little data. Tweed would have appreciated Marin.

Eventually Marin decided this man did not concern him or his country. French security was too tight. Germany was the next likely target. He scribbled a note in French on the last page. *Not for us, could be for you.* He then told an assistant to send a copy of the file by courier to Otto Kuhlmann, chief of the Federal Police in Germany.

Kuhlmann, a quick-witted man, read the file once, read the comment Marin had scrawled on the last page. Taking out a pen he scribbled through the comment, wrote one word next to it. *Dummkopf*. Which is the German word for 'idiot'.

On the same day, at Park Crescent, Tweed received a call from his old friend and sparring partner, Superintendent Roy Buchanan. At times they agreed, then disagreed, but Buchanan was probably the most efficient detective in Britain.

'Come over now if you want,' Tweed suggested.

'That's me knocking on your door. I've something to show you.'

No more than fifteen minutes later he walked into the office, carrying a large cardboard-backed envelope. In his forties, Buchanan was a tall, lean-faced, lean-bodied man. His hair was dark brown and below his long nose was a neat moustache of the same colour. His eyes were shrewd, swept round the room at its occupants, all of whom he knew. Monica, Paula, behind her desk, Newman in an armchair and Marler, leaning against a wall.

'I've left Sergeant Warden downstairs,' he remarked.

Tweed invited him to sit down and Monica bustled out to fetch coffee. A stranger's impression of the lanky Buchanan would have been that he was relaxed, easygoing – which was a mistake many a villain had made.

'Is it about the riots, Roy?' Tweed enquired.

'Yes and no. I would appreciate your account of what you saw. One of my men recognized you near Reefers Wharf.'

'We didn't see any uniformed police until it was nearly all over,' Newman said caustically.

'That was because I took an unorthodox decision. I sent in teams in plain clothes so they didn't become a target. They ended up arresting twenty thugs.'

'That was clever,' Tweed commented. 'What did we see . . .'

He gave Buchanan an abbreviated report. Buchanan was writing in his notebook. He had just put his notebook away – Tweed had made no mention of Lisa – when Monica arrived with the coffee. He drank half a cup, asked his question.

'Any clue as to who is behind them? Here? On the continent? In the States? Pity we hadn't an American contact.'

Mark Wendover had once more not arrived. Nor had he contacted Tweed, who was getting used to the American's independent habits. He shook his head as he answered the question.

'Not a clue. I'm investigating possible sources of finance.'

'Good idea. Very. Jumping to another topic, ever heard of a Mr Blue?'

'Yes,' said Marler. 'What do you know?'

'Only the name. One of my undercover men heard a reference to him in a sleazy nightclub. Made by a man who knows things no one else knows. I only asked because the name struck me.' He looked at Marler. 'Your turn.'

'Mr Blue,' Marler began, 'is the strangest case I've ever come across. Rumour hath it – no more than rumour – that he's a top-class assassin. The weird thing is he's not for hire, no matter how much the money offered on the grapevine. He selects his own targets. That really is weird.'

'So we know nothing,' Buchanan commented. 'Jumping now to a third topic, a murder case. Here in town. In a flat off Ebury Street. I was nearby so I went and interviewed the landlady who rents out the flat. The victim, a Helga Trent, was shot dead from a window across the street. So was her dog.'

'Sounds unusual,' said Tweed quickly.

'I've got here . . .' Buchanan took a thick sheet of paper, cartridge, from his envelope, gave it to Tweed. 'That's a picture one of our artists drew from the landlady's description of a sister Helga who was visiting her. The sister who rented the flat has since vanished.'

Tweed, his face expressionless, looked down at the drawing. It was a head-and-shoulders portrait of a woman with long red hair. It was a surprisingly good likeness of Lisa.

Tweed stood up. He walked towards Newman and Paula with his back to Buchanan. He was frowning a warning at them. Paula looked at the portrait, shook her head.

'Can't help you.'

Tweed presented the portrait to Newman, who took his time studying it. He handed it back to Tweed.

'A good-looker. Wish I did know her.'

'Well, it was a long shot,' Buchanan remarked as he returned the paper to its envelope. 'But you lot mix with a whole variety of people.'

'We do,' Tweed agreed. 'If you'd like to have a copy of the portrait reduced to a small size – something I could carry in my pocket - we just might spot her here in town.'

'Make you three copies. One for you, one for Paula and one for Newman.'

'Before you go,' Marler interjected as Buchanan started to stand up. 'Any news from Dorset?'

'I knew there was something else.' The superintendent sat down again. 'The Chief Constable down there had a chopper up all night. They changed crews and the chopper tried its luck in daylight. Not a thing. No sighting of a crowd of men like Tweed described – from what you saw. No buses, but they could have hidden them in old barns.'

'I don't suppose this Mr Blue could have killed Helga Trent?' Marler suggested.

'It is a very strange case,' Buchanan ruminated. 'The landlady said Helga was older than her sister but also had long red hair and looked a bit like her. The body was lying under a window with heavy net curtains. Two bullet holes in the window. One for Helga, the other for the dog. It crossed my mind that maybe the killer had shot the wrong target – that he was after Helga's sister and thought he saw her as Helga stood behind the curtains, with the light on behind her.'

'Anything to back up that theory?' Tweed asked.

'The fact that the younger sister has vanished – and made no attempt to call the police. Mind you, the landlady said they didn't get on. Helga tried to dominate her younger sister – the landlady heard arguments. I must go now . . .'

Monica held the door open for him, peered down the stairs. Sergeant Warden was sitting motionless on a chair facing George, the guard. As usual, Warden looked like a wooden Indian.

When Monica came back into the room Paula had shifted her desk chair in front of where Tweed was sitting. She sat down.

'That gave me a shock,' she said. 'That drawing is a perfect likeness of Lisa.'

'Almost,' he said. 'I congratulate both you and Bob for reacting the way you did.'

'You don't want Lisa bothered by police while she's ill,' Newman suggested.

'That comes first. Is most important. But I also think she is the key to this huge crisis building up. I think Buchanan is right in his theory. Lisa was the killer's target. We must keep her guarded night and day.'

'Harry has just gone over to the clinic to relieve Pete Nield,' Newman reported. 'I'm next on duty. No one will get at her.'

'I'll phone the clinic, see how she's progressing,' Tweed decided.

While he was speaking to Master neither Paula, Marler, nor Newman said a word. Paula sensed an atmosphere

128

of tension in the room. After a while Tweed put the phone down.

'Master says she has severe concussion. He wants to keep her there until she's completely recovered. Warned me it could take weeks and he'll keep me informed.'

'I'd hoped for more,' Paula said quietly.

'I'm sure we all did. There's no skull fracture, thank God. Master also said he's sure she was exhausted and that has not helped.'

'She would be, after last night,' Newman commented.

'I have an idea,' Marler began. 'I'd like to go and check out that area round Ebury Street. The killer knew where Lisa was staying. That means he followed her. Might have located her pad days ago. That's what I'd have done in his place.'

'So what would you be looking for?' Newman enquired.

'His base – where he shacked up while he waited for the ideal opportunity. I might get a description of someone. It could take me days.'

'Do it,' Tweed decided. 'It's the only lead we've got to this mysterious business.'

Paula reached for his doodle pad. He had added another name, put a loop round it. Mr Blue.

'And I can't link him up with anyone.'

Tweed put a hand on the top of his head. He began to stand up, then rested both hands on his desk for support. Paula reached out, grasped both hands in hers. He sank back slowly into his chair, sagged.

'You're feeling rotten, aren't you?' Paula said, coming round to his side of the desk.

'Headache's been building up . . . pounding like a drum. It's so damned hot in here . . .'

Monica swiftly produced a thermometer, handed it to Paula. She inserted it gently into Tweed's mouth, looked at her watch, felt his temple. When she took out the thermometer she showed it to Newman.

'He's got a fever,' she whispered.

'He certainly has. That's diabolically high,' Newman whispered back.

'We're taking you to the clinic,' Paula said, leaning over Tweed. 'You're not . . .'

'Not the clinic . . .' Tweed was having trouble speaking. 'You know I . . . hate all medical things . . . hospitals, nurses fussing. Get me home . . . That's an order . . . Then get Dr Abbott . . .'

Tweed made a supreme effort. Resting his hands on his chair, he hoisted himself upright, swayed as Paula and Newman each grabbed an arm. He slowly walked towards the door as they held on to him.

'The stairs,' Monica warned, horrified.

'Bring the . . . pad on my desk,' he ordered Monica, then started coughing.

'Not a good idea . . .' she began.

'*Bring the pad on my desk!*' he roared.

Everyone was startled by the ferocity and strength in his voice. Monica hastily ran and picked up the pad.

'I'm going down the stairs immediately ahead of him,' said Marler. 'The hatchback is outside.'

'Water . . .' Tweed called out, his voice now croaking.

Monica poured a glass, handed it to Paula. Tweed tried to take it but Paula held on, guiding it to his lips. He drank the whole glass in two draughts, coughed again. They half-carried him down the stairs, step by step. Once he bumped into Marler who grabbed hold of both banisters, stiffened himself to take the weight. They reached the hall. George grasped the situation at once, ran to unlock and open the front door. Marler ran out to unlock the hatchback, open the rear door.

Tweed paused on the pavement, took in a deep breath. He looked at Paula, gave her a half-smile.

'Air's good . . .'

When they had Tweed flopped against a rear seat, Marler

ran round to take the wheel as Paula climbed in the back. Newman waited.

'I'll keep the roster on you-know-who going,' he called out.

Upstairs, Monica had already phoned Dr Abbott, explained the situation, that Tweed was being taken home. In the Crescent the car moved off.

12

They had another battle when they arrived at Tweed's flat on two floors, ground and first. Tweed told Paula where to find his keys, she fished them out of his pocket, unlocked the two Banhams, then the Chubb. Marler had held on to Tweed and Paula took the other arm and they entered the hall.

'On the couch in the sitting room,' said Paula.

'No. Upstairs in my bedroom . . . be comfortable there,' Tweed insisted.

'For God's sake,' Marler burst out. 'You don't want to climb more stairs.'

'I said my bedroom. I can make it myself.'

Tweed released himself from their grip, took hold of the banister with both hands, began to haul himself up. Paula and Marler leapt forward, grabbed his arms again, hoisted him up.

Inside the large bedroom Tweed sat on the edge of the bed, bent down to take off a shoe. Paula took over the job and took off both shoes, his jacket, tie, loosened his shirt collar. Between them they had him undressed, in pyjamas and under the sheets, blanket and old-fashioned eiderdown when the door bell rang.

'That will be Dr Abbott,' said Paula. 'Go down and let him in, please, Marler . . .'

Tweed had flopped his head on the pillow, closed his eyes. Then he opened them and, despite Paula's protests, eased himself up on one elbow.

'My pad,' he demanded.

'You don't need that now,' Paula said firmly.

'It's in my pocket. Put it in the bedside drawer. Then get a fountain pen out of the other pocket . . .'

'You're not going to work . . .'

'Put the pad and pen in the drawer. That's an order.' As she did so he continued talking. 'No one is to know about this silliness. Anyone phoning, I'm away, can't say when I'll be back. Tell all the staff. That's another order . . .'

He flopped back on the pillow as Dr Abbott came in accompanied by another man carrying a machine. Abbott had a brisk manner, an amiable smile. He knew Tweed well as a friend. *And he knows how to handle him*, Paula thought as Abbott spoke.

'What's all this nonsense? Decided to take a holiday at long last, Tweed?'

Paula went downstairs to join Marler in the living room while the examination took place. She raised her eyes to heaven as she sat down.

'He'll make one hell of a patient.' She told Marler what Tweed had said. 'See what I mean.'

'That's what keeps Tweed going. Iron will-power . . .'

Abbott joined them about fifteen minutes later while his assistant went out to their car, carrying the machine. Paula also knew Abbott.

'He's got a virulent fever, a form of flu, but I suspect it's a rare strain. Has he mixed with anyone from abroad recently?'

'Yes. He toured the riot areas with us. Every conceivable nationality.'

'That's where he's picked it up, a quick-acting strain which I yet have to identify. I've given him an antibiotic and he's fallen asleep. I wanted him to be put into a clinic, but there's no budging him. Says he prefers his own bed, that he won't stand for a lot of chattering nurses fussing round him. Someone should be with him.'

'I can sleep here on that couch. You've met Monica – she can come here to relieve me.'

'Monica is a very capable woman. If there's an emergency – I don't expect one – whichever of you is on duty must call me at once. Now I'm going. I want to get the results of certain tests.'

'You'll keep me informed I hope?'

'Of course – or Monica if she's here. I have the phone number. He must not get out of bed. I slipped a bedpan under it.'

'Dr Abbott, how long do you think this will take until he has recovered completely?'

'The usual question.' He smiled. 'I never guess. But I will tell you it could be a long haul . . .'

Marler stood up when they were alone. He slipped on his topcoat.

'I'm obeying orders. I'm off to my flat to pack a few things, then I'll trawl Ebury Street, find that place where someone tried to bump off Lisa. I may stay in the area for several days. Something has just struck you.'

'It has. I wonder where the devil that Mark Wendover has got to?'

It was a quiet time in The Hangman's Noose. Herb was polishing the bar counter when Mark Wendover walked in, asked for a dry Martini. Herb looked dubious.

'I get a hint of American from the way you speak.'

'British mother, American father. Spent half my life here. Educated here and in the States. Get the picture. What's the problem?'

'Do my best, but Americans are perticular about Martinis. Saw you mixing it with those rioting swine,' Herb remarked as he took great care over the Martini. 'Saw you with a pal of mine, too. I'm Herb.'

'I'm Mark.' Wendover paused. 'I'm looking for a man called Delgado. Have a hunch his pad is somewhere round here.'

'You try your luck with some dangerous villains. Don't know where Delgado kips down – but I've seen him prowling round 'ere quite a bit. Especially down Reefers Wharf. That's across the street to the left. Any good? Don't mind if you won't pay for it.'

Wendover had just sipped his Martini. He licked his lips, took another sip, then raised the glass to the barman.

'This is the best Martini I've had since I was in New York. They couldn't do any better over there.'

'Thanks. Tries to oblige.'

Herb started polishing the bar again. Wendover had hoped his genuine compliment about the drink would get Herb talking but the British were careful what they said to visitors. He tried another tack.

'Just between us, the reason I'm after Delgado is I'm CIA.' He produced the folder he had deliberately omitted to hand in when he'd left Langley. The open folder he held up showed his photograph. He slipped it back into his pocket. 'I need to know as much about him as I can.'

'That's just beween you and me. The CIA business. And so is what I'm going to tell you. Delgado is an ugly customer. He was in 'ere one day, chatting to a pal at this very bar. I've got good 'earing. He said "I wish we can find out more on Rhinoceros".'

'That's an animal,' Wendover commented.

'I know. But 'e made it sound more like a person. Which I thought was strange. I s'pose that's why it stuck in my mind.'

*   *   *

Wendover left the pub, headed for Reefers Wharf. On his way he went into a phone box, one of the old red boxlike types, which he preferred to the new modernistic horrors. Newman answered the phone.

'Mark here, Bob. Ever heard of a guy called Rhinoceros?'

'Where did you hear that name?'

Newman's tone was sharp. *At least*, thought Mark, *I now know it is someone's name.* He asked to speak to Tweed. Always talk to the top man, or as high as you can go, had been Wendover's experience.

'He's not here. He's away on a trip. Don't know when he'll be back. Now, once again, where did you hear that name? And where the hell are you? With this outfit you work as a member of a team . . .'

Newman was talking into nothing. Mark had broken the connection. He'd try to get hold of Tweed later. At the moment he wanted to explore Reefers Wharf. He paused at the entrance to a very wide street leading towards the distant river.

There were very large five-storey buildings with the fifth storey in the sloping roof. The buildings furthest away had a modern look, renovated by a so-called architect in a feeble attempt to preserve the original warehouses' appearance. They had large opaque blue-glass windows you couldn't see through. They reminded Wendover vaguely of a miniature version of Park Avenue in New York.

The buildings closest to him had not been touched. They were still the warehouses that had stood there for heaven knew how many years. Their walls of slatted wood had a decrepit look, as though uninhabited. The dormer windows perched on the sloping fifth floor looked as though at any moment they might slide into the street.

He walked a short distance down the street, paused. The sun had come out, was a blinding glare on the buildings, but on his side of the street were dark shadows, alleys leading off, very narrow, cobbled and twisting. Then he saw Delgado.

The giant, holding a bottle in one hand by its neck, was walking unsteadily towards him on the sunny side. Wendover slipped into the shadows of an alley, peered out. Delgado had passed the renovated buildings, which Wendover could now see were occupied by companies, was strolling past the old warehouses.

A single-decker bus came crawling along the street, hiding Delgado from view. When it was near the top of the street Mark could no longer see Delgado. He had vanished into one of the old warehouses. But which one? It could have been any one of four. He went back to The Hangman's Noose, told Herb what had happened.

'I'll have to hang around here until I spot him again. Maybe for days. Know anywhere I can get get a room?'

'Here. Upstairs. The one I gave Lisa, the attractive girl I saw you with during the riots. A taxi arrived this morning to collect her case.' Herb looked at the American. Tall, fair-haired, with a large body to match. But it was the clothes Herb was looking at. 'Hope you don't mind me sayin' so – but you're too smartly dressed to mooch around here for days. You stand out from the crowd. There's a shop just down the road called Wingers. They'd have the kit you need.'

'Thanks. I'll go there now . . .'

He returned later, holding a carrier bag with his new suit inside. Herb looked at his new get-up approvingly. Mark was clad in a shabby camouflage jacket, well-worn denims, a Para's discarded red beret on his head.

'You'll do. I'll show you the room . . .'

Marler had found the flat where Helga Trent had been

murdered. It had not been difficult. Police tape still cordoned off the building and on the first floor he noted two
bullet holes in a window.

Earlier, carrying a hold-all, he had found a 'hotel' – no
more than a boarding house – but it had a small bar. It
also had a vacant room which he'd taken.

Now, just before dusk, he stepped over the tape, rang the
bell of the flat. A middle-aged woman with a disagreeable
expression and suspicious eyes opened the door, stood in
the entrance like a guardian, beefy arms folded.

'Are you the landlady?' Marler enquired.

'I'm the owner, if that's anything to do with you.'

'I'm a friend of the late Helga Trent.' Marler smiled
and when he did so the opposite sex usually took to him.
'I would very much appreciate it if we could have a few
minutes' chat about her . . .'

'You're another bloody reporter. I can smell them a
mile off.'

'No, I'm not. Just a few minutes of—'

'Go jump off Beachy Head.'

She slammed the door in his face. He heard her bolt and
lock it. Marler decided he wasn't going to get far with this
paragon of the female species. He went back to his hotel
and into the bar. Officially he was a solar-energy salesman.
He didn't think he would run into anyone else in that line
of business.

A peroxide blonde wearing a miniskirt sat on a stool next
to him. She lit a cigarette, looked him up and down.

'Care to buy me a drink, darling?'

'You live round here?'

'I might.'

'I don't think you do.'

'Bloody well drink on your own.'

She got off her stool, walked away swinging her hips,
then out of the front door. Marler was trying to contact
someone who knew the area.

He had to wait five days before he struck lucky. It was dark outside when a big man in a shabby suit walked in as though he owned the place, sat on a stool. He shouted his order at the girl behind the bar.

'Double Scotch. Neat. No muckin' about.'

'Coming up now, Mr Barton.'

'You seen anythin' of that girl with the long red hair I asked you about last night? Slim, good figure, a real looker.'

'No,' the girl said as she served the drink. 'She hasn't come in here.'

'I'll pay for that drink,' Marler said suddenly.

He moved to the stool next to Mr Barton, noticed he had very large hands with hair growing on their backs. Lifting his glass, Barton turned to study Marler with hostile eyes. The girl had moved to the far end of the counter, now Marler had given her the money for the drink.

'An attractive girl with long red hair,' Marler whispered. 'I'm looking for her too. I'll pay for information. What do you know about her?'

'Let's go outside,' the big man suggested. 'Walls 'ave ears 'ere . . .'

It seemed very dark outside. The street was ill-lit. They came to a corner, walked round it. Barton was gradually dropping behind Marler. Out of nowhere a youth on a skateboard was speeding towards them. Marler felt something hard and round rammed into his back.

'This is a gun,' Barton growled menacingly. 'So you tell me what *you* know about the red-haired tart . . .'

A car backfired. The youth glanced back over his shoulder, wasn't looking where he was going, cannoned into Marler who twisted his body as he was hurled back against Barton. He stamped his foot down with great force on Barton's foot. The big man dropped his gun, limped, groaned. Marler stooped swiftly, picked up the gun. It was a .455 Colt automatic. From its weight Marler knew it was loaded, with seven rounds probably. Charming. Barton, still limping, yelled out the words.

'Come an' 'elp me, Skinny . . .'

Marler slammed his attacker across the jaw with the barrel of the Colt. Off balance, the big man tumbled down the steps into an area below street level, hit his skull against a brick wall, sagged down, moaning. Marler switched his gaze to the small lean streak of a thug charging across from the opposite side of the street. In his right hand he gripped a flick knife, the murderous blade exposed. Marler waited until he was close, on the pavement, looked behind him, called out.

'Take him, Larry . . .'

The oldest trick in the world but it worked. As Skinny looked back Marler used the barrel of the Colt again, but this time he aimed it at the side of Skinny's head. It was a businesslike blow and threw Skinny hurtling down the steps after Barton. He remained still at the bottom. Marler checked the street. Empty. Skateboard had long since vanished round a corner. Marler went down the steps.

He checked Skinny's pulse, which was beating steadily, but he was unconscious. Lifting him out of the way, Marler dumped him in a far corner, returned to Barton, still moaning. He bent down, aimed the Colt.

'What were you going to do to the red-haired lady?'

'Rough her up . . .'

'Open your mouth or I'll blow your head off.'

Terrified, Barton flopped open his mouth as blood dripped from his jaw. Marler shoved the muzzle of the Colt inside the open mouth. Barton's eyes nearly popped out.

'Again,' said Marler, his tone steely. 'What were you going to do with her? Three seconds and I'll pull the trigger.'

He removed the muzzle from the big man's mouth so he could speak. It took him half a minute to get the words out and then they were a mumble.

'We was goin' to kill her.'

'Right. Who paid you to do it?'

'For Gawd's sake, Mister . . . don't know. One like us . . . wore dark glasses. Paid cash . . .'

Marler was convinced Barton didn't know. In any case, the man who had instructed him, who had paid the cash, would be only part of a chain, extending back who knew where. He looked carefully at Barton. The big man was lying motionless, his eyes half closed, a real mess. And Skinny was out for the count.

Climbing back up the steps, he walked a short distance away, took out his mobile, called Buchanan's private line. The Superintendent answered at once.

'Yes?'

'Marler here.' He had already noted the street name, the number of the house above the area. He gave them to Buchanan. 'In the area at that address you'll find two criminals, knocked about a bit, waiting for your collection by a patrol car . . .'

'Hang on.'

Marler knew Buchanan was already dispatching the patrol car. He spoke quickly so he could get away before the police arrived.

'The big fellow is Barton, if that's his real name. The other one has the nickname Skinny. Barton admitted they tried to kill a certain girl, muffed it . . .'

'Knocked about a bit, you said. Your work?'

'Have to go now. Run out of coins . . .'

He hurried back to the hotel, went up to his room, locked the door. About five minutes later he heard the sound of a police siren. Taking out his mobile, he called Newman at Park Crescent, explained what had happened.

'I can't keep out of trouble, can I? Now, how is Tweed?'

'Bearing up, I gather. Not the easiest patient in the world.'

'Good for him. And Lisa?'

'Still at the clinic. The consultant doesn't seem worried, but like Tweed it could be a slow recovery.'

'OK. By the way, when I spoke to Buchanan I didn't let slip we even knew Lisa, didn't mention her name.'

'That's the way Tweed would want it, I'm sure. Go out and find some more thugs you can chat to . . .'

'I'm sorry I'm late relieving Monica,' Paula said as she sat down by Tweed's bedside. 'How are you feeling?'

'Better.' Tweed was perched up against a pillow. 'I think the first antibiotic Master gave me is doing the trick. I won't need the second one.'

'Yes, you will. Master says that's the vital one. Behave yourself.'

'You've been up to something. You're an hour late. You're never late except for a very good reason. Tell me,' Tweed snapped.

'All right. I thought you'd get it out of me. Since Monica took over this afternoon I've been trawling London – in the hope I'd see something – or someone – which would tell us what is going on. Partly walking, partly moving from area to area by taxi. I may have struck gold this evening,' Paula ruminated.

'Get to the point.'

'A taxi dropped me near Santorini's, that expensive restaurant with a platform projecting over the river. I saw the Brig. – Lord Barford – and his disgusting son, Aubrey. The one I had lunch with. They had just got out of a taxi and Aubrey was carrying a large suitcase plastered with labels. The sort of thing you collect travelling abroad . . .'

'I know,' Tweed said impatiently.

'I got the distinct impression they'd just got back from Heathrow – because of the suitcase. Which one made the trip to somewhere I don't know – Aubrey could have been carrying his father's suitcase. They went into Santorini's.'

'And?'

'I had a mad idea,' Paula informed him. 'I followed them in a few minutes later. They'd be in the restaurant by then. I looked at the hat-check girl's cubbyhole and saw the Brig.'s suitcase with the labels showing. Went up to her and told her Mr Swanton had sent me because he owed them ten pounds on his dinner bill. Held out my hand, full of ten pound coins, reached over the counter, pretended to drop them by mistake on her floor. She bent down to scoop them up and I took a pic of the suitcase with my non-flash camera, then took a taxi back to Park Crescent where they developed the print.'

'Which you've got with you.'

'Yes. I really think this can wait . . .'

'Give.'

She handed over the print, took a magnifying glass out of her shoulder bag, handed that to Tweed. He studied the print.

'Hotels in Brussels, Berlin, Paris and Stockholm. Those were the places Aubrey, while drunk in Martino's, told you his father visited.'

'Exactly.'

'But it looks as though one label has been removed.'

'It has,' Paula agreed. 'And it must have been recently. Those labels stick like the devil if they're left for a while.'

'The missing label must show where he has flown back from. Today. Why the secrecy?'

'I wondered that.' She watched as he placed the print in the drawer of his bedside table. 'You haven't been working on your pad, I hope?'

'Added one name. Rhinoceros.'

M. Bleu had left France. Following the car with his target, Louis Lospin, at the wheel, he had been surprised when the car headed in a different direction, eventually arriving at the airport.

After parking his car in a crowded multi-storey, Lospin had, carrying his bag, checked in for a flight to Corsica. Bleu had shrugged, realizing Lospin was taking a holiday. Air travel did not appeal to him this time – the airport swarmed with security men. The President was due in on a flight. Bleu had left his motorcycle in the multi-storey, had taken a taxi to the Gare du Nord.

From there he caught an express to Amsterdam. He would have been very difficult to detect, let alone to follow. And he had not even considered waiting in Paris for Lospin to return. He could have become conspicuous, been intercepted by French security.

Arriving in Amsterdam, he took a taxi to a hotel near Schiphol Airport. Registering under one of the several names in his collection of different passports, he went up to his room, phoned the airport for flights to Britain the following day. To his surprise he found he could catch an early evening flight to Heathrow if he left the hotel immediately. He did so.

13

Weeks sped by. Tweed had a relapse, then staged a steady recovery. In the clinic, Lisa endured a slow return to normal. All his team had been summoned to Park Crescent on the morning Tweed roared in. It was now late June. He sat erect behind his desk, gazed round.

'Welcome back,' said Paula.

'Hear, hear,' called out Newman.

'Enough of that, I have a clearer picture of what is happening. Still vague, but clearer. We must get moving . . .'

He broke off as the door opened and Lisa walked in. Newman, Paula, Mark Wendover, Harry and Pete, Monica and Marler all stared at her. The colour had come back to her face, she was the picture of vibrant health. No one had heard that she had left the clinic. She looked at Tweed.

'I discharged myself.'

'Was that wise?'

'*I* know when I'm fit. I have to go somewhere at once.'

'No point in asking you where?' Tweed said.

'None at all.' She bent down, kissed him on both cheeks and headed for the door. 'Goodbye, everyone. For the moment. Thank you for all you've done for me.'

'Not even a hint?' pressed Tweed.

'You know where I'm going.' She opened the door. 'I told you. Tweed, you're a bit thick.'

Then she was gone. Tweed reached into his pocket, took

out the doodle pad, extracted a page. He again gazed round the room.

'I *am* a bit thick. It was staring at me all the time. Those words she managed to utter when she arrived at the clinic. "Ham . . . Dan . . . 4S." Hamburg. The famous Four Seasons Hotel, which I know. That's where we're all going.' He looked at Monica. 'Book Club seats for all of us – on a flight for tomorrow. And pack light clothes, now this heatwave has hit us.'

The heatwave had started two days earlier, not predicted by the forecasters, of course. Not only Britain was affected. It was scorching the whole of northern Europe. Tweed was wearing a fawn linen suit. He had already taken off his jacket, hanging it on the back of his chair.

'Thick is the word for me,' Tweed continued. 'Buchanan confirmed it when he told me Lisa's murdered sister was called Helga.'

The phone rang. Monica answered, told Tweed Keith Kent was calling.

'On the phone?'

'No, he's turned up downstairs, most unusual behaviour for him . . .'

'Wheel him up.'

Keith Kent walked in. He smiled at Paula, pulled a funny face at Newman, sat down, refused the offer of coffee from Monica.

'Can't stay long. Thought of another contact who could be helpful with information about Rhinoceros. Should have thought of him weeks ago.' He passed a sheet of paper to Tweed. 'Name is Dr Kefler. That's his phone number and address. He's lived in Hamburg all his life. Regarded in Germany as a financial genius. Rightly so.'

'We're off to Hamburg tomorrow, as it happens, Keith. I'd prefer to call on him.'

'Oh. Then be careful. That address is down by the docks, overlooks the river Elbe. A tricky place at night.

You can bump into some pretty rough characters. Wish I was coming with you. I like Hamburg.'

'Come, then. Join us. We'll be at the Four Seasons Hotel.'

'Now you're making my mouth water. Can't make it tomorrow. Might – just might – fly over there in a few days' time.'

'What sort of a man is this Dr Kefler? His personality?'

'Shrewd as a barrel of monkeys. Personality? Reminds me of a chuckling teddy bear. I must go now. Enjoy the holiday.'

'I suspect it may be anything but a holiday.'

'See you all . . .'

Kent was gone as swiftly as he had arrived. Tweed held up the sheet of paper Kent had left him.

'There we go. Further confirmation. Germany. Before you scuttle off to buy new clothes, which I expect some of you will need to, I'll summarize the state of war up to now – my thinking when I was lying in bed for ever. I can't explain why, but I'm convinced we're involved with two very powerful forces battling with each other. I can't yet work out which character we've met – there are plenty of them – belongs to one force and which to the other. Lisa could be on the good side – but she could also be on the bad one. And this is very big. It involves governments, power. Two top aides to powerful men have been murdered – Jeremy Mordaunt, and Jason Schulz in Washington . . .'

'Pause for breath,' Newman called out. 'Permission to speak.'

'Well, get on with it. What is it?'

'I don't think you've read the newspapers today.' Newman held up a copy of the *Daily Nation*. 'Yesterday, in Paris, the closest man to the Prime Minister, a certain Louis Lospin, was murdered on his front doorstep.'

★   ★   ★

Paula had rarely seen Tweed take a minute to absorb the implications of a new development. He sat quite still, his expression one of great gravity. He pursed his lips.

'Which further confirms what I just said – that governments and power are involved. At the highest level. We must tread carefully. I'm convinced that someone decided these men – Mordaunt and Schulz, and now Lospin – knew too much.'

'I've got another morsel,' Newman told him.

'Then spit it out.'

'While you were lolling in bed I spent part of my time renewing contacts with old reporter chums. Lots of alcohol. One chap is a specialist writing on security. Used to be with Special Branch. Told me there's a top secret international conference planned soon now . . .'

Tweed interrupted. 'Attended by who?'

'Do let me finish. One candidate is your old friend . . .' Newman smiled. 'Gavin Thunder. Another is the American Secretary of State . . .'

'Their Foreign Secretary,' Paula chimed in.

'Do you mind?' Newman snapped. 'A third one is the Prime Minister of France. Number four is the Deputy Chancellor of Germany. They'll all to fly to the Bahamas, land, transfer by boat to another island, name unknown. An SAS unit is being flown out, plus a whole regiment of security wallahs. The stage is yours.'

Tweed stood up, walked briskly over to a large map of the western hemisphere hanging on the wall. Paula noticed he was studying the Bahamas.

'One hell of a lot of islands,' he commented. 'You said this conference will take place soon now. How soon?'

'My contact said it could be any time within the next month. He also guessed – or so he said – that it was linked with the riots a while ago. The secrecy is quite incredible.'

'It's all adding up to the picture I built up,' said Tweed,

returning to his desk. 'The vague picture. Huge forces are on the move. Forces that, I suspect, could transform our lives.'

'And the answer could be in Hamburg?' Mark enquired. 'I'm fluent in German, if that would help.'

'I hope to find the key in Hamburg. This Dr Kefler might help. Paula and Marler are also fluent in German. I know a little myself . . .'

'You're damned well so fluent you could pass for a German,' Paula snapped. 'And you know it.'

'The more the merrier,' Tweed replied.

'Seats all booked for Hamburg,' Monica called out. 'You're to be at Heathrow at noon tomorrow. I've sent a courier to collect the tickets – I'll hand them out this afternoon. I did book return.'

'Yes, we do hope to return,' Tweed told her grimly.

Paula thought Tweed had never been more vigorous – and doom-laden. *This is going to be no picnic*, she told herself.

'Seating. How do we travel?' Harry asked, the first time he had spoken.

'Good point,' Tweed agreed. 'I sit with Paula. Away from us, Newman sits with Mark. Near the back of the plane Harry will be with Pete – to keep an eye on us. Marler behind all of us.'

'Weapons?' drawled Marler, propping up a wall.

'You ask that question?' Tweed rasped, leaning forward. 'We know three top government men have been murdered. Paula told me she'd heard from Buchanan that one of the two thugs he's arrested admitted their job was to kill Lisa. Somebody tried to kill me on our way back from Alfriston a century ago. And you ask that question?'

'So I gather the answer is yes,' replied Marler, quite unperturbed. 'Lucky I have a contact in Hamburg. Nice little chap. In a not-so-nice little street off the Reeperbahn.

151

For that I'll have to take ninety thousand deutschmarks.'

'So you're buying an artillery piece?' Harry joked.

'Thought it might come in handy,' Marler joked back.

Paula did a quick mental calculation. Ninety thousand DM – about thirty thousand pounds. But she knew obtaining illegal weapons – with the serial numbers filed off and that had never been used by anyone else – came expensive.

'Oh, Tweed, I didn't tell you the full story about Louis Lospin's murder. That's London's version. The French papers are calling it suicide. Gave a graphic description of how he waited until his chauffeur had raced off – probably to see his latest girlfriend, which is my bit – and then blew his head off and slumped down the front door of his apartment, still holding the gun.'

'Echoes of Jason Schulz,' Mark commented. 'Found slumped down at the bottom of a tree trunk, the gun clasped in his hand. He should have toppled sideways.'

'Echoes of Jeremy Mordaunt,' Tweed said. 'And I saw the body. I've just decided – after what Bob told us – that I'll call in at the Ministry of Armaments on the off chance Gavin Thunder is behind his desk.'

'Want me to come with you?' Paula suggested.

'No. From what I've heard of Gavin, a married man, no less, he'll ask you for your home phone number. I'm going now.'

Lord Barford was sitting in his study in the manor. From the windows he could see the sweep of the rolling Downs, the sun reflecting off a quarry face. He had unlocked a drawer in his desk and was studying a ticket he had bought at Heathrow the previous evening. Yet another journey into Europe loomed. He shoved it quickly inside a large leather wallet as his younger son, Aubrey, came in.

'Well, Pater, I was early to meet you at Heathrow last

night,' Aubrey remarked as he sat down and languidly crossed his legs.

'What's that red mark round your forehead?' Barford growled. 'You haven't been tearing around on that motorcycle with a filly on the pillion, I hope.'

'Given up the old motorbike. That red mark is a riding cap I wore which was too small for me.'

'So you say. How can I believe one bloody word you say? Incidentally, I'm off again on business tomorrow. An early start. Not sure how long I'll be away.'

'Can I drive you up to Heathrow, Pater?'

'No. The chopper will get me there.' Barford made sure the drawer containing the leather wallet was locked. 'I'm off to bathe . . .'

When Lord Barford had gone, Aubrey began poking round the study. For the second time he picked up the French newspaper which had arrived a week ago. His father had several foreign papers delivered to him by air mail.

Settling himself comfortably, after raiding his father's cocktail cabinet and helping himself to a double Scotch, he reread the item. It reported the return of Louis Lospin to Paris after conferring with the police in Corsica about the bandit problem on the island.

Inside the control room of his house, Eagle's Nest, below the quarry on the Downs, Rondel pressed the lever that elevated the apparatus up the chimney-like tower. Then he went outside into the warm night and watched and listened.

The device rose smoothly, noiselessly appeared out of the chimney's mouth, continued to rise until its targeting apparatus focused above the rim of the Downs. Satisfied, Rondel returned to the control room, pressed another lever which withdrew the system down and inside the chimney.

'Is you ready for dinner, sir?' Mrs Grimwood asked when he walked into the spacious dining room. 'Cook has roasted a nice chicken for you. She left you to choose the wine, as usual.'

'Good. I shall be going abroad tomorrow. May be absent for quite a while. Phone you when I'm returning.'

'My. You do travel, sir. I'd be tired out if I had to travel as much as you do. All those trips by airplane.'

'That's modern business. And I think I'm ready for a meal.'

When he was away Mrs Grimwood often used one of his older cars in the evening to drive to a pub in Alfriston. She loved the gossip. 'Was it true Mildred was expectin'? And 'er not married . . .'

There were times when a friend would ask her where Rondel had gone to this time. Always seemed to be gallivantin' off, the friend would comment hopefully. Then Mrs Grimwood, after taking another sip at her strong gin, would look mysterious.

'Now, Elsie, you know I can't talk about me employer. Not right 'an 'e 'as secrets. Mum's the word.'

The truth was that Mrs Grimwood hadn't an idea on earth where Rondel disappeared to.

14

The junior civil servant seated behind his desk in the entrance hall of the Ministry of Armaments stared stiffly at Tweed. His attitude suggested some sacred protocol had been abused.

'The Minister cannot possibly see anyone who has not made an appointment.'

'Tell him my name. He will see *me*.'

'I have to tell you that is impossible. Without an—'

'Look at this.' Tweed produced his SIS folder, opened and closed it before it was possible to see what was inside. 'Now, if you want to keep your job, stop wasting my time and get on with it. You will find yourself in a most difficult position if I report your obstruction.'

Tweed's manner was autocratic, a pose he rarely adopted. He did, however, know how to deal with government officials full of their own self-importance. He twirled the rolled umbrella he rarely carried. His whole aura suggested someone who was a high-ranking member of the Establishment.

'I'll see what I can do,' the arrogant young man said, getting up slowly from behind his desk. 'Tweed, you said the name was?'

'Didn't you hear me the first time?' Tweed snapped.

Thoroughly cowed now and uneasy, the young man hurried up the large staircase Tweed had mounted on his earlier visit. When he glanced down from the first floor, Tweed was making a ceremony of checking his watch.

A minute later, Tweed was ushered into the Minister's large office. He came forward from behind his massive desk, hand extended.

'My dear Tweed, how good to see you. Do sit down. Coffee – or something stronger?'

'No, thank you, Gavin.'

'You're here, I'm sure,' Thunder said, sitting on a couch facing his visitor, 'to tell me whether you're still investigating the case of the unfortunate Jeremy Mordaunt. I know you asked Superintendent Buchanan to attend the coroner's inquest.'

'I was called away on a very urgent matter.'

Thunder was in his most amiable mood. He had a habit of stroking people he wished to use, stroking them verbally.

'Of course. You have so much responsibility. As you wanted, Buchanan asked for – and obtained – an adjournment, pending further investigation. Or have you now decided it was suicide and therefore the case is closed?'

'No. And it wasn't suicide. It was murder.' Was it Tweed's imagination or had he detected a flicker of disappointment in Thunder's large dark eyes? 'In fact,' he continued, 'I suspect Mordaunt's murder was part of a far larger picture which may well have international implications.'

'International?' Thunder's long foxy face went blank. 'How do you make that out?'

'Because the same man who killed Mordaunt had earlier murdered Jason Schulz in Washington. Now we hear Louis Lospin has been assassinated in Paris.'

'I see.' Thunder took out a gold cigarette case, lit a menthol. 'This is so startling I can hardly believe it.'

'You'd better,' Tweed went on relentlessly. 'Exactly the same *modus operandi* was used in all the murders.

I won't bore you with the details. Take my word for it.'

'Of course, if you say so.'

There was a long pause. Then Tweed continued.

'Furthermore, another strange matter I'm investigating has led me to think it could be linked with the three murders.'

'And . . . ?' Thunder reached for a crystal ashtray, stubbed out his cigarette. '. . . Can you give me a hint of what you referred to as another strange matter?'

'Only when I have solved the whole mystery. Then I will be able to give you a full report.'

'I see . . .' The gold case appeared again, another menthol was lit. 'Have you any idea when that will be?'

'You never can tell. But I expect you'll be here if it is solved quickly.'

'I could be away.' Thunder was choosing his words carefully. 'Not for more than a week, I expect. A visit to a country interested in negotiating a big arms deal with us. A lot of money could be at stake for Britain. If that happened I'd call you when I got back.'

He was stubbing out his second cigarette, hardly smoked, as though the interview was nearing its conclusion.

'Are you prepared for the second – and much more dangerous – outbreak of riots?' Tweed asked suddenly.

Thunder's right hand went towards the pocket containing the gold cigarette case. He changed his mind, relaxed, folded both hands behind his neck.

'You really think this is on the cards?'

'Don't you?'

'I was going to tell you, Tweed. When we had those riots weeks and weeks ago I had a small SAS team ready. We did not need to call on their services.' He smiled. 'It was based not five hundred yards from where we're sitting.'

It would be, Tweed thought, *so it could protect Downing*

Street and the Ministries, including your own. He looked at his watch.

'I think I should go now. Thank you for your time.'

'And you will keep me informed of your investigation into what you called another strange matter?' Thunder said as he followed Tweed to the door, opened it for him.

'Only when I have solved a very complex mystery . . .'

As Tweed left the building he was satisfied that he had left behind a thoroughly rattled Gavin Thunder.

'Bad news, Tweed. I'm furious.'

The phone call from Roy Buchanan had come through within five minutes of Tweed returning to Park Crescent.

'What is it, Roy?' Tweed enquired. 'You do sound livid.'

'I am. You recall those two thugs who were going to kill Helga Trent's sister, Lisa? Barton and Panko?'

'Yes.'

'Well, they've escaped from custody already and they're on the loose. I had given strict instructions they were to be held in a top-security prison, Parkhurst on the Isle of Wight. Some idiot ignored my orders, sent them to a certain prison in London noted for its *in*security.'

'When did this happen? How did they manage it?'

'Last night. They put a warder in hospital – seriously injured and recovery unlikely. How? The old trick – they smuggled themselves inside the laundry truck just before it was leaving. The driver ran into traffic, had to stop several times, so obviously they left the truck during one of those stops and vanished. I have put out an alert – armed and dangerous.'

'Armed with what, Roy?'

'A knife. They stabbed the warder seventeen times. Some of the thrusts were because they enjoyed it, I suspect.'

'We're leaving the country tomorrow. I'd sooner not say where at the moment. May phone you from abroad,' Tweed suggested.

'Care to tell me how many of you are going?'

'Sooner not, if you don't mind.'

'Secret is the appropriate word for your lot. You take care. Are you still feeling all right?' Buchanan asked.

'Fresh as a daisy.'

'Take good care of Daisy . . .'

No one in Tweed's team who had encountered Delgado would have dreamt of his living conditions. On the fourth floor of one of the old warehouses in Reefers Wharf his living room was expensively furnished with tasteful sofas and armchairs. The old floorboards were covered with a pearl grey wall-to-wall fitted carpet. A large TV set was hidden inside a mahogany cabinet.

His kitchen was equipped with the latest dishwasher, a modern oven and cupboards. A large American fridge stood against one wall. His bedroom was lavishly furnished, as was his bathroom.

And no one in Tweed's team would have easily recognized the giant. Clad in a lightweight suit from Aquascutum, he gave the impression of being a successful businessman. He had visited a barber he had never patronized before, remarking he had just returned from a safari in Africa. Hence his long greasy hair. The barber had transformed his appearance. His hair was now trimmed neat and short.

He had also purchased a rubber-tipped stick and practised stooping when he walked, which made him seem a shorter man. It was the following day when he received the expected phone call from Heathrow at lunchtime.

'Donau here. I can tell you where they're going – flying from Heathrow.'

Donau, the German name for Danube, was the code

name Delgado had given him. A short man, thirty years old and frisky in his movements, Donau had watched Park Crescent with a pair of field glasses while he crouched in a shrubbery on the edge of Regent's Park.

Seeing the cars leave before eleven in the morning, with Tweed inside one of them, he had jumped into his car parked nearby at a meter. He had followed them to the long-stay car park at Heathrow.

Carrying his case, which contained nothing but a selection of his clothes, Donau followed Tweed and his team with his frisky walk. Arriving in the concourse, he had bought a ticket to Paris because there were no passengers at the Air France counter. He had told the check-in girl he would carry his small case onto the plane.

Walking more slowly – you always changed your way of walking when tailing a target – he was just in time to see Tweed's team moving through the formalities. It was holiday time so when he held up his passport in the name of Donaldson he was waved through.

His only discomfort was the heat. The sun had glared down on him all the time he'd hidden behind the shrubbery. He was sweating profusely when eventually he followed his target to the departure gate. *Hamburg*.

He retreated immediately the way he had come. In a toilet cubicle he smeared white chalk over his face. He was trudging when he explained to officials near the exit that he was feeling very ill, had decided to go home. A ghastly stomach upset, but he had eaten lobster which had tasted odd late the previous evening. After checking his suitcase and searching him thoroughly, the officials allowed him to depart, after making a note of data on his passport.

Once outside, he had walked slowly to a phone – in case he was under observation. He had then called Delgado.

'So where the hell are they flying to?' Delgado had snapped.

'Hamburg. I saw them enter the departure lounge.'

'This is good. You do well. Stay there and I arrive. We catch later flight to Hamburg. Moment – I check airline table . . .'

Delgado had a collection of international rail and airline timetables. After a few minutes he gave Donau instructions where to wait. Then he called Oscar Vernon. Pink Shirt answered immediately.

'I will come with you,' Oscar said. 'Now I have the time and number of the flight I will phone Heathrow to book three tickets to be kept for collection. The instruction is the same. Kill Lisa, kill Tweed . . .'

'Lisa left clinic. We lose her . . .'

'Where Tweed goes, so does Lisa. We will find them.'

'B and P have made it,' Delgado informed his boss. He was referring to Barton and Panko escaping from prison. 'I tell them go express train Newcastle. From Newcastle ferry go to Hamburg. I give address Hotel Renaissance, Grosse Bleichen.'

Unlike his fractured English, Delgado spoke fluent German. It was a talent he shared with Oscar, but the latter had been careful not to let Delgado know this – he might later hear Delgado say something in German he didn't wish Oscar to understand. Also, the Renaissance was where Oscar would stay when he arrived.

'You have done well,' he said.

'We have no defenders,' Delgado protested.

'Defenders' was the code word they used when phoning each other for weapons.

'I have a friend in Bremen,' Oscar assured him. 'I will phone him, tell him to bring defenders to Hamburg main rail station. Bremen is close to Hamburg. I must go now.'

Oscar did not think it wise to explain that at Bremen, being a port, weapons were smuggled in from arriving freighters. He kept to a minimum vital data passed on to subordinates.

Delgado put down the phone, went into the bathroom, looked at himself in the mirror. He did now look like a successful businessman. Once again he wondered who was the man Oscar took *his* orders from.

15

Hamburg.

Tweed and Paula walked out of the Fuhlsbuttl Airport and the heat hit them like walking into a brick wall. The limo from the Four Seasons was waiting for them. The young chauffeur was pleasant, welcoming them with a warm smile. Soon they were well inside the great city and Paula stared out, admiring the stately villas as they drove down Rothenbaum-chaussee.

Despite the fact that it was late June the plane had been more than half empty so they had been able to talk without any fear of being overheard.

'We were followed at Heathrow,' Paula commented. 'Right up to the departure lounge.'

'I know,' Tweed replied. 'A small man carrying a small case. Quite professional. He varied his walk – sometimes bouncing along and then walking slowly. We could have a reception party waiting for us in Hamburg.'

'Have you any idea yet who is behind all this?'

'None at all . . .'

Mark Wendover had wandered down the aisle from behind them and jogged the tray of Tweed, sitting in the aisle seat.

'I'm so sorry, sir,' he apologized.

'That's all right. Been a smooth flight so far.'

'I spent hours, days at Reefers Wharf watching for Delgado to return – so I could identify where he lived.

163

He never reappeared. Mentioned this to Harry and he said I should have checked the street at the back of the warehouse. The backs have fire escapes – so he thinks Delgado spotted me and used the fire escape from then on. Enjoy the flight . . .'

They were driving down the Neuer Jungfernstieg when Paula caught her first glimpse of the Binnenalster, the smaller of two lakes in the centre of the city. She glowed with delight and excitement as she gazed at the blue water, rippling and glittering in the sunlight. Single-decker ferries were shuttling back and forth, some heading back for the landing stage at Jungfernstieg.

'We're just about there,' said Tweed.

As they alighted on the pavement in front of the Four Seasons hotel a motorcyclist, who had trailed behind them since they left the airport, sped past and disappeared. Tweed shrugged as they entered the spacious reception hall and they registered.

'It's a long time since we've had the pleasure of seeing you, Mr Tweed,' the receptionist greeted him.

'We both have suites on the third floor,' Tweed told Paula. He lowered his voice. 'Let's take a quick look round. For generations this hotel was run by the same family. It's been taken over by a foreign chain. I just want to see if they've had the sense to preserve its wonderful character.'

As they strolled into a spacious sitting area a curious incident occurred. One of the elevators reached the ground floor. The doors opened. Inside stood a late-middle-aged man of medium height, well-built and wearing gold-rimmed glasses. His eyes met Tweed's briefly, then he stayed inside, pressed a button and the elevator climbed to the second floor.

'That was odd,' Paula remarked.

'Probably forgotten something in his room.'

He showed her a gallery with portaits in gilt frames hung

from the walls. Luxuriously covered chairs were placed close to the walls so people could sit and take their ease. He then took her through another spacious room, where men and women sat drinking, and into the Grill Room.

'This is magnificent,' said Paula. 'I wouldn't mind eating up there.'

She pointed to a balcony on the first floor overlooking the main restaurant. On their way back to the elevators Tweed peered into a smaller room with tables laid. 'The Café Condi,' he explained. 'More than a café – you can get lunch here. The service is excellent and the food very good. I think we should go up to our suites now. I want to phone Dr Kefler, the financial genius as Keith Kent called him. The sooner we see him the better . . .'

They were passing reception when they saw Marler registering. He had come from the airport on his own by taxi. He looked up, saw them, looked away as though he didn't know them.

'Did you say I'm in Room . . . ?' he called out in a loud voice to the receptionist.

He had now told them where they could find him. Tweed was shown into his suite while another porter took charge of Paula. Alone, he walked to the balcony and stood there a moment. The trees which lined the far side of the road were in full leaf but, on the third floor, he could see over the tops and had a clear view of the Binnenalster. Peace.

Going back inside he sat down, checked the number Kent had given him, pressed the number for an outside line and then the German's number.

'Who is this?' a gruff voice demanded in German.

'My name is Tweed. We have a mutual acquaintance . . .'

'Ah! You have arrived quickly. Keith phoned me that you were coming, gave me your description. A necessary precaution. I am Kefler.'

The German was speaking in English now. A necessary precaution? It had an almost sinister sound.

'I'm at the Four Seasons, Dr Kefler.' He gave him his suite number. 'I would like to see you as urgently as possible. Also, I would like to bring my assistant, Paula Grey – and Robert Newman, the foreign correspondent.'

'All will be welcome. But you must come well after dark. Take a taxi, tell the driver to drop you just before he reaches the Fish Market. Then walk along Grosse Elbstrasse. Soon, on your right you come to a high grassy bank. There is a footpath up to a terrace of old houses. Climb up the footpath. I am number 23. Keep in the shadows as you walk. I suggest we meet at eleven o'clock.'

'Tonight?' Tweed asked.

'Yes, tonight. Who can guarantee there *will* be a tomorrow? Thank you for calling . . .'

Someone tapped on his door. When he opened it, Paula walked in. She looked round the suite, walked out on to the balcony, took a deep breath of air, although it was still hot. She turned round.

'I should have asked if this is a convenient moment.'

'Very. Sit down. Listen.'

He relayed to her every word of his conversation with Dr Kefler. She frowned, gazing at him as he spoke from an armchair. He waved a hand.

'That's it,' he concluded.

'We're going, then?'

'Yes.'

'It all sounds rather menacing, downbeat. "Come well after dark. Keep in the shadows. If there's a tomorrow",' Paula commented.

'On the contrary, Kefler sounded very jovial, very warm.'

'Well, Keith Kent did say Kefler reminded him of a teddy bear. But don't you think there was a grim element?'

'Yes, I do. We shall therefore take heavy protection.

Later we'll walk to the Hotel Renaissance where Harry Butler and Pete Nield are staying. I want Harry to guard our rear,' Tweed decided.

'And Mark?'

'Would be one too many.'

He went to the door. Someone had rapped hard on it. Opening it, he looked at the tall figure standing outside.

'Mr Tweed. I am Victor Rondel.'

Paula looked with curiosity as their visitor entered, was introduced to her. He held on to her hand only briefly and his grip was firm. She was rather struck by him.

Six feet tall, slim, athletically built, he was clean-shaven and had blond hair neatly brushed back from his forehead. His brown eyes had a humorous hint and his smile was attractive. In his late thirties or early forties, he was clad in a pale blue polo-neck sweater, fawn slacks with a razor-edged crease and white trainers. He accepted Tweed's invitation to sit down, paused when Tweed gestured to the champagne in an ice bucket the management had provided.

'It's not been opened. You might like to keep it for later.'

'The ice in the bucket is almost water now,' Tweed commented. 'I think you'd do us a favour if I opened it now.'

'Then I will be happy to do you that favour.'

He smiled again as Tweed took the bottle into the bathroom to open. He was smiling at Paula, who had perched herself on the arm of another chair.

'Would this be your first trip to Hamburg, Miss Grey?'

'Paula, please. No, it isn't. I was here quite a few years ago when the old family was running it. In this hotel, I mean.'

'Ah. The end of a dynasty. I fear a lot of that is happening these days. Thank heavens the new owners – a chain – have

167

preserved its original character. I understand you are Mr Tweed's close assistant.'

She didn't reply because Tweed had returned with the bottle opened. He poured champagne into three of the six glasses laid out on a table, raised his glass.

'To peace and propserity.'

'I will certainly drink to that,' Rondel agreed.

'How did you know I was here?' Tweed asked suddenly, still standing.

'I saw you and Miss Grey . . .'

'Paula, please,' she said again, smiling.

'I saw you and Paula come in when I was having coffee in the lounge downstairs. The gentry in Hamburg patronize that room.'

'But how did you know it was me?' Tweed persisted.

'Information is one essential element in my job. Sometimes more valuable than gold. You are the Deputy Director of the SIS.'

'And may I ask you what your job is?'

'You just did.' Rondel laughed pleasantly. 'I am one of the two partners who control the Zurcher Kredit Bank.'

'With a reputation of being the most trustworthy bank in the world.'

'I would hope so. I would most certainly hope so.' Rondel emptied his glass. 'Thank you for the drink. That champagne is a most superior brand. Now, I have taken up enough of your time. This was in the way of a first introduction. We would be most happy if you could be our guests at one of the best restaurants in town.' He extracted from his chamois wallet a long off-white card, handed it to Paula. 'We have reserved a good table for you for tomorrow night. I hope that is acceptable. The table number is on the back.'

'Very kind of you,' replied Tweed. 'Would I be out of order if I brought someone else as well as Paula? A man called Robert Newman.'

'Ah! The world-famous foreign correspondent. He would be most welcome.'

'I will, of course, pay for him . . .'

'You won't be able to.' Rondel laughed again. 'The manager will have been instructed to put three guests on my account. No argument, please. Oh, I hope you will not think it unfriendly, but you will be dining by yourselves. I shall be at another table with my partner – by tomorrow evening an urgent cable will have arrived and we must make a decision.'

'That is quite all right. You refer to "we", and mention your partner.'

'That, as I think I mentioned, is who I shall be dining with.' Rondel stood up. 'Soon we may well wish you to visit us at our headquarters.'

'Which are where?'

'Information never disclosed in advance.' Rondel smiled again, shook hands with both of them. 'We will keep in touch . . .'

Alone with Paula, Tweed looked at her. Taking off his glasses, he polished them with a clean handkerchief, perched them back on his nose.

'What did you think of him?'

'Bit of a whirlwind. I liked him. Never met anyone like him before. I've heard of this restaurant.' She handed him the card. 'It is supposed to be super.'

'Fischereihafen Restaurant,' Tweed read aloud. 'Grosse Elbstrasse 143. That means it's not so far from where Dr Kefler lives. *Hafen*, you know, means harbour.'

'What did *you* think of him?' Paula asked.

'Very secretive. Rondel cleverly evaded giving us the name of his partner – and where their headquarters are situated. I wonder how he found out who I was, that we'd be coming here? Paula, on this journey into a mirage we can trust no one except our own team. No one.'

'You found Rondel suspect?'

'I didn't say that.' Someone knocked on the door. 'Maybe that's Newman. He's staying here, of course, as is Mark.'

Tweed opened the door, was taken aback. Standing there with a half-smile on her face was Lisa Trent.

16

'Welcome to Hamburg,' said Lisa as she walked in, went over to hug Paula. 'Amazing,' she said, turning to Tweed. 'Truly amazing. You worked out my message, you clever man,' she ended cheekily.

'Interested in a glass of champagne?' Tweed suggested.

'Buckets of it,' Lisa rapped back after checking the bottle. 'Can I sit down? It's bloody hot,' she remarked, sitting down.

She wore a white blouse, khaki shorts. Her feet were clad in sandals. No jewellery – not even one ring on her fingers. Tweed gave her a glass of champagne. She drank half of it straight off.

'How did you know we were here?' Tweed asked casually.

'I make it my business to know what's going on. Thought you'd have caught on to that when I made it my business to come to London – to warn you where the imminent riots were going to take place. Wake up, Tweed,' she rapped out, again saucy.

'Why have you come to see us now – glad as we are of your restrained presence?'

'*Touché!* My guess is you're hunting Rhinoceros.'

'Is it?' Tweed sat down facing her so as not to miss any nuance of expression. 'And supposing that *was* one of the reasons we are here?'

'Then you're in the right place. Germany.'

'Rhinoceros is in Germany? Whereabouts?'

'No damned idea.' Lisa refilled her glass, knocked back half of her fresh drink. 'You really will have to do some of the work yourself.'

'I have been known to exert a little energy. What about a hint?'

'I haven't a clue.' She suddenly dropped her flippant attitude, stared at Paula. 'But I can tell you that all of you are in grave danger.'

'From who?'

'This interrogation has gone far enough.' She flared up, her face flushed with anger. She turned on Tweed. 'I do *not* know. Don't you bloody well think I'd tell you if I did?' Standing up, she confronted him. 'There's a quality called trust. Ever heard of it? *Trust!*' she shouted at him. 'As you obviously don't trust me we have no more to talk about.' She reached for the champagne glass, saw it was empty, threw it onto the table where it shattered. 'When I think of what I went through in London to help you and you treat me like this!'

'I remember that well, Lisa . . .' Tweed began.

'Don't "Lisa" me. The name is Trent. Got it? T-r-e-n-t. So forget about me,' she shouted, heading for the door. 'Paula, I pity you, working for this man . . .'

Then she was gone.

'I blew it,' said Tweed.

'She didn't have to rave at you like that.'

'I blew it,' Tweed repeated. He went on to the balcony and Paula followed. 'She is just out of the clinic and probably needed a few more days, but she's gutsy. In her place I'd have walked out of that clinic. We've lost one important key.'

'I could go and try and find her . . .'

'Don't. She has to simmer, then quieten down. Her sister Helga was murdered. She probably realizes the bullet was meant for herself.' He took a deep breath. 'At least we still have Dr Kefler tonight.'

'And maybe Rondel.'

'Funny idea. His inviting us to dinner and then not sitting with us. Something odd there.'

'We'll find out tomorrow night,' Paula said quietly.

'Meantime, I think we should go now to the Hotel Renaissance and contact Harry for tonight. We just don't know what may be waiting for us down in the docks area.'

As if on cue, Marler arrived, carrying a large hold-all. He grinned, refused a glass of champagne.

'Just back from the Reeperbahn. I've seen Newman, given him his favourite, a .38 Smith & Wesson with holster and spare ammo. Said he felt better now.'

'Why? Was he nervous?' Tweed asked, not believing it.

'This is a nervous city. Also visited Mark. His bedtime companion is a 7.65mm Walther.'

'How did you know which rooms to go to?'

'Followed them discreetly when they arrived separately. They didn't know I was there.'

'Must be losing their grip,' Paula joked.

'You said,' Tweed recalled, 'this is a nervous city. What prompted that remark?'

'My contact off the Reeperbahn who supplied the weaponry. He said they had enough of their own thugs, but on the grapevine he'd heard more were coming from Britain – some by ferry, some flying in. I bought enough weaponry to deal with a small army. Now, Paula.'

He handed her out of the hold-all what he knew she wanted. A .32 Browning automatic with ammo. She checked the empty weapon, checked its mechanism, pushed a magazine inside the butt, slipped the gun into the special pocket inside her shoulder bag.

'Now I feel fully dressed,' she announced.

'You're as bad as Newman,' Marler commented. 'How about a couple of grenades, two compact containers of concentrated tear gas?'

'Give,' she said, holding out her hand.

'And then there's yourself, Tweed. A Walther, if I remember rightly.'

'You know I rarely carry a weapon,' Tweed objected, staring with distaste at the automatic held out to him.

'Take it,' snapped Paula. 'I sense we are in for a very rough ride on this one. Don't you want to save my life when the time comes?'

'You are diabolically persuasive. You should be kept locked up.'

But he accepted the Walther, hip holster and ammo from Marler. Then he checked his watch.

'Paula and I were just going out to make contact with Harry and Pete, staying at the Hotel Renaissance.'

'Then, since I was going there next, I'll give you a thirty seconds start, then stroll after you to guard your rear . . .'

It was still daylight as Tweed and Paula walked out of the hotel, turned right and strolled like a couple of holidaymakers. The sun, which had glared in at the windows of Tweed's suite, still roasted them even though it was mid-evening.

They had reached the end of the street, crossed over. Paula paused, staring across the street at the wide pedestrian platform of Jungfernstieg. The ferries, far fewer in number than earlier, were still plying their way from the landing stage over the Alster.

'In the early morning and at the end of the day,' Tweed told her, 'commuters who live in houses or apartments near the Alster commute by ferry. Saves them worrying about parking cars.'

'It's heaven,' sighed Paula, looking at the beautiful big buildings on the opposite shore.

'We must keep moving,' Tweed decided. He glanced back the way they had come. Marler was overtaking them. He had just called Harry's mobile on his own. His lips hardly moved as he spoke when passing them.

'I've got Harry's phone number, so now I know his room. Just follow me a bit behind when we reach the Renaissance . . .'

They were passing department stores in tall massive buildings which looked as though they had stood there for ever. Marler turned right down Grosse Bleichen, a narrower street. Very few people about. They followed Marler, entering the Hotel Renaissance, a quiet comfortable place. Paula glanced into the entrance to the restaurant, turned away quickly.

'What's the matter?' Tweed whispered.

'In the restaurant. You're not going to believe this. Remember Pink Shirt, fat-faced with a large head – on the pavement opposite The Hangman's Noose during the riots?'

'Yes.'

'He's sitting in the restaurant we've just passed. And I think he spotted me . . .'

'Hurry, Marler is waiting . . .'

Harry Butler opened the door of his room after Marler tapped in a certain way. He hustled them inside, closed, locked the door.

'What's the rush?' Tweed asked.

'Bad news,' Harry announced. 'Pink Shirt, big man, ugly. Directing the thugs at Reefers Wharf. Staying here.'

'We saw him,' Paula said.

'The news gets worse,' Harry went on. 'Delgado is staying here. Well disguised, hair trimmed short, stoops, carries a rubber-tipped stick. I saw his eyes. Always tell a man by his eyes.'

175

'How on earth did they get here so quickly?' Paula wondered.

'Easy. Caught a later flight.'

'But how could they know we were coming *here*?' Paula persisted.

'The frisky little runt who followed us to the departure lounge at Heathrow,' Tweed reminded her. 'There was a board outside with "Hamburg" in big letters. He'd beetle off, call his boss.'

'Oh, I'd just forgotten him. They're horribly well organized.'

'So we'll be better organized,' Tweed replied.

While they were speaking Marler had taken a Walther out of his large hold-all, handed it to Harry. He gave him another one for Nield. More presents followed. Grenades, tear gas canisters, smoke bombs, an Uzi machine pistol. Marler then produced more – for Pete Nield.

'Starting a new Gulf War?' Paula asked mischievously.

'Could be like that,' Harry warned.

'Where is Nield?' Tweed asked.

'In the next room.' Harry jerked a thumb to his right. 'It was lucky. We arrived separately. He's outside somewhere – prowling round to get the feel of the place.'

'I have to tell you something . . .' Tweed began.

Harry listened, arms folded across his powerful chest, saying not a word. Tweed explained in detail about their visit to Dr Kefler at eleven that night, gave him the address, showed him the area down by the docks on a map of the city he'd acquired from the receptionist at the Four Seasons.

'I'll be there,' Harry said, glancing at the marksman's rifle Marler had given him. 'I've bought a motorbike. Follow the taxi in that. When you get out I'll hoof it. Don't like the sound of what this Kefler said at all. Don't like where he lives. Docks. At night . . .'

'I feel reassured Harry is coming,' Paula said as they left

the Renaissance. She squeezed Tweed's arm, whispered. 'Look who's ahead of us.'

A stooping man plodded along about twenty yards ahead of them. He carried in his right hand a rubber-tipped stick. His hair was trimmed very short. Tweed grabbed Paula's arm and swung her round so that, like himself, she was pretending to gaze into a shop window.

'That's how Harry described the new Delgado – I would never have recognized him.'

'We have things to do,' Tweed warned. 'Get back to the Four Seasons – personally I want a quick shower – have dinner, then we go see Dr Kefler.'

'The shower's for me, too. I'm not very hungry.'

'You will be if you don't eat – hungry in the middle of the night.'

'He's gone!'

She had stolen a glance up the street and it was deserted. Tweed looked, grunted, took her arm, guided her across to the pavement on the other side of the street. A whole line of vehicles, many of them large trucks, were parked for the night.

'He's gone into one of the arcades we passed on our way to see Harry,' Tweed explained. 'Walking up this side of the street we're almost invisible behind these trucks if he reappears . . .'

They reached the main street running past the platform and landing stage. Tweed was about to turn left when Paula tugged at his arm. She nodded to her right.

A short distance away a tall man in a straw hat was operating a video camera. Mark Wendover. As they watched, with his back to them he swivelled the camera to take pictures of the Alster, of a ferry coming in. Then he quickly swivelled it into a different direction, aiming the lens at a building – the entrance, the ground floor windows, higher up to the first floor. The imposing building was the Zurcher Kredit Bank.

'He's at it again,' Paula protested. 'Doing his own thing. Mavericking.'

'Well, if that's the way he works . . .'

'Something I've been meaning to tell you,' Paula said as they approached the hotel entrance. 'Kept slipping what passes for my mind. Before we left Park Crescent – you were out of the room – Monica told me that when that awful screaming started on the Internet the phone went dead.'

'It did?' replied Tweed dismissively. 'I thought she was calling various contacts to see if their systems were all right.'

'That was later,' Paula said emphatically. 'She reckons the phone was dead during the whole awful experience. Afterwards, too. For a couple of minutes.'

'A glitch . . .'

'Listen, do! The Internet is linked to the phone system.'

'Intriguing.'

Annoyed, Paula gave up. When she reached her room she dived into the bathroom to take the shower she would have welcomed hours earlier.

In his room Tweed postponed the shower while he called Cord Dillon at his private number in his apartment.

'What is it, Tweed?' a sleepy voice enquired. 'It's morning here – and I'm not an early riser unless I have to be.'

'Mark Wendover. What kind of a detective agency does he run in New York?'

'Corporate work. Embezzlement. Someone dipping their hand into the till. In a big way. How is Mark?'

'Thriving.'

'Is that all? Good. Thank God . . .'

Tweed took out his doodle pad, scribbled Zurcher Kredit, put a large loop round it, joined Rondel's loop to it, then Mark's. He stared at the pad for a few minutes, the non-working end of his pen in his mouth. He grunted, then went into the bathroom for his shower.

Earlier that evening, after shouting her head off at Tweed, Lisa had stormed back to her room. When she opened the door she saw an envelope had been slipped under it into the room. She took it out of the envelope, saw it was a hotel record of a phone message.

Call me urgently. Go to the main railway station to make the call. Rocco.

She left her room immediately. Leaving the hotel, she walked. Every now and again she paused, fiddled with one of her sandals as though it had picked up a stone. This gave her the chance to glance back, to check she wasn't being followed.

The station wasn't crowded when she arrived. It was Germanic, vast and with a very high roof. She went into an empty phone cubicle, called the number. A familiar voice answered.

'Lisa, would you like to make a hundred thousand marks?'

'What did you say?'

'I think you heard me. I want you to gain all the information you can from Tweed from now on. How many in his team? Where is he going? In Hamburg. Outside Hamburg? And the only person you report this information to is me . . .'

'Just a minute,' she said. 'Someone is trying to get in here.'

She turned round. A man she had never seen was holding a white envelope. He thrust it into her hand, said it was for her, then departed.

'You've got the envelope,' the voice on the phone commented. 'Now count the contents. I'll wait.'

She opened it. A thick sheaf of 1,000 DM banknotes. She

checked. 10,000 DM. She checked again. No, 100,000 DM. In English money, roughly £30,000. She slipped the envelope inside her handbag.

'Remember, you report only to me . . .'

She had never had so much money in her life.

17

Tweed and Paula were having dinner in the Grill Room. They had the only table occupied on the balcony, which gave them a good view down into the restaurant below. There were just a few guests, even though they were on the edge of July.

'Not so many people as I'd have expected,' Paula commented. 'I think it must be the heat – it has even penetrated up here.'

She was eating scrambled eggs – not on the menu but she'd explained to the waiter she wasn't very hungry owing to the heat.

'Most unusual, Madame, for Hamburg,' the waiter replied. 'A heatwave is something we rarely experience.'

'I see Newman is sitting at a table over by the wall and has Mark with him,' Tweed remarked. 'As we came in I heard Mark asking if he could join him, as he hated eating alone.'

'Keeping up the pretence they don't know each other,' Paula observed.

'And Marler is having sandwiches and a drink in the lounge by himself. From that position he can observe anyone who comes in here. Doesn't miss a trick, our Marler. Don't look now, but you'll never guess in a hundred years who has just sat down at a table by himself. By the wall,' said Tweed.

'Tell me – or I'll have to look.'

181

'The Brig. Bernard, Lord Barford. Wearing a white dinner jacket.'

'On a sweltering night like this?' Paula exclaimed.

'Oh, typical of him. You dress for dinner whatever the temperature. He'll have done that hundreds of times in the mess when he was in the Army.'

'Heavens.' Tweed's observation had just sunk in on Paula. 'He's the last man on earth I'd have expected to turn up here. What's going on?'

'I haven't any idea.'

'You don't believe in coincidences. And Hamburg wasn't one of the places Aubrey, his drunken son, included when he told me over lunch at Martino's where the Brig often flies to. I wonder why he keeps Hamburg so secret?' Paula said.

'I simply couldn't even guess.'

Tweed was making short work of his Dover sole. He was famished. Both of them had avoided alcohol, were drinking water to ward off dehydration.

'Has he spotted us?' Paula enquired as she finished off the last of her scrambled eggs.

'No. He didn't look up here as he came in. Now he's concentrating on reading some documents.'

'He probably will see us when we leave, go down the steps from this balcony.'

'We'll try and choose a moment when he's surrounded by waiters serving him. They do have plenty of waiters.' Tweed put down his knife and fork, checked his watch below the table cloth.

'What's our next objective – after we've visited Dr Kefler?'

'To locate and identify Rhinoceros. Coffee? Dessert?'

'Not for me,' Paula decided.

'Then now might be a good moment to leave.'

As they descended the stairs into the main restaurant, Paula had a good look at the unexpected arrival. A covey

182

of waiters hovered round him as they served a steak. She thought he looked very alert, his hand movements agile, very much in command of himself, sitting erect as a ramrod.

'He didn't see us,' Paula said as they walked into the lounge.

'Don't kid yourself. He's a spry bird. Doesn't miss much.'

Marler was seated by himself, shielded from other guests by a palm tree. Tweed walked slowly, dropped a crumpled piece of paper into his lap, continued walking.

'What was the note about?' Paula wondered.

'To tell Marler we're going out to see someone. And also that Harry is going to guard our rear.'

Newman, as arranged, caught them up as they entered the hall. He kept his voice down as he spoke.

'Mark handled that cleverly. Anyone near us who knew English would have heard him talking about New York, then asking what my job was. He's astute. Look who's here.'

They were about to walk down the steps into the street when Lisa appeared from nowhere. She was dangling her shoulder bag by its strap and smiling as though all was well with the world.

'Going somewhere?' she asked Paula.

'Just a long stroll,' Tweed replied quickly. 'We have something we want to talk over in confidence.'

'Can I come with you?'

'You look really tired,' said Paula, having a go at her. 'I'd suggest you go to bed and get some sleep . . .'

They reached the street and started walking along the pavement towards the landing stage. Lisa ran after them, caught up with Tweed.

'I really am sorry I blew my top. I didn't mean—'

'Lisa,' Paula snapped, 'go back and get some sleep. Didn't you hear Tweed say we had something confidential to talk over?'

Lisa blinked, turned on her heel, went back and climbed the first few steps. She stayed there, waited a short time, then peered after them.

'That wasn't very nice of either of you,' Newman protested. 'I could have shooed her off much more politely.' He frowned. 'I sense good relations with Lisa have broken down. Had a row?'

'She was very rude to Tweed in his room,' Paula told him.

'It isn't that,' Tweed said, glancing over his shoulder. 'I want to see how much of an effort she'll make to get back into our good graces. And here's a taxi coming . . .'

With the aid of a map he explained to the driver exactly where they wanted to be dropped. The driver looked at them as though surprised, then nodded.

'Don't think he thought it was a good idea,' Paula whispered.

They stopped talking and Paula gazed out of the window as the cab drove at speed deep into Hamburg. Huge solid buildings loomed above them and there was no one else about. At long intervals the streets were lit by tall lamps and then they again plunged into shadows. Paula slipped her right hand inside her shoulder bag to make sure she could grab her automatic quickly. Tweed was following their route, studying his street plan.

'They go to bed early,' Newman commented. 'Not a soul about.'

'They work hard, get up early,' Paula replied, to say something to keep her nerves in check.

The cab stopped in the middle of nowhere. Weird modern buildings hemmed them in. The driver looked back uncertainly, kept his engine running.

'Is this where you want to get off?' he asked in German.

'It is,' Tweed assured him.

'You're certain?'

184

His manner was uneasy. Paula noticed he had kept the doors locked. He peered at her, frowning.

'This is exactly the point,' said Tweed, handing him the fare plus a generous tip.

'Thanks very much,' the driver said. 'You are coming back?'

He scribbled his name, Eugen, on a card giving the firm's name and phone number. Tweed slipped it into his wallet. The cab disappeared quickly.

'I heard a motorcyclist behind us,' Newman remarked. 'Now he's stopped somewhere.'

'That's Harry,' Paula told him. 'I'm glad he's come.'

They started walking past the weird buildings that reminded Paula of gigantic modern sculptures. It was very quiet, very humid. She thought she smelt a whiff of oil.

'How far to the Elbe?' she asked.

'Not far,' Tweed told her, having put his map away.

It was disturbingly quiet as they walked downhill. Not a soul in sight anywhere. She looked back, hoping for a comforting sight of Harry. Nothing. But when Harry followed you he was the Invisible Man. It was unnervingly silent, then she heard the faint swish of water as they reached the bottom of the hill. They had reached the docks, the Elbe. Tweed led them to his right. She saw a street sign. *Elbstr*.

To her left as they walked slowly in the heat she had her first sight of the river. About as wide as the Thames in London. Above them loomed immensely tall cranes. Halfway up the huge structures she saw control cabins. There seemed to be dozens of the cranes. All motionless. She thought they looked like Martians which had just landed. She saw one vast structure, squatter, resting on railway lines so its position could be moved when barges arrived. Lights high up gave spasmodic illumination, emphasizing the black shadows. There was no moon to see – the sky had a heavy overcast which must have drifted in recently.

185

She felt tiny, and a little nervous, walking below these monsters.

'When the Germans build they build big,' she commented.

'Hence the enormous Panther tanks they used in the Second World War that I've read about,' said Tweed. 'I've seen pictures of them. They fought like tigers and caused us a lot of trouble during the Normandy landings.'

'Just so long as we don't see one coming down the street,' she retorted.

'Rather unlikely,' Newman assured her.

Across the far side of the river Paula saw another army of cranes deployed. More lights glowed from a great height. Two freighters were moored for the night with several large barges.

'It just goes on and on,' she commented.

'They are,' Tweed informed her, 'the second largest docks on the Continent. The only bigger system is Europort down in Holland. But these docks are catching up.'

A chain clanked in the night. She nearly jumped out of her skin. It was the first sound she had heard since they'd begun their long plod along Elbstrasse.

'Just a barge being moved by the current,' Newman remarked. 'That would be its mooring chain.'

'Creepy down here,' Paula commented.

She had stopped looking up at the cranes. But she found herself very aware of their presence. At least they were immobile. Tweed raised an arm, pointed ahead.

'See that grassy bank, the row of terrace houses on top of it. That's where Dr Kefler must live. And there's the footpath he told us to climb. All we have to do is find No. 23.'

'Lovely view he's got,' Paula said. 'Looking out on those cranes which rise up higher than the houses.'

They began climbing the narrow footpath with Tweed in the lead. The huddle of small old houses bunched together along the terrace did not look very upmarket. Paula was wondering why a man of Kefler's eminence lived like this.

No. 23 was close to where they had left the footpath, where they were perched on top of the slope. Tweed looked up at a first-floor window where lights shone behind net curtains. A window was raised. Before Tweed could see the figure leaning out, the beam of a powerful torch shone in his face. It was switched off quickly.

Very quickly he heard steps running down stairs inside. Behind him Newman was shuffling his feet impatiently. Their position, standing on top of the slope, was very exposed. His eyes swept the metal forest of cranes but he could see no movement. Then the two new locks Tweed had noticed on the heavy old wooden door of Kefler's house were turned from inside. The door was pulled inward and a small figure stood in the dark. Why no lights?

'Come in immediately, please,' a deep voice said in English.

They filed into the gloom, the door was closed, locks turned. Light flooded a small hall. The small plump man held out a hand to Tweed.

'I apologize,' he began in English, 'for shining the torch in your eyes. I had to be sure it was you. Keith Kent's description fits you perfectly. Oh, I am Dr Kefler . . .'

Tweed introduced his two colleagues. Paula thought Kent's picture of Kefler as a teddy bear was perfect. The German had brown hair *en brosse*, eyes like buttons which gazed at her through glasses with the thickest lenses she had ever seen. He smiled warmly, was cuddly, she felt, then dismissed the word as silly but appropriate. He wore a velvet smoking jacket, his short legs were clad in dark blue slacks and he almost danced with pleasure as he ushered them into a room on the first floor at the front. They had to be careful climbing the narrow twisting staircase. Paula guessed that the room he showed them into was his study.

'I have bought a jar of English coffee,' he confided to her. 'I know the German coffee is very strong . . .'

'That was very thoughtful of you,' she told him.

'It is nothing. I turned on the kettle before I came down. I will fetch it now. Yes? Make yourselves comfortable. Sit down everyone. I fetch the kettle. I have the papers for you, Herr Tweed . . .'

Before Tweed could ask what papers he was referring to, Kefler had trotted off into the kitchen. Relaxing in her armchair, Paula looked round the room. You can tell a man from his study. On a large old desk, which didn't look German, was a fax machine, a computer, a printer – and an ancient Remington typewriter which looked out of place. She also thought the modern equipment looked very new, hardly used. Along one wall were floor-to-ceiling bookcases. She stood up to look at them.

'Not my choice of armchair,' Newman whispered.

'You're too tall,' Paula whispered back.

Which was true. The armchairs had low seats and Newman had to stretch out his legs in front of him. It struck Tweed, who was just about comfortable, that Kefler with his short legs had chosen furniture that suited himself. An understandable lack of thought for guests – domestic matters would be a nuisance to him.

'He's got six old volumes on the history of the Frankenheim Dynasty,' Paula observed, indicating the bookcases.

'I am so sorry I take so long time,' Kefler began as he reappeared and laid a tray on a low table. The coffee pot, the cream jug, the cups and saucers were Meissen. He's got out the best china, Paula thought. 'You serve yourselves, please? Then you have the coffee the way you like it,' the German suggested, smiling all the time. Paula did the honours.

'You know something?' Kefler said as he perched on a stool. 'You noticed the two new locks on my front door, Mr Tweed?'

'Yes, I . . .'

'Refugees. Turks, Croats, Kosovars – God knows who else or why we ever let them in. Many are criminals. A house near mine was burgled a week ago. They take everything. And would you believe it . . .' Once again the teddy bear was in full verbal flood. '. . . they take a parrot!'

'A parrot? Difficult to take away . . .' Paula began.

'No, not at all . . .' Kefler gave a bubbling laugh. '. . . It was a cheap piece of pottery. Now where they sell a thing like that? Crazy. Is the coffee any good?'

They all agreed sincerely it was marvellous. Kefler nodded dubiously as though he thought they were just being polite.

'You're well equipped,' Paula remarked, looking at the old desk.

'I don't use any of it. I do like my Remington, though. Scientists are dangerous. They invent things without first thinking: what will be the consequences? That time bomb, the Internet. Great, they say. Brings the world closer together. Nations get too close to each other, disagree, quarrel, then make war.'

'I'm inclined to agree with you,' Tweed slipped into the pause. 'Now, earlier you mentioned some papers.'

'Ach! The Zurcher Kredit Bank is the best, the most honest in the world. It is *not*! Miss Grey, you were looking at my old desk. Not so German, eh? I bought it in your Portobello Road in London. I love it. But I divert . . .' Kefler stared at Tweed as though making sure he trusted him. '. . . Vast sums of money are being laundered through that bank – or they do the walk with the money from rich clients, maybe send it to a secret account at Vaduz in Liechtenstein . . .'

'You know that definitely?' Tweed interjected.

'No, *nein*. I only know three hundred million marks walk off.'

Paula did a quick calculation in her head, was stunned. Very roughly, one hundred million pounds sterling. Hardly chicken-feed.

'I give you papers now,' Kefler decided.

He jumped off his stool, stooped down under the cherished desk from the Portobello Road. Reaching under the knee-hole, his pudgy hands jerked, brought out a small leather folder which had obviously been attached with sticky tape. He carefully removed the tape before handing the folder to Tweed.

'Open it! Please do!'

He was almost dancing with enthusiasm. Tweed extracted a sheaf of folded stiff papers, unfolded them. They appeared to be German bank statements with *Zurcher Kredit* printed at the top of each sheet. The contents on the sheets baffled him – lists of figures with code letters such as *GT*.

'You don't understand them, of course,' Kefler advised. 'So you show them to the clever Keith Kent. He will decode . . . Did I say three hundred million marks? . . . My British numbers go wrong. I should say *seven* hundred million marks walk.'

Paula did another quick calculation in her head. Roughly £230,000,000! She stared at Newman, who obviously had also converted marks into pounds. He had a blank look.

'Dr Kefler,' Tweed said calmly, 'are these papers really for me?'

'Of course! I tell you. Keith Kent decode, show you.'

'You haven't a briefcase – or something like that – I could carry this folder away in?'

'The docks. I know your meaning . . .'

Kefler reached down the side of his desk, produced a briefcase of a type no longer in fashion in Britain. He opened it, fumbled inside and clearly it was empty. He lifted both short legs up and down, in need of exercise, Paula realized. He walked over to the window.

'In the daylight the view is interesting. Great barges come here. Large freighters. The ferry from Newcastle in Britain will arrive at 12.30 the pm – in the—'

The report was shockingly loud. Kefler staggered, fell backwards, face up. Blood streamed over his chest, spilt over his smoking jacket. Newman dashed to the body lying on the floorboards, crouching low so he was below the sill of the window. The glass had been shattered by one star-shaped hole with another ragged hole in the net curtain – where the bullet had come through.

'Is he . . .'

Paula barely found herself able to frame the question.

'No pulse,' Newman reported. 'He's dead. Don't look. The left side of his head is blown away. Explosive bullet.'

'Oh, God! No.' Paula covered her face, with her hands. She stood up, looked down across the room. 'Horrible. He was such a nice man . . .'

Newman reacted quickly. Crawling, still well below the windowsill, he reached up, pulled one heavy dark curtain across the window, then the other. When he stood up, away from the window, Paula was standing beside him, staring down at what remained of Kefler.

Only half a teddy bear, she said to herself, then dismissed the thought as obscene.

She sat down in her armchair again, tears in her eyes. She looked at Tweed, choking as she spoke.

'He was *such* a nice man,' she repeated. 'Wouldn't hurt a fly. In life you sometimes meet someone you know *is* good, even at a first meeting. You like him – or her. Trust them. So rare.'

'Same technique, same situation,' Tweed said in a very quiet voice, 'as the murder of Helga Trent off Ebury Street. Night-time. A figure silhouetted against net curtains, the light behind them. I should have realized . . .'

'I'm going downstairs,' Newman said, his revolver in his hand. 'There should be a back door. I can get out that way . . .'

'Stay where you are,' rasped Tweed.

Newman was ignoring the command, heading out of the study, when his mobile buzzed. He snatched it out of his pocket, faced them, standing in the doorway.

'Yes?'

'Harry here.' The voice was very low. 'No one leaves that house till I call back. That's an order . . .'

Newman, still holding the revolver, repeated what Harry had said.

'We all stay here then – until Harry calls back,' Tweed replied. 'Harry knows what he's doing . . .'

Harry Butler, sweating from the heat in his motorcyclist's black leather kit, had been crawling on his hands and knees to get closer to where he'd seen Tweed and his companions disappear into No. 23. A short way ahead he heard a sound, like the squeak of an old wooden door being opened. Looking up, he saw a door close on the control cabin of a monster crane a few yards away.

He was inside the wire that fenced off the docks from Elbstrasse. Earlier he had picked a padlock, opened a gate. He continued his crawl, his rifle with the sniperscope in his right hand, his left hand testing the ground ahead for loose chains or oil drums.

Arriving at the base of the crane, which reminded him of a slimmed-down version of the Eiffel Tower, he peered up at the cabin way above him. A ladder led down from it to the ground. He was uncertain what to do next.

It could be a spy, keeping an eye on Tweed. On the other hand it might be a stupid vandal. He checked his watch. Tweed and the others had been inside the house for a while. He settled down to wait.

He switched his gaze frequently from cabin to house and back again. There was neither sight nor sound of any activity from the control cabin. It could be a drug addict – they did the craziest things, were totally unpredictable. Again he looked at the house. There was the same light in the first floor window, but he'd seen no sign of anyone inside the place.

He wiped his sweaty hands on his trousers. His grip would slip if he ever had to use the weapon. He looked back at the house, saw a small figure silhouetted against the light behind the net curtains. He looked up. He never heard the sound of any movement above him; but he saw the muzzle flash, jerked his head back to the house, saw the small figure topple out of sight. The report of the rifle being fired echoed across the Elbe river.

Taking out his mobile, he rang Newman, gave him his message. Bracing himself against the base of the crane, he raised his rifle, aligning the cross-hairs on the cabin. Nothing happened. He crawled to the far side of the crane, looked up at the ladder.

The cabin door opened. A figure appeared, stood on a small platform, closed the cabin door, which squeaked again. Harry could have shot him then but he decided perhaps there was a chance to take him alive, to extract information. The figure began to descend the long ladder, his back to Harry, a rifle strapped huntsman-style across it.

Harry waited, his own rifle held in both hands. Less than halfway down the ladder the figure stopped, looked down. Holding on with his left hand, his right hand dived inside his jacket, came out holding a handgun.

'All right, chum, have it your own way,' Harry said to himself.

In less than a second the figure appeared in his cross-hairs. He pressed the trigger. His target stiffened, lost his grip, came tumbling down from a considerable height.

Harry jumped aside, fearing his target would crash on top of him. Instead it hit the ground near the foot of the ladder with a sickening thud. The assassin's rifle had slipped off his back, had fallen a few yards away.

Harry stepped forward, his weapon aimed. You never could be sure. He checked the twisted neck's pulse. Nothing. The corpse lay on its back, both legs broken. To Harry's surprise the right hand still gripped an automatic. Reflex action.

He shone his torch on the upturned face. Slavic cheekbones, hawkish nose, thin cruel mouth. Long hair. Harry called Newman on his mobile.

'You can come out now. Down the footpath. Find me by watching for my torch flashing.'

While he waited he put on latex gloves, searched pockets he could reach for identification material. Nothing. From the mess on either side of the head he guessed the fall had crushed the back of the skull.

He went to the gate he had opened, flashed his torch when he saw them coming. Tweed was carrying an old briefcase. Harry led them in, shining his torch on the ground so they didn't trip over discarded rusty chains. He waved Paula back, but she came over.

Butler shrugged. These days you couldn't tell Paula anything. He led the trio to the base of the crane, switched on his torch – after glancing down deserted Elbstr. Paula found she had no feelings at all about the corpse. This was the man who had killed Dr Kefler. Butler had aimed his torch at the face.

'He was up in the control cabin,' Butler said, pointing. 'Did he kill someone?'

'Yes.' Tweed paused. 'Dr Kefler, the man we went to consult. Who is he?'

'No idea.' Butler extended his hands, showed they were covered with latex gloves. 'I've searched him as best I could. Traces of identity? None.'

194

'Probably a Croat,' Newman commented.

'That would be my best guess,' Butler agreed. 'Shall I chuck him into the Elbe? His rifle's over there.'

'Certainly not,' Tweed ordered. 'Leave everything as it is. The police will have to come into this – because of Kefler. Their ballistics people will prove the Croat shot Dr Kefler, which is why we must leave the weapon over there. But I don't want you mixed up in their investigation, Harry. Not if we can help it. So chuck your own rifle well out into the river. Or is that the only one you've got?'

'Another's back at the Renaissance.'

'Good. You do what you have to do quickly, then go back to your hotel. Where's your motorcycle?'

'Well hidden twenty minutes' walk from here. Lights have come on in the house next but one to Kefler's. Upstairs and downstairs.'

'Time for us to get moving. I'll call a cab when we get to the point where the cab dropped us earlier. You look queasy.'

'Yes, he does,' Paula agreed. 'Harry, I've got some stomach-upset pills which work fast.'

'Don't need them. It's the oil stink from empty drums. I'm off to dump my rifle . . .'

It was unfortunate, but when Tweed later checked the card he'd been given and called the taxi firm on Newman's mobile who should arrive but Eugen, their original driver.

'Are you all right?' he called out in German when Tweed told him to take them back to Jungfernstieg.

'Why shouldn't we be?' snapped Tweed. 'We're shipping agents. We wanted to check the Hamburg docking facilities.'

'Pretty good, eh?'

'I think we prefer Europort . . .'

It was Paula who spotted him as Tweed paid the driver near the Jungfernstieg landing stage. No point in advertising where they were staying.

'Now what is it?' he asked as the taxi drove off.

'Mark Wendover. Mavericking again. At this hour.'

The American was coming towards them – from the direction of the Zurcher Kredit Bank. He was carrying his video camera. He began walking back with them.

'I see you've been shopping,' he said, pointing to the briefcase Tweed was carrying.

'In a manner of speaking. What have you been up to?'

'Raiding safety deposit boxes – lock-boxes, as we call them in the States.'

Tweed almost stopped dead. He stared at him, then at a dark woolly cap protruding from a pocket. In fact, Mark was clad in black from head to foot.

'You are joking, I hope?'

'No joke. Their security is good, but not that good. And I did pick up a few tricks of the trade while I was with the CIA.'

'What the devil did you think you were doing? I do like to know what's going on.'

'Well, you do know now I've told you,' Mark rapped back. 'I opened almost every box. You wouldn't believe the amount of 1,000DM bills they have stashed away there. To say nothing of jewellery worth a king's ransom.'

'And you helped yourself?'

'I did not. I was looking for records. Found something in almost the last box I prised open. Can't understand it. A blue leather-bound book full of coded stuff. I'll give it to you when we get back. Well, here we are . . .'

As they approached the elevators a woman sitting in the room beyond the hall, smoking a cigarette, stood up, walked over to them. Lisa Trent.

18

Lisa was dressed to kill, Newman thought. She was wearing a close-fitting green dress which went perfectly with her flaming red hair. She was smiling as she approached Tweed, who paused briefly on his way to the elevator.

'Mr Tweed, I have important information for you . . .'

'Not now. I have an urgent phone call to make.'

The elevator door was open. He walked inside, followed by Paula and Newman, who smiled back at Lisa. Just before the doors closed Lisa slipped into the elevator with them. No one spoke. As the elevator doors opened at the third floor Tweed marched out, holding his room key which he had taken with him. He opened the door of his suite without a glance back. Paula followed him. Newman hesitated and Lisa walked past him into the suite. Tweed, still in his coat, stared at her.

'I can't see you tonight.'

'Not very nice of you,' she said softly. 'I have been paid to spy on you . . .'

'Tell me about it in the morning. I must ask you to leave now.'

'All right, be bloody-minded.' She was flaring up again. Tweed had returned to the door, was waiting to open it for her to go. 'I was asked to phone a number from the main station.' As she spoke she was delving in her handbag. She dropped a sheet of paper on a couch. 'That ruddy note, you oaf. While that suggestion was being made to me over the phone – by a voice I didn't recognize – a scruffy type pushed this envelope into my hand. My fee for spying on you.' She threw a bulky envelope on the couch. 'One hundred thousand deutschmarks. Give it to your favourite charity – probably yourself . . .'

She smiled at Newman, glared at Paula, walked out through the door Tweed opened for her. Pursing his lips, Tweed locked the door, rushed over to the phone after checking the directory on the desk for the number he needed. Police. Paula had opened the unsealed envelope, quickly counted the banknotes inside. She called out to Tweed.

'Lisa was right. There *is* a hundred thousand deutschmarks in the envelope. It's a fortune . . .'

'She's clever, damnit,' he responded as he began pressing numbers. 'A confidence-building tactic . . .'

'For heaven's sake,' Paula protested.

She was going to say more but Tweed held up a hand. She kept quiet.

'Polizei?' Tweed began.

'Who is calling? And why?' a gruff but faintly familiar voice demanded in German.

'My name is Tweed . . .'

'Hell! I thought it was you,' the voice of Otto Kuhlmann, chief of Federal Police, answered in English. 'I was about to phone you – just tracked you to the Four Seasons.'

'What on earth are you doing in Hamburg, Otto? I'm calling to report a murder . . .'

'I'm in Hamburg on another matter. Who has been murdered?'

'A Dr Kefler. At No. 23 . . .'

'I've just come back from there. Were you there at roughly 2300 hours?'

'Yes, which is why I'm phoning . . .'

'Anyone with you?'

'Paula and Bob Newman . . .'

'Fits the description I have here. I'm coming to see you immediately.'

'It might be better if we came to see you,' Tweed suggested. 'If it's not too far away.'

'Five-minute walk. I'm speaking from the 12th District – *Polizeirevier* 12 is on the sign outside, under a white star. It's in a section of the Rathaus. From where you'll come it's on the far side, an entrance you can easily miss.'

'We're on our way . . .'

It was a little cooler but still humid. They were walking past the Jungfernstieg landing stage when Paula made her comment.

'You were pretty rough on Lisa.'

'Have you forgotten my earlier warning? On this trip we trust no one, absolutely no one.'

Paula let it go for the moment. Back in the suite Tweed had said 'Damnit' twice. He was a man who rarely swore, even mildly. She suspected Lisa had rattled him, something very few people could do. They crossed the bridge over the canal which led from the Binnenalster and eventually reached the Elbe. Then across an eerily deserted square alongside the great Rathaus, its highly decorated towers rising up towards the moon. She was thankful for the moonlight. They walked round the far side of the building.

'What do we tell Otto?' Paula asked.

'The truth, but only as much as we have to. Not one single word about Rhinoceros . . .'

Kuhlmann was right – it was easy to walk past the entrance but Tweed spotted it. An arched opening wide enough for one car to pass through and, beyond, the large interior square hemmed in by the inner walls of the

Rathaus. The large white star and the wording were on the left-hand wall and as they entered the opening Kuhlmann appeared, as usual wearing a civilian suit.

Once again the police chief, short, wide-shouldered, heavily built and with a large head and a wide mouth, reminded her of Edward G. Robinson, seen in repeats of old films. He threw his arms round Paula, hugged her, stared at Tweed.

'This time you could be in big trouble,' he rasped.

'I like you too,' Tweed replied.

'Come in. Bob, you look younger,' he said to Newman.

'Softening me up from the very start.' He waved a hand. 'I think that remark should have been intended for Paula.'

'But she always looks younger . . .'

He escorted them into a bleak room with a metal table in the middle. Four tall upholstered chairs were placed on different sides of the table. Tweed suspected this was the interrogation room – except for the chairs. During normal interrogations the suspect would be seated in an uncomfortable metal chair. A policewoman in uniform brought in a tray with a coffee pot, a jug of cream and cups and saucers. She offered to serve, but Kuhlmann waved her away. He poured coffee as his guests sat down, let them add their own cream, sat down himself.

'I've seen Dr Kefler,' he began, 'laid out on his back with a bullet – explosive – in his head. What's left of it. I knew him, liked him. Now the stage is yours, Tweed,' he concluded, folding his arms.

Tweed started with Keith Kent in London – without naming him – and then explained what had happened inside the house. How they had then returned to the Four Seasons so he could phone the police.

'What about the second body?' Kuhlmann asked, gazing at the ceiling.

'Which second body?'

200

If he possibly could, Tweed was determined to keep Butler out of it. Otherwise Harry could be kept in Hamburg for weeks – interrogated and Lord knew what else.

'You're saying you didn't see it?' the German asked, now looking straight at Tweed.

'Where was it?'

'Inside the enclosed docks area. At the foot of a large crane. Shot once. That was enough. I suspect he was the man who murdered Kefler. Ballistics will confirm that – we have his rifle. My reconstruction is that the killer – from the Balkans, I'd say – fired from the control cabin. We found imprints of his boots inside that cabin. Perfect view of No. 23. Where was Kefler when he was killed?'

'Standing in front of a window behind net curtains – with the light on behind him.'

'Then I'm right. The Balkan thug, I'm sure, had left his cabin, was climbing down the ladder, when he noticed someone below. He was still gripping an automatic when he was shot. Since the back of his skull was smashed in he must still have been pretty high up. Marksman's work. Is Marler with you?' he asked casually.

Paula had already realized that Kuhlmann was still the experienced, shrewd policeman, the way he had worked out the sequence of events. His question worried her.

'Oh, yes,' Tweed said agreeably, 'Marler is with us – but he wasn't when we went to see Dr Kefler. He'd had a hard day and we left him fast asleep in his room at the hotel.'

'Tweed, why did you go to see Kefler? I know you have told me but I think there's something else.'

'He gave me some papers.'

'Can I see them?'

'No.'

Kuhlmann drank more coffee. Then he folded his hands behind his neck.

'I could get a warrant for them, you know.'

'Yes, I do know. But if you took them from me you

201

might well hinder my investigation – which could affect your investigation.'

'Which investigation?'

'The other matter you referred to on the phone – the one that brought you to Hamburg.'

'Oh, that one.'

'Yes,' said Tweed firmly. 'And I doubt that you're going to tell me what that investigation is about.'

The German grinned, broke out into peals of laughter. Then he looked at Paula.

'You know something, Paula? Talking to your chief is like getting lost in Hampton Court maze. Or playing verbal chess. Why do I always lose?'

'Well, are you going to tell him about the other matter?' she asked with a smile.

Kuhlmann pushed his chair back. He then paced slowly round the table. He looked at none of his guests and his large hands were clasped behind his back. Returning to his chair he drank more coffee, refilled his cup, looked round but they all shook their heads.

'Something very strange is happening is Germany,' he began in a quiet voice. 'A team of our special forces – like your SAS, if you like – is being assembled secretly in certain suburbs of this city.'

'More riots?' suggested Paula.

'No. I hear rumours from influential contacts . . .' He paused. 'This is strictly between ourselves. For no other ears. Rumours of a coming highly secret meeting between certain top international figures to be held soon and never announced afterwards.'

'London, Washington and Paris,' Tweed said, as though talking to himself.

'And one other capital in a certain country, an important country.'

'A meeting on a remote island in the Bahamas.'

Paula was startled. She was careful to remain expressionless. Tweed was really going overboard in a big way. She was careful not to look at Newman, remembering he had suggested the Bahamas when they were back in London.

'I've heard that rumour,' Kuhlmann said slowly. 'Systematically spread among key members of the press and security organs. A very clever smokescreen – to conceal the real meeting place. Someone is acting as liaison between the men who will attend that meeting. Someone I can't identify. Of course there had to be liaison lower down to start with. A risky role, that one.'

'Jason Schulz, Jeremy Mordaunt, Louis Lospin,' said Tweed.

'I did say risky,' Kuhlmann ruminated, studying the ceiling again. 'And now they're dead. They knew too much.'

'But how could this link up with the riots?' Paula wondered aloud.

'Shrewd lady.' Kuhlmann went silent for a short time. No one interrupted the silence. 'I have a theory. It is nothing more. Supposing there was a second wave of riots – far more frightening and widespread than the earlier ones. What would the public reaction be in the West?'

'Well . . .' Paula wondered whether she was talking too much. Oh, hell – in for a penny, in for a pound. 'The public in all the countries suffering them would want a fierce clampdown. A drastic resurgence of law and order.'

'Shrewd lady,' the German repeated. 'I mustn't keep you up all night.' He paused, stared at Tweed. 'Have you heard of the island of Sylt – in the far north of Schleswig Holstein, well north of Hamburg?'

'Yes,' Tweed replied. 'You can only reach it by rail across a large dyke. Cars can also go there – aboard the special wagons.'

'So why, I ask myself,' Kuhlmann said dreamily, 'are

some of the inhabitants of large houses on Sylt being asked to leave their houses for a month. Which they are doing – due to the huge sums in compensation they have been promised.'

Kuhlmann stood up, stretched his arms. The conference was over. As they all stood up he went to Paula, gave her another bear hug.

'It's about power, isn't it?' she said.

'Shrewd lady,' Kuhlmann said for the third time. He looked at Tweed who had moved near the exit door. 'I wish I had her on my staff.'

'Go on wishing,' said Tweed.

They walked back across the Rathaus Square. Leading the way, Paula decided she'd like to stroll on the platform close to the landing stage to get a good view of the lake at night. A small launch drifted a few feet away with a single man aboard, fishing.

'Liaison,' said Paula. 'A word used more than once. It almost sounds like Lisa.'

'Now you're being fanciful,' Tweed told her.

The rifle report echoed in the night. The bullet hit the water. Where it had vanished was a pool of swirls. Tweed grabbed hold of Paula, hauled her across the platform, sat her down under cover of the ticket building. Newman stayed in the open, revolver in his hand, scanning the buildings across the road. The bullet had missed Paula by about ten feet. The lone fisherman used a paddle to bring his craft up against the landing stage. He was waving an envelope. Newman ran across the platform, bent down, tore the envelope from his hand, opened it.

'Who gave you this?' he shouted.

It was too late. The fisherman had used a boathook to push his launch beyond reach. He started an engine, guided the craft towards the middle of the Alster. Livid,

Newman handed the note, typed on a blank sheet of paper, to Tweed. Reading it once, Tweed stuffed the sheet into his pocket. Its message was clear, brutal.

Go home. Get out of Germany within 24 hours. The next bullet will blow Paula's skull to smithereens. That one was a deliberate miss.

Tweed took hold of Paula, lifted her up, hustled her off the platform down into the street. Newman stayed on the platform, his revolver swinging slowly across the buildings opposite, searching for any sign of movement. Then he joined Tweed and Paula, so she was sandwiched between them as they hurried back to the hotel.

'What was in that note?' Paula asked.

'A threat. They have declared war. So, as from tomorrow, we will give them war in all its hell.'

She had never known him so angry, so forceful, wearing such a ruthless look.

19

The three of them had just returned to the hotel, were heading for the elevators, when a tall distinguished-looking man appeared. Bernard, the Brigadier, still clad in his dinner jacket. He came up to Tweed.

'Just the chap I want to talk to. Meet you in the lounge. What's your tipple?'

'Thank you, but not tonight. I have phone calls to make. I could spare a few minutes tomorrow evening. Early, though.'

'It will have to wait, then.' He was not best pleased. 'The lounge tomorrow. 1800 hours. Right.'

'He didn't like that,' Paula remarked as the elevator ascended.

'He's a Brigadier. Used to people jumping to it when he gives an order . . .'

Newman said goodnight while Tweed and Paula walked towards their rooms. Tweed paused outside his door, looked along the corridor, which was empty.

'I'm worried about you. That bullet came within a dozen feet of you. I know I won't sleep tonight. Mind's whirling. Would you feel more at ease if you used my bedroom? I'll be in the living area. Can always sleep on the couch if I do feel I'm dozing off, which is unlikely.'

'I would feel safer,' Paula admitted. 'I'll fetch my things from my room . . .'

She returned quickly with her night attire and cosmetics case in a hold-all. Looking at the couch she frowned.

'Not sure this is a good idea. You'd never sleep on that couch. Think I'll go back.'

'Take over my bedroom area, pull the curtains. Sleep well.'

He sat down at his desk, took out the papers Kefler had given him, studied them. He soon realized it was hopeless – he was no accountant. And he suspected it would need a first-class one to sort out the tangle. Picking up the phone, he called Keith Kent. He knew he worked through the night.

'Tweed here, Keith. Speaking from Hamburg, Four Seasons Hotel.' He gave Kent his suite number. 'I have some very complex financial papers given to me by your German friend – and I want them analysed. It concerns the company which you mentioned in our conversation in London. No chance, I suppose, of your coming over here?'

'Hang on . . .'

Tweed straightened up the papers, put them back inside the envelope, then Kent was back on the line.

'I'm catching an earliest possible flight tomorrow. Should reach you by lunchtime. Say noon or soon after.'

'I'm very grateful. I'll book you a room here.'

'See you. Very soon . . .'

Tweed sat facing a wall, recalling all the events that had occurred from the beginning. Less than half an hour later Paula appeared, wearing a belted dressing gown over her nightdress and slippers, sat in a chair by the side of the desk.

'Can't sleep. Or am I interfering with your thoughts?'

Someone tapped on the door. Paula reacted swiftly. Standing up, she vanished into the sleeping area. Before she went she whispered, 'Don't want to give anyone the wrong idea. You know how people are . . .'

As Tweed approached the door, his right hand slipped into his pocket, gripped the Walther automatic. Before using his left hand to remove the chain and unlock the door quietly, he stood by the wall on the opening side, grasped the handle, flung open the door. Mark Wendover stood outside, holding a large manila envelope.

'Come in, Mark.'

'I knocked on your door earlier but you were out,' explained Mark as Tweed re-locked the door.

'I *was* out. What can I do for you?'

'I thought you should have this urgently.' Mark handed him the envelope. 'It's the blue leather-bound book I took from the lock-box at the Zurcher Kredit.'

'Thank you. That was very good of you.'

Tweed placed the envelope on the desk. Then he turned round and faced Mark.

'Are you sure no one saw you enter or leave the bank?'

'Yes. The street was deserted on both occasions. I was very careful. They have an advanced alarm system but we have the best in the world in the States. I neutralized every one.'

'What about video cameras?'

'I took in with me several children's water pistols. But instead of water they were filled with a certain substance I squirted at each camera. It blots out the lens completely.'

'What about guards?'

'Three of them.' Mark grinned. 'I passed the control room. They were sitting watching a boxing match on TV. Hadn't even noticed their screens had gone blank.'

'You sound confident,' Tweed said sceptically.

'Not confident. Cautious. Friggin' cautious all the time I was inside.'

'Sounds as though you're safe. Better get to bed now . . .'

Paula reappeared after Mark had left, sat in the same chair. She stared at the Walther Tweed had put on the desk when Mark had gone.

'You're not taking any chances, are you?'

'This is possibly the most dangerous assignment we've ever undertaken. Now, a brief recap. It started in Alfriston when we investigated the murder of Jeremy Mordaunt . . .'

'You've missed something. Before that we had dinner with Lord Barford – and he's turned up in this hotel. And that was when Lisa Trent first appeared on the scene.'

'You're right. I got that out of sequence. And Lisa also is staying in this hotel. Going on to Alfriston, Bogle tried to say it was suicide – an idea put into his head by Gavin Thunder. Sergeant Pole tells us about the Invisible Man – Rondel. We visit Eagle's Nest, Rondel's weird house, see a communications mast raised above the chimney. We return to Park Crescent . . .'

'After a bullet has been fired through the windscreen, aimed at you.'

'True. Mark Wendover arrives, goes off, does his own thing.'

'Just as he's done at the Zürcher Kredit here.'

'Let me go on. I see Gavin Thunder, who accepted Mordaunt *was* murdered. Albeit reluctantly. Lisa's sister, Helga, is shot dead. Target was probably Lisa herself . . .'

'And you still don't trust her.'

'Really?' Tweed looked surprised. 'I thought you didn't.'

'I'd forgotten about Helga.'

'Doesn't prove anything . . .'

'She gave us the list of targets the rioters would hit – and she was right,' Paula reminded him.

'Might have been another confidence-building exercise – so she could infiltrate the SIS. Our opponent – whoever it is – has audacity. Now we come to the guts. Newman hears rumours of a highly secret meeting to take place somewhere in the Bahamas . . .'

'Which now looks more like the island of Sylt, according to Kuhlmann,' Paula interjected.

'I think,' Tweed said decisively, 'three factors are keys to what is going on. One, the huge amount of money which is disappearing from the Zurcher Kredit. Keith did say billions of marks. Two, this absolutely top secret meeting of very powerful men somewhere in the world. Three, who is running this show? Finally, I'm still convinced two tremendous forces are arrayed against each other. Trouble is, I don't know who belongs to which one. But I'm sure one is good and the other is evil.'

Paula put a hand to her mouth, suppressing a yawn. Tweed, who had taken his doodle pad from a drawer, noticed it, of course.

'I really think you ought to get to bed, leave me to it. I think you could sleep now.'

'I think I could.' She stood up. 'They are all mysterious characters. Gavin Thunder, Lisa, Rondel, Lord Barford. I even wonder about Mark Wendover sometimes.'

'Get to bed.'

'And,' she persisted, 'really it all started with the murder of Jason Schulz in Washington – to say nothing about the murder of Louis Lospin in Paris.'

'Do go to bed.'

She flip-flopped in her slippers towards the sleeping area, then turned round.

'And don't forget the Internet glitch that scared the wits out of Monica when the screen went crazy. And the phones went dead at the same time.'

'What do you mean?' He grunted. 'Monica was phoning all the world to see if the same thing happened.'

'That was later. She told me that when she picked up the phone after the glitch stopped it was dead for at least two minutes. I thought the Internet worked off the phone lines. We've talked about this before.'

'If you say so,' he mumbled.

'And I keep thinking of that man in the elevator here who went up again when he saw us. I was closer to him.

His eyes behind those gold-rimmed glasses. He radiated energy, will-power, personality.'

'For the last time, go to bed. What I want is to locate and meet Rhinoceros.'

20

Tweed woke with a start. Not knowing the situation, he kept quite still, half-opened his eyes. Daylight was streaming into the suite. Someone had pulled back the curtains and he was lying on the couch, a cushion behind his head. He listened, heard nothing, got up.

He stretched, remembered that before he'd felt obliged to sprawl on the couch he'd taken off only his jacket and shoes. But he hadn't bothered to place a cushion behind his head. He recalled he had felt something underneath the cushion. Removing it he stared at his Walther, the papers and the blue book Mark had brought him. He'd been so tired he hadn't put them there.

'Paula,' he called out. 'I'm awake.'

No reply. Cautiously, he peered between the curtains into the sleeping area. No Paula. Rubbing the back of his neck he saw two envelopes on the carpet, obviously pushed under the door from the outside. He tried the door. It was locked. Bending down, he retrieved the two envelopes.

One had the hotel name on the outside. He opened it. The room key. Of course, Paula had woken before him, had gone back to her room, not forgetting the precaution of locking his door, then pushing the key under it. He opened the second envelope, a stiff, plain white affair. He read the message inside.

Meet me at the Turm for coffee – and information. Turm, Lagerstrasse 2–8. Lisa.

He frowned. 'Lisa' was also typed, not signed in her hand.

He thought about it after checking the time – 8 am – and while he bathed, shaved and dressed in another suit. He put the note in one pocket, the Walther in another. Going down in the elevator he asked for a safety deposit – he almost said lock-box – and when he had signed the form, a male member of the staff accompanied him up a short flight of stairs.

Producing a key, the hotel man opened a door it would be easy not to notice. Once inside he closed the door which was automatically locked. He led Tweed into another room where the walls were lined with safety deposit boxes in varying sizes. He used his master key to turn the lock, invited Tweed to take his time and then vanished so his client had privacy.

Tweed turned the other key, took out the metal box, opened the lid. Inside he put Kefler's papers and Mark's filched blue book. Sliding it back, he turned his own key, then tried to open it again without using his key. He couldn't. The compartment automatically locked and could not be opened again without use of the master key. Excellent security.

He had also put in the box Lisa's envelope containing the 100,000 DM. He went into the breakfast room. There was quite a party at one table – Paula, Newman, Mark and Lisa. There was laughter, a jolly atmosphere of people enjoying themselves. Lisa wore a sleeveless pale green blouse, a white pleated skirt and trainers.

'Welcome to our working breakfast,' said Paula with a warm smile. 'Did you sleep well?'

'Like a man with no conscience,' Tweed replied as he sat in an empty chair, next to Lisa, facing Paula.

'Oh, come on,' Lisa chaffed him. 'You mean a man with nothing on his conscience.' She cocked her head. 'Or am I wrong?' she continued with a grin.

214

Tweed ordered his breakfast. Orange juice, coffee, toast and marmalade. He produced the note about the Turm, gave it to her.

'Did you slide this under the door of my room?'

'I damned well did not,' she replied indignantly after a swift perusal. 'What's going on? I had a note slipped under my door, too. Do read it.'

She produced a stiff white envelope, the replica of the one Tweed had received. The message was typed.

Go urgently to the main railway station. Wait in the small cafe. You will be approached by a man wearing a carnation in his buttonhole. Wait until he arrives.

'No signature,' he commented.

'Exactly,' she said. 'I decided not to cooperate. Now I'm wondering if someone was trying to get me out of the way so you couldn't check with me about your note.'

'My conclusion too.'

'Would you excuse me for a few minutes?' she asked. 'I have spilt coffee on my new skirt. Won't take me long to change.'

When she had gone Tweed lowered his voice. First he checked to make sure no one was sitting near them.

'Paula, I said last night I'm ready for war. And I am. The rendezvous at the Turm – or tower – gives us an opportunity to hit back hard. Here is the plan . . .'

When he had explained it he left them to make a call to the Renaissance. He spoke to Pete Nield, who said Harry Butler had just arrived in his room. His instructions were precise and terse. Arriving back at the table in the breakfast room he found Lisa had returned, wearing another plain white skirt.

'Sorry, I had to make a phone call,' he told her.

'Your orange juice is getting cold,' she said with a grin.

At 11 a.m. the six of them walked down the hotel steps

and found the two cream Mercedes Newman had hired waiting for them. Earlier, in the breakfast room, Tweed had brought over Marler from his solitary table in a corner, had introduced him to Lisa.

'I do the odd jobs, like carrying luggage,' Marler had told her.

'I've never seen a porter look so smart,' she had commented with a warm smile as they shook hands.

Marler was wearing a pale linen suit, blue shirt and was sporting a Valentino tie. He grinned at her as he sat down with them.

'The luggage I carry,' he had explained, 'is expensive. So it needs an expensive porter to carry them,' he joked.

'You are making fun of me,' she had replied, then laughed.

On the pavement a uniformed porter opened the rear door of the first Mercedes. Tweed gestured for Lisa to take a rear seat. Paula took Marler by the arm.

'Go on, join her. She likes you.'

'If you say so.'

When the porter had closed the door Paula thanked him, gave him a tip, said they didn't need him any more. Alone with Tweed, she spoke softly.

'You're driving this one? I thought so. Tell me the real purpose of this trip to the Turm.'

'I've already explained it to Newman, who will travel with Mark in the second car behind us.' His expression became grim. 'I have reached the point where I think we should tackle the enemy very roughly. Put as many of them out of action as we can.'

'So you also think, as I do, that this invitation to the Turm is a trap?'

'Yes. We'll turn the trap on them.'

'It's not to do with the bullet they fired at me last night?'

'Partly, yes. But also it's strategy . . .'

Paula was sitting beside Tweed as he drove off and headed for their destination. In the back Marler was making Lisa laugh again. They had travelled some distance and Tweed had been glancing frequently in his rear-view mirror.

'We have company,' he whispered. 'Two BMWs are following Newman, keeping their distance. I'm sure Bob also has spotted them.'

'What about Harry Butler and Pete Nield?' Paula wondered.

'They were waiting on the other side of the street, across from the hotel – shielded by parked cars. As soon as I drove off they jumped into the back of Bob's Merc.'

'What are you two whispering to each other?' Lisa called out. 'Or is it something rather personal?' she suggested cheerily.

'Coming from you two canoodling in the back that's a real joke,' Paula called back and laughed.

'At least we are behaving ourselves,' Lisa shot back.

'And here,' Tweed said in his normal voice, 'is Fernsehturm. I've seen it before but I don't think you have, Paula.'

She was already staring up out of the window in amazement. Soaring up above them was a thick white needle-like tower, climbing up to an incredible height. Perched at its summit was a wide observation crest, circular like the needle below it. At the very top was a red-and-white signals mast.

'The revolving restaurant is up there,' said Tweed. 'Takes about an hour to complete one revolution – so you're not aware of any movement. I'm parking here, illegally.'

They stepped out of the car on to the pavement and the sun burned down, furnace-like heat even in mid-morning. Marler held out his hand and Tweed gave him the key. Lisa looked at him.

'Aren't you coming with us?'

'No. I'm staying with the car . . .'

Tweed led the way along a concrete path, crossing trimmed grass and then running round the base of the Turm. His legs were moving like pistons and Paula wondered why he was in such a hurry. Glancing back, she saw Newman's car parked a short distance behind Tweed's. Bob and Mark were standing on the pavement but there was no sign of Harry or Pete. They must be hunched down out of sight in the back she speculated. Why?

After a long walk they reached the entrance. Tweed bought three tickets and the girl receptionist told him a car was just leaving. They entered, had the car to themselves. Paula tensed, prepared for a rocket-like elevation like the one she had experienced in New York – going up the Empire State Building. She was wrong. The car ascended steadily without a blast-off. The girl operator looked at Tweed.

'It was the café you wanted?' she said in English.

'It was . . .'

The doors opened and they walked straight into the café, a spacious circular room with viewing windows, an upraised section in the centre with cloth-covered tables. Tweed stepped up, chose a table on the far side. A waitress appeared the moment they were seated and he ordered coffee.

'You take these,' Lisa said, producing a compact pair of binoculars from her shoulder bag. 'They're very powerful.'

'What about you?'

'I have another pair. See.' She looked at Paula. 'We can share . . .'

Tweed left the platform, stepped down on the far side, gazed below, focused the binoculars. Paula and Lisa followed him. Paula drew in breath as she stared down the sheer drop. The two parked Mercedes looked like toys.

'This is a devil of a height,' she commented. 'Good job I don't suffer from vertigo.'

She took the binoculars Lisa handed her, focused them, saw Newman's face, quite passive as he stood still. Mark was pacing back and forth. No sign of the two BMWs which had followed them. No sign of their occupants. She remarked on this to Tweed.

'They'll be taking their time, planning their approach. I would, in their shoes. Let's go drink some coffee . . .'

Paula remained standing while she drank. She was gazing at the view through the windows on the opposite side. Beyond parks with green trees a large stretch of blue water, glittering in the sunlight, spread out. Tiny white triangles, which were yachts, dotted the blue surface.

'Is that the Elbe?' she asked.

'No, not with yachts on it. That's the Aussenalster,' he said, standing beside her. 'The outer *alster*. "Binnen" is "inner". Why am I saying this? You know German.'

'It's heaven,' she said dreamily. 'Pure heaven.'

Lisa had taken her coffee, put it down on a table near where they had looked down. She was standing by the window. She called out urgently, peering down through her binoculars.

'I've spotted Pink Shirt. Remember him? At Reefers Wharf. Now he's wearing a bright yellow one. Could he be directing an operation? His fat face looks savage, he's just checked his watch . . .'

'Where?' Tweed was beside her, Paula on her other side.

'See that road curving over to the right – well away from our cars? Half behind a tree on the pavement.'

'Got him.' Tweed was peering through the binoculars she'd handed him. Paula now had the other pair. 'Yes, that's him,' Tweed agreed, 'keeping well away from the action. And I agree – he looks as though he *is* directing an operation.'

'Never expected to see that bastard over here,' Paula remarked. She moved next to Tweed as Lisa walked several yards away. 'Could he be Rhinoceros?' she said quietly.

'Possible, but we simply don't know.'

'Here they come,' called out Lisa. 'Give me the glasses. Thanks.' She didn't change the focus and her next words were almost hissed. 'Simply don't believe it. Two men, carrying sledgehammers. Barton and Panko. The thugs who followed me in London. Just escaped them in Bedford Square.'

'Don't like the look of those Balkan-type thugs who are coming,' said Paula, binoculars pressed against her eyes.

'Shouldn't we go down and help?' Lisa demanded.

'How could you – against that lot?' Paula asked.

'Look what Marler gave me.' She had opened her shoulder bag. When Paula looked inside she saw a 6.35mm Beretta pistol. 'And he gave me ammo,' Lisa went on.

'Lisa has a Beretta,' Paula warned Tweed.

'We stay here,' Tweed ordered in a strong voice. 'Newman has ordered on no account is there to be a shooting party. Dead bodies in the city would pose a problem for Kuhlmann, who has enough on his hands.' He looked down. 'They'll cope.'

As Barton and Panko, leading the assault, approached, holding their sledgehammers, with the foreign thugs not far behind, Newman remained where he was, his arms folded. Mark attached something to the fingers of his right hand. Knuckleduster.

Barton reached the second car, was starting to lift his weapon when the rear door was flung open on the pavement side. It slammed into him, knocking him off balance as Butler jumped out. His right foot, booted, swung up like a spring being released, hit Barton a savage blow between the legs. Barton dropped the sledgehammer, groaned in agony, bent forward. Butler grabbed his hair, swung him round, rammed his head against the car. It sounded as though his skull had cracked.

Panko dropped his sledgehammer. A long-bladed knife appeared in his hand. He was grinning. Newman had skipped to the side of his attacker. His right hand, stiffened, struck Panko on the side of his scrawny neck. Karate chop. Panko dropped, lay motionless close to the unconscious Barton.

Then it became a mêlée as the foreign thugs rushed forward. Marler appeared behind them. Earlier, seconds before they parked, he'd seen an old metal railing sagging away from the pavement, probably hit by a car. His gloved hand had tugged at a rail, twisted it, forced it free. Running up behind the thugs, he stooped, swung the iron rail at the back of the legs of one thug, hitting him behind the knees. The thug screamed, sagged, wriggled on the pavement. Marler administered the same treatment to another thug.

A ferocious-looking bandit was wielding a vicious machete. He swung it behind him for the blow which would have taken Mark's head off his shoulders. Mark's knuckleduster smashed into his exposed face, broke his nose, a cheekbone. Blood streamed from his face. Mark hadn't finished – he hammered the knuckleduster into his jaw, broke that. Pete Nield had jumped out of the other side of the car, plunged into the gang. Two stood close together for protection, their backs to him. He took a swift, firm hold of them by their hair, jerked them apart, jerked them together, the heads colliding with tremendous force. Both men sank to the pavement.

Another bandit, holding a knife, had come up behind Newman, was preparing to drive the knife into his back. Marler hoisted his iron bar, brought it down, hitting the elbow of the thug, breaking it. There was a scream of pain, the knife clattered on the pavement. Newman swung round, hit the thug in the face. He staggered back, his right arm limp. Newman followed him, hit him again, then once more. He toppled over backwards.

The first bandit Marler had dealt with was still screaming, wriggling on the pavement.

'You're making too much noise, buddy,' Mark told him.

Stooping, he hit the culprit on the side of his head with the knuckleduster. The wriggling stopped, the bandit lay motionless, silent.

Newman rubbed his hands together, looked all round. No more. And there was not a single pedestrian in sight. He remembered reading in a magazine in the hotel lounge that an erotic exhibition was being held. One day only. This day. He pictured long crocodile queues waiting for ever to get into the place.

'Clearance time. Anyone know where they parked the BMWs?'

'Just round the corner,' Marler said. 'Follow me.'

'Harry,' Newman called out. 'Gloves. We're fetching the ambulances.'

Harry held up his hands, covered with latex gloves. He followed Marler and Newman. The cars were parked only a few yards out of sight. And in each they'd left the ignition keys. For a quick getaway, Newman guessed.

They worked quickly. The moment they had parked the BMWs a few yards behind their own cars, leaving the pavement side doors open, Operation Clearance began. The bodies, all alive but unconscious, were tumbled inside the BMWs without ceremony. The doors were closed. Butler suggested a refinement. Together with Pete, he picked up the sledgehammers that were then used to batter in the windscreens.

'Job's done,' Newman announced.

Gazing down from the café windows way up in the Turm,

Lisa and Paula had watched, fearfully at first, then with astonishment, the scene below.

'Reefers Wharf was a children's party compared to that,' Lisa commented.

Tweed had been aiming his binoculars at Fat-Face, Pink Shirt, watching the débâcle with his arms folded. As it ended he straightened his jacket, wandered out of sight. It was his expression that intrigued Tweed. Rage? No. Disappointment? No.

'We'd better get down,' Paula said. 'Newman's waving at us.'

'We'll go down and away from here as fast we as we can . . .'

When they arrived back at the hotel, Newman asked the porter to garage their cars. Tweed ran up the steps with Paula close behind him. He had checked his watch. Keith Kent stood in the hall, waiting for them.

'Welcome, Keith. I'll get the material out of the hotel safe.'

Then he noticed the man sitting at the back of the hall, facing the staircase up to the security room. The Brig sat erect in his chair, motionless as a graven image, observing their return.

'I've changed my mind,' he said suddenly. 'We'll go up to my suite . . .'

Newman had joined them in the elevator and Lisa slipped in just before the doors closed. Kent carried a dispatch case, explained he'd occupied his room a few minutes before seeing Tweed arrive.

'That chap,' he continued as they walked to the suite, 'by himself in the lounge area. Surely it was Lord Barford?'

'It was.' Tweed turned to Lisa who said she was going to her room. 'Could I see you in about ten minutes? I'll call you in your room.'

'Can't wait . . .'

'She strikes me as excessively intelligent,' Kent remarked inside the suite. 'Quite a personality. Attractive, too.'

'Keep off the grass,' Newman said amiably, nudging him in the ribs.

'Lord Barford,' Tweed began.

'Hold on,' chided Paula. 'What would you like to drink, Keith? The management have put another bottle of champagne in a fresh bucket of ice. Care for a glass?'

'Nice of you. Just one glass, please.' He accepted Tweed's invitation to sit down, then raised the glass Paula handed him. 'Here's to success to your present enterprised – and damnation to the villains.'

'Had some of that last bit this morning,' Newman commented.

'Lord Barford,' Tweed began again. 'Sounded as though you know him.'

'Know about him,' Kent replied. 'Like me he's a member of a very select organization, the Institute of Corporate Security. Membership confined to twenty at anyone time – and you're vetted first. Can't imagine why they asked me.'

'Have you talked to Barford? We call him the Brig.'

'A bit – at meetings of the ICS. He puts up a front as the pukka Brigadier, a purely military type. But there's a lot more to him. He has a vast knowledge of what's going on in the world. Has some very top contacts back home, in Europe and in the States. I've heard he's consulted when there's a major crisis. Travels all over the place.'

'Shall I pop down and see if the coast's clear?' Newman suggested.

'If you would, Bob,' Tweed agreed.

Newman was back in no time. He gave the thumbs-up signal.

'He's vanished. Probably gone to lunch.'

'Then I'll be back in a minute . . .'

'Keith,' Paula said thoughtfully, 'I've just remembered an incident when Tweed and I met Gavin Thunder at a club in Pall Mall. As the meeting ended and we were leaving the library I glanced back. Thunder was collecting his coat and his jacket wasn't fitting him properly. So his right lapel was turned and I could see the inner side. Clasped to it was a metal symbol I thought at first was Greek – but on reflection I don't think it was. It was like a capital letter "E" – but turned the wrong way round . . .'

'Could you draw it for me?'

Kent's normal relaxed and easy manner had changed. He had stiffened, was leaning forward. His expression had become very serious, concerned. Newman came closer – he had noticed the transformation in Kent. Paula took a pad, thought for a moment and drew the symbol.

'My God!' Kent exclaimed. 'He's a member of the Elite Club . . .'

Tweed returned shortly afterwards, holding a large white envelope containing the Kefler papers and the blue leather-bound book Mark had stolen. He was immediately aware of the strange atmosphere. Kent looked shocked. Paula had a puzzled expression. Newman waved his hands, as though to say 'I haven't a clue what's going on.'

'Something wrong?' Tweed asked quietly, sitting down so he faced Kent. 'You look as though a bomb had dropped on you.'

'It has. Paula, would you first tell Tweed what you told me?'

She began with when they were leaving the library of

the Pall Mall club. She recalled how she had glanced back at Thunder, what she had seen, that she had forgotten to tell Tweed in her haste to meet the drunken Aubrey at Martino's. She showed Tweed the pad with the symbol she had drawn, quoted Kent's explosive reaction.

'What does it mean?' Tweed asked Kent. 'What is the Elite Club? Never heard of it.'

'Few people have,' Kent replied grimly. 'I only heard of it by pure accident when someone had drunk too much – the late Jeremy Mordaunt.'

'Like a glass of water, Keith?' Paula suggested. 'They have left a carafe on ice. You've lost your colour.'

'Yes, please.'

They waited while Kent sipped water, then drank the whole glass, held it out for a refill.

'This is terribly dangerous,' he said.

'Why?' Tweed pressed. 'What *is* the Elite Club?'

'A very small club.' Kent's glass trembled as he replaced it on the table. 'I gather it has either four or five members selected from the most powerful men in the world. Men who will stop at nothing to gain whatever they want. Evil men. If they knew what has just been said in this room I'm sure none of us would stay alive for more than twenty-four hours.'

There was a long silence. Kent waved aside an offer from Paula of more champagne, a curt gesture. He sat with both hands clasped, his fingers moving. Tweed realized they were seeing a Keith Kent they had never seen before. A very frightened man. Tweed spoke quietly.

'Take your time, Keith.'

'My only thought now is that I want to wake up tomorrow morning as usual. Alive.'

Tweed took out a packet of cigarettes. He projected one out of the packet, took from his pocket the jewelled lighter

226

Paula had once given him when he recovered from having a bullet taken out of his chest.

'I know you rarely smoke, Keith,' he said in the same quiet tone.

Kent looked up at him. He took the cigarette and Tweed lit it for him. He took a small drag, expelled smoke, looked again at Tweed.

'You must think me a coward.'

'Nonsense. Only a fool doesn't fear great danger.'

'Thanks.' He licked his lips. 'I had no idea that this business involved that lot. Shook me up a bit.' He was speaking more normally now and the colour was coming back into his face. 'I've never told you about them before, Tweed, because there never seemed to be a reason to.'

'Who are "them"?'

'No idea. Except obviously Gavin Thunder is one of the group. Mordaunt was really in his cups that night. One remark he did make. The members of the Elite Club are not necessarily Presidents or Prime Ministers. They are the strong men. I quote his exact words. A few minutes later he blacked out. I think he was an alcoholic.'

'Embarrassing situation for you, Keith,' Tweed remarked.

'In my world you run into these situations. I called a cab, got him into it with the help of the barman, took him to his flat in Eaton Square. Of course, he couldn't find his key, so as there were lights on inside I rang the bell. A statuesque blonde with the brains of a peanut let us in. Between us we got him into bed, fully clothed. She said she'd undress him later.'

'Was probably used to doing that,' said Newman.

'Next thing I knew,' Kent continued, 'the blonde says she feels like some fun and who was I? I said just a friend. What was my name? Morrison, I said and I had to leave to meet a businessman coming in from abroad. Heaved a sigh of relief when I got out of the place.'

'So that was it?'

'Not quite,' Kent grimaced. 'Next day phone rings at my office. It's Mordaunt – phoning from a call box. Was my phone secure?'

'I said yes, it was, and what did he want? He thought he had maybe blacked out the previous night. Couldn't remember a word he'd said. What had he said? I told him the truth – that he'd nattered on trying to get stock market tips out of me. That I'd told him I never touched it and didn't want to know about it. Then he'd collapsed. He seemed relieved, put the phone down suddenly – he was like that.'

'And how did you first get to know Jeremy Mordaunt originally?'

'The night before at a party.' Kent smiled. 'A short acquaintance. Fool who introduced me to him called me a financial genius, so he latched on to me. Arranged to see me the following evening at this upmarket bar. A pretty quiet place. I went because at the party he'd told me he was Under-Secretary at the MoA. Thought I might pick up something. Instead, he detonated his bomb.'

'Ever heard of the Elite Club before then?' Tweed asked.

'Once. Brief reference to it from an informant I've never trusted. So I dismissed it as hot air. But Mordaunt . . .' Kent shuddered. 'He is – or was – close to the inner circle. I believed him.' He looked at Tweed. 'I'll take those papers now, go back to my room, start working on them.'

'Here they are.' Tweed handed him the envelope. 'Don't let anyone see the blue book. Not staff. Not anyone. And don't leave this hotel under any circumstances. If the phone rings pick it up, say you're in conference, slam it down.'

'Don't worry.' Kent stood up. 'And I'll get a safety deposit box for this stuff while I'm downstairs eating.'

'I'll come with you to your room,' Newman said.

'You don't have to . . .'

He didn't sound at all convincing. When he'd taken the envelope perspiration from his hands had stained the outside. He was still shaky.

'I'm calling Kuhlmann,' Tweed said when they had gone. 'Pink Shirt worried me – the way he reacted to the collapse of his attack at the Turm. You're good at describing people. I may put you on . . .'

'Morning, Tweed . . .' Kuhlmann's strong voice came down the line. 'I was going to call you. Visited the Turm today? A witness who has a flat nearby watched one hell of a fight in the street just before noon. You wouldn't know anything about that?'

'Yes. I was in the café with Paula. We watched from a mile up. One lot – foreigners – took a beating.'

'Your people wouldn't have been involved?'

'What a question, Otto. Now you're on the phone, we did see a strange individual standing clear of it – as though he was the boss. We had binoculars. Paula can describe him better than I would. Here she is . . .'

Paula spoke for several minutes. Tweed poured himself a glass of water, stared out of the window. The sun streamed in, the lake looked as though it were boiling. The heatwave was intensifying. Paula called to him.

'He wants to speak to you again.'

'Here, Otto . . .'

'That Paula is something else again. She paints a perfect picture of a man. So much so, it struck a chord with me. Oskar Vernon. Oskar with a "k". Very distinctive appearance. Known to us, as we say.'

'In what way?'

'Bit of a mystery man. Loads of cash, dresses in an outlandish way, but very expensively. Suspected of being the mastermind behind an international money-laundering operation. Also of smuggling refugees in a big way. We have two million Turks in Germany. Two, I wouldn't mind, but two *million* . . .'

'Arrest him.'

'No chance. No evidence. Works through a chain of men which runs down a long way from him. Powerful, ruthless, smart.'

'Works on his own?'

'Don't think so, but could be wrong on that. He travels the world, knows a lot of powerful men. Don't ask me for names. Haven't got any. If I had a photo I would be certain this is Oskar Vernon. Spends a lot of time in Britain and in the States.'

'Nationality?'

'Travels on a British passport but I'm damned sure he's not English. Could have come from anywhere.'

'Otto, I might just be able to get you a photo of him.'

'That would decide it. Tweed, if you're up against him be very careful. Several agents who tracked him ended up in hospital.'

'Going back to the Turm. What we saw was a real dogfight. A lot of bodies. Lying on the pavement. Injured, I'd say. I suppose you've got them?' Tweed asked.

'Like hell I have. By the time we arrived there was blood on the pavement – and nothing else. If you're right about Vernon he'd have foreseen that might happen, would have organized transport to move the evidence fast. Very fast.'

'He did.'

'You watch not only your back, but your front and both sides. Don't make one mistake about Oskar. One is all he needs . . .'

Tweed put the phone down. He relayed everything Kuhlmann had said. Paula looked thoughtful.

'Could he possibly be Rhinoceros?' she suggested.

'Go along and see Newman. Explain the situation. If Oskar is still at the Renaissance Harry might get a photo of him. But he'll need your camera. Then please stay in Newman's room until I call you. I have to interview Lisa,' Tweed said.

'You'd better be careful with her too. She's clever.'

'Maybe too clever by half . . .'

Tweed checked his watch after Paula had left. Lisa was due in two minutes. Sure enough, she arrived on the dot. Tweed asked her to sit down, offered a glass of champagne.

'Yes, please.' She smiled warmly. 'I won't drink too much. I think there's nothing more disgusting than a woman who is drunk.'

She wore the same clothes but had put her hair up. Round her forehead she wore a green bandanna, had added lipstick and a touch of mascara. Seated in an armchair, she stretched her bare arms along the sides. Newman would have said she looked very sexy. It was water off a duck's back to Tweed, who was in a grim mood. He sat facing her across a small table.

'Lisa, there are some questions I have to ask. About your background. That is, if you want to stay with us.'

'I do . . .'

'Where were you educated?'

'I won a scholarship to Roedean. I did make friends but I found the atmosphere too rarefied. Then later I won another scholarship, this time to Oxford . . .'

'Studying?'

'Languages. French and German. I was the odd one out – I didn't mix much. I concentrated on work. Too many of the others fooled around. I got a Double First.'

'Impressive.' Tweed smiled, his manner deliberately becoming more relaxed to gain her confidence. 'When you left Oxford?'

'Became an air hostess, so I could travel. If you obey the

231

rules, keep to your schedule, you see damn-all. I missed several return flights so I could explore places. New York, Singapore, Paris, here – Hamburg. They put up with my missing flights back for a while because I was good at the job. Then they chucked me out. That covered about two years.'

'After that?'

'Went to New York, joined a security agency for a couple of years.'

'Doing what?'

'Tailing businessmen suspected of embezzlement. I learned quite a bit about accountancy to do the job properly – studied in my apartment at night.'

'Did you know Mark Wendover before you met him in London?'

'I beg your pardon?'

'I said, did you know Mark Wendover before you met him at my office in Park Crescent?'

'No.'

Tweed was sure that if she'd been attached to a polygraph – a lie detector – the machine's needle would have jumped. For the first time he felt she had told a lie. Nothing in his expression changed. He went on switching the questions' subject matter.

'What was your father's job?'

'He was in the Intelligence Corps. Shortly after he was transferred to Cyprus he was shot in the back. My mother flew with him on their way home. The plane crashed and my father was killed. My mother survived, later remarried.'

'Must have been a terrible shock for you.'

'Yes.' She paused. 'It was. But by then I was an air hostess, so I was reasonably mature, had been around, had learned to fend off unwanted attentions from men. I carried on with the job for a few months before they threw me out.'

'Where were you born?' Tweed asked quietly.

'Place called Pinner in Middlesex. Lived there for a long time. Until I went to Roedean. Address – Shoals Cottage, Orchard Tree Road.'

Tweed smiled. She had anticipated his next question. He was taking no notes. Writing things down inhibited the subject he was interrogating.

'You got on well with Helga, your late sister?'

'I did not. We fought like cat and dog. Since she was older she thought she could boss me about. To be fair, I think it was simply her temperament. My mother had married a German professor in Freiburg, went to live with him there. Don't know why she did that.'

'So,' Tweed smiled warmly, 'we got through that without a tantrum.'

'I really am sorry about that. I occasionally get worked up. Usually when I'm tense. But not in an emergency.'

'And you can handle a Beretta,' he said casually.

'Well.' She chuckled. 'I don't shoot myself in the foot with it.' She reached for the glass of champagne Tweed had poured for her earlier. 'And I'm familiar with the Walther and the Browning.'

'Where did you learn all this?'

'By chance. Had a boyfriend who was mad keen. He took me to a shooting club in London, showed me what he could do – which was no more than passable. Gave me a Beretta. I scored six bull's-eyes and three inners. He said it was a fluke. We went back the following day. I scored five bull's-eyes and an inner. He said beginner's luck. So I tried again. Six bull's-eyes. We went back to my flat off Ebury Street, had the emperor of a row, which he started. Couldn't stand a girl beating him at anything. End of friendship. Some men are like that.'

'And now you're working for Rhinoceros?'

She chuckled again, re-crossed her legs, sipped more of her drink.

233

'In an interrogation always save the heavyweight punch for the end.' She stared at him, her eyes fixed on his. 'For your information, Mr Tweed, I've no idea who I'm working for. But the money is good. And I think it's in a worthwhile cause.'

'What does that mean?'

'I'm sure there are two powerful forces confronting each other. One good, one very bad. I'm on the side of the angels, as they say.'

Tweed lit one of his rare cigarettes. This was the first indication that his theory of two opposing forces had been confirmed. He looked at Lisa and she leaned well forward, much closer to him, arms folded, waiting.

'Ever *heard* of Rhinoceros?' he eventually asked.

'Overheard a reference to him, which I wasn't supposed to hear at the time. No idea who he is, where he lives.'

'How are you instructed? Paid?'

'A typed note is slipped under my door inside an envelope – it started like that in my flat off Ebury Street in London. At the time given I have to be standing inside a certain phone box. At Waterloo in London, when it was quiet. Here at the main railway station. He uses the name Olaf, speaks slowly, enunciating every word carefully. Sometimes in German, sometimes in English.'

'I wonder . . .' Tweed blew a smoke ring. '. . . how he came to know about you?'

'No idea. Oxford, Double First in two languages, air hostess, my stint with the security agency in New York. Thought I'd be highly suitable for the job.'

'And,' Tweed stood up, clapped his hands, 'I'm sure he was right. Thank you for being so patient.'

She stood up, plumped up the cushion she'd leant back against, walked to the door which he unlocked. She put a hand on his shoulder to make him pause.

'Now.' She smiled very warmly. 'You have the data to

check up on me. I'm going out shopping now. Need some better shoes. You can let me out, sir . . .'

Tweed stood by the closed door when she had gone. He had almost a dazed look. *You have the data to check up on me.* Which was exactly what he was going to do.

Oskar Vernon stood in the ward of the out-of-the-way clinic where he paid the doctor a lot of money to keep his mouth shut. Delgado, clean-shaven, hair smartly trimmed, wearing a good business suit, half-listened as Vernon talked to the doctor.

Barton sat on the edge of the bed. Delgado had earlier dragged him out of it. He was tenderly feeling a bandage between his legs under his pyjamas. Another bandage swathed his forehead where it had been slammed against the Mercedes. Panko, fully dressed, was trudging slowly down the large ward they occupied. Round his neck was a collar where the karate chop had felled him.

'I want these men fit by tomorrow morning,' Vernon snapped. 'Fit for anything.'

'That asks for a a miracle,' the doctor protested.

'That's why I pay you all the money I do. For miracles.'

They were speaking to each other in English. The doctor, a small fat man with greedy eyes, wore a white coat, had a stethoscope dangling over his ample chest. Delgado felt it was time to stir the pot. He went up to Barton.

'What are you moaning about? Kick in crotch? Nothing. I've had it – killed the man who did it.'

'My head . . .'

'Kissed the car. Headache? We all get headache. So start walking, damn you. Now!'

Barton heaved himself up, took a few steps, stooped, stopped. Delgado grabbed his arm, forced him to walk.

Panko grinned savagely. He straightened himself up, began pacing round the ward, adjusted his collar.

'Leave me with them,' Vernon ordered the doctor. 'They're leaving tomorrow. Fit as fiddles.'

The doctor nodded, took the sheaf of banknotes thrust into his hand, shoved them into a pocket, left the ward with a glum expression.

'Now!' Vernon said in a savage voice. 'You listen. Listen good. When we can lure Tweed and his team into the country we kill them all. I have ten tough men who came off the ferry from Newcastle.'

'They walk off?' Delgado asked incredulously. 'They walk off. No trouble? How that?'

'How you think?' Vernon's thick lips puckered. 'Come ashore as seamen. This time of year ferry full of passengers from Newcastle and a big crew.'

'Only refugee toughs?'

'You'll never do what I done.' Vernon lit a cigar despite the 'No Smoking' sign, blew out a cloud. 'They been trained in secret camps – Slovakia. When we come to kill them, you, Barton and Panko, lead. Attack force in three sections, each of you leading one section.'

'So how we get them into country?'

'I'm moving into Hotel Atlantic. You three stay Hotel Renaissance. I visit you. You no come to me.'

'So how we get Tweed team into country?' Delgado persisted.

'How?' Vernon's smile was sinister. 'We use Lisa's gambit.'

21

Tweed was alone in his suite. About ten minutes earlier Lisa had left 'to go shopping'. He picked up the phone, rang Mark Wendover's room. No reply, even though he kept on the phone for several minutes – plenty of time for him to get out of a shower. He gave it up.

Settling himself in his chair, he lit another cigarette. So, Lisa was out 'shopping'. And Mark was not in his room.

'I wonder,' he said, half aloud.

He stood up again, took his doodle pad out of a drawer, went back to the phone, called Monica. He phrased his wording carefully, as though 'Trent' had applied for a job and he wanted Monica to check references.

'I'll get on it right away,' Monica responded. 'Call you back . . .'

Then he decided he'd go out for a stroll. Walking helped him to think. He had almost reached the landing stage when an Opel, with Pete Nield at the wheel, parked in a slot a woman had just left. Nield hustled after him, drew alongside Tweed.

'You shouldn't be out on your own. This city is dynamite.'

'You make me feel like royalty,' Tweed grumbled. 'What have you been up to?'

'Touring the city, keeping my eyes open for hostile forces. I know Hamburg backwards by now. Could be useful. What's the next move?'

Tweed was heading towards the Zurcher Kredit Bank. 'I have an appointment for drinks with the Brig at six this evening. At 1800 hours. On the dot.' He had imitated the Brig's manner. Nield grinned. Few people knew that Tweed was a first-rate mimic. 'Then at 8.30 p.m. Paula and Bob are coming with me for dinner with the mysterious Rondel – except we aren't having dinner with him. He's booked a table for us but he's dining at another one with his partner.'

'Curious idea.' Nield flicked a speck off his smart suit. 'I don't get it.'

'Neither do I. We'll just have to see.'

Tweed had paused, was staring up at the nearby Zurcher Kredit Bank. Behind a balustrade on the first floor was a very well concealed camera, covering the front entrance.

'Mark broke in to that bank at night,' he recalled. 'Opened every security box, may have found gold in one of them – a book of ciphers which may help Keith Kent, ensconced in a room at the Four Seasons – to crack the papers Dr Kefler handed me.'

'Harry told me about the Kefler murder down at the docks. I'd have thought Mark took a big risk, breaking in there.'

'He killed the alarms, blotted out the internal cameras. His CIA training must have helped. I'm just hoping that he spotted that camera on the balustrade up there. In daytime it's not easy to spot, but at night . . .'

They had reached the entrance to a side street, the Grosse Bleichen. Glancing down it, since it led to the Renaissance Hotel, Tweed froze. Instinctively Nield stood very still. Further down the street a single shaft of sunlight illuminated the outside of the hotel. Standing in the sunlight, arms folded, was Oskar Vernon. Paula stood close by.

He appeared to be gazing up at the building opposite while waiting for something – or somebody. What had caused Tweed to freeze, his nerves to tense, was the scene taking place. Vernon lowered his eyes, watched as a short wide-shouldered man scrabbled in a dustbin. Harry Butler was clad in a shabby jacket, torn denims, a tramp searching for treasure.

Tweed held his breath. Paula, wearing a straw hat pulled well down, was using a camera to photograph Vernon while Butler attracted his attention. Vernon had only to glance to his left to see her.

'Paula, you're taking too long. He's bound to turn and see you,' Tweed said to himself.

He sighed with relief as Paula vanished down an alley. At the same moment a porter came out of the Renaissance as a cab pulled up. Vernon climbed inside, gestured for the porter to give him the bag.

The next development was the appearance of a well-built man emerging from an arcade, just below the hotel on the opposite side of the street. He too wore a straw hat, wrapround dark glasses. Only the way he walked told Tweed it was Newman – so he'd escorted Paula on her mission as protection.

Tweed backed away from the corner as the taxi drove slowly towards them, edging its way past parked trucks and cars. Harry shoved an empty cigarette packet retrieved from the bin in his pocket, ambled rapidly up the street towards the landing stage.

'Pete,' Tweed said urgently, 'could you follow the cab coming up Grosse Bleichen?'

'Piece of cake . . .'

Nield streaked across the road where traffic was held up by a red light. He kept running until he was behind the wheel of his Opel. Which was when the cab with Vernon inside emerged, turned left past the landing stage, then right up Neuer Jungfernstieg and past the Four Seasons. Nield performed an illegal U-turn when a small white van drove behind the cab, masking him. Then he followed van and cab.

Tweed saw all this from inside the department store he had slipped into. He faced the street, appearing to study the window display. Once Nield's car had disappeared he went outside, turned down Grosse Bleichen, just in time to meet Paula hurrying towards him. Behind her Newman followed and Butler had stopped on the far side.

'You took one hell of a chance,' he chided her.

'Oh, shut up.' She was triumphant. 'I've got six shots of the bastard. Decided to use the small Polaroid-like camera the boffins at Park Crescent developed. Look at these.'

Tweed flipped through the six prints she handed him. His eyebrows rose. Leaning forward, he kissed her on the cheek.

'I expected more,' she said with a grin.

He leaned forward, kissed her on the other cheek. He gave Newman three of the prints, then gestured to Harry to come over. Butler had removed his disgusting jacket, rolled it up, tucked it under his arm. He now wore a linen jacket and, despite the torn denims, looked reasonably respectable.

'Harry, there's a police station on the far side of the Rathaus. Not easy to see . . .'

'I've seen it. While Pete's toured a bigger area in his car I've walked my feet off. Why the police station?'

'Because I want you to give these to Otto Kuhlmann.' He handed him two prints. Paula fiddled in her shoulder bag, brought out an envelope, took the prints, slipped them inside, wrote 'Otto Kuhlmann' on the outside, gave them back. 'No,' said Tweed, 'you hand them personally to Otto.'

'Heard you the first time.'

'You might have difficulty barging past inferiors.'

'Me?' Harry was indignant. 'You're joking. I'll trample over them . . .'

Then he was gone, walking very fast towards the Rathaus.

As the three of them walked back towards the hotel Tweed held Paula's arm, squeezed it.

'You're brilliant.'

'I know. But it's nice to be told . . .'

They had walked slowly along the edge of the Alster. Tweed talked fast, bringing them up to speed on his interrogation of Lisa, then his phone call to Monica.

'I just wonder about Lisa,' he ruminated as they neared the hotel. 'Going out shopping . . .'

'I suppose she's allowed to do that,' Paula said indignantly.

'You remember I've just told you the one factor where I felt sure she was lying? When I asked her if she knew Mark before she came to us? Well, after she'd gone out I called Mark for about five minutes. He wasn't there.'

'Oh, I see. Casts a doubt over her. Can't we trust anyone? No. You warned us earlier. We can only trust the team. I told Bob about Oskar Vernon, what Kuhlmann said.'

'So now,' Newman remarked as they reached the hotel steps, 'Pink Shirt becomes Oskar Vernon. Which spells "Danger" – with a capital "D".'

At the top of the steps the Brig appeared, obviously on his way to the coffee lounge.

'1800 hours,' Tweed called out. 'On the dot.'

The Brig paused, glared, opened his mouth, closed it again, as though uncertain how to reply to this sally. He nodded, proceeded towards the lounge.

'So whose side is he on?' Newman mused.

'No idea. Yet.'

The phone was ringing when they entered Tweed's suite. He grabbed hold of it.

'Otto here. Want to say a thousand thanks for the pics – the first we've ever had of him.'

'Thank Paula sometime. She took them under risky circumstances.'

'Give her my love . . .'

'Oh, there's one other thing,' Newman reported. 'When I took Kent along to his room he glanced at the papers and the blue book. Said it could take up to a week to sort out the financial position – and that the book would be a great help.'

Paula poured three glasses of water from a fresh carafe that had been put in the suite. She sat down, drank the whole of her glass.

'This heat is getting ferocious. The forecast says it will continue, but get hotter. I'm off to my room in a minute for a shower.'

'So what is the next move?' Newman enquired.

'I think I can read Oskar Vernon now,' said Tweed, pacing between the balcony and his desk. 'I got a good look at his face when we were up in the Turm. Saw his reaction to his men being bashed about. I think he'll try and get us well outside the city to wipe us out.'

'From what we did to his troops I shouldn't think he has many of them left,' Newman commented.

'Don't count on it,' Tweed warned. 'He'll have reinforcements – either already here or brought in. I predict a battle royal which will make this morning's episode look like a mild punch-up. An extermination attack this time.'

22

Tweed and Newman were leaving the suite when the phone rang. It was Monica, reporting back on the results of her investigation of Lisa.

'She checks out OK,' she told Tweed. 'The only place which I couldn't check was New York – not knowing the name of the security agency she worked for.'

'I'm amazed at how quick you've been. Don't know how you do it.'

'By getting on with it, talking fast. Take care . . .'

'We'll get out of here now,' Tweed decided. 'It's like a steam bath. Go for a walk by the Alster.'

They had just left the hotel steps behind when Tweed spotted an Opel parked just beyond the entrance, on the Alster side. Butler was in the passenger seat with Nield behind the wheel. His two subordinates reacted sensibly. Instead of getting out to meet him they stayed in the car.

Tweed glanced up and down the street, saw no one suspicious. They crossed, strolled along the pavement by the lake. It seemed hotter than in the suite. Tweed could feel sweat running down inside his shirt. When they reached the Opel he opened the rear door, climbed inside, followed by Newman.

'I have news I was bringing you,' Nield announced. 'I was going to call you on the mobile, code it. I can now tell you Oskar Vernon has moved to the other five-star hotel, the Atlantic, facing the Aussenalster.'

'Now why would he do that?' Newman wondered.

'Let's go for that walk,' Tweed suggested.

'I'll come with you,' Nield said firmly. 'Trail you.'

'Don't do that. Walk with us. I'll bring you up to date on recent developments.'

'I'll stay with the car,' Butler said as they were alighting. 'Oh, Otto Kuhlmann told me he was having copies made of the Oskar pic. Distributing them to officers all over Hamburg.'

'Which is what I hoped for,' Tweed told him. 'Now we have the whole might of the police on our side.'

'Just before you go,' Harry continued, 'he said it would be a careful surveillance. No one must approach Oskar.'

'Better and better . . .'

They walked along a mostly deserted pavement, Tweed in the middle with Newman and Nield on either side. If you could stand the heat it was a glorious summer's afternoon. A clear blue sky, ferries hustling back and forth, rippling the glasslike calm of the water. Trees in full leaf lined the walk above them. They came to a bridge and Tweed led them across a road, then down a curving footpath and along a tunnel leading to a park alongside the Alster.

'So that's how ferries pass into the big lake,' Nield remarked. 'I hadn't been able to work it out. They go under the road bridge . . .'

'Which is also a separate rail bridge. Bob, we've been riding round in two cream Mercs. Stretch limos at that.'

'I didn't know how many of us would be travelling in them.'

'But Oskar saw them, parked near the Turm. So I want you to return one cream limo, then hire a blue version. Park it in the nearest underground garage. We continue to use only the cream job.'

'No point in asking why?'

'Forward planning, I think the military call it. Or used to.'

244

'You still haven't answered my question about why Vernon's moved to the Atlantic.'

'He's very smart, so very dangerous. So just when someone is sure they've located him he whisks off elsewhere.'

They continued walking along the shore path. A large woman in a floral dress and with blue-rinse hair bent down as she fed some ducks. Her glasses had thick lenses and when she looked up she stared at Tweed, went on staring. Then her thin mouth smiled at him.

'Glorious day,' Tweed said to her.

'Pure paradise.'

Her English had a foreign accent. Newman looked back but she was concentrating on her ducks. He frowned.

'That woman was studying you,' he said.

'Not my type,' Tweed responded jovially.

'No, she really was,' Newman insisted. 'And she noticed the bulge of that Walther you transferred to your trouser pocket.'

'Just a local.' Tweed had earlier removed his jacket and carried it. Under his armpits were damp circles. 'You see the enemy everywhere. Don't get paranoid.'

'Bob could be right,' Nield interjected. 'Before we got there I saw her get out of a car on the road, then she scuttled across to where we met her.'

After only a few minutes Tweed suggested they turned back. He had the appointment with the Brig for drinks. When they reached the point where the large woman had been feeding ducks she had gone. Nield glanced across at the road between the trees. Her car had also gone. Newman bent down, retrieved a brown paper bag full of broken bread.

'Floral Dress didn't stay long after she'd given you the once-over. And this bag is still full of bread.'

'Well, we're not feeding ducks.'

'Don't you see?' Newman was annoyed. 'She saw us earlier when we were leaving the hotel, watched us, then

245

drove ahead so she'd intercept us. Now she'll know you on another occasion. And these days women use guns. Not only Paula . . .'

Before meeting the Brig, Tweed dashed up to his suite, took off his clothes, had a shower, put on a fresh suit, gave the spoilt one to a porter he'd summoned and asked for it to be cleaned.

He had ten minutes left before the 1800 hours deadline. He picked up the phone on the second ring. It was Kuhlmann, in a towering rage.

'What's happened, Otto?'

'The grapevine tells me that Mr Blue murdered Jason Schulz in Washington weeks ago, tried to make it look like suicide. Then he kills Jeremy Mordaunt down in Sussex. Next M. Bleu, as the French call him, murdered Louis Lospin in Paris. Ditto suicide. All these men were close aides, confidants, to powerful people in their respective governments . . .'

'Slow down, Otto. You're not driving the IC train . . .'

'Now!' Kuhlmann rasped. 'Herr Blau has murdered Kurt Kruger in Berlin this morning. Clumsy attempt to make it look like suicide again. Revolver clamped in his fingers, in a manner no one would hold a gun and fire it . . .'

'Hold on. Who is – or was – Kurt Kruger?'

'Only chief aide and closest consultant to the Deputy Chancellor. Travelled all over the globe at the behest of his master.'

'In Berlin, you said. Whereabouts?'

'In the Zoo Garden – *Zoologischer Garten*. A quiet day due to the heat, the stink of animals. Kruger, married, met his girlfriend there in a secluded spot. Found slumped at the foot of a tree.'

'Like Jason Schulz – in a park. Did Kruger meet his girlfriend there regularly?'

246

'We think he did. The girl's as much as admitted it.'

'So Herr Blau could have followed him over a period to make sure Kruger kept to his routine?'

'*Ja*! I mean yes. All hell has broken loose. They want me to go to Berlin. I've refused, appointed a top detective to be in charge of the investigation.'

'Any leads at all?' Tweed asked.

'Not a sausage.' Kuhlmann was proud of his command of idiomatic English. 'Herr Blau is a very careful killer. I've checked with informants in the underworld. What gets me is he doesn't seem to be an assassin for hire. Just chooses his own targets. Which I find very strange.'

'Very strange. It could be the key to his actions.'

'Go on. Tell me.'

'I've got to think it out first.'

'Thanks a lot . . .'

Tweed arrived in the bar on the dot. The Brig was seated behind a small table in a corner. Tweed almost expected him to check a stopwatch. To his surprise the Brig was clad in a German jacket, German slacks and a German shirt open at the collar, exposing his bull-like neck.

'Two double Scotches. On the double,' his host barked at the barman.

As he sat down Tweed noticed an almost empty glass on the table. This wasn't the first drink the Brig had enjoyed. His complexion was a brilliant red, the veins in his nose prominent.

'I phoned your room during the day but you were out,' Tweed remarked.

'Went to Bremen, didn't I? Shipping. They showed me a new destroyer. Lots of gimmicks. Played the buffoon. So they boasted about their new toy. Took more in than they realized.'

'But you're not Admiralty.'

247

Tweed thought his companion was explaining far more than he usually did.

'They knew that. Which was why they talked. Got a naval chum back home. Do my bit when I can. Cheers!'

Tweed sipped while the Brig swallowed half the contents of his glass. Not drunk, he decided, but not sober, either.

'Been to Berlin?' Tweed enquired.

'Berlin?'

'Yes. The new capital of Germany.'

'I know that. Made the odd trip there. State-of-the-art architecture. Horrible new jargon. It's chaos over there. Never stop building. Crazy tubes and cubes going up to the sky. Get vertigo. Looking up.'

'It's a comparatively short flight from here to Berlin.'

'Is it? Sort of thing you'd know, I suppose.'

The Brig seemed nervous. He kept looking at the entrance to the bar, as though he expected the Devil to walk in.

'How's your investigation going?' the Brig asked when he'd ordered another couple of double Scotches.

'Not for me,' Tweed said firmly. 'And this one is mine.'

'You'll accept when I say so,' Barford said in the manner of addressing an awkward subaltern in the officers' mess. 'And I did ask how your investigation is progressing.'

'What investigation?'

'Oh, come on,' the Brig said roughly. 'You're always up to your clever neck in an investigation.'

'What do you think about the riots we endured?' Tweed asked suddenly.

'Riots.' He took a long drink – while he thought out how to react, Tweed said to himself. 'Shoot the lot of them, I would – and not with rubber bullets. We've gone soft. What we need is strong government. We . . .'

He faded out. Tweed felt he had pressed a button. Someone came into the bar. The Brig jerked his head

248

to see who it was. Just a relief barman coming to take over. Visibly, the Brig relaxed. Tweed stood up.

'I must go now. Thanks for the drink.'

'Do it again. Do it again. Soon . . .'

For the first time since he had sat down, Tweed suspected the Brig was nothing like as drunk as he'd pretended to be. At the exit he turned round, just in time to see Barford getting up, striding across to the bar to demand more service. No sign of a stagger. He'd moved as erect as the soldier he had once been.

In his suite Tweed had just taken another shower and dressed for dinner when there was a tapping at the door. Paula and Newman walked in, ready for departure. Paula was clad in a stunning blue, form-fitting belted dress, slashed on one side up to the knee and with a high collar.

'You look terrific,' Tweed told her.

'Everyone says that.' Her tone was self-mocking. 'Which means Bob said something similar. What about transport?'

'We're taking a cab,' Newman announced.

'What?' exclaimed Paula. 'To the dock area?'

'Cool it.' Newman put a hand on her shoulder. 'Behind us will be two four-wheel drives. One with Harry at the wheel and Marler beside him. The second with Nield at the wheel and, I hope, Mark beside him.'

'But what the devil has happened to Mark?' growled Tweed. 'I will only take so much more of his mavericking.'

As if on cue there was a knock on the door and when Newman opened it Mark walked in, smiling broadly.

'Hello, folks,' he greeted them. 'Bet you've been cursing me,' he went on, looking at Tweed.

'I have. Where have you been? From now on you tell me or you go home.'

'Fair enough. Not going home. I'm wondering whether you're all feeling your age, going soft . . .'

'What does that mean?' Newman bristled.

'In case you've forgotten we knocked hell out of the thugs during that little escapade at the Turm. I was there, so maybe I'm losing it.'

'What are you talking about?' Newman demanded.

'I've been spending time keeping an eye on the Renaissance. Who should turn up late this afternoon? Two gentlemen you may recall. Barton and Panko. They have a drink at the bar and then leave again on foot. I follow. Still with me?' he asked, grinning at Newman.

'Yes,' Newman said shortly, his tone rather subdued.

'Like I said, I follow. They go to a nearby gym. I pay the fee, hide myself up in a balcony. Then I watch Barton beating hell out of a punchball. Did some fancy footwork, too. While he's doing that, Panko is on his back, lifting weights. In other words, our friends are back in business.'

'I can't believe it,' Newman said.

'You'd better believe it, buddy,' Mark told him.

'Vernon's men are tough,' Tweed said quietly. 'So we'll have to be tougher.' He quickly explained to Mark who Oskar Vernon was, that he'd moved to the Atlantic. Then he asked Newman to put Mark in the picture about the trip to the Fischereihafen.

'I imagine,' Mark speculated when Tweed had explained, 'that when we get to this place you're dining at, the rest of us stay outside, scatter, take up positions watching the entrance. I've been down to the docks. At night they won't be the most fun place to be.'

'They're not,' Paula said, with feeling.

'One more thing I have to tell you before we go,' Tweed began.

He told them about the call from Kuhlmann, the murder of Kurt Kruger, confidential aide to the Deputy Chancellor. Then he looked at Paula and Newman.

'You realize what that tells us?'

'No,' said Paula as Newman shook his head.

'Well, work it out,' Tweed snapped as he moved towards the door. 'You have the same data I have . . .'

Paula did not enjoy the journey to the docks. She glanced back several times and felt better when she saw the two four-wheel drives following them as the cab entered Elbstrasse.

Again, she had the illogical fear that the enormous cranes would topple down on them. She made a point of not looking at No. 23, the late Dr Kefler's residence. Tweed did look, saw there was still police tape cordoning off the property.

The moon was hidden by a heavy overcast and the humidity was trying. They reached yet another large ware-house located on the river bank and the taxi stopped. The driver pointed to a side entrance with light streaming out. Tweed led the way inside and an arrow pointed up a long staircase. Tweed leapt up it. At the entrance Paula had glanced back, had seen Marler directing his troops to their positions. The vehicles had disappeared.

'Have you worked it out?' she asked Newman. 'Tweed said we had all the data. Was he talking about Rhi-noceros?'

'No idea,' Newman replied in his easy manner.

'Or maybe he was referring to the Elite Club?'

'Still no idea.'

'You're not trying,' she accused him.

Tweed was waiting in the reception area just beyond the top of the stairs. A dinner-jacketed manager had welcomed him.

'Mr Tweed? A friend of Herr Rondel. You are most welcome. May I lead the way . . .'

Paula was impressed as they walked inside the converted warehouse. The restaurant was enormous and on two levels. The main level was below, stretching across to large windows overlooking the Elbe river at night. The upper level, like a narrow balcony, was smaller. The place was packed with people, the men wearing either dinner dress or business suits while the women, many very attractive, wore a variety of expensive evening dresses. The restaurant was a hive of activity, with waiters moving rapidly among the tables. The atmosphere was joyful, a constant chatter, clinking of glasses. The manager led them to the balcony, paused by a table near the far end, pulled out chairs and they settled in. Tweed had a chair at the edge of the balcony. Paula was given the position opposite him while Newman sat next to her. Tweed told a waiter his suggestion was acceptable. Champagne.

Looking down at the table below them on the lower level he saw the blond-haired Rondel, seated with his back to him. Opposite him was a shorter man, well built and, like Rondel, in a dinner jacket. Tweed knew he'd seen him somewhere before, then remembered the man at the Four Seasons who had descended in an elevator and then gone back up again. The man looked up at him, said something to Rondel. He was still looking at Tweed, who felt he'd reached a decisive moment.

23

Tweed went on looking at the man. His eyes. They were like glass marbles but there was no hint of a lack of humanity. He was simply scrutinizing Tweed, who felt he could see right inside his head. Earlier, while listening to Rondel, the eyes had swivelled, in short penetrating scans of different tables in the restaurant. Now they were motionless as he gazed at Tweed.

About five feet four inches tall, he had wide shoulders and a wide chest. His head was large, his complexion healthy, his skin smooth. He had neatly brushed white hair, thick eyebrows of the same colour. His nose was prominent, almost Roman, the mouth below it firm, the lips compressed above a strong jaw. In his fifties, sixties, early seventies? Impossible to tell.

He eventually lowered his gaze, produced a small silver box. Lifting the lid he took out a toothpick, used the box to conceal his usage of it. Paula had glanced down, realized the toothpicks were made of ivory. Rondel rested his hands on the table as though to leave it. His companion said something and Rondel stood up, disappeared. Watching him seated alone, Tweed recalled Paula had said he radiated dynamic power. He agreed with her. Tweed was sipping champagne when Rondel appeared.

'Welcome to the Fischereihafen. I personally think it is the best restaurant in Germany. May I join you?' He sat next to Tweed. 'My partner sends you his greetings. Yes,

I will taste the champagne,' he said as a waiter brought a glass. He looked across at Paula, smiled warmly. 'I want to see if it's any good.'

'I can assure you it's delicious,' Paula replied, smiling warmly.

'Then I bow to what I am sure is your excellent judgement.' He smiled at her again, took a sip. 'And I was right – you have a subtle taste, Miss Grey.'

'Please call me Paula.'

'And I am Victor.' He smiled at Newman, turned to Tweed. 'And now we come to the important question of selecting something which will justify your visit. Of course . . .' He laughed. '. . . It really should be fish. But they have the greatest variety. Waiter, another bottle of champagne.'

Paula thought he was a handsome man. The table light gleamed on his smooth blond hair. His sea-green eyes kept glancing at her. His nose and other features reminded her of a bust of Apollo she had once seen. But his main attraction was his bubbling personality, his manners, his way of speaking English with perfect articulation. He would be easy to go out with, she thought.

Paula chose a soup, followed by sole. She had started a trend. After studying the menu, both Tweed and Newman ordered the same. Tweed looked down again at Rondel's partner. He still held the silver box close to his mouth while he worked his teeth. His eyes were again swivelling round the restaurant, pausing now and again, then moving on.

'You must excuse our bad timing,' Rondel said to Newman. 'We arrived early, were voraciously hungry, so we dined before you arrived. My apologies. My partner,' he went on, glancing at Tweed, aware of his gaze downwards, 'is quite happy to linger for hours over coffee. He drinks it by the litre. And he does not mind being on his own for a while. It gives him the chance to think. He never stops thinking.'

'He lives round here?' Tweed enquired.

'A good question.' Rondel was leaning forward, refilling Paula's glass. 'He lives everywhere. He travels so much. London, Paris, New York, San Francisco. And he takes the trouble to preserve his privacy. Tweed, you strike me as a very private person.'

'Yes and no. Depends on the circumstances.'

'He can be extremely sociable,' Paula said. 'Depending on who he is with and, as he just remarked, on the circumstances.'

She liked the way Rondel kept the conversation going fluently. The way he included everyone in what he said.

'Has your partner a home in Hamburg?' Tweed asked when they had ordered.

'Yes, he has. On the main road to Blankenese, if you know where I mean.'

'Millionaires' Row.'

'Yes, some still call it that.' Rondel laughed gently. 'But times have changed. I have nicknamed it Crooks' Road.'

'So such people have arrived there?'

'I'm afraid so. As you clearly know, it is a rather expensive area for property. But some of the *nouveau riche*, to be a shade more polite, have accumulated fortunes by questionable means. Going close to the edge of the abyss, as my partner would say.'

'Two sets of ledgers,' Tweed suggested.

'Pardon?'

'There are corporations, some large ones, who use clever accountants to create two ledgers recording the financial activities of their company. One ledger for the tax man – another for themselves.'

'Oh, I see.' Rondel chuckled. 'Yes, I am sure there is a lot of that about these days.' He looked across at Paula as the soup was arriving. 'You ride as well as you can handle a gun, Paula?'

'What makes you think I can handle a gun, Victor?'

255

Secretly, Newman gave her top marks for swift verbal reflexes. The question had been thrown at her without warning.

'The answer to that is simple.' Rondel smiled very warmly. 'It is part of our business to know things about key people on this planet. Information is more valuable than diamonds.'

'I didn't know I was a key person,' she fenced.

'But you are the close and confidential assistant to Mr Tweed. Need I say more?'

'You can if you wish to. I'm fascinated.'

Top marks to you again, Paula, Newman thought to himself. *He's clever but you're more than a match for him.*

Paula began to drink her soup. She looked across at Rondel, raised her eyebrows, inviting him to take the conversation further. He grinned, shook his head in a 'You win' gesture.

'It's gone very quiet,' said Tweed, then sipped more soup.

'I might be on firmer ground,' Rondel began, 'if we discussed the state of the world. We've heard rumours that far bigger riots are being planned in the near future to take place all over the West.'

'Lots of rumours floating around all the time,' Tweed commented.

'We have very good contacts,' Rondel insisted amiably.

'Did these very good contacts warn you about the imminent murder of Jason Schulz in Washington, then of Jeremy Mordaunt down in Alfriston?'

'No, they didn't. But you know what America is like – people are getting shot almost every day over there.'

'And in Europe. So what's next on the agenda, to use an ugly word?'

'Chaos, if much larger riots do take place.'

'And then?' Tweed enquired.

'We all go and live in Nepal.'

Tweed had glanced down at the table below them. Rondel's partner had perched a pair of gold-rimmed spectacles on the bridge of his nose. He was checking the bill. Without looking up he made a gesture towards Tweed's table, signed, sat back while the waiter took the bill away.

'My partner would like to meet you tomorrow at his house on the way to Blankenese,' Rondel said suddenly. he took out a notebook, scribbled with a gold pen, tore out the sheet, handed it to Tweed.

'There is the address. It's on the right-hand side as you head for Blankenese. The timing is of your choice. At your convenience. But my partner is anxious to meet you.'

'Eleven o'clock tomorrow morning any good?'

'Agreed. Splendid. I'm sure my partner will be pleased. And Paula and Bob Newman would be most welcome to accompany you.'

Paula glanced down at the table below them. The chair previously occupied by the man equipped with gold-rimmed glasses was empty. He had gone, like a ghost at daybreak.

'Before I leave,' Rondel said as he stood up, 'I want to say how much I have enjoyed the company of everyone at this table.' He held out his hand, leaning across to Paula. 'Maybe we can find some activity we have in common. Like ping-pong.'

'I'll murder you,' Paula replied with a smile.

'There have been too many murders already,' Tweed said.

Rondel shook Tweed's hand, squeezed Newman's shoulder as he passed him, then he also was gone.

'Don't discuss anything while we're in this place,' warned Tweed.

They were outside the Fischereihafen, about to get into

a waiting taxi, when Marler appeared, took Tweed aside, spoke softly.

'Damnit, he's done it again. Mark Wendover. Gone off on his own.'

'Did he say where he was off to?'

'Yes. Four Seasons. He'd got an idea in his head that Keith Kent needed guarding. I suppose he had a point – with Kent working on those papers. But he didn't ask me – he *told* me. Said he knew you'd agree, so I didn't argue.'

'How long ago since he pushed off?'

'Very soon after you entered the restaurant.'

'I'll have a word with him. The last thing Keith will want while he studies what I gave him is a bodyguard hanging round his neck . . .'

During the journey back no one spoke, probably because Tweed had earlier warned them to keep quiet. At that hour Elbstrasse was deserted but there was a moon. By its illumination the towering cranes seemed to Paula even more menacing. She found her eyes drawn to look up at No. 23. The police tape still closed off the house and a uniformed officer stood in front of it. Much good that would do now.

They were very close to the hotel, proceeding up Neuer Jungfernstieg, when Tweed noticed that a section of the pavement on the hotel side was cordoned off with police tape. Patrol cars, their blue lights flashing, were parked opposite the hotel. He had an awful premonition.

'Wait for me,' he told the others while he paid the driver.

He sprinted up the steps, followed closely by Paula and Newman. Heading for the elevators, he saw a familiar figure seated in a chair at the back of the lounge. Otto Kuhlmann had a uniformed police sergeant by his side.

An elevator was waiting, its doors open. Kuhlmann jumped up. As they entered the elevator the German slipped in behind them, waited until the doors had closed. His tone of voice was as grim as his expression.

'Your suite. I'd like everyone to join me there.'

'What has happened?' Newman asked.

Kuhlmann didn't reply. Instead he stared up at the ceiling of the elevator. When they entered the suite Tweed waved the German towards a sofa but instead he sat in an upholstered chair, waited until everyone was seated.

'I fear this may come as a shock to you, but I always come straight out with it. I believe you know Mark Wendover, an American. He was shot dead outside the hotel. With a rifle. Explosive bullet.'

'Oh, no!'

Paula covered her face with her hands. Tweed poured a glass of water, held it for her while she drank, trembling. She looked up at him gratefully after a short time, took hold of his sleeve. He smiled down at her, refilled the empty glass she held out with her other hand. She drank more, then spoke.

'He was such a decent man,' she croaked throatily.

'One of the best,' said Newman, who had sat beside her on the couch.

She became aware that Kuhlmann, seated above them in his chair, was watching her closely. She stiffened, sat erect.

'I'm all right now,' she said in a firmer voice.

'I have to ask some questions,' Kuhlmann began. 'Paula, it might be better if you went to your room. Stay if you wish.'

'That's the last place I want to be now. On my bloody own.'

'Where was he shot from?' Tweed, asked, still standing.

'Across the street. The marksman probably hid behind

259

one of the cars parked by the Alster. We've checked. Found nothing.'

Standing behind Kuhlmann, Tweed frowned at Paula. She understood his message immediately. Say nothing about the break-in at the Zurcher Kredit – that would lead to Kuhlmann demanding that they hand over the vital blue book Mark had brought them which was needed by Kent to crack the code.

'Any idea of the time he was shot?' Tweed went on.

'A couple of hours ago. The doorman called the police immediately. He claims he didn't see anything suspicious before the shooting. Tweed, I need to hear all you know about Wendover – who, incidentally, was carrying a CIA identity folder. So I'm anticipating all hell will break loose when the news reaches Washington.'

Tweed paced around, told Kuhlmann most of the story about how they'd come to know Mark Wendover. He emphasized he'd left the CIA some time ago, had set up his own detective agency in New York.

'That covers the whole story,' he concluded.

'So,' Kuhlmann began, 'you were having dinner in the Fischereihafen and your team was outside, keeping an eye on things. Why would Wendover come back here on his own?'

'As I've explained, Mark had maverick habits. I gather he decided to come back to see what was happening here. After all, it is our base for this operation in Hamburg.'

'And if you had to make a guess, who would you say was behind this murder?'

'Oskar Vernon and his gang spring to mind. Oskar's moved to the Atlantic. Maybe he didn't want to be anywhere near here if they got the chance to kill one of us off.'

Kuhlmann stood up. He looked at Tweed as though he didn't believe he had the whole story. Which he hadn't. Then he pursed his lips before speaking again.

'I need someone to go to the morgue to confirm the

identity of Wendover. It's not a pretty sight.'

'I'll go,' Newman responded, jumping up.

'Thank you. Then please come downstairs with me and I'll introduce you to Sergeant Brand. He was sitting beside me in the lounge and will escort you. I want to check that pavement by the Alster. Never met a detective yet who was as thorough as I'd like . . .'

'Why do you think they shot Mark?' Paula asked when she was alone with Tweed.

'My guess is he missed blotting out one camera – the one up on the balustrade on the first floor outside the building. Difficult to see by daylight. Probably impossible to detect after dark. Also, I think Oskar's mood has changed. He has become more ruthless, more audacious. He's resorted to picking us off one by one. But someone may have given him a specific order to target Mark – because they're livid that the blue book has gone. Take your choice.'

'Strange that it occurred while we were at the fish restaurant. I wonder if the dinner was a lure to get us out of the way.'

'That thought had occurred to me, but I rejected it. They'd hardly foresee Mark would turn up here on his own.' Tweed decided to change the subject, to get her mind off what had happened. 'What was your reaction to our hosts tonight?'

'I liked Victor Rondel. I think he's very intelligent and has a hypnotic personality. I thought he was fun.'

'I noticed.'

'Was I that obvious? Oh, Lord, I'll have to learn to control myself more. Do sit down.'

He sat on the couch in the position Newman had occupied and she squeezed his hand, then released it. He drank more water, urged her to do the same.

'You weren't obvious at all,' he assured her. 'It's just that I know you so well. Did you enjoy the meal?'

'Best I've had in ages. Marvellous restaurant.'

'And what did you think of Rondel's companion?'

She hesitated, leant her head back against a cushion. She took her time to answer.

'Weird the way Rondel kept referring to him as "my partner" and never gave us a name. Highly secretive.'

'I noticed that. Maybe we'll learn more tomorrow when we visit his mansion on the way to Blankenese. He struck me as being exceptional, the sort of person you rarely come across. What about the relationship between them?'

'Good question. Difficult to come up with a good answer.'

'On the surface, I had the impression they are equal partners. But, thinking it over, the relationship could be different. I should be able to be more positive after we've seen them tomorrow. And now, I think it's time you went to bed.'

'Frankly, I'm dropping. See you in the morning . . .'

Newman returned a little later. He walked over to a cabinet, opened it up, took out a bottle of Scotch.

'Excuse me, but I need a stiff drink.'

'Like that was it?' Tweed said.

'I can talk frankly, now Paula's gone.' He poured a strong neat drink, swallowed half of it, sat down. 'It wasn't a picnic.'

'Tell me.'

'Poor Mark. The left side of his face – and his head – had been blown away. Explosive bullet, Kuhlmann said. He was right. To identify him I had to look at the other side of his face and head. Not a pretty sight, as Kuhlmann pointed out.'

Tweed had sat down at the small table near the sofa

Newman had sunk into. He picked up the mobile phone Paula had left in her state of shock. He pressed the numbers of Pete Nield's mobile from memory.

'Tweed here. Where are you?'

'Parked no more than a score of yards from your hotel.'

'Can you come up to my suite? Right away. See you . . .'

'You're looking very grim suddenly,' Newman commented. 'I'd say you've just taken a major decision. Have you?'

'Yes. Wait until Nield gets here.' Within five minutes Nield was tapping on the door, entering the suite. Tweed told him to sit down, asked him if he'd like a drink. Nield, cool and calm as always, sat down, crossed his legs and shook his head.

'I'm driving. And I'm sorry about Mark. Very sorry.'

'How did you know it was Mark they shot?'

'I followed you into the hotel when you got back from the fish restaurant. You didn't see me. When Kuhlmann had disappeared in the lift with you I went over to the sergeant who had been with Kuhlmann, showed him my identity folder, asked him what had happened. I only knew it had been Mark when the sergeant described what he'd been wearing. Now, what do you want me to do?'

'Go back to Butler. Tell him to be ready to bring over here the armoury Marler obtained. Stun grenades, tear gas, smoke grenades and all the weaponry – except what Harry needs for himself. What about guns? Tell me again.'

'Three Uzis, several automatic rifles, a whole array of handguns. Lord knows what else.'

'We'll need all three Uzis here when the time comes, plus the rest. Where is Marler staying?'

'He's moved into the Renaissance with us now Oskar has left.'

'Consult Marler. He may want to make extra purchases. We shall be outnumbered, I suspect. So we make up for that in firepower. That's it.'

'Right. On my way . . .'

'You're planning all-out war,' Newman commented. 'Was it the killing of Mark that stimulated you to arrange all this?'

'I suppose it was a factor.' Tweed stood up, started pacing. 'It underlined how vicious Oskar Vernon is. And I think I'm beginning to sort out the good side from the evil. I'll be more certain after our meeting with Rondel and his partner tomorrow.'

Newman had opened the door to leave when he bowed, turned to Tweed, winked.

'You have a visitor. Don't stay up all night.'

Lisa walked into the suite as Newman left, closing the door carefully behind him. Tweed stared as he stood up. She was wearing a close-fitting strapless white evening dress. Round her waist was a green lizard belt with a lock ornament dangling from it. She carried a green evening bag no larger than a foolscap envelope.

'Well,' she said, with a wicked smile. 'Do I pass inspection, sir?'

He knew then that she was in a whimsical mood, which clashed with his own reaction to the recent tragedy. He managed a quirky smile.

'Not bad. Would you like a drink?'

She sat down on a couch against the wall, crossed her shapely legs and a slash in her dress exposed one leg almost to her thigh. Looking at him from under her eyelashes she spoke in a mock-indignant voice.

'Not bad? Is that all? And I would like a drink.' Glancing at the table, she saw the bottle Newman had left. 'I'd like a terrific double Scotch. Please. Sir.'

He found a fresh glass on a lower shelf under the table and poured Scotch slowly.

'Say when.'

'Keep going.'

He continued pouring. He looked at her and she was watching him quizzically, one bare arm stretched along the back of the couch. He used tongs to cram the glass with ice, hoping it would dilute the Scotch, then placed it on the table close to her.

'Any more,' he remarked, 'and you might spill it down that glorious dress you're almost wearing.'

'That's better. Much better. You are drinking with me? I hate drinking alone.'

He found another fresh glass, poured himself a modest drink. She patted the space beside her, raised her eybrows, patted the space again.

'You are going to sit with me.'

I don't think so, he thought. If I get any closer to her now, heaven knows where we'll end up. He sat in the upholstered chair, raised his glass.

'Cheers!' He took a small drink. 'Now where the devil have you been for the past few hours?'

'You missed me. I like that.'

'Where?' he growled.

'I like you when you growl.'

He began to realize she was going to be hard to handle. He decided not to mention Mark's death. He felt sure she had not heard.

'What are all those policemen doing outside the hotel?' she asked.

'Maybe there was a traffic accident. Lisa, where have you been?'

'You went off to dinner without me this evening.' She pouted, then waved aside the reaction as childish. 'That's why I got all dressed up. I was hoping.'

She'd had another mood change. Tweed, for the second time, decided she *was* going to be difficult to handle. He was damned if he was going to apologize. Then he went ahead and said the wrong thing.

265

'It was a private dinner. A business dinner . . .'

'About the coming crisis?' she said quickly. 'I had a weird idea I was involved. Or are you shutting me out now?' She was annoyed. 'Give me a cigarette.'

He took out his packet, held it out. Then he leaned forward, lit the cigarette for her. She thanked him, sitting stiffly erect, taking several deep drags, then carefully tipping the ash into a crystal glass ashtray. He kept quiet until she had stubbed out the cigarette, leant back against the couch cushion, her chest heaving. She folded her arms.

'What crisis?' he asked quietly.

'The big one . . . the one that's going to blow up in our faces out of nowhere.' She was talking rapidly. 'The one you should be making preparations for . . . although, knowing you, I expect you've already made them.'

He was having to concentrate to follow her. He wondered if she'd take off again if he, once more, asked her where she had been. He decided she would. She seemed to read his mind.

'When I realized I wasn't included in the party I hit the town. Oh, you're probably wondering how I knew you'd gone out to dinner.' Which was exactly what Tweed had been wondering. 'I saw Newman further down the corridor when I was coming out of my room. He was standing in front of a wall mirror, brand new suit, fresh shirt, new hand-made shoes, fiddling with his Chanel tie to get it just right. Going out to dinner, I thought. Why didn't Tweed warn me, I thought. Because I'm not included on the menu.'

'Well, you know why you weren't included now.' He spoke quietly. 'I agree we might be close to a major crisis, but what gave you that idea?'

'Sixth sense,' she snapped.

'You can, I suspect, do better than that.'

'Lisa,' she said, 'he says do better than that. OK, I will.' She half-smiled at him. 'I trawled the Reeperbahn – don't

266

look like that. Wait till I'm finished. I used taxis to move from one bar to another . . .'

'In that outfit?' he asked in a worried tone.

'Just watch me.'

From her small evening bag she took out several hairpins. She lifted her red mane, coiled it on top of her head and held it there with the pins. She picked up the scarf she'd carried in, now spread over a couch arm, wrapped it round her head, tied it under her chin. The next item from the evening bag was a pair of large spectacles with thin horn-rims. She perched them on the bridge of her nose. Finally she took out a very small metal case, extracted a slim cigar, placed it in her mouth. She was unrecognizable and none too attractive.

'Well?' she said.

'I'm amazed. I suppose you learned tricks like that when working for the security agency in New York.'

'Right on the button, Mister.'

Her accent was convincingly American. Tweed waved both his hands in admiration.

'I got lucky,' she said, after removing the cigar, 'in the sixth bar. I'd left my drinks hardly touched in the other bars. In the last bar I found myself sitting next to Blue Shirt, Pink Shirt, whatever . . .'

'He's been identified as Oskar Vernon, now staying at the five-star Atlantic facing the Aussenalster.'

'Now he tells me.' She smiled. 'Oskar, then, was whispering to my old friend, Barton, last seen in Bedford Square while I was with my friend, the tramp. I have very acute hearing. Oskar said, "We're going to have a bloodbath with that bastard Tweed and his whole team. Wipe them off the face of the earth. Soon now. We just have to trick them, get them well outside Hamburg. I've worked out how we do it." Having heard that, I thought I'd better make myself scarce. Oh, Oskar was wearing a violet shirt. Hideous.'

'So now we know.'

She reached for her half-empty glass of Scotch, put it down untouched. She pulled the scarf off her head, dropped it on the floor, removed the spectacles which had made her look like a schoolmistress. She looked as though she had squeezed the last drop of energy out of herself. She swayed. Tweed grabbed her by the shoulder. She closed her eyes, opened them again with an effort.

'I'm flaked out,' she said hoarsely. 'Can't move my legs. Sleep. I need sleep. For a week . . .'

She swayed again. She was half asleep already. He moved to the end of the couch. He just had time to grab a cushion, lay it on his lap, before her head fell on it. Leaning forward, he got hold of her legs under the knees, spread them along the couch. She half opened her greenish eyes, looked up at him.

'Thanks,' she mumbled. 'I know poor Mark is dead. Saw his body on the pavement when I got back . . .'

Then she fell into a deep sleep. Tweed understood now her erratic moods. The sight of Mark, half his head shot away, had shaken her up badly, accounted for her swift changes of emotion. He leaned back against the high end of the couch and fell fast asleep.

He woke in the morning to find her still fast asleep, her head in his lap. Daylight filtered through the closed curtains. His back felt stiff as a board but he had slept non-stop. He couldn't move without disturbing her so he stayed still until, after a few minutes, she opened her eyes, stared at him, smiled. Lifting her head, she sat up, planted her legs on the floor.

'A shower,' she said, suppressing a yawn. 'My kingdom for a shower.'

Tweed pointed to the bathroom, told her to take her time, that he'd have a shower when she had gone.

'I'll order breakfast for us from room service,' he called out.

'But won't they think . . .'

'Who the hell cares what they think? What do you fancy for breakfast?'

When she had gone into the bathroom, he ordered orange juice, coffee, toast, scrambled eggs and tomato, croissants, marmalade for two people. Then he tidied himself up, checked in a wall mirror, decided he wouldn't have time for a shave but he didn't look too bad.

'Bathroom's yours,' she said, emerging more quickly than he'd expected.

She was wearing a white flannel robe she'd found in the bathroom and looked herself again. She smiled at him.

'Excuse the robe. I do have the dress on underneath.'

'I'd better hurry. Breakfast will come soon . . .'

During the first part of breakfast they didn't say much to each other. Lisa had said she was ravenous. Then Tweed, keeping off serious subjects, described to her the Aussen – or Outer – Alster. How the ferries zigzagged across it, moving from one landing stage to another, picking up and dropping off passengers. How, at the extreme distant end, it narrowed into little more than a wide stream with willows drooping into the water with small parks behind them.

'Sounds heavenly,' she said, watching him.

'We ought to take a trip sometime,' he suggested.

'I'd love to. Sounds so peaceful – you described it in such a graphic way. I think I'll get back to my room now.'

She returned the robe to the bathroom, straightened her creased dress, went to the door, looked back.

'Am I still on the team?'

'You were never off it.'

24

Paula tapped on Lisa's door. She heard it being unlocked and approved of the caution. Lisa opened the door, looked pleased, invited her in.

'My face is a mess,' she explained. 'Do sit down while I try to make it look half decent.'

'You look OK,' Paula replied as she sat down next to the table with the phone.

'Don't feel it.'

'You have heard,' Paula began tentatively.

'About Mark being shot last night? Horrible, isn't it? I saw him on the pavement. I must have got back just after he had been killed. I felt sick.'

The phone rang. Lisa asked Paula to see who it was so she could finish her renovation. Paula picked it up, was about to ask who it was when a creepy voice spoke.

'Oskar here. I have news . . .'

Paula put down the phone as though it were red hot. She was careful not to look at Lisa, who turned round on her dressing table seat.

'Was it Tweed again?'

'Wrong number.'

'Tweed rang me a few minutes ago to tell me you and Newman were going with him to a business meeting. Said he hoped you'd be back in a couple of hours. You know I'm still feeling ill about poor Mark. You don't look too good yourself.'

'I'm all right. I'd better go soon. I just called to see if you had heard – and if so how you were.'

Paula was in a state of shock. Why had Oskar Vernon – she felt sure it had to be him – phoned Lisa of all people? She let herself out, saying nothing in case her voice might betray her.

In the corridor the same small chunky uniformed hotel cleaner was still operating his vacuum cleaner. She noticed that the trousers he was wearing flopped over his shoes. His jacket wasn't a wonderful fit. She walked towards Tweed's suite.

'Good morning,' she said as she passed the cleaner.

He grunted, didn't look up. Which was unusual. She'd found all the staff so polite. Maybe he was new. She knocked on the suite door and Tweed, wearing a new business suit, a coat over his arm, ushered her inside.

'You won't need a coat this weather,' she told him. 'It's a boiling day outside already.'

'You're right. Can't think why I took it out of the wardrobe. Had my mind on something else.'

The death of Mark, she thought. Or, more likely, working out his strategy for the meeting with Rondel and his partner. She sat down, couldn't think of anything to say. Shouldn't she tell him about the weird phone call in Lisa's room?

'Lisa,' he said, 'has had a bad time of it. She actually saw Mark's body on the pavement when she got back to here. From Bob's description, when he visited the morgue, it must have shaken Lisa up badly.'

'I can understand that.'

She was still trying to decide whether to tell Tweed when Newman arrived. He smiled at her, squeezed her shoulder.

'I can do without any more grim shocks today. What are the tactics for this morning?'

'Leave me to do the talking,' Tweed replied. 'You

272

two keep your eyes open. You might just see something interesting.' He looked at his watch. 'Time to go. Nield has told the porter to have the Merc ready for us – the cream one, of course.'

When they entered the corridor Paula noticed the man using the vacuum cleaner had disappeared, but half the carpet still needed attention. Tweed had gone ahead, turned to call to Paula.

'I'm having a brief word with Lisa, then Keith . . .'

He tapped on Lisa's door and stood half inside when she opened it. Paula heard every word that was said.

'Lisa, I'm off to a meeting with Paula and Bob. Expect to be back in about two and a half hours. I hope you can then join us for lunch. You can? Good.'

He hurried on to Keith Kent's door, beckoned Paula and Newman to come with him. A heavy-eyed Kent let them in. Paula thought he looked as though he'd had no sleep. His desktop was scattered with Kefler's papers and he had a small ledger open. The page was a jumble of figures. He took the blue book out of a drawer and it had a marker inside it.

'Didn't know who it was,' he explained. 'So I hid the book.'

'How is it going?' Tweed asked.

'I'm breaking it, but haven't got there yet. The blue book Mark provided is invaluable.'

It occurred to Paula that Kent didn't know Mark was dead. He was in his shirt sleeves and on another table was a tray of coffee, remnants of croissants. Tweed looked at it.

'When did you last eat a proper meal?'

'Can't remember. Been at it all night. It's absorbing.'

'Go down now and get a decent meal at the Condi,' Tweed told him.

'I can't leave these papers, even locked up . . .'

'Lisa could come and keep guard while you eat,' suggested Tweed.

'Lisa,' Paula said hastily, 'is fagged out. She told me,' she lied, 'she didn't get any sleep – probably after her long day yesterday.'

Tweed glanced at her, bewildered. There was nothing that he could say, that it would be wise to say. He looked back, saw Newman standing inside the closed door, turned to Keith.

'Any hint as to what you've found so far?'

'Oh, there's a ton of money missing. But whether it's still somewhere inside the bank or has been moved elsewhere I just can't fathom yet. Nor who is responsible for the movement. I'll crack it, but it may take a few more days.'

'Promise you'll phone room service, order a proper meal as soon as we've gone.'

'I'll do that. I've just realized I'm hungry . . .'

The cream stretch limo was waiting for them and Newman took the wheel. Paula sat beside him and Tweed rode in the back. Tweed had once visited Blankenese and navigated for them.

It didn't seem to take long for them to leave behind the massive, stately buildings which were Hamburg and then they were driving along a rustic road with trees in leaf. Paula gazed out and to each side they began to pass imposing mansions set back from the road with manicured lawns in front of them. The architecture varied enormously – there were mansions in the old style, square and solidly built, but others were more imaginative with long frontages, thatched roofs and strange turret-like towers. Each property, she guessed, would cost a fortune to buy.

'Marler and Nield are not far behind us in the Opel,' Newman remarked. 'Not a bad idea, maybe. It's rather lonely out here.'

'We're approaching the house,' Tweed warned from the back. 'I can see a sign ahead pointing to a side road. Taxusweg. Rondel scribbled that as a landmark when he gave me the address.'

Newman slowed, indicated right. A warning to Marler they were close. As he had anticipated, Marler turned down Taxusweg. To park discreetly, Newman guessed.

'This big house well back,' Tweed warned. 'Turn along the drive.'

Newman swung into the wide entrance, flanked by two pillars, each surmounted with an elegant lantern. The front garden was like a small park with lawns and beautiful specimen trees. *But no electronically powered gates*, Paula thought – *and no sign of guards. You just drove in.*

There were other lanterns perched on steel posts scattered amid the trees. This place must look even more glorious after dark with the lanterns lit, she mused. A large long mansion built of white stone came into view. Newman parked close to the main entrance, a pair of heavy oaken doors.

'Well,' said Tweed, before alighting. 'Let's hope here is where we find the key to what is really going on.'

Both doors were opened with a flourish by a tall uniformed chauffeur. A Daimler was parked near the corner of the mansion. Tweed studied the chauffeur intently. Not the usual chauffeur – even by the standards of those working for rich men. He had brown hair trimmed short, a strongly featured face, and was in his thirties, but it was the eyes that caught Tweed's attention. They were exceptionally intelligent, and the man moved athletically.

'Yes, I'm Tweed.'

'You are expected, sir,' the chauffeur replied in faultless English. 'If you would wait in the hall for just a few moments . . .'

Left to themselves in the spacious hall, Tweed noticed a Louis Vuitton case standing against a wall. He bent down. Someone had tucked in below the handle a *Bordkarte*, or a boarding pass. Lufthansa. *From BER to HAM*. Dated

275

the previous day. Someone had flown back from Berlin to Hamburg in the afternoon – on the day Kuhlmann had reported that Kurt Kruger, aide to the Deputy Chancellor, had been murdered.

Tweed was holding the pass in his hand when Rondel entered like a whirlwind, clad in riding gear.

'Welcome! Welcome! Welcome!'

He bowed, took Paula's right hand, kissed it, looked up at her with a broad smile. She found she rather liked a gesture she would not normally have found acceptable. Tweed held up the printed slip.

'I found this boarding pass from Berlin to Hamburg lying on the floor. It must have slipped out of the case.'

'That belongs to Danzer, the chauffeur who greeted you. He flew to Berlin and back again yesterday.' Rondel grinned. 'He has a new girlfriend. He collects and dismisses them as though they were playing cards . . . Please excuse my attire. I have an engagement to go riding . . . Want to come?' he asked Paula.

'It's a long time since I sat on a horse. Thank you, but I think I need a quiet day. Yesterday was rather hectic. I did enjoy the dinner, though.'

'You couldn't have enjoyed it as much as I revelled in having a chat with you . . . I couldn't sleep last night. Your image kept coming into my mind . . .'

He was talking as he had at the restaurant. In rapid bursts that demonstrated the extraordinary quickness of his mind. He waved towards the interior of the house.

'My partner is waiting for you. Or rather, he would like to see Tweed alone, if that is not too impolite . . . Paula, you and Bob can come with me . . . we will enjoy a drink together: I am hoping Bob, the famous international foreign correspondent, can tell us what is wrong with the world. If both of you would like to make yourselves comfortable in this room . . .' He was leading them towards a closed door. '. . . I will be back in a tick.'

276

He turned to Tweed, who had slipped the boarding pass under the handle of the case.

'Please, Mr Tweed, let me escort you . . .'

Inside the room she had been shown into with Newman, Paula remained standing. It kept going through her head. Lisa concussed, after the blow Delgado had struck her back home at Reefers Wharf. The message she had desperately tried to get across, hardly able to speak.

Ham . . . Dan . . . Four S.

Ham had been Hamburg. *Four S* had been Four Seasons Hotel. *Dan.* Couldn't that have been Danzer, the chauffeur who had shown them in?

After opening another door at the rear of the hall, where gilt-framed portraits of men of earlier times were hung, Rondel accompanied Tweed down a long hall to a door at the far end. This opened on to a large conservatory full of different plants. His partner sat facing them in a wickerwork chair with a high straight back.

In front of the chair on a glass-topped table were the remains of a meal. His partner had been holding the silver box close to his mouth while he manipulated one of the ivory toothpicks. He closed the lid quickly, tucked it inside a pocket of his linen jacket.

'The gentleman you are so anxious to see,' Rondel said.

'Thank you. Do not let his two colleagues leave. I wish to pay my respects to them later,' the seated man ordered.

'Let us go into the garden, Mr Tweed,' the partner suggested, rising, holding out his hand. 'There we can talk without inhibition. May I offer you a drink?'

He was speaking slowly, each word enunciated with clarity. Not from age, Tweed guessed, but from temperament. A very careful man.

'Just water, please . . .'

His host opened a door, ushered Tweed, holding his glass of water, into what seemed more like a beautiful park with an abundance of flowers. Especially hydrangeas. Paved walkways wended their way in all directions, disappearing round curves. They strolled slowly and Tweed kept quiet, leaving his strange host to choose a subject.

'I will tell you something very few people in the world know. My name is Milo Slavic. Which shows I trust you.'

'Why should you?' Tweed asked outright.

'Because before I get even a little close to someone I have him checked out meticulously.' He drew out the word as m-e-t-i-c-u-l-o-u-s-l-y. 'I have had you checked out on two continents. You are a unique man. I never flatter.'

'So what did you want with me?'

'Direct, too. Do you believe that, with all the weakness of present Western governments, we need something stronger?'

'Depends on how strong. In the last century we have had Adolf Hitler, Benito Mussolini, Josef Stalin. Do we need men as strong as that?'

'There was chaos when those men took power. The masses were frightened, looked for strength. Perhaps it may have to happen again?'

'Are you related to an earlier member of the Frankenheim Dynasty?' Tweed asked suddenly.

'Ah!' His host chuckled, an odd sound. 'History sometimes does repeat itself. You know about the Frankenheims – I can tell. The first Frankenheim took the name, pretended to be a Jew, made himself indispensable to Mayer Amschel, that brilliant man who created Rothschild. We are back in the late 1790s. Frankenheim, as he continued to call himself, then learnt all the tricks of the profession from his mentor – left him, founded his own bank in Paris. Jump forward to 1940. As a very young man I met the last of the Frankenheims, who had no son, no heir. I was naturally gifted in mathematics, in accountancy and solved for him a problem he had found insoluble. He obtained a Swiss passport for me, as he had for himself, and soon I was Director of his bank in Zurich. When he died I found he had appointed me his heir. I have simplified a rather complicated history.'

'So where do you come from?'

'Slovenia.'

'The northernmost state of what used to be Yugoslavia in the time of Marshal Tito. Adjoins the border with Austria. Has gained its complete independence.'

'Not everyone would know that. Are you concerned with what is happening?'

'Yes. We could be on the edge of a catastrophe.'

Tweed looked at Slavic. He was broader across the shoulder than he had realized, looking down on him at the restaurant. He emanated physical strength as well as mental power. Tweed was still unsure.

'Your mutual chauffeur is an unusual man,' he remarked.

'Danzer. He is my chauffeur. Blondel prefers to drive his own Bugatti, Maserati – whatever is his latest toy. Shall we turn back? We are close to the house.'

'You said "Blondel". I thought your partner's name was Rondel.'

'Ah.' Slavic chuckled unpleasantly. 'Vanity. He has blond hair, so dislikes his real name. Calls himself Rondel. Had a French father, a German mother. We must meet again soon. My headquarters are in the far north. I like privacy.'

'How shall I know where you are?'

'I, Mr Tweed, will always know where *you* are.'

'I may need to call you something to the closest members of my team. So what name do I use?'

'Simply call me Milo. It sounds as though they are enjoying themselves.'

They had almost reached a side door open to the park.

Tweed could hear Paula laughing with Rondel. A middle-aged woman with blue-rinse hair appeared out of nowhere, carrying in her hands large clusters of hydrangeas. Milo Slavic waved her away. She looked disappointed as she retreated.

'That is Mrs Gina France, my chief accountant. A most professional accountant but with a volcanic personality.' He paused. 'You do believe, then, in iron governments?'

'Depends on how strong they are,' Tweed replied.

'We must meet again.' Slavic sounded urgent. 'I will contact you when the moment arrives. Then you must come quickly.' His voice changed, became mellow as they walked in through open doors into the room where Rondel sat with Paula and Newman. Slavic remained standing.

'I think we should leave now,' said Tweed.

'So early!' Rondel jumped up. 'This charming lady and I are just getting to know each other.'

'There will be another time, Victor,' Paula said, smiling as she stood up and Newman followed.

Tweed turned to thank his host, but the man from Slovenia had vanished. Instead he looked at Rondel.

'Please tell your partner I found the conversation most illuminating. I look forward to the possibility sometime of repeating the experience . . .'

Rondel led the way along a devious route through the complex mansion until they emerged into the hall and he opened the double doors. As he did so, another figure appeared at the back of the hall, watching them. The chauffeur. Danzer.

'Safe journey,' Rondel wished them and then they were outside and the doors closed behind them.

They were moving slowly down the drive when Tweed glanced back, saw Mrs France dashing after them, still clutching her hydrangeas.

'Stop the car,' he ordered, lowering his window.

'It's Floral Dress,' said Newman, looking back. 'The

280

lady who was feeding ducks, who spoke to you as we walked along the edge of the Alster.'

Mrs France was almost out of breath when she reached them. She thrust the flowers through the open window and Paula took hold of them. She smiled at the plump-faced lady who had a high colour. Mrs France peered through her huge thick-lensed spectacles.

'These are really beautiful.'

'That is very kind of you,' said Tweed, smiling.

The woman pushed her face inside the window. She was very nervous and her hands were trembling. She tried to speak, then had to start again.

'Mr Tweed, I need to come and see you on my own. Something is happening which is very serious, which you should know about. I expect they are watching me from the house.'

'Four Seasons Hotel,' Tweed said quickly, keeping his back to the house. He gave her his suite number. 'You would like to come and see me soon? This afternoon? Three o'clock any good to you?'

'I will be there at three. Oh, thank you so much. You are a nice man. I must go now. They will question me. I will say I heard Miss Grey comment when you arrived how much she admired the hydrangeas.'

'I do . . .' Paula began.

Mrs France didn't hear her. She was hurrying back up the drive to the house.

'That,' said Newman, 'is one very frightened lady.'

281

25

On the day Tweed was driven to Millionaires' Row, in London Gavin Thunder stood in his Whitehall office and gave orders to Montagu Carrington, the aide who had replaced Jeremy Mordaunt.

'You will, nominally, be in charge while I am away. I am flying abroad on holiday for five days. Try not to make too big a mess of things in my absence.'

The heatwave was intensifying and Thunder wore tropical kit. His sharp features seemed even more pronounced, as though he was in a state of tension. His temper was on a short fuse.

'A sudden decision, sir,' commented Carrington, a pale-faced man in his thirties who regarded himself as a high-flier. 'May I ask where you are going so I can contact you?'

'You damned well may not. How can I get a quiet holiday if people like you are bothering me? My destination is both private and secret. Has your thick head grasped that?'

'I can at least arrange for a limousine to drive you to the airport . . .'

'You bloody well won't. I'm driving myself. Got it?'

Carrington, clad in a grey suit quite unsuitable for the weather, frowned. He shifted his feet.

'You are a Minister, sir. You should at least have two bodyguards wherever you are going. Somewhere hot?'

'I know I'm a Minister, you idiot. Has anyone ever told you that you're like a mangy dog which keeps on chewing its bone?'

'No, sir, they haven't . . .'

'Well, I'm telling you now.' Thunder's mouth was tight, his eyes impaled Carrington's. 'No bodyguards. No limousine. No nothing. Shall I write it down for you?'

'Not necessary, sir.' Carrington had been told wrongly that as a civil servant it was important to stand up to a Minister. 'Supposing there's an emergency while you're away,' he suggested in a subdued voice.

'An emergency!' Thunder exploded. 'In that case I would have thought your reaction was obvious. Clearly it isn't. You pass it straight to the PM,' he roared. Then his tone became casual. 'If I have any more of your foolish chatter when I return you will be fired. You may be anyway when I get back. Now get out of my room!'

Alone, he unlocked a cupboard, took out his packed case, left the room. He departed by a back entrance, got into the parked modest Ford car waiting for him, drove off.

Aware that his appearance was well-known, due to the many times he had blasted inerviewers out of the water on TV – a popular act with the public – on his way to Heathrow he parked in a deserted side street. It took him only a moment to perch a Jewish skullcap on his head, concealing his hair. He checked his fake passport in the name of Rosen, then strapped a dark patch over his left eye. Checking himself in the rear-view mirror, he decided he was unrecognizable, drove on to the airport.

After passing through the controls he looked at the monitor. His flight would be leaving in fifteen minutes. His flight to Hamburg.

'I saw Marler while I was walking with our host in the park

behind the mansion,' Tweed remarked as Newman headed back for the hotel. 'I thought it was a shadow, then, as he was vanishing, I recognized his walk.'

'He takes good care of you,' Paula told him.

'The odd thing was I couldn't see any guards at first. A man like that would have guards, I thought. Then I noticed a couple of gardeners. One of them was bent over and his holstered gun was exposed.'

'Incidentally,' Newman called out from behind the wheel, 'Marler and Nield are only a little way behind us in the Opel.'

'How did Rondel's partner strike you? 'Paula asked. 'Would you trust him?'

'I can't say that, one way or the other. We were talking about the present state of chaos. He mentioned strong government being needed. I responded by recalling Hitler, Mussolini and Stalin. His reaction was ambiguous.'

'You mean he approved of those three terrible dictators?'

'In one way he seemed to, but I did say he was ambiguous. He wants me to meet him again. He said he had his headquarters in the far north. That could mean north of Hamburg or even further north. Scandinavia.'

'He doesn't tell you much,' she observed.

'He's a very wily man. Oh, Rondel's real name is Blondel – had a French father, a German mother. Milo explained it was vanity, that Blondel is conscious of his blond hair.'

'So,' she mused, 'I'd better be careful if I meet him again. To call him Rondel, not Blondel. Safer if I just use Victor.'

'You rather like him, don't you?' Tweed suggested.

'He's a charmer.'

'I always did mistrust them. Maybe because I lack charm myself.'

*   *   *

Tweed had lunch in the Condi with Lisa, Paula and Newman. He sensed that Lisa was ill at ease, although she chattered quite animatedly to Paula. They were having lunch when the Brig appeared. He dragged a chair over to their table.

'Mind if I sit with you?'

'You are doing.' Tweed smiled. 'And welcome too. You do look serious.'

Paula thought Tweed was right. The Brig, clad in khaki drill, looked grim. It seemed to her that his hawklike face was even larger, more ferocious than when she'd last seen him. They had reached the coffee stage and the Brig said he'd like some too. He remained oddly silent until coffee had been served.

'You've heard there was a fatal shooting outside here late last night?' he said suddenly.

'We have,' said Tweed.

'I saw the body when I was coming back from a walk. I may have been the first person to see the corpse. Head blown clean off.'

'We know,' Tweed said, annoyed at the brutal description when Paula and Lisa were present.

'I called the police.' He paused. 'I thought what was left of him looked like one of your people.'

'It was.'

'Might be wiser if you went back home. Hamburg has become a dangerous place.'

'Coming from you I find that suggestion surprising. Since you were in the Army you must have seen worse in the way of casualties.' Tweed leaned forward. 'Much worse. So why are you so anxious that we should leave Hamburg?'

'Anxious?' The Brig drank some of his coffee. 'I'm never anxious. But what was lying on the pavement did rather hint that Hamburg is – or may be – not a healthy city for any of you.'

286

'I'm fairly experienced in unhealthy situations,' Tweed said in the same even tone.

'You are. But what about the ladies here?'

'What about them?' snapped Paula. 'I don't wish to sound callous but it goes with the territory.'

'Very dangerous territory,' the Brig told her.

'Just how dangerous?' enquired Tweed. 'Maybe you could tell us, since you seem to be on the inside track?'

'I'm just here on business.' He stood up. 'Must go now . . .'

Newman had been studying their guest. He waited until he had left the Condi.

'That was very odd. The way he spoke it was almost as though he was giving us orders. I didn't like it.'

'I didn't like *him*,' Lisa said. 'Back at Barford Hall down in Sussex he was the soul of courtesy. He's like Dr Jekyll and Mr Hyde. Today Mr Hyde was in control. I'd been in the lounge when I saw you coming in and joined you for lunch. It's sweltering. I'm going up to my room for a shower. Thank you for the lunch – and your company . . .'

'Changing the subject,' Paula began, 'at least Rondel's partner didn't urge us to leave town. Just the opposite, he suggested you must meet again, didn't he, Tweed?'

'Yes, he did. I'm wondering why Mrs France wants to see me. Milo told me she was his chief accountant.'

'Milo?' Paula queried. 'That's the second time you've used that weird name.'

'It's what Rondel's partner suggested I call him.'

'Sounds Balkan,' Newman commented.

'He did say he was from Slovenia. Remote country.'

'And difficult to check someone out coming from there. You think he could be Rhinoceros?'

'My best bet for Rhinoceros is the Brig,' Paula suggested.

*   *   *

287

Gavin Thunder had arrived inside his suite at the Atlantic. Earlier, after disembarking from the flight, he had slipped into a lavatory, locked himself in a cubicle, and removed the skullcap and eyepatch. He had then walked through Passport Control, had stuffed the skullcap and the eyepatch in a rubbish bin. He had never appeared on German TV, nor had his picture been printed in the newspapers, so recognition was unlikely.

He took a taxi to the Atlantic Hotel, registered as A. Charles, was escorted to his suite. Once alone, he checked the time. His visitor should arrive soon. He poured himself a stiff Scotch from the drinks cabinet, looked round, decided that he would dominate the discussion best if he sat in a high-backed chair behind an antique escritoire.

He then decided he would dress in a more formal lightweight suit to emphasize who was in control. He moved quickly, remembered to attach the reverse letter 'E' symbol to the inside of the jacket's lapel. He had just sat down again when there was a heavy hammering on the door. He called out.

'Come.'

Oskar Vernon entered, wearing an orange shirt and a fawn suit. The fact that he wore his jacket unbuttoned at the front emphasized his weight. Thunder stared at his outfit as his visitor closed the door, then surveyed the suite.

'You're pretty conspicuous in that wild shirt,' Thunder observed critically.

'Ah! It is a double bluff. Staying in a hotel, people see me at first. But soon they get used to the sight and I am hardly noticed. A matter of psychology.'

'Sit down, then. We haven't got all day.'

'We have indeed got all the rest of the day if we needed it.'

Oskar was not a man easily intimidated. He had already

noticed how Thunder had positioned himself. He was invited to sit in a low chair placed in front of the desk. He selected another high-backed chair from against the wall, carted it over, shoving the lower chair aside. Sitting down he crossed his long fat legs, gave a beaming smile.

'The problem,' Oskar announced, 'is Tweed. He is here and has based himself in the Four Seasons Hotel, roughly a mile closer in to the city . . .'

'I know that,' Thunder interrupted. 'Delgado phoned me at my home. We have to deal with him – permanently and immediately. We must make preparations . . .'

'They are already in the process of being made.' Oskar's tone was lofty. 'To eliminate him and his team.'

'How many in the team?' Thunder snapped, feeling he was losing control.

'That we don't know, have no idea. But Delgado has twenty men, which should be more than enough to do the job.'

'I would certainly hope so.'

'It will be simple and easy,' Oskar assured him.

'You think so?' Thunder leaned across his desk, lost control. 'Now listen to me, you complacent buffoon. Tweed is very clever, very experienced, very dangerous.' He raised his voice. 'So you make damned sure he doesn't come back alive.'

'You are tense,' Oskar replied calmly. He folded his arms over his ample chest. 'Tension causes a man – or a woman – to make bad mistakes. You must remain calm. Incidentally, they may never find the bodies.'

'That would be the best solution.'

'I thought you would like that.' Oskar gave his beaming smile again. 'And you will never again insult me by using that word "buffoon". Never! You have understood that?'

'I heard you.' Inwardly Thunder was struggling for control. He had to remember he was not back home now. 'So now can we talk about the arrangements?'

289

'I was just about to explain them. You stay in this hotel at all times. You do not go outside. You will travel to your destination, the island of Sylt, by helicopter . . .'

'I never travel in them.'

'You will this time. Or you will not go. It is a large machine which will fly from a remote part of the airport. A taxi will call for you. The driver's name is Thomas. The other four members . . .'

Oskar paused and Thunder was appalled. Surely Oskar wouldn't know about the Elite Club, about who belonged to it?

'Members?' Thunder croaked.

'The other four members of the party will arrive in separate taxis close to the machine. It will fly you to a secret airfield close to Sylt. From there you will board a train which will take you across the embankment to your rendezvous. It could be tomorrow or the day after.'

Oskar stood up, straightened his jacket. Then he replaced his high-backed chair by the wall and put the small chair in front of the desk.

'Is that all?' asked Thunder.

'Isn't it enough?' Oskar enquired and left the suite.

26

Tweed had just returned to his suite with Paula and Newman when someone hammered on the door non-stop. Newman waved the other two back, approached the door with the Smith & Wesson by his side. He opened the door a few inches, then wide.

Pete Nield walked in. He was his normal cool self but Tweed noticed he was fingering his small moustache. That, added to the urgent hammering, told him Nield was excited.

'Take a seat, Pete,' Tweed suggested. 'Relax.'

'Like a glass of nice cold water?' Paula asked him.

'Thanks. Yes, I would. I'm dry as the Sahara.'

He drank the whole glass in two swallows, accepted a refill. He leant back against the couch and grinned.

'I have a little news to report.'

'Now why did I get that idea?' Tweed chaffed him.

'Gavin Thunder has arrived in Hamburg. He's staying at the Atlantic.'

There was a short silence. Newman folded his arms, standing up. Paula sat on a couch, curled her legs underneath her, whistled.

'In a double-length stretch limo,' she said. 'With a flare of trumpets and a band playing.'

'Don't you believe it,' Nield told her. 'He sneaked in like a thief in the night. Comes in an ordinary taxi. Must have paid the driver as the cab was nearing the hotel. Leaves the porter to get his bag, hustles up the steps and he's out of sight.'

'Sure it was him?' queried Newman.

'Bet my pension on it. I was parked in the Opel not far from the hotel entrance. But far enough back to use binoculars. It was him. I've seen him often enough blasting away at an interviewer on TV. Now I'd better get back there – see who else turns up.'

'You've done well,' Tweed said. 'Yes, go back, keep checking.'

'Well, that's some development,' Paula commented.

'The eagles gather,' Tweed said, half to himself, standing on the balcony, gazing into space.

Less than a minute later there was a gentle tapping on the door. When Newman opened it Lisa walked in very quickly. She was holding a folded sheet of paper in her hand.

'You'll never guess what I found slipped under my door. It could have been there a little while. I spent ages in the shower. Here it is.'

She handed Tweed the piece of paper. He unfolded it, took his time studying it. Nothing in his face showed what his reaction was to the contents. They were typed.

Drive to Flensburg tomorrow. You will find important information waiting for you there. Very urgent. Lisa.

He handed it to Paula. While she was reading it Lisa was walking back and forth, couldn't keep still.

'The only thing wrong with that message,' she said, 'is I didn't write it. So why has someone put my name on it?'

'Maybe because the sender doesn't like you,' Tweed suggested. 'But the interesting point is it was typed on the same machine as the earlier message inviting us to assemble at the Turm. The letter "i" jumps on both typed messages.'

'It's a trap,' said Paula, who had handed the paper to Newman.

'Oh, it's a trap all right,' agreed Tweed as he took a map from a drawer. 'If I remember from a trip I made quite a few years ago, the direct route up through Schleswig-Holstein is along autobahn No. 7. Yes, I'm right, it is. And, I have a good memory for routes I've driven along in the past. I can see a lot of it in my mind. The A7 to Flensburg is a very lonely route. Mile upon mile of farmland and nothing else except for the odd dwelling all on its own.'

'Ideal country for an ambush,' Newman observed.

'It is that. But that could be turned to our advantage.'

'You do believe,' Lisa began nervously, 'that message is nothing to do with me?'

'Of course we do,' Tweed said with a smile.

'Then I think I'll go back to my room. I threw on clothes to bring that to you. I need to get dressed properly.' She hesitated. 'I can have dinner with you tonight?'

'Let's make sure nothing else develops. Keep in touch . . .'

Paula, again on a couch with her legs curled under her, was trying to make up her mind. *I can't keep this back any longer,* she decided.

'Now Lisa's gone I have something you ought to know . . .'

They listened in silence as she described her visit to Lisa's room, how she had answered the phone. The voice which had said 'Oskar' before she had broken the connection.

'And,' she concluded, 'while she was here we let slip the idea that maybe we could plan an ambush.'

'Puts a different complexion on a lot of things,' Newman commented grimly. 'We have a spy who knows too much about us.'

The huge underground room, beneath an unoccupied warehouse and alongside the river Elbe, had twenty men

293

of varying nationalities assembled. It was a bleak chamber with an ancient roof constructed of giant beams. The floor was paved with old stones, the sound of seeping water added to the unsettling atmosphere. The water was trickling in between gaps in a massive stone wall which looked as though it had stood there for a hundred years. An uneasy feeling was apparent among the villainous occupants. Perched on a heavy wooden crate Delgado watched them, keeping them in suspense deliberately. Barton broke the eerie silence.

'Don't like this place. Supposing that wall breaks?'

'We drown.'

Delgado grinned wolfishly as he saw Barton's expression. As a method of controlling his brutal gang he was enjoying it. Despite their weird appearance – Slovaks, Croats and men from other parts of the world most Westerners had never heard of – they had all been well trained in the use of weapons. All had been given large sums of money and promised more when they had accomplished the massacre.

'Tomorrow,' Delgado said, 'we do it. Here.'

He pointed with a long thick finger to the map of Schleswig-Holstein pinned to a blackboard beside him. He was pointing to the autobahn which eventually led to Flensburg. Then he glared at Barton and Panko.

'You have the trucks?'

He was referring to four Discovery Land Rovers, vehicles capable of traversing almost any kind of territory.

'They're in the garage you hired,' Barton said sullenly.

'How we know they go up autobahn?' demanded the frisky Panko.

'Is quickest way. They will go.'

'What do we do to them?' Barton asked. 'Like the Turm?'

He was being sarcastic, recalling the fiasco. Delgado

could have smashed his face in. He breathed heavily and then told them.

'We kill all Tweed men. Kill. Kill. Kill. OK?'

There was a growl of approval from the men assembled below him, a growl like that of predatory animals. Several raised their hands in a clawlike gesture.

'What wrong with you, Barton?' Delgado demanded, glaring at his target.

'People outside may hear us.'

'You think this?' Delgado gave his wolfish grin again. 'I ask you, clever Barton. You hear ships' sirens?'

'No.'

'Beyond that wall river Elbe. Ships moving all time. Using sirens. You do not hear? They do not hear us. Idiot!'

Delgado paused. 'Now, tomorrow, this we do . . .'

It was evening when Tweed summoned Marler, Butler and Nield to his suite where they joined Paula and Newman. In his shirt sleeves with the windows wide open, Tweed had the map of Schleswig-Holstein spread out on a large table.

'We've had a mysterious invitation to visit Flensburg tomorrow,' he explained. 'It is a trap. We will walk into their trap. Marler, you will be in charge of the operation to destroy our attackers once and for all. To use a certain phrase, we take no prisoners.'

Paula was startled. She had never heard Tweed issue such an order before. She looked at him as he stood, crouched over the map, arms wide spread. His mood was one of deadly and controlled determination.

'We drive up,' Tweed continued, 'in the cream Mercedes which the enemy has now become accustomed to seeing us use. All except you, Harry. You will leave half an hour later, after we have gone, driving after us up the A7. In the blue Mercedes. You will carry one of the advanced mobile phones – so you can contact Marler if you see something he should know about. You are our distant rearguard.'

'We drive up this direct route, then?' Marler queried. His finger traced the autobahn from the northern outskirts of Hamburg all the way to Flensburg in the far north.

'That's the route.'

'So the distance from here to Flensburg is . . .'

'One hundred and eighty kilometres,' Tweed replied. 'Driving at normal speed, not like a bat out of hell, it takes about two hours to reach Flensburg.'

'Traffic. How much of it?' Marler wanted to know.

'Hardly any – even at this time of year – once we've left Hamburg and its suburbs behind. It's lonely and pretty much deserted.'

'We'll hope they follow us in some kind of convoy. They'll then overtake Harry in his blue Merc and he can warn us they're coming. But they may not do that. They may instead set up an ambush ahead of us.'

'I'll be driving,' Newman remarked.

'If you run into an ambush,' Marler ordered, 'you reverse like mad. If there's a wood close by you back into that. We all then abandon the car *toute-de-suite*.'

'Weapons?' queried Newman.

'Everyone will carry grenades, the more deadly type, tear-gas canisters, automatic rifles, handguns and then there are the three Uzis. One for you, Newman, another for Nield and I'll take the third.'

'I'd like an Uzi,' Harry piped up. 'I'll be coming up behind you, may get there in time to take them in the rear.'

'Agreed. You can have mine. Now, tactics . . .'

It was almost dark when everyone had left the room except for Tweed and Paula. Butler and Nield were going to fetch the rest of the armament to conceal it in the blue Mercedes. Paula checked her watch.

'Doesn't look as though Mrs France is coming. She was due hours ago.'

'She may have been delayed – or not be coming at all. If she does turn up I've warned Keith about her. I shall bring her in at a certain stage – to make sure she isn't fooling us.'

'It struck me Marler has a good grasp of strategy. When he wanted to know the geography of the land on the way to Flensburg and you said flat as a billiard table. He seemed to be happy about that.'

'Because he realizes we shall be fighting a peasant army – even though well-trained. But trained in the mountains of the Balkans or the Tatra Mountains in Slovakia. They are accustomed to having rocks to shoot from behind, very rough country. Exposed out in the open, their training may well be useless.' He paused. 'How do you feel about it?'

'Excited. Now don't worry. I'll be as cold as ice when it really starts. We could have done with Mark Wendover,' she added sorrowfully.

'I talked to Cord Dillon in America when I was alone. He was appalled. But the grim arrangements have to be made. I've also spoken to Kuhlmann. Now the autopsy has taken place, Kuhlmann is arranging for the body to be flown back to the States. Dillon will meet the flight at Dulles Airport.'

The phone rang. Paula answered, then called out to Tweed.

'It's Mrs France. She's downstairs in the lobby. So I've asked her to come up. I'll go and fetch her . . .'

Mrs France entered in her usual fuddle, grasping a folder under her arm. She was waving her hands about and wore a floral dress.

'Oh, Mr Tweed! How can I apologize enough? I am so very sorry to be so late. Quite dreadful behaviour. But

I had no choice. Rondel gave me some work which he insisted I should deal with at once. I told him I was going shopping but he said I could go to a late-opening store. Will you ever forgive me?'

Tweed waited until his plump visitor had run out of breath. Then he seated her on a couch and she placed the folder on a coffee table in front of her. He suggested she might like a drink.

'A brandy and soda?'

'That would be lovely. Really lovely. And so kind of you. The moment I saw you I knew you were a kind man. Such a very kind man.'

Paula poured her a drink. Her hand slipped and she poured more brandy into the glass than she had intended. She smiled as she handed it to her visitor.

'It may be too strong. I made a mistake. I can pour a milder one . . .'

She stopped speaking. Mrs France had swallowed half the glass at one go. Her eyes, behind the atrocious spectacles, sparkled with pleasure.

'Oh, I feel so much better. I had to rush to get here in my VW. But I had to be careful I was not followed.'

'Who would follow you?' Tweed enquired, sitting opposite her.

'The chauffeur. Danzer! He creeps about the house, appears at my side like a ghost. A peculiar man. Not the sort I'd expect to be a chauffeur. A hard man but intelligent.'

'You have something to tell me, to show me?'

'Yes. Something is wrong at the Zurcher Kredit.' She was opening her folder, producing a sheaf of bank statements. 'There is no one in Germany I dare talk to about this.'

'Mrs France.' Tweed stood up. 'I have a close friend over here for twenty-four hours. Would you mind if he joined us?'

'Of course not. If he is a close friend of yours then he can be trusted. That is so important. Trust . . .'

Tweed called Keith Kent, asked him to come along. When he came in, Tweed introduced him.

'This is Mrs France, chief accountant at the Zurcher Kredit. Mrs France, this is Peter, financial director of a company in London.'

'I am pleased to meet you,' Kent said, sitting beside her. 'I may say that anything you tell us will be treated in the strictest confidence.'

'You are a friend of Tweed's, so of course I trust you. Now, I am taking too long.' She spread the statements, a number of which had on them circles in pen. 'These are photocopies you may keep. A huge sum of money has been extracted from important clients' accounts. Then, if you can follow me, the money was wired electronically to a bank in the Bahamas. The strange thing is the money was immediately returned – again wired electronically – back to the Zurcher Kredit in Hamburg. The original wire carried this symbol. That means the transfer was a mistake and must be returned immediately. Which it was. Do you understand?'

'Yes,' Kent said after studying the documents, 'I think I do.'

'Is that technically possible?' Tweed asked.

'Yes, it is,' Kent assured him. 'Not everyone knows how to do it. But I can see that's what happened here.'

'Why on earth would someone take all that trouble?' Tweed wondered.

'It's very mysterious,' Kent agreed. He pondered. 'It is possible that the vital "return immediately" symbol was inserted at the very last moment. Just before transmission.'

'By someone else?' Tweed pressed. 'Rather than by whoever started the movement of the money originally?'

'That is possible. It would require a swift and secret action – to insert the symbol at the last moment.'

'Who at the bank would know about the system, Mrs France?'

'The two partners.' She tapped the rim of her half-full glass against her teeth. 'Of course, Danzer has a large account at the bank.'

'Why mention Danzer?' Tweed enquired.

'Because he has a lot of qualifications. He was once the head accountant at another bank. Then he is an engineer. And he is also an expert on explosives. I overheard that bit.'

'Explosives?' Tweed was taken aback. 'Has he ever used that expertise while in the employ of Rondel and his partner?'

'Not so far as I know.'

She checked her watch, finished off her drink, climbed to her feet.

'I do hope you will excuse me. I must go now to buy something before the late-night store closes. It is my excuse for coming here.' She looked at Kent. 'Please keep those papers for Mr Tweed. Now I *really* must go. Mr Tweed, I am so very grateful to you. I simply must go . . .'

When she had gone Kent went back to his own room, taking the photocopies with him. Tweed later picked up the phone and called Lisa.

'Tweed here. We are leaving early in the morning. Could you pack your things? You can do that in five minutes? Good. Later we'll all have dinner . . .'

'That's a mistake,' said Paula. 'A big mistake, taking her.'

'No, it isn't. Then we can keep an eye on her.'

Paula opened the door cautiously when someone tapped on it. Nield walked in and his manner suggested he was in a hurry.

'First, hours ago I saw Oskar Vernon walk into the Atlantic.'

'Did you see any contact between him and Gavin Thunder?'

'None at all. He arrived a while after Thunder rushed in. But recently another VIP, American, was smuggled in.'

'Smuggled in? What do you mean?'

'Rushed him in via the service elevator. Big tough guards galore. One came up to me, said "Staying long?" I was eating an apple, pretending to read a book. I snapped at him, said I was waiting for my girlfriend, if it was any of his business. He pushed off. Must get back now. May see more . . .'

Tweed wandered out of the suite onto the balcony and Paula followed. It was dark and across the water buildings were illuminated mistily, more like a beautiful painting. On the opposite shore two tall church spires glowed in the illumination while street lamps were reflected in the still water, like small daggers of light. They stood there, admiring the beauty of it all.

'It's like a ghost painting,' Tweed said, half to himself. 'And now we have Gavin Thunder and one of the most powerful men in America slipping into the Atlantic Hotel. On top of that we have Oskar going into the Atlantic not so long after Thunder arrived. You know something. Looking at that wonderful view, which is a bit muddled, I'm wondering if I've got everything the wrong way round, back to front.'

27

Nield was sitting behind the wheel of his Opel when it happened. He had his window open since the heat seemed more torrid than ever. The barrel of the Magnum revolver appeared inside the window. He froze.

'Now get out very slowly. And keep your hands away from any pockets. Otherwise this cannon is likely to take on a life of it own.'

Nield opened the door carefully as the muzzle of the gun retreated a foot or so. He was livid. He recognized who was speaking. The same American who had approached him earlier.

It was only when he stood on the pavement that he realized the guard, clad in civilian clothes, was built like a quarterback. Over six feet tall, his face a fixed mask. Not someone to underestimate.

'Now, buddy, turn so that your back's to me. Again, very slowly. No sudden movements. They make me nervous, trigger-happy.'

Nield revolved in slow motion, stopped when he had his back to the guard. He felt the muzzle rammed into his back. He swore inwardly. No one else appeared to be about and the street, so far as he could see, was deserted. He took a deep breath to cool his anger.

'Next move, buddy, is I'm going to check you. First for weapons. Then for identification. Get it? Because if you don't there'll be one big bang. Don't want you getting brave, do we? The gun is in my right hand and will stay there. Guess I'll use my left hand to check you out. Your girlfriend should have come earlier. Much earlier.'

Nield stood stiffly. His Walther was clamped under the dashboard. He'd grown sloppy, sitting in the car too long, staring at the entrance to the Atlantic. The bastard had crept up behind his car.

'One false move and I'll blow your spine in half.' Another voice. Harry's. Cold as the Arctic. 'This, chum, is an automatic jammed into your back. So maybe you should drop the piece, as I believe you call it, on the pavement. *Now!*'

The gun hit the pavement with a dull *clunk!* Hearing the sound, Nield spun round, stooped quickly, picked up the weapon. He held it close to the American's face. His expression worried the guard. It was so devoid of emotion.

'Now,' Nield began, 'let's get something straight before I blow a hole in your head. You're guarding someone important at the Atlantic. We need to know who he is. Talk.'

'Top secret,' the guard mumbled.

The muzzle of his own gun moved closer to his right eye and he blinked. If anyone knew the devastating result of pulling the trigger it was the guard.

'I'll ask you once more,' Nield continued in the same neutral tone. 'Who did you hustle in, using the freight elevator? We may be on the same mission. We're Special Branch, controlled by New Scotland Yard. You tell us who you're guarding and we'll tell you who we're protecting. Deal? Or shall I pull the trigger? We could always dump you in the lake. It's close enough.'

'Just between us?' The guard licked his lips. 'If my guys get to know it's court martial for me.'

'Just between us. My trigger finger is getting itchy.'

'The Secretary of State. Who are you protecting?'

'Winston Churchill.'

304

Nield stood several paces back from the American who looked furious. He knew Harry was still behind the guard with the Walther pressed into his back. He emptied the huge revolver of bullets, threw them one by one across the road into the park at different angles. The American was appalled.

'How do I explain to my sergeant that I've lost my bullets?'

'Easy. You don't. Surely you can slip into your ammo store and load up again?'

'Guess mebbee I could at that.' The guard took back from Nield his weapon, tucked it down a holster inside his jacket. 'Special Branch? I heard of you guys.'

'The CIA would.'

'That's right . . .'

The guard stopped speaking suddenly. He had given away the organization he belonged to. He walked back to the hotel slowly, taking long strides. When he reached the Atlantic he ran up the steps, disappeared. He hadn't risked looking back once.

'You really can talk on your feet,' Harry said.

'I had to pressure him to make him talk. Now I'm going back to tell Tweed the news. I think he'll be interested in the confirmation.'

'I'll drive you to the Four Seasons, then take over the watch. But I'll have to park in a different place.'

'Very British,' Nield remarked as Harry started the car, 'the way Gavin Thunder sneaked in on his own. Whereas the Secretary of State has a small army to look after his precious hide.'

Nield arrived outside the door to Tweed's suite at the same moment as Paula, who was carrying a coloured brochure.

'I have news for him,' she said.

'I have a little news myself . . .'

305

Tweed, still in his shirt sleeves – the humidity had become even worse – ushered them both inside. Nield drank two glasses of water and sighed with relief.

'We have news,' Paula reported. 'I think Pete should speak first.'

'The American Secretary of State is staying at the Atlantic,' Nield announced.

'So it's all coming together. Paula, you'll recall how this has happened in the past. Suddenly everything accelerates and the pace never lets up until we reach the climax. We are at that stage now.'

He listened while Nield swiftly told him the circumstances under which they had obtained the information. Tweed said nothing but he was frowning as Nield completed his report.

'Pete, do you think that CIA guard will talk when he is with his pals?'

'I bet he won't,' said Paula. 'Not with his career on the line.'

'I agree,' Nield commented. 'Now I'd better get some sleep.'

'Harry also needs some,' Tweed decided. 'Bring him in and then both of you go straight to bed.' When Nield had left he turned to Paula. 'Something on *your* mind?'

'You remember when Lisa was in the clinic and desperately trying to tell us something? *Ham . . . Dan . . . 4S?* Recently we thought she was trying to say "Danzer", the chauffeur. I was going through some brochures I picked up downstairs. Look.'

She held up a coloured brochure. It folded out but she had it closed. On the front were three large letters. DAN. She opened it out and the complete word appeared. DANEMARK.

'The German word for Denmark,' she said. 'I think that was what Lisa was trying to say. There's something significant in Denmark.'

'Better ask her when we're all together in the limo in the morning. You could be right. And Denmark is in the far north from here – Milo said that's where his headquarters are.'

Marler arrived just when Paula had finished speaking. He looked as though he'd just had eight hours' sleep, when actually he hadn't had any. He looked at Tweed.

'You've had time to think over the battle plan we worked out. Any doubts?'

'None. It's a flexible plan, allowing for several different situations. I reckon if it's Delgado who is commanding their attack he may have between fifteen and thirty men. And we only have six.'

'Seven,' Marler corrected him. 'Lisa will be with us and I gave her a Beretta automatic with plenty of ammo. Don't look like that, Tweed. I took her to a shooting gallery here I know of. She scored six bull's-eyes twice, the third time it was five bulls, one inner. Not bad. I was staggered.'

'You're in charge.'

Tweed didn't look at Paula. He knew she would be pulling a sour face, expressing doubt. They then had another visitor. When Paula opened the door Nield came in again.

'More news. I'd just climbed into the Opel Harry had parked in a different position when we saw someone come out of the Atlantic and walk briskly back here. You'll never guess who it was.'

'Come on,' Tweed snapped.

'The Brig. Bernard, Lord Barford.'

'Probably went up to have a drink at a different place.'

'So why was he carrying an old-fashioned briefcase?'

Tweed walked out onto the balcony as Nield left. Paula joined him as he stared into the distance. He drank the rest of the Scotch from a glass he had picked up, lit a cigarette.

'It does look as though I've got it all back to front,' he said eventually. 'And tomorrow – prepare for a day of undiluted hell.'

28

The cream Mercedes was moving along the autobahn but keeping within the speed limit. It had left Hamburg and its suburbs well behind and the wide road ahead was deserted, crossing open country. There had been traffic in the city and for a distance beyond it – huge juggernauts and a few private cars. Now they had the world to themselves.

Newman was behind the wheel of the stretch limo, with Marler beside him. In the middle section Tweed sat behind Newman with Paula next to him, while in the rear Nield was behind Tweed with Lisa alongside him. No one had spoken for some time and there was an atmosphere of tension inside the large car. Paula kept wiping the palms of her hands on paper handkerchiefs so, when the time came, her fingers would not slip as she gripped the butt of her Browning.

The sun glared down on them mercilessly out of a clear blue sky and, despite the air-conditioning, the heat was building up inside the Merc. Paula was gazing out at the endless fields of crops which spread out to the horizon.

'Maize,' said Tweed. 'Scores of acres of it. And because of the heatwave it's almost ready for harvesting. It's really very tall.'

'Is that a point in our favour?' she asked.

'It could be – unless they've laid an ambush ahead of us.'

'It's just what I would have ordered,' Marler called back. 'It could turn the tide for us.'

Newman kept the car moving. One private car passed them coming in the opposite direction, the first they had seen for a while. Then the autobahn ahead was clear again and they ate up more miles.

'How far are we from Flensburg?' Lisa called out.

'A very long way yet. Over an hour's drive, easily,' Tweed replied. 'We're in the middle of nowhere.'

'I've only seen the very occasional farmhouse,' Lisa remarked.

Paula studied the fields again. They came almost up to the edge of the autobahn. The thick plants of maize had large leaves and there were no gaps between them. It was a sea of uninterrupted green. She had never before seen such a continous mass of crops.

'They're taking their time,' Paula said.

'Have patience,' Tweed advised. 'They will come.'

Fifteen minutes behind them Harry was driving steadily up the autobahn in his blue Merc with tinted windows. He couldn't see the cream limo – it was too far ahead of him. He was constantly checking his rear-view mirror, seeing nothing. On the seat beside him rested the Uzi machine pistol. It was fully loaded.

He checked the rear-view mirror once more and stiffened. Out of nowhere a four-wheel drive had appeared. He thought it was a Discovery Land Rover. It was coming like a rocket. Then he saw another vehicle of the same type racing up behind the lead vehicle. Then a third. Then a fourth.

He maintained the same speed. The first vehicle was about to overtake him. He glanced up as it raced past him, saw the man at the wheel, wearing a black beret and a camouflage jacket. Delgado.

The second vehicle passed him. The third. The fourth. All the Land Rovers were crammed with villainous-looking men. Some were holding automatic rifles. He picked up his mobile, called Marler.

'Harry here. Four Land Rovers coming up behind you – packed with armed thugs. They're really moving. Saw Delgado driving the first one . . .'

'Thank you, Harry,' Marler's calm voice responded. 'How far back?'

'Could reach you in five minutes. Even less . . .'

Marler reported Harry's warning to everyone in the car. As he did so, Tweed was studying the topography. To his right the surge of maize. To his left they were close to a rare copse of trees.

'Drive into that copse,' he ordered Newman. 'Leave the car so it can be seen. When we stop everyone dives into that maize field, go deep inside. Three separate sections as we planned . . .'

Paula checked her hands, found they were dry. Inside she was ice-cold. Newman reached the copse, a small wood, backed the limo into it, leaving its bonnet exposed to view from the autobahn. Doors were flung open. The moment they left the car was like entering an inferno, the sun roasting them as though through a burning glass. At different points they plunged into the maize.

Newman and Marler were on the right flank, facing the autobahn. Tweed and Paula were in the centre. Nield and Lisa, a distance away, were on the left flank, again facing the autobahn. A second before she dived in Paula heard, then saw the helicopter, flying in from the direction of Hamburg.

'There's a chopper,' she shouted.

'It's seen us. It will inform Delgado,' Tweed shouted back so everyone heard him.

They shoved their way in among the maize, the crop almost as tall as they were. The heat was intense. They heard the chopper hovering, trying to detect where they were, Paula guessed. Then she heard the racing engines of the Land Rovers, their sudden braking.

They couldn't see, but Delgado drove his vehicle a fair distance up the autobahn beyond where the other three had parked by the cream Merc. Men piled out of the vehicles, rushed into the maize as they saw movement. Tweed had shaken plants to attract their attention. Twenty men pushed their way into the maize, seeking their targets.

Paula heard the chopper move away to the south. It had done its job, had pinpointed the location of Tweed's small team. But it had left too early. Tweed and his team had pushed well back from the autobahn into the maize until they dropped into a small gulley – probably an irrigation ditch to carry water during the rainy season. It gave them cover.

'Here we stand,' Tweed said.

He had just spoken when two of the attackers appeared almost above them. One was wielding a machete, which he swung in a vicious circle. He almost beheaded his companion when he was shot in the chest by Tweed. Paula fired twice at the other man. Both fell sideways, crashing into maize plants, then lay still. In the distance they heard Delgado's voice screaming.

'Kill. Kill. Kill.'

'All right, if that's the way he wants it,' Tweed said.

To their left, well over, Lisa was wiping her damp hands on her jeans when another attacker with a machete saw her, grinned gleefully, hoisted his wepon. Nield shot him in the throat. He went down.

Delgado's men had moved through the maize more quickly than either Marler or Tweed had expected. Marler realized it would soon be close combat, so something had to be done about it. He stood up after taking the pin out

312

of a grenade from his satchel. Four grim-looking men were advancing shoulder to shoulder, rushing forward to overwhelm their opponents. Marler hurled the first grenade, took the pin out of another, hurled it. Three of the men fell down. The fourth had moved sideways, understanding their mistake. The second grenade landed at his feet. He threw his rifle into the air, dropped.

Marler grabbed two tear-gas canisters, threw both where he saw movement in the maize, then hoisted his Armalite. Two men jumped up as though electrocuted, hands clasping their eyes. Marler took swift aim, shot them both. By the side of Lisa, Nield had dropped his Walther, had grabbed hold of his Uzi. Not a moment too soon. Five men were charging *en masse* through the maize in a frontal assault. Nield pressed the trigger. A deadly sweep of bullets cut across them, then back again. All five went down, dead as dodos. An eerie silence fell over the battlefield. No sign of movement, no sound. Paula began to stand up and Tweed grabbed her shoulder, hauled her down again. He was sure it wasn't over.

After the four Land Rovers had got well ahead of him, Harry had pressed his foot down. The Mercedes roared up the autobahn. A few minutes later he saw three Land Rovers parked in front of a small wood, heard the sporadic sound of shooting.

He braked, switched off the engine, grasped the Uzi, left the car. Then he went back, climbed on top of the Merc. Well over to the right he saw five men with automatic rifles crouching down as they moved steadily forward. He realized they were outflanking Tweed and his team, were going to come up behind them.

Harry lowered his head, charged through the maize like a mad bull. When he felt he must be close to the five men he nearly fell into a ditch, stood up briefly, saw the back of the five killers as they began to circle. He crept forward swiftly, making as little noise as possible. When he stood up he was within yards of them. One turned round, saw him, raised his rifle. Harry fired non-stop, swinging his weapon in an arc. All five dropped to the earth, all with several bullets in them. Harry walked forward carefully, stared down at the blood-soaked bodies. He had foiled them.

Then he heard sounds from the autobahn, the sounds of running feet. He began rushing back.

Delgado had been careful to stay at the rear, to have his escape vehicle ready, parked further along the autobahn. He reached the road, ran along it, jumped into the Land Rover. He had reached for the ignition when he heard something. Turning round, he saw Barton and Panko about to jump aboard. He waved them away. Then he saw Barton's automatic, aimed at him point-blank. He swore foully but let them join him. Turning the ignition, he pressed his foot down and the vehicle shot forward like a shell from a gun.

Harry reached the road just in time to see them speeding off. Much too fast for him to bother taking a shot at them.

29

The blue Mercedes was travelling towards Flensburg, a long way north of where the battle in the maize had taken place. The autobahn ahead and behind them was deserted. Butler was in the rear, seated between Nield and Lisa. He held up another sandwich he was about to eat.

'This was a great idea of yours, Lisa. I like to eat regularly when I can.'

'It was a brilliant idea,' Paula called back over her shoulder to Lisa. 'Arranging with the hotel kitchen last night to make up cartons of sandwiches, some fruit and litre bottles of still water.'

'Litres and litres of it,' said Marler, sitting in the front next to Newman who was driving. 'Absolute life-saver in this heat.'

'The chopper's back,' Paula said suddenly. 'It's a fair way off across the fields, doesn't seem interested in us. Looks to be flying on to Flensburg.'

'That's because we're in a blue Merc,' Tweed said. 'Back in Hamburg they got used to us travelling in two cream cars.'

'So you foresaw this might happen,' Paula commented. 'Hence getting one car switched to this blue job.'

'I like to change the image from time to time.'

'Well, at least we can look forward to peace and quiet when we reach Flensburg,' Paula remarked.

'Don't you believe it,' Marler warned. 'You heard Harry

describing the three men who escaped in a Land Rover and headed north. You heard Lisa describing Barton and Panko and Harry agreed he'd seen them jump aboard the vehicle. And he also saw Delgado behind the wheel. My guess is those three make a lethal combination.'

'Except,' Newman objected, 'they wouldn't expect us to go on to Flensburg after the job we did. They'd probably think we skedaddled back to Hamburg.'

'Maybe,' said Tweed. 'Maybe.'

Flensburg. An old town and port where Germany runs out, close to the Danish border. They had hidden the Mercedes in a car park crammed with vehicles. They wandered into the centre of the town. Paula was surprised at the difference in atmosphere from Hamburg. Instead of massive block-like buildings there was a country-town feeling. They entered the Grosse Strasse, a pedestrian-only street. The buildings were only three or four storeys high, the ground floors occupied by small shops. Many had picturesque arched windows and trees, in full leaf, were growing on either side, their trunks protected with wire cages.

Tweed had earlier ordered they should not bunch, that they should walk as couples not too close to each other. Paula, alongside Tweed, breathed in fresh air coming off the nearby fiord which led to the Baltic, or Ostsee – the East Sea as the Germans called it.

'It is peace and quiet,' Paula said. 'There's hardly anyone about. Not even tourists.'

'That's why,' Tweed told her.

He pointed to a poster with a picture of a fair and the name of a place he'd never heard of.

'They've all gone there,' he said. 'All the fun of the fair.'

'They can keep it. Crowds and noise. I like it here. It must look lovely at night. Quite dreamy.'

At intervals they passed a lamp standard with a large glass globe perched on top of it. There were little market stalls but hardly any customers for the wares displayed. Paula looked up as a helicopter droned low overhead. She stared at it. Inside the control cabin the man next to the pilot was peering down through binoculars. Then the machine vanished.

'You know,' she said, 'I meant to mention it earlier, but I'm sure the second chopper that passed us on the way here was not the same machine as the one which tracked us to the maize field. Now I think the same chopper, that is the second one, which was smaller, has just flown over us.'

'Lots of choppers about these days.'

A distance behind them Marler strolled with Newman. He stopped abruptly, his hand grasping the Walther inside his jacket. He was sure he had just seen Barton. When the man turned round he saw he was wrong. He resumed his stroll.

'False alarm,' Newman commented and grinned.

A little way behind them Nield was walking with Lisa. He had too much in one of his pockets. His hand was trying to sort out one thing from another when he pulled out his Walther. It fell down on to the smooth paved area of the pedestrian street. Lisa wandered ahead as he scooped up the gun, slipped it into his hip holster, where it should have been anyway. He looked round to see if anyone had noticed his mistake. The few people who were about were staring into shop windows.

Lisa came to an archway on her right. She walked under it into a small deserted square with an opening beyond. She passed the Tourist Office on her left, continued on and through the second exit. It was very quiet and there were narrow alleys leading off at intervals. She peered into one stone-paved alley, saw another at the end running at right angles, guessed it would lead her back into the Grosse Strasse.

317

She passed an open door in one of the long terrace of old buildings. She heard a noise behind her, then a gloved hand covered her mouth. She kicked back but it was like kicking a tree trunk. She saw another hand holding a cloth appear, caught a whiff, sucked in a deep breath a second before the cloth was pressed over her nose. She'd detected the smell of chloroform. Then the cloth was pressed hard over her face.

Her assailant used one hand to keep the cloth in place, his other to slam the wooden door shut, then to drop a lever which locked it. Both hands and arms were now free to hold her round the waist and she made her body go limp to fool him into believing she was unconscious. Even so, her mind was swimming and she felt she was living in a nightmare as he switched on a feeble light. Forty watts maximum. Then he gripped her under her knees and began climbing what she thought was a narrow staircase. She could hear the clump of his heavy boots on stone steps, which pounded through her head like the tolling of some dreadful bell.

He stopped briefly, used his shoulder to push open another door. Everything seemed to be happening in slow motion. Moving inside a dark room until he switched on another light. She saw the room through a mist. She quietly let out the breath she had held, now he had removed the cloth from her face. Although she had only absorbed a whiff of the foul stuff she was feeling nauseous, addle-headed.

She was vaguely aware that he had sat her down in a chair and she slumped forward more than she need have done. She was terrified and she was furious. He straightened her up so her back leant against the chair. Then he was doing something with her hands, her wrists. She felt the cold metal of handcuffs clamped over her wrists. When he released them she realized there was at least a foot of chain linking one wrist to the other.

318

Now she felt him tying her ankles together with a length of rope. Then he stopped messing about with her. She heard his feet clumping away from her and took the risk. She began to take in long deep breaths.

The next thing she knew he was pouring cold water over her face. It drove away the lingering nausea. She still remained limp. Without warning he slapped the right side of her face a hard blow, then the left side. She let her head swing with the blows. Her terror was giving way to a murderous fury. She opened her eyes and gazed at her captor. It was Delgado.

She wanted to kill him. It was not a momentary emotion. If she ever got the chance she was going to kill him, using whatever method presented itself. She took the opportunity to study her prison. It was an old room built of wood, with two weird wooden doors alongside each other in the wall she was facing. She could see daylight filtering between the joins. What the hell was this place? Doors on the first or second floor? She had been carried up a lot of steps.

Lisa glanced round the room. The only furniture was a large old wooden table which Delgado was standing in front of a few feet away from her. In corners of the room were short lengths of heavy chain, rusted, looking as though it had lain there for years. Another corner was stacked with old canvas sacks. One sack had fallen over, tipping some of its contents on the planked floor. It was caulk.

She recognized the blocks of caulk like these she had once seen in a maritime museum. They had been used years ago to seal up seams in bulwarks with oakum and melted pitch. The door he had carried her through into the room was closed with a wooden bar dropped into place. The room smelled musty and she felt trapped.

Very carefully, she worked her toes inside her shoes to keep and strengthen, the agility in her legs. She stared at

319

Delgado as though he were a filthy creature, which was the way she saw him. He had a dirty black beard and greasy hair. He was wearing a shirt which had once been white, the short sleeves cut off below his wide shoulders, exposing his hairy chest, with denims that carried the traces of spilt food and maybe beer.

'Ready to talk, lady?' he sneered.

'What did you say? I didn't hear,' she lied.

Anything to give her more time to work out how she was going to kill him. He came forward, slapped her face on both sides again. She twisted her head to minimize the force of the blows. Her face was stinging. Then, for the first time, she thought of her companions. They would never find her. She wanted to blow her nose. Just before he had grabbed her she had been going to do that, had her handkerchief in her hand. She sniffled and he mistook her action for fear. He grinned, exposing bad teeth.

'You got plenty worry. I play rough, lady.'

He gave her his dirty grin. Then he came forward, stooped, took out a knife, cut the rope binding her ankles together. He looked up at her.

'No good with legs tied together. Get in way later. After you talk.'

She could have spat in his hideous face. She didn't, since that would be bad tactics, might trigger him off. He stood up, stepped back close to the table. She was careful not to move her freed feet. She wanted him to think she was terrorized, limp as a doll, still not fully recovered from the drug. The chain between the cuffs was wide enough for her to clasp her hands over her knees, working her fingers, making sure they had strength.

'Talk, lady. How many men Tweed have?'

'Most were shot. By your men.'

'Good.' Then suspicion came into his yellowish eyes. He came forward, raised his hairy hand as though to strike her yet again. 'You lie.'

320

'Why should I? What difference, now you've got me?'

He liked that. He grinned. He rubbed his hands together like a man contemplating some great pleasure to come. She read his mind, kept her expression blank. Keep him talking. Buy time.

'I got you,' he said and grinned again. 'Nice for me.'

'All right. What else do you want to know?'

'How many men come with you here Franzburg?'

The ignorant swine couldn't even pronounce 'Flensburg', she thought. How many should she say? Too many might worry him, cause him to attack her and then get away from this strange room.

'Only one. He went to have a long lunch. He was hungry.'

'Only one?' He clenched his right hand into a claw. 'Break his neck. OK?'

'He has a gun.'

'Gun!' Delgado exploded into raucous laughter. He produced a long-bladed knife. 'I cut him. Small pieces. OK?'

'Whatever.'

'Now you talk. Not lie. Nice face.' He gazed at it. 'Not nice if burned. Then you tell truth.'

From a jacket thrown across the end of the large table he extracted a crumpled pack of cigarettes, a match-book. For a moment she was flooded with fear. Then the urge to kill him submerged the fear. She watched as he fumbled with the matches, a cigarette hanging loosely from his cruel lips. He lit the cigarette, puffed at it. The cigarette went out. He wasn't a smoker. And he had made one mistake. Perhaps two.

He lit another cigarette, grinning at her. It went out. He dropped the match-book, bent down, picked it up, stood up. Her legs were already stiffened. She stood up, leapt at him, threw him off balance, toppled him across the table. She hoisted her handcuffed wrists high, brought them down behind his neck, jerked her hands forward, then twisted one wrist over the other. The chain was round his neck, pressing savagely into his throat. She pulled her wrists closer together, digging the chain into his air passage.

She was on top of him, his head pressed down on the table. She held on as he struggled, lifted an arm to reach the knife he had dropped on the table. His fingers touched it, pushed it over the edge. She held on, staring down at him as he choked, his eyes bulging out of his head.

'Bastard!' she shouted. 'Bastard! Bastard!'

The arm that had reached for the knife slumped on the table with a heavy thump. His movements were becoming feeble, pointless. Gritting her teeth, she pulled the chain even tighter. He opened his mouth to scream and no sound emerged. She held on, watching him closely. Spittle appeared on his lips. He made one final effort to heave her off him, but it was a faint muscular movement. His eyes closed and he lay still. She continued to hold the chain tight against his bruised throat where streaks of blood had appeared. Only when she was quite sure he was dead did she lift herself off, standing on the floor. She was breathing heavily with the supreme effort she had made. Then her breathing returned to normal.

'God! What I wouldn't give to have a shower, a complete change of clothes.'

30

'Lisa has gone. She just vanished. I should have kept a closer eye on her. We've got to find her.'

Pete Nield was in the Grosse Strasse. Tweed had never seen him look so panic-stricken. He was staring everywhere, his face distraught.

'Calm down,' said Tweed as they were joined by Paula and Newman. Marler and Harry arrived a moment later. 'Now where was she when you last saw her, Pete?'

'I dropped my Walther out of my pocket. I stooped to get hold of it and out of sight before anyone saw it. When I looked for her again she'd gone. I seem to remember she walked on ahead of me.'

'Harry, Marler, you come with me,' Tweed ordered. 'I want the rest of you to stroll up and down this section. She could have gone into a shop.'

'No, she wouldn't do that,' Nield protested. 'Not without telling me.'

'She walked ahead of you.' Tweed repeated what Nield had recalled. 'So we'll go that way slowly . . .'

He led the way while Harry and Marler followed close behind him. Tweed was walking slowly, trying to reconstruct what could have happened. It did occur to him that Delgado, Barton and Panko could be within the area. He stopped by an archway, looked through it, saw the small square beyond.

'This looks nice. Could have attracted her attention.'

He continued plodding along, frequently looking down at the ground. He passed the Tourist Office, went on through another archway. His old instincts from the days when he had been a detective were coming back. His eyes missed nothing. He'd glanced into the Tourist Office but hadn't expected to see her there.

'She'd be entranced by the beauty of this square,' he said aloud. 'Then she'd arrive here. What's that?'

Just beyond an entrance to an alley he'd seen a spot of colour at the foot of a closed wooden door. He picked up a handkerchief with lace edging and a bluebell in one corner. From his own pocket he took out a replica, complete with a bluebell in a corner. He showed it to Harry.

'In the car I wanted to blow my nose, found I hadn't got a handkerchief. Lisa gave me one. She's in here.' He pushed at the closed door but it was as solid as a rock. 'We've got to get in there and quickly.'

'Leave it to me,' said Harry.

He moved the short distance to the other side of the alley, took a deep breath, then threw his bulk against the wooden door. It gave way, came off the hinges, the whole door falling inwards, exposing a long stone staircase. Tweed walked in over the door, his Walther in his hand, listened. He heard nothing. Harry shone the powerful beam of the torch he'd taken out of his satchel. It illuminated a closed door at the top of the long flight of steps. Tweed ran up them, followed by Harry and Marler.

They made a lot of noise hurrying up the old stone steps. Standing by the door Tweed heard a faint knocking, then an equally faint voice.

'Help me. I can't get out. Help me . . .'

'Stand well back from the door,' Harry shouted. 'As far back as you can . . .'

He had no space to manoeuvre and Tweed was now holding his torch. Harry put his shoulder to the door on the opposite side to the hinges. He leaned into it with all his strength. The hinges held fast but the door split on the other side, flew open. Tweed walked in and Lisa was standing at the far end. She pointed to what lay on the table.

'It's Delgado. I killed him. He was going to torture me. I strangled him with the handcuffs he'd put on my wrists. I found the key in his pocket and freed myself,' she said calmly, too calmly for Tweed's liking.

'Marler,' he said quickly, 'take her back to Paula, then . . . get back here fast . . .'

'This is a problem,' he said to Harry when Marler had escorted Lisa out of the building. He felt Delgado's neck pulse and there wasn't one. 'The problem is someone could notice the smashed door downstairs, come up and find the body. We want to be well clear of Flensburg before that happens.'

'We'd better get rid of the body, then.'

'How?'

Harry was examining the thick canvas sack that had fallen over, spilling caulk. Then he went over to the strange double doors on the far side of the table. He fiddled with a rusty metal catch, carefully opened both doors, looked down.

'This is one of those ancient warehouses,' he told Tweed. 'They used to – ages ago – bring cargo in on horse-drawn wagons and haul it up here for storage.'

Tweed went over, looked down the drop into a deserted street. Then, without hope, he cranked a wheel attached to the wall. It was stiff, but it turned. Rust fell on the floor and outside a hook at the end of a chain began to descend. He stopped turning the wheel.

'Newman brings the car round into this street,' Harry suggested. 'Parks it below here. I can put the body into that sack, attach the hook to it, lower the sack into the boot of the car.'

'It's risky . . .'

'It's more risky leaving the body here . . .'

Three-quarters of an hour later Newman had found his way through the labyrinth of old streets and parked the car below the hoist. In the meantime, Tweed had held open the large sack while Harry thrust the body inside. He then added sections of old chains he'd picked up off the floor.

'Why the chains?' Tweed asked.

'There's a river or a harbour nearby. The chains are to add weight so when we dump the sack in the water it will sink immediately.'

'That won't be easy . . .'

'None of this is easy but we've got to do it . . .'

Marler had explained the situation to Newman, who had co-opted Nield to stand as watchdog in the street with a whistle Harry had produced from his satchel. He would sound the alarm if anyone was approaching. Harry had tied up the top of the sack firmly with lengths of rope lying on the floor. They were now coming to the really nerve-racking part – lowering the sack attached to the hoist's hook down into the open boot of the car below. Tweed had dropped the handcuffs which had imprisoned Lisa into the sack.

Harry kept looking down as he motioned Tweed to operate the hoist. The sack swung out of the open doorway and Tweed cranked the handle. Would the hoist work properly? Would it stick half way, leaving the sack suspended in mid-air? Tweed secretly wished, as he started to crank the handle, that he hadn't agreed to this mad idea. The sack swung out into space. It stayed there. Tweed grabbed the crank handle with both hands, gave it a mighty twist.

Without warning, the handle started turning at high speed and Tweed had to let it go. The sack plunged down, landed just above the boot of the car with a heavy jerk. The sack and contents had ripped free from the now suspended hook. Newman closed the boot quietly, his hands dripping with sweat. Tweed had peered down the long drop, hardly able to believe they had managed it.

Then he started to reverse the handle to haul the chain back up. The handle wouldn't move. Harry, wearing the gloves he'd put on to deal with the body, grabbed hold of the handle, tried to force it to rewind the chain. It wouldn't move an inch.

'We can't leave the chain dangling over the street,' said Tweed.

'We can't do anything else,' Harry told him. 'We just want to get the hell out of here so Newman can drive us to the river, wherever it is. You go down now and get into the car. I'll close the doors.'

'Where are Lisa and Paula?' Tweed asked Marler who had just re-entered the room.

'In a restaurant in the pedestrian street. Lisa's OK now. I'll go and fetch them.'

'Don't say anything about what's in the boot,' Tweed warned.

'And you get out of this damned room,' Harry growled.

When they had gone, he was very careful closing the double doors. He didn't want them giving way and collapsing down into the street. He gave a sigh of relief when he'd closed them. Leaving the room, he stood outside on the top step and pulled open gently the door he'd broken. It was still held by the hinges and swung shut without any trouble. It might be splintered but he couldn't do anything about that. He used his torch to see his way down. The last thing he needed now was a sprained ankle.

As he walked over the flattened street door Marler arrived with Paula and Lisa. Tweed had the car door open for them to get inside. Lisa looked up at the hook at the end of the chain swinging just above her head.

'What's that?'

'Don't ask silly questions,' Harry said quietly. 'Get in the car. We're leaving Flensburg.'

Guided by Tweed, who had the street plan open on his lap, Newman drove round the end of the *hafen* – or harbour – and along Hafendamm. They had entered a new world. The town was across the water from them and there were hardly any buildings on this side of the water. Instead, they had a view of little old houses across the water, houses freshly painted and well looked after.

'The body's in the boot, isn't it?' Lisa suddenly asked.

Tweed turned round and looked at her. She seemed to be her normal self. Her brain was ticking over very well. 'Yes, it is,' he said. 'We lowered it, using an old hoist, into the boot. Inside a canvas sack. Then I couldn't manage to haul the chain back up again, the one you saw hanging over the street.'

'How are you going to get rid of it?'

'Dump it in the harbour, which is why we drove round here.'

'So it will be gone.' She sounded relieved. 'For ever . . .'

A little further on they passed a cluster of fishing craft, then some pleasure boats. No one was about on the barren shore. Newman drove on and then slowed. A group of ramshackle huts and sheds stood just off the road on the harbour side. He stopped behind them, masked from the houses on the distant shore opposite.

'Did you see what I saw?' he asked.

'Yes,' Harry replied. 'A large old rowboat. Ideal for the purpose. Let's get on with it . . .'

At Tweed's suggestion Paula left the car with him and they strolled further along the road. Behind them Lisa followed with Nield. It gave a reason for the car stopping, just in case someone across the water had noticed. Marler had stayed behind to help Newman and Harry.

They first inspected the rowboat, lying behind the first hut.

'Looks pretty ropey,' Newman observed. 'The bottom could fall out.'

'We'll have to risk it,' replied Marler, opening the boot.

Between them they lifted the heavy weight out of the boot, transferred it to the inside of the boat. Harry checked the top of the sack. When the sack had been lowered to within six feet of the boot it had ripped itself away from the hoist's hook. That was when the hoist stopped working. Harry decided the top of the sack was very secure.

'It's a narrow beach,' Newman reported, 'but it's made up of pebbles and stones. They could rip the bottom out before we reach the harbour.'

Harry had found a pair of old rubber boots behind the hut. He managed to get them on. He got back to the others in time to hear Newman's remark.

'So,' he told them, 'we carry the boat to the water. I'll take the stern, one of you takes the port side, the other the starboard. Do let's get on with it.'

In the blazing heat it was a physical ordeal as the three men slowly carried the boat with its cargo towards the water line. When they reached it and the prow was in the harbour, Newman and Marler, still holding on, moved further back. The boat was in the water when Harry, in his boots, kept pushing, then gave it a mighty shove. He nearly went under as the slope shelved steeply. He stepped back quickly, joined the others on the shore as they watched.

'Lord,' said Newman, 'it's keeping going, heading for the far shore. This harbour leads out into the Baltic. There could be a current keeping it moving.'

It was another nerve-racking experience as the boat drifted steadily across the harbour. Newman took out a pair of binoculars and scanned the opposite shore. No one was in view in front of the neat little houses but there was a restaurant with people sitting outside at tables. Luckily a deep blind obscured their view. Not that this would make any difference if the boat reached the shore.

'Sink, you devil. Sink,' Harry growled.

It must have heard him because at that moment, watching the boat through his binoculars, Newman saw the bottom give way, the sack plunging down out of sight. With no bottom, the boat began to break up and soon was no more than shards of driftwood.

'I vote we move off,' said Harry. 'Where has Tweed got to?'

He looked along the road and the four strollers were quite a distance along it. Paula turned round and Harry waved frantically for them to come back fast.

The strollers changed partners for the walk back. Tweed joined Nield while Paula and Lisa followed a distance behind them. Tweed had thought one advantage of walking away was that Lisa wouldn't see what happened to the body. Despite her outward calm he felt sure it would take several days for her to get over her hideous experience with Delgado.

'Lisa,' Paula said quietly, 'there is something I've wanted to ask you and this is a good opportunity. If you don't mind.'

'Ask away.'

'When you were badly concussed and in the clinic back in London you tried to tell us something. You made such an effort I really admired you. What you said was *Ham . . . Dan . . . 4S*. We eventually worked out *Ham* meant Hamburg and *4S* meant the Four Seasons Hotel. But what did *Dan* mean?'

'I said that? I've got no recollection of this.' Lisa looked at Paula. 'I can see the Hamburg bit and the hotel. Even though it's all gone from my memory.'

'Could *Dan* have been Danzer, the chauffeur to one of the partners controlling the Zurcher Kredit Bank?'

'Never heard of Danzer. Chauffeur to which partner? The one with the gold-rimmed spectacles?'

Paula almost missed a step. Lisa had, they thought, no knowledge at all of the partners. And the only time Paula had seen Milo wear gold-rimmed spectacles was when he had paid the bill at the Fischereihafen restaurant down by the Elbe docks. She had to say something.

'I don't know which partner he's chauffeur to – Danzer, I mean. It's a detail.'

But as they walked back all Paula's earlier doubts about Lisa flooded back into her mind. She was badly shaken.

The Sikorsky helicopter was within half an hour of taking off from its remote location at Hamburg's airport. All four VIP passengers were aboard. They were waiting for permission from the control tower to start their flight. The aircraft was luxuriously equipped with leather armchairs and the armed guard had brought down the wide aisle a trolley of every kind of drink imaginable. Gavin Thunder had asked for a stiff brandy.

He was seated next to the American Secretary of State, squat and with a high-domed forehead and a hard face expressing great intelligence. Not surprisingly, the Prime Minister of France and the Deputy Chancellor of Germany sat together several rows ahead.

'You seem nervous, Gavin,' the American remarked.

'I'm not too keen on helicopters.'

'Use them frequently. Useful for short urgent trips in the States. Something important in that case in your lap?'

'Only the complete operational plan.'

Thunder had the executive case open and inside were sheaves of typed papers, clipped together so there were seven copies of the document. He extracted one sheet and the rest came loose from the clip and scattered. He handed the sheet to his colleague.

'That's the important one. The rest are details.'

The American read the close-typed page divided methodically into sections. He was a fast reader.

'I like it. We're thinking on similar lines. You've divided up your country into six control areas, each commanded by a Governor with wide powers. And a secret apparatus of informers to report to the governor any dangerous protesters. Plus a Bill for Parliament which declares martial law without appearing to do so. Who is this Supreme Governor – Brigadier Barford?'

'A very experienced soldier who has also run Special Branch, our equivalent to your FBI. His views coincide with ours.'

'So all we need, which will happen soon, are riots such as the world has never seen. Then the Elite Club will take over. I presume preparations for the outbreak are well advanced. I have been informed they are.'

'Very well advanced. They are an essential element in our plan – to scare the populations of our countries witless to such an extent they will accept anything. Rather like the way Hitler came to power because the German middle classes were desperate to stop the Communists assuming power. I have replaced the man in charge of the earlier riots. A man I have great faith in witnessed them and thought they were feeble. I have put him in sole charge.'

'Anyone I know?'

'I doubt it. A man with a brilliant brain called Oskar Vernon. With Vernon and Brigadier Barford running the operation we cannot fail.'

31

'There's a windmill,' Paula said, 'and the sails are turning.'

'That's because for the first time since we arrived in Germany a wind has blown up,' Tweed told her. 'It's a south wind so it will be warm. Don't expect any relief from the heat.'

'You're so encouraging. Now we're leaving Flensburg behind where are we heading for?'

'As close as we can get to the island of Sylt in the North sea – or the Nordsee as the Germans call it. Sylt is the last in the chain of German Frisian Islands. Immediately north of there and you're in Denmark.'

'Why Sylt?'

'Because I want to see if there are signs of preparations for a rendezvous of international statesmen.'

'You mean politicians, don't you?' suggested Newman behind the wheel of the blue Mercedes. 'There aren't any statesmen these days.'

'I stand – or rather sit – corrected. We're now on Route 199. In a while we move on to small country roads. I'll continue guiding you.'

Paula was staring out on to the sun-scorched countryside. Its character had changed from the monotony of the endless maize crops. It was becoming hilly, with copses of trees often growing by the roadside. More intimate and varied. Again the road was free of any other traffic and she welcomed the atmosphere of peace, the feeling that nothing awful could happen here. Tweed turned round to look at Lisa.

'You really are back to normal, I'd say.'

'Shall I tell him why?' Paula wondered and giggled.

'Go on,' Lisa urged her. 'Why not? It was funny.'

'We went into a restaurant in the Grosse Strasse after the incident,' she explained tactfully. 'We ordered coffee but Lisa was, naturally, dying to have a real wash-down. So she pretended to be ill and I escorted her to the ladies'. Then I stood on guard outside to stop anyone getting in. One unpleasant middle-aged woman tried to push past me. In German I told her the position and said she'd have to find somewhere else. She stormed off.'

'In the meantime,' Lisa took up the story, 'I'd stripped off, used up four flannels washing myself all over. I felt tons better when I'd dried myself even though I had to put on the same clothes.'

'That was a good idea,' said Tweed.

'Oh, there was something else,' Paula recalled, her tone of voice serious. 'I'm sure that while I was standing there looking through the windows into the street I saw someone we know. You're not going to believe this.'

'Try me.'

'I'd bet a lot of money I did see him. Striding down the street. It was his walk which caught my attention. You can always tell a person by his walk.'

'Who, for heaven's sake?' asked the exasperated Tweed.

'The Brig. Bernard Lord Barford.'

'What on earth is that gigantic aqueduct thing?' Paula wondered.

They had travelled quite a distance when the massive structure came into view. At the bottom of a slope leading up to it stood a stationary train.

'That,' Tweed said, 'is the famous Hindenburg Dam which carries the railway – the only access to the island – to Sylt. The train appears to be waiting for something, which is odd.'

'I can hear a machine flying in the air a long way off,' remarked Lisa.

'Bob!' Tweed's instruction was urgent. 'Take this turning to the right. We're nearly on it.'

Newman slowed, swung the car skilfully just in time to drive up a hedge-lined lane which climbed steeply. Ahead of it was the summit of a small hill with a dense copse of trees to the left. On top of a slightly higher hill behind the copse stood a windmill, its sails motionless.

'Keep it moving,' Tweed urged.

'Which way now?' shouted Newman as he came to a fork.

'Take the right turn.'

Paula leaned forward. As far as she could tell this lane would lead close to the windmill. They topped a rise and saw a smaller copse very close to the windmill on the edge of the road.

'Get under those trees, then stop,' Tweed ordered.

'Like me to turn a somersault?' asked Newman.

He drove along a track under the trees, came to a glade, turned the car round so they faced the way they had come but were still sheltered under the trees. They could all now hear the sound of a large aircraft beginning its descent. Tweed grabbed his binoculars, looped them round his neck, dived out of the car. He called out to Paula to bring her camera.

Out in the open they were hidden but perched high up, looking down on the other copse. Paula stared, then whipped up her own binoculars, pressed them against her eyes. She was aiming the lenses at the edge of the larger copse below. She sucked in her breath.

'Look at the edge of those trees down there. A tall man. Not in uniform but I'm sure it was Danzer.'

'Where?' asked Tweed.

'He's gone now. I just caught a fleeting glimpse. He's slipped back out of sight inside the wood.'

'Pretty unlikely that Danzer would be in this part of the world.'

'I *know* it was Danzer,' she said stubbornly. 'The same dark hair, the same figure, the same way of standing very erect, the same way of moving. What more do you want?'

'A photograph would help . . .'

'If we'd damned well got up here earlier I might have been able to take a shot of him with my camera.'

'Cool it,' Newman advised. 'There's a lot more to watch if you'd just look.'

The large helicopter was landing very slowly on a round pad. Then from nowhere a horde of Americans came running to the pad, some in uniform, some in civilian clothes. They were careful to stand well back while the rotors slowed, stopped. Then the wind returned, blowing strongly. Paula could feel its warmth on her face. Now the Americans were moving forward to the landing pad.

'I don't know that the Germans would be pleased at having a load of uniformed American troops on their soil,' Newman remarked. 'Unless they've got permission. And they're all carrying automatic rifles. We'd better stay just where we are.'

Tweed and Paula had their binoculars focused on the machine. A door opened, a staircase, electrically operated, descended. The wind was blowing Lisa's hair all over the place. A man, carrying an executive case, walked gingerly down the steps. As he did so the lid of his case fell open. A paper flew out, was caught by the wind, carried up the hill close to where they stood.

'Get that if you can,' snapped Tweed.

Harry took off. Close to the road they had driven up

was a gully, which looked as though water flowed down it during wet weather. He slid down the gully, out of sight, reached the errant sheet, grabbed it, worked his way back up the gully. He handed it to Tweed who, holding his binoculars with one hand, took the paper with the other, folded it once and put it in his pocket.

'That was Gavin Thunder who lost a sheet from his case. Here, behind him, comes the American Secretary of State, followed by the German Deputy Chancellor and the French Prime Minister. The gang's all here. The Elite Club has arrived.'

'A limo's driven up,' Newman reported, 'to take them to Sylt. At the back of the train there's a ramp the limo can go up to put them aboard the train. Hang on . . .' He paused. 'Before getting into the limo Thunder's giving some instructions to a small stocky man in civvies. He's pointing up this way.'

The limo drove off, heading for the ramp. A crowd of men in boiler jackets and wearing baseball caps had flooded out of nowhere. The stocky civilian went to meet them, pointed up the hill to the wood where Tweed and his team were sheltering from view. Several of the men in boiler suits, accompanied by uniformed troops, started climbing up the hill. At that moment the pilot of the helicopter started up his rotors – checking the engines prior to maintenance. The engine row was deafening.

'They're coming up here,' warned Newman. 'I'm going to back the car out of the other end of this wood. The track goes right through it . . .'

'He's chosen the right moment to move the car,' Paula said, her mouth close to Tweed's ear. 'The roar of the rotors will drown the sound of the engine – and we'd better get moving . . .'

The Americans, with the stocky man in the lead, were coming up the hill fast. Tweed and the others ran deeper

337

into the wood, following the Mercedes which was backing at speed. Reaching the end of the track they emerged into the open, dived inside the car.

'Head for that windmill,' Tweed ordered. 'There's nowhere else to hide,'

Paula agreed. Below the hill a vast flat area spread out, a plain which went on and on and which she felt must be Denmark. To the left they could see the brilliant blue of the North Sea stretching away to a distant horizon.

'That windmill may be occupied,' Newman objected. 'The sails aren't moving and there's a strong wind.'

'Just do it,' ordered Tweed. 'They'll be here in a minute and won't like our presence.'

The windmill, very large, was six-sided and on the ground floor were windows. Tweed imagined they were the living quarters. The tips of the giant motionless sails were suspended only a few feet above the ground – at least two of the sails were in this position. The front door was closed. Tweed thought the mill looked deserted.

'The ground floor is where people live,' he told Paula. 'It also has the machinery which operates the sails in a wind.'

'You sound as though you've been inside one.'

'I have. Once stayed twenty-four hours with a friend in a mill he owned in East Anglia.'

'There's a big shed next to it,' she called out. 'Maybe we could park the car inside.'

'Provided it's empty,' Newman told her.

'Hurry it up,' snapped Tweed, who had glanced back.

There was still no sign of the Americans coming through the wood. But they would appear soon, he felt sure.

'I'm going as fast as I can over this rough ground,' Newman retorted.

It was a race against very little time, if this windmill was to be a refuge. Newman pulled up close to double wooden

338

doors at the end of the shed. Tweed jumped out, followed by Paula. Running up to the heavy wooden front door he looked for a bell push. There wasn't one. He turned the handle, pushed the door inwards and there was a musty smell. Steppping a few paces onto a wooden floor he called out.

'Anyone at home? We're English.'

A brooding silence in the half-light. No sound of movement. And a place like this would creak if occupants started to walk about.

'I think it's empty,' whispered Paula.

'Everyone inside here. Move like lightning,' Tweed shouted from the doorway.

As the team was piling inside Marler opened both doors of the shed. It was empty. He stood aside, motioned to Newman to drive forward. With the Mercedes inside they shut the doors, fastened the crude latch, ran into the mill and Tweed closed the front door.

'Watch yourselves,' he called out. 'There's dangerous machinery in this place.'

'We're going up to the top,' said Nield.

With Harry at his heels, he began cautiously climbing a crude wooden staircase circling the wall of the mill. With no protecting rail on the open side it felt hairy the higher they climbed. Looking down was not a good idea.

'Don't show yourselves by a window,' Tweed called up to them.

Reaching a platform high up, again without a protective rail, Nield peered quickly through a tiny window covered with a net curtain. He nudged Harry.

'See what I see?'

What they had feared had appeared. Rushing into the open, from the end of the track through the wood, were American uniformed soldiers, holstered guns at their hips, led by the stocky civilian. One very big soldier had attracted

Nield's attention. It was the American they had encountered back in Hamburg on the pavement not far from the Atlantic Hotel.

'There's a soldier who could recognize Harry and me,' he called down the long drop.

'Shut up. Keep still. Don't make a sound,' Tweed called up.

He had seen them coming through a ground-floor window covered with a net curtain in need of cleaning. He picked up an old straw hat and crammed it on his head. Paula blinked as she looked at him taking off his jacket so he was in shirt sleeves.

'You look like a peasant.'

'That's the idea.'

'What's that grim-looking thing?'

She was pointing to a huge wooden wheel mounted parallel to the floor with savage-looking teeth at regular intervals and close together. A very thick wooden pole rose up from its centre and ascended vertically until it vanished from sight. Near it were several wooden levers.

'That operates the grinding system if the sails are turned by a wind – once I've pulled one of those levers. Now keep quiet, for heaven's sake. Is everyone hidden?'

He looked round and couldn't see a single member of his team. Near where Tweed had found the hat Paula saw an old pinafore. Obviously a woman had been here at one time. Swiftly she slid off her jeans, wrapped the pinafore round herself. Fortunately it had been used by a larger woman. Tweed peered out of the window again.

They were almost here. The stocky civilian was leading the troop of soldiers as he approached the front door. Tweed opened it before he could reach it. Wearing his straw hat he stepped outside, gave a beaming smile. He began jabbering away non-stop and Paula understood not one word. He seemed to be uttering several words containing the letter 'k.' The stocky man stood still, held up an open folder.

'FBI.'

'What was FBI?' asked Paula, who appeared by Tweed's side.

'You speak English, ma'am?' the FBI man demanded. 'What language was he speaking?' He pointed at Tweed.

'Please?' Paula seemed confused. 'You say?'

'What language was he speaking?' The FBI man worked his thick lips rapidly, as though speaking, pointing again at Tweed.

'Ah!' Paula smiled. 'Speak? Him. He speak the Danish.'

'Jesus!' The FBI man took a step back. 'We could be in Denmark. The border is just north of Sylt. The last goddamn' thing we want is an international incident – considering what is happening on Sylt.'

He had looked up at the huge American soldier by his side as he said this. The soldier stared at Paula with interest and she had trouble maintaining her demure expression. She could see he was aggressive, used to pushing his way in anywhere he chose to.

'I say we search the dump. We gotta find that piece of paper.'

'Yo', said Tweed.

'You've seen a piece of paper blowing round here?' the FBI man asked.

Tweed started his non-stop jabbering again. He waved his arms in a friendly gesture, then opened the palms of both hands and made a pushing motion in the friendliest manner. He kept on jabbering.

'I think he's telling us we ought not to be here,' the FBI man said.

'I say we go in and rip the guts out of the place,' the soldier snarled.

He took two steps forward and Tweed decided more drastic action was needed to get rid of them. His head and

341

wide shoulders were three feet away from the tip of one of
the sails. Tweed jabbered to Paula, disappeared inside the
mill. Paula didn't know what he was going to do but felt
she must stop the soldier entering the mill. She was still
smiling when she spoke.

'He work. Work. You know work?'

'Yeah, baby,' the soldier told her. 'We work but we like
a little fun too.'

Inside the mill Tweed was crouched over the three
wooden levers, trying to remember from his short stay
in East Anglia which was the correct one. He couldn't
remember. Closing his eyes, he reached out with his hand,
grasped a lever, pulled it down.

The wheel began to turn with an aching grind. He
opened his eyes and saw the vertical column also revolving.
Outside the sails, caught by the wind, began moving. The
sail close to the soldier hit his head. He yelled, automatically lifted both hands, felt the sail, grabbed hold of it. He
was lifted off his feet as the sail began its ascent, continued
to rise higher and higher. Peering through the window
Tweed saw what was happening. *Right, you asked for this*,
he thought. He waited, then pushed up the lever he had
pulled down. The wheel and the vertical spindle stopped.
Outside he heard yelling, then laughter. He ran out.

The sail had stopped at its uppermost height. The soldier
was clinging to it, terrified, staring down. Below him the
other soldiers were roaring with laughter, prodding each
other, pointing up at the suspended soldier who was
shouting in fear.

'Get me down. Can't hold on much longer . . .'

Tweed stared up, looked at the FBI man who was
suppressing a smile. He began jabbering, waving his arms,
as though to say why has he gone up there? Tweed
looked amazed, ran back inside. Grasping the lever he
had operated earlier, he rammed it down as far as it would
go, then ran outside.

The sail rocketed downward. The soldier hit the ground with a hard thump, let go and the sail continued its swift climb. Nobody helped him to get up. He was the bully of the unit. He clambered painfully to his feet.

'Need first aid,' he gasped. 'Shoulder broken . . .'

'No, it isn't,' snapped the FBI man. 'For God's sake get him out of here. He's caused enough trouble.'

Two soldiers grabbed hold of the injured man, practically dragged him away towards the wood. As they did so, another man in civilian clothes appeared. He called out to the FBI man.

'The fifth man hasn't come. Sent a message he can't be here.'

'Then forget Number Five.' He turned to Tweed and Paula and for the first time had the ghost of a smile on his hard face.

'OK. We're going. OK?'

'Yes,' said Paula.

They watched the FBI man until he'd disappeared inside the wood. Paula gave a great sigh of relief.

'What was that incredible language you jabbered?'

'Incredible is the word. I've heard Finnish spoken and so I mimicked that. The language of Finland is a trainload of k's – without that letter there is no Finnish. And you put up a remarkable performance, backing me up. Couldn't have done it without you. Let's go inside.'

Tweed adjusted the levers until the sails stopped spinning round at frantic speed and moved normally. They were met by Harry who didn't mince his words.

'We have to get out of here fast. Let me show you something. This mill does have an occupant.'

He carefully opened a large wooden drawer, sliding it open gently. They peered inside. There was a large black box of metal with a muddle of wires protruding.

'That,' Harry told them, 'is a very powerful bomb with magnetic strips to attach it to something. Like a car bomb but much bigger. Then there's something else.' He closed the drawer with the same delicate care, opened a second deep drawer.

'What on earth is that?' Paula wondered.

'It's a mechanic's boiler suit, American model. Plus a baseball cap. I won't take it out again. I had to fold it back the way I'd found it. I also found a pretty fresh half-eaten croissant under that table. Don't you think we ought to move now?'

'If not sooner,' agreed Tweed.

They took trouble leaving the place just as they had found it. The front door to the mill was closed. When Newman had backed the car out of the shed they closed the double doors.

Harry had returned from checking the track through the wood. He reported they couldn't go that way.

'Maintenance men in boiler suits are swarming round the big chopper.'

Inside the car Tweed had been studying the map. Newman looked over his shoulder.

'Any other way out?'

'Yes. Drive ahead and we'll find a little country road which will take us direct to Tonder.'

'And where is Tonder?' asked Lisa.

'Across the border in Denmark. I stayed the night there quite a while ago. It's one of the most attractive villages I've ever seen. The people are nice, too. It's the essence of peace and quiet.'

'Famous last words,' said Newman.

32

The light aircraft with a blue insignia on its tail swooped down to the landing strip at Tonder airfield. Outside a small building Oskar Vernon stood, arms folded, as he watched it land perfectly. Skimming along the ground it came to a halt, propeller slowing, then stopping.

'Barton is a good pilot,' Oskar said to himself, 'but then, he does belong to a flying club in Britain . . .'

Barton, clad in flying gear, carrying his case and helmet, walked across as Panko followed him after dropping agilely from the cabin, also carrying a case. In his usual rough manner Barton said nothing to Vernon as he walked inside the building and checked that it was unoccupied. Panko went straight up to Oskar.

'We arrive good time,' he greeted Oskar.

'You're expected to.'

'We lose Tweed team in Flensburg. Delgado gone.'

'Do keep your trap shut,' snarled Barton who had come out of the small building in time to hear what he'd said. 'I do the reporting.'

'Then report,' Oskar ordered. 'What's all this about "Delgado gone"?'

'He insisted on searching Flensburg on his own. He was hoping to find one of Tweed's women on her own. He planned to torture her to get information. He never came back.'

'Strange. Well, we can't waste time over him. Did you see Tweed in Flensburg?'

345

'Yes,' Barton replied hesitantly. 'Walking on a street with some of his men. We slipped inside an alley so we wouldn't be seen. When we came out they had all gone. We never saw them again.'

'You were supposed to kill them all on the way to Flensburg. I take it from what you've just said you didn't?'

'They outnumbered us heavily,' Barton said quickly. 'We were ambushed and they killed all our men. Only Delgado and the two of us escaped.'

'Really?' Oskar's tone was skeptical. 'Outnumbered. Now you're here, well out of the way as a reserve.' He tapped his mobile phone. 'I expect to hear tomorrow where to send you. I have booked rooms for you at the Hotel Tonderhus. That is my Audi in the road. I'll take you to your hotel.'

'You'll be staying with us?' asked Barton.

'I will not. I'm staying with a Danish friend who knows nothing about my activities. After a meal you can walk round the little town. It's quite pleasant. But get to bed early. Tomorrow will be a day of activity and you will need all your energy. Come on, let's get moving so I can drop you off at the Tonderhus.'

Newman was driving inland and they had a panoramic view over vast flatlands. A short distance from the sea Paula saw a very large concrete structure like a long dyke close to the water.

'What's that?' she asked.

'Tonder,' Tweed explained, 'is known as Capital of the Marshlands, although actually we'd call it a large village. Many years ago there was a great storm and the sea flooded inland. The Danes took measures – they built that dyke to prevent another catastrophe. Like the Dutch, they are good engineers.'

'Looks like the biggest billiard table in the world. It just stretches away to the north as far as the eye can see.'

346

As they drove on, Tweed took out the typed sheet of paper which had flown out of Gavin Thunder's case. Paula was watching him as he read it. His expression became very grim as he folded it and returned it to his pocket.

'Trouble?' she enquired.

'Catastrophe would be a better word. We're facing the most dangerous problem we've ever tackled, plus the fact we're up against incredibly powerful opponents.'

'That's encouraging.'

'I'll explain later.' Tweed was checking his map. 'Bob, we turn left just ahead. Another narrow lane, I expect.'

Soon a number of woods appeared by the side of the lane, blotting out the view of the vast tableland which Tweed mentioned was the westernmost province of Denmark, Jutland. They came to a frontier post where a red-and-white-striped pole stuck up at an angle. There were no guards.

'We're in Denmark now,' Tweed remarked.

'I feel much safer,' said Paula.

'We're fairly close to our destination. We shall have to find a hotel to stay the night. I prefer Hostrups Hotel – it overlooks a large stream. But it may be full up. If it is we'll stay at the Tonderhus.'

'I wonder who Number Five is?' Lisa asked.

'Number Five?' queried Tweed, his mind elsewhere.

'Yes. When those Americans were about to leave the windmill a soldier came running out of the wood – no, it was a civilian – and he called out to the FBI man that the fifth man wasn't coming. So the FBI man told him to forget Number Five.'

'You're right,' agreed Tweed, 'he did. So far there are four of them. Gavin Thunder, the American Secretary of State, the German Deputy Chancellor and the French

Prime Minister at the secret meeting on Sylt. So who could be Number Five?'

'Rhinoceros,' whispered Paula.

Hostrups Hotel was a large three-storey white building of character facing a wide stream with banks of reeds. It was on the edge of Tonder. Tweed got out with Paula to see if they had rooms.

'If they haven't there is always the Tonderhus,' he reminded her.

'I do like the look of this place . . .'

The receptionist, who spoke perfect English, said yes, they did have enough rooms for Tweed's party.

'We would not have normally,' she explained, 'but so many people fly abroad to crazy places like Thailand and St Lucia, wherever that might be. You would like a meal after going up to your rooms?'

'Yes, please,' Paula replied. 'I'm ravenous.'

When the others were brought in, Lisa asked if she could eat later.

'I want to have the longest bath I've ever had.'

Paula understood. After her experience with Delgado Lisa would want to wash every part of herself and change all her clothes. Everybody else voted for dinner.

After being shown to their rooms and having a good wash they trooped down into a large and pleasant dining room. It had an atmosphere of hygienic cleanliness. The meal was first-rate and they ate almost in silence. Paula noticed that Tweed hardly took his eyes off his plate and had a very serious look. He first spoke as they were drinking coffee.

'Do you think you could all stand coming to my room while I talk to you? Good.'

Going upstairs they met Lisa coming down. She wore different clothes and carried a laundry bag.

348

'The food's marvellous,' Paula said.

'Great. I could eat a wild boar. Bet that's not on the menu. Bob, I've put everything I was wearing in this bag and I want to dump it.'

'Give it to me. I'll find somewhere to get rid of it . . .'

In Tweed's room some sat on chairs while others perched on the edge of the double bed. He closed the window, turned, began talking.

'There are three major factors we must never forget. One is the Elite Club now meeting on Sylt. *Plotting* on Sylt would be a better way of putting it. To establish dictatorships in each of their countries. The second factor is the money – a huge sum – missing from the Zurcher Kredit Bank in Hamburg. I have little doubt they plan to use that to finance the enormous number of riot groups they are linking up with. The third factor is the Internet.'

'What about the Internet?' asked Newman.

'Someone has found out how to manipulate it, how to use it to communicate by weird codes with the riot groups. Maybe to inform them when and where to act.'

'Can't do much about that, I'd have thought,' said Nield.

'We'll see. There is a fourth element. Rhinoceros. Who is he? Where does he fit into the picture. Could he be Number Five? There are other factors but I've simplified the horrific danger down to the main ones.'

'Don't see how it all fits in,' said Nield.

'It will. Now I'm going to read extracts from the sheet Gavin Thunder lost from his executive case. It's clear, it's methodical. Gavin has a first-rate brain, unfortunately.' Tweed took the typed sheet from his pocket, unfolded it. 'One, to create iron governments in our countries there must be chaos on such a scale the people will accept any system which brings back peace. That has been arranged – the imminent arrival of chaos everywhere. Two, each country must be divided into large military areas, each area controlled by a strong Governor. Three, any opposition must be ruthlessly and immediately crushed. Special prisons will be established on remote islands off the mainland. In the case of Britain an Enabling Act will be rushed through Parliament overnight, giving the new Government supreme powers. The Governors of the six military areas in Britain will be commanded by a Supreme Governor, Brigadier Bernard, Lord Barford. That's it,' he concluded.

'My God!' gasped Newman. 'It's a dictatorship backed up by martial law. And Barford's in the conspiracy.'

'Now you see how serious the situation is,' Tweed replied. 'I hope you noticed the use of the word "imminent" – so we have very little time left.'

'I'm stunned,' said Paula. 'What next?'

'I am convinced there is another powerful force determined to counter this conspiracy. I expect to be contacted here by a representative from that force at any moment.'

'How will this other force know we are here on Tonder, away from anywhere?' she wondered.

'Because they have known where we were most of the time. I did hear another light aircraft flying a long way behind us when we left the windmill. But we mustn't underestimate Gavin Thunder and his friends. Now, I want this village trawled for sight of the enemy while it's dark. Armed, we split up into three sections of two people. I will take Paula, Newman will accompany Marler, Butler will accompany Nield. We all go in different directions. We do not enter any hotel, bar or restaurant. Too risky. Lisa I will persuade to go to bed. She needs sleep. Any questions?'

There were no questions. Paula was staring at Tweed, impressed and a little taken aback by the forceful way he had spoken. It had created in her a feeling that they were on the eve of war.

★   ★   ★

The three pairs had left the hotel, strolling off in different directions. Tweed chose to walk up Sondergade, which he knew would lead them to the centre of the small town. Then he wandered into narrower side streets. At distant intervals they were illuminated by small lamps but between them were long areas of deep shadow. The side streets were cobbled. It was very silent and not another soul was to be seen.

'Tonder is so beautiful, the houses so quaint,' Paula observed.

Little more than cottages, the buildings were hunched together in terraces. Some had brick walls, some were covered with plaster, painted in different colours – ochre, pink, blue or yellow. Some houses had bay windows on the ground floor and above a window in a steep gable. The silence was total, with only the tread of their feet on the cobbles punctuating it.

'This is Dreamland,' Paula remarked. 'I really can't imagine any danger in a place like this.'

'You know me – I take every precaution. What happened on the autobahn on our way to Flensburg showed how determined the enemy is to wipe us out.'

'We're too far away from them. This is Denmark.'

They followed a complex route. Tweed had obtained a street map from the receptionist and carried it now in his head.

They were walking on through the maze and Paula felt relaxed. Not so Tweed, she noticed. The temperature had dropped and he had his right hand inside his coat pocket, gripping his Walther. Paula secretly thought he was overdoing it. They were approaching the edge of the town when Paula pointed ahead.

'Look. That big red building. It's the Tonderhus, the other hotel you mentioned.'

As they drew closer a tall, well-padded man, smoking a cigar and looking the other way, came out and paused under a lamp. Paula grabbed hold of Tweed at the same moment he slipped an arm round her waist. They dragged each other into a side street.

'I don't believe it,' gasped Paula. 'That was Oskar Vernon.'

'It most certainly was. What were you saying earlier about feeling safe in Denmark?'

'How on earth can he have turned up here?'

As she spoke they were hurrying down the side street, then along into another which led away from the hotel. Paula was breathing heavily, almost in a state of shock.

'It must be a coincidence,' she said eventually.

'You know I don't believe in coincidences.'

'There must come a time,' she argued, 'when we do actually run into a coincidence.'

'And where Oskar is,' Tweed persisted, 'Barton and Panko may not be far away.'

'I wanted to shoot him,' she said wildly.

'No shooting here – if it can possibly be avoided. I think we'd better wend our way back to our hotel.'

'It's such a jewel of a little town,' she protested. 'Not for filthy villains like Oskar.'

'Keep moving – and keep alert. We're not too far from our hotel.'

They crossed the wide stream and the moon appeared. It was reflected in the water and Paula thought it was paradise – paradise lost because of the appearance of that fat pig of a killer. It would have looked so romantic, she thought wistfully. Yes, she could have shot the pig. They re-crossed the stream and were outside their hotel. Tweed hustled her inside. He ordered a brandy for Paula and a glass of wine for himself. They went up to his room where she flopped on a couch. Then she pressed her lips together, sat up straight, took a sip of her brandy.

'Sorry I lost my cool,' she said.

'You didn't. You reacted, grabbing me to get me under

cover. Look at it this way – we saw him but he didn't see us.'

There was a tap on the door. Tweed had his Walther by his side when he unlocked and opened the door a fraction, then opened it wide. Newman came in with Marler. Both men looked very serious.

'We have bad news,' Tweed told them. 'We've just seen Oskar Vernon coming out of the Hotel Tonderhus.'

'We have our own . . .'

Newman broke off. He had just noticed Paula had lost some of her normal high colour. Paula looked up at him, smiled.

'Do go on with what you were saying.'

'All right. We have our own bad news. We spotted Barton and Panko drinking in a bar. They didn't see us.'

'What might be called the last straw,' Paula commented. 'On the other hand, isn't it fortunate we know they're in town?'

'So what do we do now?' Newman enquired.

'I'll tell you what you three do now,' Tweed said cheerfully. 'You all go to bed, get some sleep, then you get up in the morning and we'll have a big breakfast . . .'

Newman and Marler had left and Paula was just about to go to her room when the phone rang. It was the receptionist Tweed found himself speaking to.

'Who did you say is here and wishes to see me?' he asked.

Paula, intrigued, paused before opening the door to leave. Tweed was now asking the receptionist to send the visitor up, that he would meet her at the top of the stairs. He put the phone down, looked at Paula.

'You can stay while I see this lady, if you feel you can hold up.'

'I can hold up all night long if necessary. Who is it?'

'Mrs Gina France, the Zurcher Kredit accountant who came to see us at the Four Seasons. The lady you received

353

that big bunch of hydrangeas from when we were leaving Rondel's mansion on the way to Blankenese. I'm wondering if the representative I said might contact us has arrived.'

'Could be a representative of the enemy,' Paula warned.

33

Paula stared in disbelief as Tweed ushered their visitor into the room. She had been expecting a woman waving her arms about, amiable and fuddled. Instead she saw a hardly recognizable Mrs France.

Wearing flying kit, including flying boots, clad in a helmet, tufts of blue rinse hair protruding, and her huge glasses, she strode briskly into the room, very erect and purposeful. She greeted Paula, accepted Tweed's offer of coffee from a pot just delivered, perched herself on the arm of a chair.

'I had the devil of a job finding you. I tried the Tonderhus Hotel first . . .'

'You didn't ask for us by name?' Tweed queried.

'Heavens, no. I just checked the vehicles in the car park, looking for a blue stretch Mercedes. I found it here.'

'Do you mind if I ask how you knew we were travelling in that car?' Tweed enquired gently as he handed her a cup of coffee.

'I don't mind at all. Right from the moment you left the Four Seasons in Hamburg we knew you had switched from your cream model to the blue one.'

'You said "we" – may I ask who "we" is?'

'Oh, that.' She smiled ruefully, swinging one leather-clad leg. 'I was once married, then had to divorce him when I found I was one of a trio. So I often use "we" – going back to the old days.'

'And how on earth did you find us in Tonder?'

'We'd picked you up again in Flensburg and I tried to follow you from there – Flensburg also has an airfield. I lost you, saw you again heading for Denmark, then you gave me the slip again. So I've been flying all over Jutland until I spotted you heading for Tonder.' She grinned. 'You do move about. This coffee is a life-saver.'

'So what can we do for you?'

'Before I come to that I'd better warn you there are some grim-looking villains in Tonder. I saw two in a bar. Certainly not Danes. I saw them in Hamburg late in the evening after I'd left you to buy something at a department store. If they were there and now they're here – just as you are – I don't think you want to go wandering round late at night.'

'Thanks for the warning.'

'And you should know that all hell is about to break loose – all over the West. I think you might be the only man who can help to stop it.'

'Why,' interjected Paula, 'do you think Tweed is the man?'

'Because we have a vast network of contacts and we have some idea of Herr Tweed's track record. How did we build up this network?' She leaned back and smiled. 'Money talks – but payment of money to the right people gets them talking. If I may say so, we also know that Herr Tweed is a man of complete integrity. Not a lot of that about these days.'

Paula was reeling. She was amazed at Mrs France's command of English – so different from the halting way she had spoken back in Hamburg, but with a foreign accent.

'What would you advise us to do?' she asked.

'Stay here for the night. Then in the morning start driving to Travemünde.' She looked at Tweed. 'Any idea where that is?'

'On the Baltic coast, just east of Lübeck. I have been to both places.'

'It's a bit of a drive from here, but the way you moved from Flensburg I know you'll make it. Just watch out for attacks the whole of the way. I have no doubt Herr Tweed and his team – including your good self – can cope with any trouble.'

'When do you want us to arrive there?' Paula asked.

'Oh, the late afternoon, I would suggest.' She smiled again. 'In any case, considering the distance, it *will* probably be late afternoon when you do reach the waterfront.'

'Why do we go to the waterfront?' Tweed asked.

'I was just coming to that. There is a section of the promenade called Vorderreihe alongside the river Trave. It is only a short walk towards the Ostsee from the police station. Just behind it is a big restaurant with a large open area with tables outside under a canopy. When you get there you sit at a table under the canopy near the promenade. Someone will meet you.'

'Who?' Tweed for the first time became aggressive. 'We are not going all that way without knowing who to expect. You?'

'No. It will be Herr Rondel – whom you have already met.'

'And,' Tweed continued in the same manner, 'what is all this about? What is going on? I need to know what you know.'

'Oh. They said you were tough.' She sat in the chair. 'There is the most dangerous conspiracy since the Second World War being planned – by powerful politicians, including one from your country. At this moment they are meeting secretly on the island of Sylt. They have to be stopped, to be killed. Before it is too late. Please do not tell the partners I have revealed this to you.'

'I knew it already.'

'I should gave guessed.'

'You *are* Milo's chief accountant? I see. I had to be sure. That is your main role in life?'

357

'Not quite.' She drank from the fresh cup of coffee Tweed had poured for her. 'I am a flier, as you now know. But also I am an expert on the Internet. That is important.'

'So,' Tweed said with a smile, 'you are aware that terrorists are using the Internet to send coded messages to trained terrorists all over the world – instructing them where and when to be ready to launch a terrible series of riots?'

'Oh.' Mrs France looked surprised. 'So you know about that.'

'I know a lot more than you probably think I do, Mrs France.'

'Please call me Gina.'

'Well, Gina, is Danzer reliable, trustworthy?'

'Danzer?'

'Oh, come off it, Gina. We're both coming out into the open with each other,' Tweed snapped. 'Now, is Danzer reliable?'

'Totally, Mr Tweed. Milo trusts him completely to succeed in any mission he is sent on.'

'And he's on a mission now. Does he speak English?'

'Perfectly. He spent several years in London training to take his engineering degree.'

'It's your own fault I have to ask you,' he said with a smile. 'When you came to see us at the Four Seasons in Hamburg you went out of your way to tell us a lot about Danzer. I couldn't be sure whether you were warning us against him, or passing on information.'

'It was the latter. At that stage I was nervous about saying too much to you. I will tell him when I get back about our conversation – but only with your permission.'

'Tell him.'

She stood up, after looking at her watch, gave Paula a great big smile.

'I have enjoyed being with you both. I must go now to the airfield and fly back.'

'You can't take off in the dark from that airfield,' protested Tweed who had also stood up.

'Yes, I can. It has lights which can be switched on from inside the hut. Lights which illuminate the landing strip.'

'You're not going to the airfield by yourself at night. Give me a minute . . .'

He went to the phone, called Newman's room, asked if he was still dressed, then told him to come over. He turned round.

'Newman is coming. He will escort you to the airfield, drive you there. He is armed. You will be safe.'

'Oh, you are so kind, so thoughtful . . . But I *insist* on going by myself. I am an independent person.'

She ran to him, kissed him on both cheeks. There were tears in her yellowish eyes. She took out a handkerchief, dabbed under her monstrous glasses.

'Do excuse me. Sometimes I get so emotional.'

'We all do,' said Paula with a smile.

Newman arrived and Tweed explained the position, that as Mrs France had been so determined to leave by herself, he had felt it best to accede to her request.

Oskar walked into the bar in Tonder where Barton and Panko sat drinking. As he sat down he knocked over Barton's glass of beer. An ugly look came over Barton's face.

'Now you can damned well buy me another.'

'Keep your voice down,' Oskar said calmly. 'You have been drinking in here instead of getting some sleep so you are fresh for tomorrow. It would be so easy to replace you. If they ever found it, your body would be floating in the sea.'

Barton was afraid of very little. But as Oskar stared at him with his bulging eyes his face lost colour.

'We haven't been here long . . .' he began.

'You should never have touched alcohol. You will both now come back with me to the hotel and go to bed. I have some instructions to give you while we walk back.'

He looked up as a waitress appeared and began to wipe up the spilt beer. Oskar's whole personality changed as he looked at her with a smile and gave her a Danish banknote.

She stared at it in disbelief, looked at Oskar.

'That is too much for the beer,' she said.

'No, it is not. It includes your tip.'

'That is so generous. I do thank you.'

He had continued gazing at her and she gave him a great big smile. Quite a lot of women liked Oskar. Barton cautiously made his comment when they were walking back along the street.

'That was a huge tip.'

'So everyone is happy – and we do not get talked about. Now tomorrow you follow the blue Mercedes Tweed and his team will drive off from here in.' He gave them the registration number. 'While you were getting sozzled I have been touring the car parks of hotels in this place. They are staying at Hostrups Hotel.'

'We go there now,' said Barton, eager to make up for his mistake. 'We kill them while they sleep?'

Panko was grinning at the prospect. He already had taken out his knife.

'Put that toothpick away, idiot,' stormed Oskar. 'You come with me to the Tonderhus, go to bed. Get up early in the morning. I will drive you to the airfield. There you'll hide until I contact you by mobile phone to warn you they are leaving. You then follow them in your aircraft, however far they go. You keep in touch with me, using your mobile, tell me where they have gone to. Report to me constantly,

360

then I can follow them in my car. We take the decision how to deal with them when they reach their destination. Don't fly too close to their car. Keep your distance. Use your binoculars, Panko. I have no more to say to you.'

'What time do we have breakfast?' Barton asked.

'At six a.m. If they don't serve it at that hour then you go hungry. Might help to keep your wits about you.'

As soon as Newman had departed with Mrs France, Paula tackled Tweed head on. Her way of speaking was emphatic.

'I don't understand what you think you're doing. You threw security and secrecy to the wind when you were talking to Mrs France. You gave her details of the whole conspiracy we have spent time, taken so many risks, to learn about. I think, if you don't mind my saying so, that you've made the one big mistake of your whole career.'

'Really, you think that?' Seated on a couch with a fresh cup of coffee in his hand, Tweed was amused. 'You do, of course,' he said casually, 'have a right to your own opinion.'

'You're not taking me seriously.' She stamped her foot. 'All our lives are at stake.'

'I would agree there.'

'Then why, in heaven's name, did you do it?' she demanded.

'Because at long last I have sorted out the negative destructive forces from the positive ones who are on our side, invisible though they may have been so far.'

'You have?'

She was taken aback. She sat down in a chair facing him, bewildered.

'I don't understand,' she said.

'You must have noticed the extraordinary change in Mrs

361

France's personality. And in her appearance and manner. How would you describe it?'

'Well, when we saw her twice in Hamburg she was a nice but fuddled lady, almost like a flower-seller behind a market stall. I felt it difficult to believe she was chief accountant at Zurcher Kredit. Do you think I'm barmy?'

'No. Your impression of her then is not far off mine. But what about her now?'

'I was staggered. Hardly seemed like the same woman. She struck me as incredibly competent with an amazing range of talents. I can now see she'd be a top accountant. But she's also a flier and I think she does have an incredible grasp of the Internet. Her manner was so businesslike, so forceful. She even seemed slimmer in her flying kit.'

'So what are you worrying about?'

'The fact that you provided her with so much information, were so frank and open with her.'

'That was because I decided she was on the side of the positive forces. I'm not bad at deciding who is trustworthy. She is trustworthy. That was why I asked her about Danzer. What she said was further confirmation for me that she was telling the truth. That and other things.'

'Sorry I blew my top. I got it all wrong.'

'We all do at times,' Tweed told her. 'I know I do. But now we are in great danger. If I were in the enemy's shoes I'd make a supreme effort to get rid of us permanently, quickly.'

'Any particular reason for fearing that?'

'Yes.' Tweed finished his cup of coffee. 'The fact that they have Brig, Lord Barford on their side. I think he planned the attack on us off the autobahn. While it was going on I had the feeling a military mind was behind it. That encircling movement by five men aiming at taking us in the rear. They could have got us if Harry hadn't turned up with his Uzi at the last moment, seen what they were up to.'

'So you think we'll face another attack?'

'I'm certain of it. And it may be more difficult to defeat.'

Inselende was a large remote house located on the western coast of the island of Sylt. It had two sections with thatched roofs linked together by a circular section in the centre. In English the name meant 'island's end'. Surrounded by a moorland, it was close to where sandy cliffs dropped sheer into the North Sea – an ideal location for a top secret meeting.

It was well guarded. At strategic points FBI men with automatic weapons crouched out of sight in the heather. Uniformed troops patrolled the outside of the house and at the beginning of the only road leading to it roadblocks had been set up.

Further precautions had been taken. Although it would have taken climbers like flies to ascend the cliffs offshore, American patrol boats equipped with machine-guns cruised a short distance from the cliffs.

In addition, helicopter gunships with searchlights flew over the house and the surrounding areas. The beams of the searchlights swivelled constantly in search of any intruders. The President himself could have stayed there safely.

Inside *Inselende* a long meeting of the four participants – without aides – had just broken up for dinner. One man did not join them. Gavin Thunder had ushered Lord Barford into a small soundproofed room where they could consult on their own.

'I have very bad news,' Barford began. 'Despite all our efforts Tweed and his team are still on the loose.'

'I thought you'd planned to wipe them out,' snapped

the disturbed Thunder. 'I know Tweed's reputation, his many successes in the past. He is the one man who could throw a very big spanner in our works.'

'I agree,' said Barford. 'I also know him well. We have to make a supreme effort to destroy him – before he destroys us. And time is short.'

'And I suppose you have no idea where he is,' Thunder commented sarcastically.

'He is at this moment in Tonder.'

'Where the hell is that?'

'Not so far from where we are sitting. On the mainland. A small town just across the border in Denmark.'

'Are you sure?' Thunder pressed. 'How do you know?'

'Because I am well organized. An hour or so ago I had a call from Barton. He informed me Tweed and his team are in Tonder. I even know the name of the hotel where they are spending the night. Hostrups Hotel.'

'Why was it Barton who phoned you and not Oskar?'

'Because Oskar likes to play it close to his chest, to take the credit. Mind you, I have no doubt Oskar has prepared a fresh attack.'

'I thought it was Oskar who planned the attack on the autobahn to Flensburg, which was a total fiasco.'

Barford thought it wiser not to reveal that he had drawn up the plan for that assault. Thunder was not a man who easily forgave mistakes.

'No, it was Delgado who planned the tactics. I met Delgado in Flensburg and he told me Tweed was in the city. Then he vanished with his whole team.'

'I don't like this.' Thunder had stood up to go to the drinks cabinet. He brought back two glasses of brandy, sat down again.

'I don't like it at all,' he rasped. 'Tweed flying all over North Germany. Appearing first in Hamburg, then in Flensburg and now just across the Danish border. He's up to something. The Americans do have the Secret Reserve

364

here but they aren't really needed. We have more guards than we need.'

Barford took another gulp of his double brandy. He was worried. The Secret Reserve was a small group of highly trained men nominally attached to the Secret Service which guarded the President. But they had a lot of independence. He'd heard they were used to liquidate awkward men – or women – whose activities were inconvenient to the US government. He'd even heard they had been responsible for a fatal 'accident' which had ended in the death of a Senator. And they would not be under his control.

'A bit drastic,' he suggested. 'I've heard about the methods they use. They don't even waste time getting rid of the bodies.'

'I have decided.' Thunder stood up again after draining his glass. 'I'll have a quiet word with the Secretary of State. I'm sure he'll agree to loan them to us.'

'If you're sure this is a good idea.'

'Damnit!' Thunder smashed his glass on the table. 'Tweed has to be eliminated. The Secret Reserve – seven of them – will do the job. They are utterly ruthless. They can travel in jeeps from the motor pool on the mainland. Tweed will be no match for men like that.'

34

Tweed was still up, studying the complex route from Tonder to distant Travemünde. Some instinct was making him look for alternative routes in case they ran into something. Someone tapped on his door and when he opened it Paula, fully dressed, walked in.

'Am I a nuisance?' she asked.

'You're never a nuisance. Sit down. Like some coffee?'

'No, thank you. I'll never sleep. It looks from the pot as though you've been drinking it by the litre.'

'Helps me to concentrate. What brought you here?' Tweed asked.

'I've been thinking about this journey to Travemünde. Could it be a trap?'

'Yes, it could. But to clean up this business we have to take the risk.'

'It isn't that I mistrust Gina,' Paula commented. 'I've come to the conclusion that you're right.'

'It's my old cocoon theory.'

'Cocoon?' she asked, puzzled.

'Well, everyone lives inside a cocoon. Their daily life, the way they think, react. Many live in a small cocoon. They go to work by the same train each day, sit at the same desk, their only thoughts concerned with their job – and their family, if they have one. They're not interested in what goes on in the wider world. Fair enough, if that rather enclosed life – cocoon – satisfies them. Others live inside a larger cocoon – men or women running big businesses, generals who command large forces, who need to know many parts of the world because they may find themselves sent anywhere there is a crisis. When I'm talking to somebody – like Mrs France – I'm trying to gauge the size of their cocoon.'

'And Mrs France's is?'

'A very large cocoon indeed. The world is her oyster. She has a wide outlook – searching for huge missing sums of money in the biggest bank in the world, tracking and recording secret coded instructions being sent via the Internet, dealing with two remarkable men. And she has ethics, is trustworthy. If our trip to Travemünde is a trap it is so because someone else has set the trap.'

'That's a thought.'

'Incidentally, I've decided everyone must be up and ready to leave by 6.30 a.m. Don't ask me why – I could only say sixth sense. I've called everyone else and luckily didn't wake anyone up. I think it could be quite a day.'

'I'd better go . . .' Paula yawned. 'I need the shut-eye. Is Lisa coming with us?'

'Yes. We can hardly leave her here.'

She told him about the incident when Lisa had mentioned a man with gold-rimmed glasses as one of the partners.

'How could she know that?' she concluded.

'That fits in too with the picture I am forming of the two massive forces ranged against each other. I won't explain now. You get off to bed.'

Paula turned at the door before opening it, waved her finger at him. 'You need sleep too, so I expect you to get to bed as soon as I've left.'

She threw him a kiss and was gone. Tweed took off his glasses, rubbed his eyes. She had a point, he decided.

*　　*　　*

At *Inselende* Barford had eaten dinner with the FBI section guarding the house. He had sat next to the head man whom he had found intelligent and interesting. They were alone now, drinking coffee. Cordell, the FBI chief, seemed in no hurry to leave.

'I find it a strain,' he admitted, 'protecting the Secretary of State and the other three VIPs. I wish the meeting had taken place back home in familiar surroundings.'

Cordell was a man of medium height, well built and very fit. He had a tough face but a warm smile which appeared occasionally. He seemed to have taken to the Brig. He showed no sign of being in a hurry to leave the table.

'It will soon be over,' Barford told him. 'How many more days?'

'They're vague about that. For security reasons. Three or four more days is the official version. My bet is we'll be out of here in one or two days.' He paused, lit a cigarette. 'I hear they're using the Special Reserve to go after some poor bastards.'

'They are. You don't sound enthusiastic.'

'I'm not. That bunch of thugs. They do things we'd never dream of doing. I heard of one case where their target was a banker who wasn't cooperating. Two men did the job. They had checked his routine and he never varied from it. Came out to lunch at exactly the same time. So one thug goes into the bank wearing dark glasses – they always wear dark glasses. He hung around for a few minutes. His pal waited outside. The banker appears, starts to walk out of the bank, reaches the door. The Special Reserve man inside shoot. him in the back. At the same moment the thug outside shoots him in the head. They go down to the sidewalk, step into the waiting getaway car and they're gone. We would never use methods like that. It's cold-blooded murder.' Cordell paused. 'I'm sure you won't pass on to anyone what I've just said – for obvious reasons.'

'Not to a soul on earth. I promise you.'

'I'd better go outside now and check the situation . . .'

The Brig lingered for a few minutes, then walked out of the dining room. Outside in the corridor he almost collided with Gavin Thunder.

'Dinner's over. We talked a lot. Everyone in agreement. Very satisfactory.'

'Could we have another private word?'

'Why not? We'll go back to the room where we talked before.'

Once inside the room Thunder headed for the drinks cabinet, came back with two glasses and a bottle of brandy. Barford thanked him but refused a further drink. Thunder poured himself a large tot, was in a jubilant mood.

'Here's to the success of our great enterprise.' He raised his glass, then noticed the Brig's expression. 'You don't look too happy.'

'I'm not happy at all about using the Special Reserve. I don't approve of it.'

'Don't approve of it!' Thunder had raised his voice. 'You know something? I wasn't aware that your approval was a factor we have to consider. The decision is taken. I want you to accompany them in the boat which will take them to the mainland tomorrow, to see them off in the three jeeps they will travel in, wish them luck, for God's sake.'

'I will accompany them in the boat. But I stress that I do not approve. I'm asking you to cancel the operation.'

'Cancel it! You know something, Bernard,' Thunder rapped out nastily, 'you're not yet Supreme Governor of the military areas Britain will be divided into.'

'I am aware of that.'

'My dear Bernard . . .' Thunder's mood changed abruptly, became very friendly. '. . . No one blames you for not wiping out Tweed. He's a cunning devil. You have been labouring under a lot of strain and stress. This I understand. Two of the Special Reserve, incidentally,

370

are British – they were in the SAS. They came to the States, adopted American nationality, were recruited into the Special Reserve. That ought to make you feel better about the whole operation.'

'I'm exhausted. I think I'll go to bed.'

'Do that. You'll feel so much better in the morning.'

When Barford had left, Thunder sipped at his brandy. He had always had a flair for talking people round to his point of view.

Tweed was still up, sitting at a desk with his doodle pad, long after Mrs France had come and gone, followed later by Paula's visit. He had added Mrs France to his pad, with a circle round her. He had drawn a line linking Lisa with Mrs France. The vast mosaic was becoming clearer to him. His mobile phone started buzzing. He swore, picked it up.

'Yes?'

'Mr Tweed?'

'Yes. Who it it?'

'You will be in mortal danger tomorrow. Lucky to survive.'

The voice sounded like that of a woman, or of someone talking with a sweet in their mouth and speaking with a silk handkerchief over the phone.

'Thanks a lot,' Tweed said.

'This is serious. Seven professional killers in three jeeps will follow your car. At the right tactical moment they will kill all of you. They are trained assassins.'

'Where are they based?'

Tweed had decided this had better be taken seriously. The phone clicked, went dead. Who the devil could that have been, he asked himself, relaxing back in his chair. Too many people had his mobile phone number. But there had been something disturbing about the warning. He wished he could call Harry, but had no intention of waking him up at this hour, despite the fact Harry hardly ever seemed to sleep.

As though in answer to his wish there was a tapping at his door. When he opened it, his Walther in his hand, Harry, fully dressed, walked in.

'Thought you'd still be up. Wanted to discuss tactics for today's expedition.'

'You should be getting some sleep.'

'Sleep dulls the brain.'

Tweed offered him coffee or an alcoholic drink. Harry refused both. He just wanted to get on with it, to work out tactics. Tweed decided to tell him about the strange warning call he'd received. Harry, sitting forward in a chair, listened.

'You take it seriously?' he asked when Tweed had concluded.

'At first I thought it was a bit of psychological warfare, to rattle me. Then I recalled how specific the caller had been. Seven men, three jeeps. I am taking it seriously. On the way we have to look for somewhere we can use as a fortress-like position. Somewhere they have to come in and attack us while we're entrenched.'

'Got myself a motorbike,' Harry said tersely.

'How on earth did you get that in Tonder at the dead of night?'

'I was prowling round, looking for trouble – any sign of the enemy. Came across this chap oiling his machine in front of a garage. Asked him how much. Thought I was joking, so he names a price. Double what it's worth. I said yes. A Dane, I think, but spoke good English. I hauled out a wad of marks, did a quick calculation, gave him the money and rode off on it.'

'You never cease to amaze me.'

'Sometimes I amaze myself,' Harry replied, making a rare joke. 'Point is, I could follow the car – then at other times overtake and ride ahead of you. Call me your scout.'

'That improves our situation enormously. I was worried that again we'd all be crammed in one car.'

'Like to go now. Want to soup up the engine a bit. Six in the morning.' He turned at the door. 'Oh, I'll have the Uzi with me . . .'

Tweed decided it was time to take a shower, then get into bed. As he switched out the light and rested his head on the pillow, his brain was still hurtling over various questions to which he didn't know the answers.

Who was Number Five – the man referred to in the exchange between the FBI agent at the windmill and the man who had run out of the wood? Was the dire warning he'd received on his mobile to frighten or in deadly earnest? Who could have called him, using his mobile number? It all went back to Monica, who had insisted once that it should be given to key people. She'd shown him the list and reluctantly he'd let her go ahead. But he was so tired he couldn't recall all the names on that list. Who was Rhinoceros?

His brain suddenly switched off and he fell into a deep sleep.

In the middle of the night Oskar was woken by the buzzing of his mobile phone. Swearing, he switched on his bedside light, picked up the phone.

'Yes? Who the hell is it at this hour?'

'Gavin Thunder. And when you are addressing me I like some polite acknowledgement of who I am.'

'You're Gavin Thunder.'

Oskar was in no mood to be conciliatory, to kowtow. Not if it had been the President in the Oval Office.

'I'm emphasizing the importance of not losing Tweed. I'm sure he will leave Tonder in the morning. You must tail him. Now do you understand my order?'

'Already dealt with. Barton and Panko will follow him from the air . . .'

Oskar switched off the mobile. Thunder was a man given to issuing the same order three times. He'd better damn well take a sleeping pill, Oskar thought, switched out the light and fell fast asleep.

Early in the morning he knocked on Barton's door. No reply. He tried the handle, walked in. No one there. Bed left like a rubbish dump. Nothing in the bathroom. Then he noticed the absence of a case. He went downstairs to enquire at reception about his two friends.

'They had asked for packed breakfasts and a flask of coffee to be ready very early. They left the hotel some time ago.' The receptionist stood straighter. 'They said you would be settling their bill.'

'And so I will . . .'

Oskar went into the dining room and deliberately had a leisurely full English breakfast. He had been up very late – or very early – and still felt sleepy. He drank two large glasses of orange juice and they seemed to start to get him going. He paid the bill, went upstairs to pack.

An hour earlier, just after dawn, Barton and Panko had left for the airfield. Not wishing to have Oskar chauffeuring them to the airfield, Barton had bribed the porter to drive them there. They travelled in an old Skoda which rasped and groaned but got them to their destination. As the car drove off, Barton approached the light aircraft.

It was surprisingly cool in broad daylight. A hint of mist like a flimsy tablecloth hung above the trees. That would go quickly when the sun climbed higher. Barton, thickset and muscular, scanned the deserted airfield. Holding a .455 Colt in his large right hand he crept up to the hut. He liked the weapon. It was self-loading and the magazine carried seven rounds.

Barton was a cautious killer. He checked out everything. He had once stalked a man for ten weeks before completing the job. He turned the handle of the hut's door slowly, then threw the door open and dived inside, swinging his automatic in all directions. The place was empty. He had thought it would be but he never took a chance.

Panko, who had carried both their bags from the Skoda, stood watching this performance from a distance. To him it was all unnecessary. He waited while Barton walked over to the plane. The previous evening, when they had left the machine, he had shut the door and attached a piece of sticky tape near the bottom, covering the edge of the door and a small part of the fuselage. The tape was still there but was curling up a fraction. Sticky tape did that in the sort of heat they'd endured the evening before. He removed it, opened the door, climbed inside, sat behind the pilot's controls.

Panko followed him, hoisting the two bags inside, climbing in after them, securing the two cases. He sat next to Barton. He guessed that his chief was glad to be rid of Oskar and have his independence again. Barton reached to turn on the machine. His hand froze in mid-air.

Glancing around, he had noticed a small black object tucked under the pedal, an object that shouldn't have been there. He took a small torch out of his pocket, bent down, examined the object with the aid of his torch beam. He straightened up, looked at his companion.

'Isn't it time we took off?' Panko grumbled impatiently.

'Oh, we'd take off all right when my foot pressed that pedal. Take off about a hundred feet into the air in small pieces. Someone during the night put a bomb on board . . .'

'A bomb!'

Panko had opened the door, dropped to the ground, fled at top speed until he was behind a wide tree trunk. Barton grinned without any mirth. It suited him that Panko had run like a scared rabbit. Now he could concentrate.

He had seen on the Internet how to make a bomb. So had someone else. It was a crude device but it would have detonated. Remembering the Internet programme which had also showed how to dismantle such a device, he looked for the switch. Behind the bomb a small red light was glowing. Taking a deep breath, he pressed the switch. The red light went out.

Several minutes later he climbed out carefully, holding the black box which had wires protruding at different angles. He carried it into the wood, hid it gently under a tangle of undergrowth, returned to the plane.

'You can come out now, Gutsy,' he called. 'The bomb is no longer on board.'

Panko slouched forward slowly, hesitantly. An ugly look came over Barton's tough face. He pulled out the Colt, aimed it as he shouted.

'Move faster or I'll shoot you.'

Panko ran. Barton was again behind the controls as Panko climbed aboard, shut the door. Barton glanced at him with an expression of disgust.

'You know something?' he began. 'There are people who would thank God I was the pilot.'

'You do great job. You great pilot. You best pilot flying in world. You great.'

'Don't overdo it,' Barton growled as he reached to switch on the engine. He paused. 'What I want to know is, who planted that bomb? When I find out whoever it was, he's going to die. Die very slowly . . .'

The propeller started whirring, built up power. The aircraft moved forward, left the ground well before it reached the end of the airstrip, gained height. Barton's plan was to fly a distance from Tonder, keeping south until he observed Tweed's blue Mercedes on the move. He was convinced the car would leave Denmark, heading south into Germany. Then all they had to do was keep their distance, follow it to its destination. He wouldn't contact Thunder to tell him where it went to. They could do the job themselves, wipe out Tweed and his team and earn another load of money.

35

Who was Mr Blue, as he was known in Britain and the States, or M. Bleu in France and Herr Blau in Germany? Tweed woke in the morning and blinked. He realized the questions had been surging through his mind while he slept.

He checked the time, forced himself out of bed, had a shower, shaved, got dressed. He packed in less than five minutes – he could pack faster than Paula. It came from years ago when he'd had to pack and leave in minutes to save his life.

Downstairs he found everyone else having breakfast in the dining room, except for Harry. He had just ordered full English when they all heard the gentle purring of a motorcycle pulling up outside. Harry, carrying a crash helmet and pulling off gloves, bounded into the room, sat down.

'I'll have the lot,' he told the waitress.

'Where on earth did you get hold of that machine?' Paula asked.

Harry told the story, making a joke of it. Then went on to explain how he'd just persuaded a garage proprietor to open up so he could get the tank filled with fuel.

'The Danes wake early,' he concluded.

'Not that early,' Nield objected. 'How did you persuade him? Half strangle the poor blighter? Knowing you, I guess you did.'

'And the crash helmet?' Tweed enquired.

'Bought that last night off the chap who sold me the bike.' He looked at Tweed. 'Hadn't you better explain the tactics?'

Tweed explained that Harry would be both advance guard and rearguard at a distance from the car. Then, for the benefit of the others, apart from Harry, he told them about the grim warning he'd received over his mobile in the night. He said he'd decided to take it very seriously.

'And I thought it was going to be a joyride,' Newman commented humorously. 'Instead it sounds as though the enemy is revving up.'

'Seems to me they always know where we are,' Lisa chimed in.

'Yes, they do,' Paula replied, giving her a look.

'We must be prepared for a really violent assault,' Tweed warned.

'Well,' Paula added on a more cheerful note, 'I arranged last night for cartons of food and fruit to be prepared for all of us. Plus umpteen litre bottles of water.'

'Maybe it will be a picnic after all,' Lisa suggested.

'It could be,' Tweed agreed. 'We mustn't let fear dominate our outlook. That could be our opponent's aim . . .'

Breakfast over, Tweed spread a map on the table. For Newman's sake he indicated the route they would follow to Travemünde. Even more important, he showed Harry, who said it seemed pretty straightforward.

'It's anything but that,' Tweed told him. 'A lot of country lanes – and we purposely cross over the autobahn at this point and continue on secondary roads . . .'

They could feel the heat starting to build up as they settled into the blue Mercedes. Everyone sat in the positions they'd occupied the previous day. Newman was behind the wheel with Marler alongside him. In the second row Tweed sat with Paula while behind them the rearmost seats were occupied by Nield and Lisa. It struck Paula that Nield was beginning to get very attached to Lisa.

Harry, astride his motorcycle, drove off first. Paula looked out of the window as they passed over the stream where a man was fishing. She'd like to have stayed longer and felt quite nostalgic about leaving Tonder.

Then the town was behind them and Tweed carefully kept an eye on the map open on his lap, navigating for Newman. They were soon out in open undulating country with copses of trees here and there. Paula looked ahead as Harry disappeared over a rise.

'What has Harry got in that big pannier?' she wanted to know.

'An Uzi,' Tweed replied. 'Plenty of firepower. Nield has the second one and Lisa the third. Because they're in the back. Now, everyone, I want you to keep an eye open for a fortress.'

'I haven't seen a castle anywhere,' Lisa pointed out. 'What do we need one for?'

'They do seem a bit spare on the ground,' Tweed admitted. 'I want a topographical area where we can hold an enemy off and make him come at us so we can see him clearly.'

'You'll be lucky,' said Marler.

On the mainland, opposite Sylt, out of sight of the railway, three jeeps were drawn up, one behind the other. Seven men in camouflage jackets stood waiting, holding automatic rifles.

Gavin Thunder appeared, accompanied by Brig. Lord Barford who had reluctantly agreed to join him. Apart from anything else, he was worried that the two ex-SAS men might be soldiers he had had attached to his forces during the Gulf War.

'That's Ed Miller, the leader,' Thunder whispered to Barford.

The American he was referring to, wearing a camouflage jacket like his men, was six feet three tall, wide-shouldered, with prematurely white hair and a face that might have been carved out of rock. Barford studied him and couldn't detect even a trace of humanity in that face.

'He was in the Marines,' Thunder whispered again. 'A born leader.'

A born killer, Barford thought to himself. A man who really enjoys his work and drives his men ruthlessly. Casualties to him would be all in the day's work. Ice-cold eyes glared at him but Barford held his murderous gaze and it was Miller who looked away.

'Which are the two ex-SAS men?' Barford asked.

Miller had heard him and gave a grin like a viper. He swung round to face his troops. They all stood stiffly to attention. Miller stared at them for over a minute and not a man moved an eyelash. When Miller gave the command his voice was a harsh grating bark, more savage than that of a British CSM.

'The two Brits take two paces forward.'

Two men did so and stood like frozen statues. Barford had to admit to himself the discipline was impressive. What worried him was the personality of Ed Miller. Clearly he ruled with cold-blooded fear. Barford was relieved to realize he had never seen the two men before. He had thought it most unlikely that he would have, but had wanted to be sure.

'Never seen either of them,' he said quietly to Thunder.

Again Miller picked up every word. He paused, keeping them standing there. Never for a second did he stop letting them know who was in command. Another minute passed and the two men remained motionless.

'Now take two paces back!' Miller roared.

He swung round, facing Thunder and Barford. He ignored Barford. His words were addressed directly to Thunder.

'Sir, time is passing. Permission to start the mission. We shall take no prisoners.'

'That's no way to fight,' snapped Barford, unable to contain his indignation.

Miller stared at him and again Barford stared back with a grim expression. This eye-to-eye confrontation lasted longer. He thought there was a hint of contempt in Miller's gaze.

'Sir,' Miller eventually said, switching his gaze to Thunder. 'Permission to start the mission,' he demanded again.

'Get moving, then,' said Thunder.

He turned to say something to Barford but the Brig was walking away. His back was erect and men who had known him in earlier times would have recognized the stiff, deliberate walk. Rare for him, he was in a state of controlled rage and cursed himself for agreeing to accompany Thunder. He was further disturbed by some of the decisions which had been taken at the meetings on Sylt. They had been far more extreme than he had expected. Above all, he felt responsible for certain events to which he had agreed. At least he had warned Tweed with his anonymous phone call in the middle of the night.

Miller organized his small convoy of jeeps very swiftly. He would travel in the leading jeep alongside the driver. A third man sat behind them. He put his deputy, Ollie, in the last jeep which would bring up the rear. Ollie would drive and have a second man with him. In the middle jeep he put two men. Then he walked up and down, holding a map as he barked orders.

'We space out. One hundred yards between my jeep

and the one behind me. The third jeep, Ollie, travels a quarter-mile behind jeep Number Two.'

'The route, sir?' asked Ollie.

'Thunder and I spent some time last night working out Tweed's likely plan. We decided that from Tonder he'll travel south over the border from Denmark, heading back into Germany. His smart way out of Tonder is down Route Five. Near a dump called Klixbull he'll turn on to Route 199, heading for the autobahn. We want to intercept him before he reaches Klixbull!'

'Any idea when he'll leave Tonder?' Ollie asked.

'If you'll keep your flapping trap shut I was just coming to that.' Miller checked his watch. 'At this early hour I doubt he's left Tonder.'

'What transport will he be using?' enquired Ollie.

'You know something, Ollie?' Miller paused and stared at his deputy. 'I'm thinkin' of puttin' a piece of sticky tape over that big mouth of yours.'

Ollie was a big man, not quite as tall as Miller. Inwardly he shuddered as Miller gazed at him. He was getting this all wrong. *Don't say another word*, he told himself. Once, during an exercise in the Carolinas, a man had talked back to Miller. One slamming fist from Miller had broken the culprit's jaw. Miller had waited until the exercise was over, hours later, before he'd called for an ambulance.

'Tweed is a nut,' Miller announced. 'He's travelling with his whole team in one blue stretch Mercedes. We locate him on a road, drive across country on either side, wait for him to pass. Ollie, you'll come up behind and punch holes in his arse. Got it? Then get aboard, get the show on the road . . .'

Newman was driving down Route Six, the direct way out of Tonder, and they were now back on German soil. Harry had sped past them on his motorcycle and vanished from view. Paula looked out of the window as they progressed through rolling, hilly country.

'There's a light aircraft way over to our left,' she reported. 'It seems to be flying on a parallel course to ours.'

'Lots of light aircraft in this part of the world,' said Tweed. 'Quite a few airstrips around here.'

'Where are we heading for?' she asked.

'Towards a place I've never heard of. Klixbull.'

'We're definitely not using the autobahn?'

'We are not. We cut across country to another place I have never heard of. Bad Bramstedt. Then we're on Route 206 which takes us over the autobahn and we go on, heading for Lübeck, which we bypass. Then we head straight up to Travemünde.'

'Sounds as though it's not too far, then.'

'It's a long way. Newman, have you got the air-conditioning turned full up? It's getting pretty warm in here.'

'Turned up as high as it will go. And Harry is on his way back. He'll let us know if it's clear ahead.'

He lowered his window, slowed the car to a crawl, then stopped as Harry reached them. Harry hauled off his crash helmet, took out a handkerchief and wiped sweat off his face.

'Road ahead seems clear,' he reported. 'Very quiet, in fact. No traffic at all. Now I'm checking behind you, make sure nothing is sneaking up. Back soon . . .'

'He's got a hot job,' Paula said sympathetically. 'And that aircraft has turned this way, is coming closer.'

'On its way back to its airfield after a morning's flight before it gets too hot,' Tweed said and returned to checking his map.

Barton had used his high-powered binoculars to scan the

385

car. He was pretty sure he could see Tweed sitting in the middle row. He used his mobile to call Oskar's number. He tried three times and made no contact.

'To hell with him,' he snapped. 'I'm calling Thunder. He can pass on the info to the Special Reserve lot.'

'No sign of them,' Panko observed.

'They'll be coming.'

He had trouble contacting Thunder. He persisted and after a few minutes got through.

'Is that Gavin Thunder? Good. Barton here. Tweed's blue Mercedes has left Denmark. Is now proceeding down Route Seven. Estimate he's halfway down it. Leave you to tell your people. Tried to contact Oskar but got no reply. I am continuing to check their progress . . .'

He turned the plane away from Route Seven so as not to draw attention to himself. He grinned brutally at Panko.

'That will earn me credit with Thunder. Meantime we'll keep well back. We'll have a bird's-eye view from up here – see the lot in that car turned into mincemeat.'

'They've survived so far.'

'Your trouble, Panko, is you think some people can go on surviving for ever. You're about to get a demonstration of what happens when the road runs out for them.'

Harry was on top of them before he knew they were anywhere near him. He rode at speed over the crest of a hill and nearly ran into two jeeps, with barely a hundred yards between them. A huge white-haired man in camouflage was sitting next to the driver. Harry waved as he roared past the first jeep.

They were still some distance from Tweed's car so he continued on past the second jeep, waving again. But where was the third one? Tweed had said there would be three jeeps. He had to find the other one. He hammered his foot down. Soon he'd have to turn back to warn Tweed what was coming up behind him.

He never saw what happened to the third jeep because the road kept curving. The third jeep, under Ollie's command, was some distance behind the other two. Ollie was smoking a cigar when, in the wing mirror, he saw a black car coming up behind them. He realized immediately the black car could be a problem.

'Slow down,' he ordered his driver. 'Then put the jeep at right angles across the road. That will block this car coming up on our rear.'

The driver acted swiftly. Stopping, he was on the wrong side of the road. He reversed, turning the jeep until it was at right angles to oncoming traffic, making it impossible for another vehicle to pass them. Ollie hauled out his automatic from his holster, stood up, facing backwards, waited.

The black car was slowing down. He could vaguely see that the driver wore a wide-brimmed straw hat. Couldn't stand the heat. It stopped about thirty feet away. Ollie tucked the automatic inside the belt behind his back. He held up both hands, formed a crude blower.

'Road blocked. Military exercise. Go back the way you came.'

The driver acknowledged the command with a brief salute. He began to turn his car. The driver of the jeep reached for his own automatic. Ollie nudged him hard.

'Leave it alone. I'll take him. We don't want a witness. I'm waiting until he's positioned at right angles to us – then I can get him point-blank.'

The driver, who had his window down, was obviously not skilled at backing and turning. First, the engine stopped. The driver got it going again. He started backing slowly, ended up with his first try slant-wise across the road.

'Friggin' amateur,' Ollie rasped. 'Going to take him all

387

day. The next time he should make it, then I'll make it.'

The jeep's driver was standing beside Ollie now, watching with his arms folded. Again sweat was dripping off his hands. He wiped them dry on his trousers. The black car's engine stopped again. The driver waved a hand out of the window as though to say *I'm not too good at this*.

'He'll get there in the—' Ollie began.

He never completed his sentence. The barrel of a Heckler & Koch sub-machine gun appeared over the edge of the open window. There was a devilish stutter of bullets which neither Ollie nor his driver heard. A spray of bullets hit both of them, a non-stop spray. Ollie fell dead at the same moment as his driver collapsed.

The driver of the black car climbed out, ran to the jeep. His gloved hands lifted one body, then the other, hurling both into the ditch by the roadside. He then reached in, put the gear into reverse, switched on the engine and jumped back. The jeep backed into the ditch, partly covering both of the bodies.

The driver ran back to his car, dived behind the wheel. With great skill, he swiftly turned the black car to face the way it had come. It sped back, vanished over the crest of a hill barely a minute before Harry arrived on his motorcycle, slowed, stopped, stared.

He dropped the strut to stabilize his machine, swung off the saddle, grabbed his Uzi out of the pannier, advanced slowly. As he stood on the edge of the ditch, looking down, he had no doubt both the men in camouflage jackets, half hidden under the jeep, were dead. He could see enough of their bullet-ridden bodies to be sure of that.

Two of the men who had been sent to kill Tweed were, instead, themselves lifeless. But why was the jeep lying on top of them? Harry decided he had no time to puzzle over what could have happened. He had to get back to Tweed in time to warn him two jeeps were coming up behind him. He shoved the Uzi back into the pannier, started the machine, turned it and twisted the throttle savagely until he was moving almost like a shell from a gun. He hoped to God he'd get there in time.

36

It struck Harry before he saw the two jeeps that he could be recognized. He pulled up, took off his crash helmet – a very risky act – and put on wraparound dark glasses to make himself look different. He could have used the glasses earlier. The glare of the sun had bothered him on the way out.

He built up speed again, still worried that he would be too late. He crested a slight rise and there ahead of him were the two remaining jeeps. He twisted the throttle still harder. At least the blue Mercedes was not yet in sight.

Aboard the first jeep, Miller saw him coming in the rear-view mirror. He frowned, which is to say his face became even more brutal. He glanced at the driver who had also spotted the motorcycle in his wing mirror.

'Don't like this,' Miller told him. 'We had a motorcyclist pass us going the other way not so long ago.'

'Not the same guy,' the driver replied. 'No crash helmet and he's wearing dark glasses.'

'I don't take any chances,' Miller snapped in his deep throaty voice. 'I'm going to let him have it.'

He had hauled his Magnum .357 halfway out of his holster when the motorcycle whipped past and was out of range. Miller stared in amazement.

'Must be doing over ninety. He'll come off, kill himself, do the job for us . . .'

Harry dropped out of sight over and down the other

side of another slight rise. No more than a mile ahead he saw Tweed's blue Mercedes. He twisted the throttle like he was trying to choke it, flew like the wind. He was sweating when he pulled up alongside the Mercedes, which had stopped for him.

'Any second,' he warned Tweed breathlessly, 'two jeeps with five men in camouflage, coming up behind you . . .'

'Bob,' Tweed ordered immediately, 'back up to that big sand quarry we just passed. That's our fortress. Drive into it.' Moments earlier they had driven past a wide entrance in the hedge leading to a very wide and high semi-circular mound with sand walls. It was like a large amphitheatre and had obviously been abandoned. A chain system with large metal buckets dangling from it ran from the summit of the mound to a rusting muddle of sheds on the right. As the car left the road Tweed glanced back, saw two jeeps cresting the low rise.

'Drive the car near the sand wall,' Marler ordered. 'I want it well back. Harry,' he shouted through the window, 'ride up the right side of the mound but keep out of sight.'

'Take the high ground,' Harry shouted back and rode off.

'The jeeps are close,' Tweed warned.

Newman drove at speed across the base of the amphitheatre, the wheels sending up spurts of sand. He swung the car round to face the way they had come, close to the base of the cliff of sand, which had to be over a hundred feet high.

Marler pointed as he issued more orders. 'I'll be in that cave on the right, halfway up the cliff. Newman, you take Lisa and shelter behind that pile of sand on the left. Tweed, Nield, Paula, get up inside the cave on the left. Keep your ruddy heads down. Everybody take weapons. Go!'

Nield grabbed hold of the heavy satchel Harry had left

in the rear section, threw back the flap. Lisa grasped one of the grenades. Paula leaned over as Harry held up the satchel, avoided the smoke canisters, clutched an explosive grenade.

'Hurry up!' Tweed snapped.

Marler, yards from the car, holding his Armalite rifle, called out to them.

'As far as we can, protect the car . . .'

Doors were flung open, hauled shut as they piled out of the car, ran towards their allocated positions. Tweed, despite being older, led the way, reached the sand wall which here sloped up to the cave, scrambled up with Paula behind him. He looked back, saw Paula had slipped, fallen down. He ran down again, grasped her arm, hauled her to her feet and she was scrambling up with him while Nield, now above them, peered down anxiously from the cave.

'You OK?' Tweed asked.

'I'm OK,' Paula replied.

She was still clutching in her right hand the grenade that most people would have dropped when they fell. They joined Nield. Tweed glanced round, surprised and relieved at what he saw. For some reason a mechanical digger had at some time scooped out a waist-high cave with plenty of space for the three of them.

'Kneel or sit,' he told them, 'but remain invisible.'

He could hear the two jeeps coming now, moving slowly. He looked round the amphitheatre. Marler had in seconds seen how he could place them all so they covered the whole area. With Harry somewhere near the summit they could command a view of every approach. Now all they could do was wait. They had found his fortress.

Miller had ordered his driver to move slowly, to stop before he came level with the entrance. The hedge was just high enough to conceal the jeeps. He jumped to the ground, a machine pistol slung over his shoulder, a grenade in his right hand.

He peered round the end of the hedge for a fraction of a second, took in the topography, went back to where his four men stood crouched below the hedge. He grinned viciously.

'We've got them. The friggin' fools are in a trap with no way out. You know I favour a mass rush against the enemy, but that won't do here. First we have to locate them, then we split up and stalk them, kill them off one by one.'

'Can you see them?' asked his driver.

'Not one. But when they open fire they'll give away their positions. Then we have them. I've seen their car. I'm going to smash that to bits first.'

He took the pin out of the grenade. Rushing forward, he stood at the entrance to the quarry, right arm well back, about to hurl the grenade at the car. Harry, perched high up on the mound, opened up with his Uzi. A rain of bullets landed inches from Miller's feet. The grenade he was holding would detonate any second. As he jumped back from the entrance he threw the grenade across the opposite side of the road, way beyond the hedge bordering it, dropped flat. The grenade exploded, hurled up masses of soil and shattered crops from the field. Miller returned to the jeeps.

'You didn't get the car,' his driver said tactlessly.

'I got something more important. The location of their machine-gunner. He's high up on the right-hand ridge. So that's one to stalk.'

Miller's back was streaming with perspiration. He hadn't felt it necessary to tell his men he was the only one wearing a bulletproof flak jacket under his camouflage tunic. It would have restricted the movements of most men, but Miller was so brawny it didn't worry him. And it gave him added protection.

'We've got to make them all show themselves,' he

decided. 'So the best way to do that is to give them something to shoot at. Brad,' he said to his driver, 'I want you to rev up your engine, hammering it until you can shoot past the entrance like a rocket to the moon. I'll be behind that hedge opposite so I can see where they all are.'

'With that machine-gunner firing like hell at me?'

'Up to you to be going so fast he misses you,' Miller told him callously. 'When you've gone past the entrance you keep going maybe half a mile, then turn round, rev up again and come back here.'

'Why not just put me in a shooting gallery?'

'What?' Miller bunched his huge fist. 'Any more talk like that and you'll lose a lot of teeth.'

He would have done it, too. But he was short of men and still was wondering what had happened to Jeep Number Three which should have arrived by now with two more men. He took a quick decision.

'Our jeeps are too close to them. I want them moved back a few yards. Don't start the engines, put the gears in reverse and we'll push them back manually . . .'

From his position, perched halfway up the ridge, Harry looked straight down on Marler, huddled in his cave, gripping his Armalite. Harry had reacted fast when Miller appeared in the entrance, but not quite fast enough. If he'd elevated the barrel of his sub-machine gun only an inch higher he'd have ripped the tall, white-haired brute to pieces.

He thought of crawling higher up until he reached the summit of the quarry. But Marler had ordered him to occupy this position. Also, Harry was sprawled inside a shallow gully and liked the position. He'd stay where he was. From where he lay he couldn't see the jeeps which had parked behind the hedge. Couldn't be helped.

Oddly enough, Marler had been thinking he'd left a dangerous loophole in his dispositions. He had no one on the other ridge opposite. Anyone crawling up that side could eventually look straight down on Tweed's cave and Newman's sandpile barrier. But Marler knew it was always a mistake to start moving men once he had them in position. Often a fatal mistake. He'd leave well alone.

Earlier, before Harry had let loose his burst of gun-fire, he had called Tweed on his mobile. Reception was very clear.

'Tweed? Harry here. Should have told you I found the third rearguard jeep well back from the other two. Found it toppled in a ditch with two of the bastards underneath it, shot to pieces, riddled with bullets.'

'That's strange . . .'

'It means now there are seven of us against five of them. So the odds are in our favour.'

'*Don't get complacent*,' Tweed warned emphatically. 'They are trained soldiers, trained killers.'

From his position inside the cave, with Nield and Paula, he could look down and clearly see Newman and Lisa crouched behind their sandpile. Lisa appeared to be talking to him.

'Nothing's happening,' she whispered to Newman. 'What can they be up to? It's so quiet. Pity Harry didn't get that white-haired tree trunk of a man.'

'It could be deliberate tactics,' Newman told her. 'They wait and do nothing. A kind of psychological warfare to play on our nerves, make us do something silly. Patience is the answer.'

It was ironic that the bull-at-gate Miller had never thought of this move. That if he waited long enough and did nothing it could shred their nerves.

'You're thirsty, aren't you?' Newman asked Lisa, who had just licked her lips.

'I'm OK.'

'So it's a good job when we left the car I grabbed a bottle of water. Here you are. Just take a few sips,' he warned. 'That may have to last us for quite a while.'

He felt sorry for the others who had no water at all. The sun was scorching down on them. If the thugs had any sense they'd wait until their opposition was in a pretty bad way. He refused a drink when Lisa offered him the bottle. He was determined to hold out as long as he could in this heat.

Above them Nield deliberately didn't watch them sipping the water. He just hoped the bastards would get on with it – whatever they were planning.

Miller had helped his four men push the jeeps further back than a few yards under cover of the hedge. He'd decided Tweed might get clever, hurl a few grenades over the hedge to destroy the jeeps.

While his driver was revving up his engine to make a Le Mans rush past the entrance to the quarry, Miller found a hole in the hedge on the far side of the road. Once through to the field he moved cautiously. Crawling on all fours, he passed another hole, but it wasn't opposite the entrance. He kept moving.

He'd have liked to take off the flak jacket under his camouflage tunic but he didn't for a moment consider doing that. He had a pair of binoculars looped over his neck, hanging down his back. They kept hammering into his body but he ignored the pounding as sweat streamed down him. Then he found another hole – facing opposite to the middle of the entrance. A perfect look-out point. He took out a handkerchief and settled down to wait.

He used the handkerchief to wipe neck and hands. When he'd finished, the handkerchief was sodden. He could hear his driver still revving up. *He's scared.* When

397

you're scared you start moving – at least, that was what Miller always did.

Head hunched well down, the driver released the brake. If he was lucky he'd be past the entrance before Tweed's men realised what was happening. As he hurtled past, Harry's machine-gun opened up, peppered the side of the jeep with a hail of bullets. Newman had fired non-stop with the automatic rifle he had grabbed on leaving their car. Lisa stood up, threw a grenade. It landed yards behind the jeep, detonating without touching the vehicle, which was gone.

Miller, who had crawled well back from the hole into the field, was jubilant, smiled savagely. Lisa's grenade, raining shrapnel into the road and the field beyond, hadn't reached Miller, who congratulated himself on crawling far enough back.

He was jubilant because he'd located their positions. The machine-gunner was still in the same place, huddled down halfway up the right-hand slope of the quarry. Another man, maybe with others, was crouched behind a sandpile on the left. And a woman was also behind the same sandpile. What he didn't know was that Marler, with his Armalite and variety of other weapons, was hidden in his cave on the right-hand side of the quarry.

Waiting for his driver to make his second run, coming back, Miller hauled his binoculars round to his chest, raised them to his eyes, focused on each location. He saw nothing. No sign of movement or men. They were keeping their heads down.

While doing this, Miller's brain was planning his strategy for the final killing assault. He was now pretty sure they had left a loophole in their defences. There had been no sign of anyone located on the left-hand ridge – to complement the machine-gunner on the other ridge. He might scale that ridge himself.

Then he heard his driver coming back. He jammed his binoculars into his eyes, ready to swivel them from location to location. The jeep seemed to be returning even faster. Miller guessed the grenade had put the wind up him.

Marler used his mobile to warn Newman, then Tweed, not to react when the jeep flashed past – unless it drove inside the amphitheatre. If it did that they'd give it all they'd got.

Harry waited for it, judging from the engine sound just how close it was. Then he opened up with another rain of bullets, aimed them just across the road. The jeep flashed past. Unfortunately Harry's hands were wet and the muzzle was aimed lower than he'd intended. Bullets hammered into the lower part of the jeep, then it was gone.

'Damn!' said Harry. 'Damn! Damn!'

'What do they think they're doing?' Lisa asked.

'Trying to make us give away all our positions,' Newman told her. 'Probably got someone behind that hedge on the other side of the road, watching. Call it a rehearsal.'

He had passed on Marler's order to Lisa earlier. To stay put. Not to show themselves. Not to open fire. It was an order which had not been received with much enthusiasm. She'd disobeyed the order, but so had he.

Inside his cave Tweed was listening, hoping to catch a sound that would give him a clue to the enemy's intentions. He heard nothing. The silence was depressing. Below them, behind the sandpile, it was getting on Lisa's nerves.

'They seem to be taking for ever to do something,' she grumbled.

'Sometimes it happens like this,' Newman said calmly. 'It probably means they don't know what to do next. We're in a strong position here.'

He didn't believe what he had just said to reassure her. He was sure the opposition were planning carefully how to deliver the final onslaught.

399

Above them, in the cave, Tweed was secretly worrying that there was a hole in their fortress. They had no one on the ridge above them. He didn't blame Marler who, almost in seconds, had established a strong defensive position. But he was still worried. Nield noticed the expression on his face.

37

Miller stood behind the two jeeps with a pad and pencil in his hands. The other four men, as he had ordered them to in a quiet voice, were gathered behind him, looking at what he had drawn on the pad.

'This is our plan of action. Everything depends on precise timing – so later we synchronize our watches. Brad, you did a good job taking our jeep past the entrance and back again.' He looked at the jeep Brad had driven. 'It's a bit bullet-spattered, but you're not. Which shows it can be done.'

'What can be done?' asked Brad.

Normally Miller would have torn him to pieces verbally for daring to ask a question. But when he was on the eve of an operation Miller always kept his temper, kept his voice at a low pitch. It was bad psychology to upset men just before they went into battle.

'Brad, you'll have plenty of help, plenty of diversion. With Stu by your side, you're going to drive your jeep straight into the quarry at speed. You can rev up again beforehand. Stu will have an automatic rifle, grenades. As you drive in, you head for their blue Merc. Go straight for it. Stu will be blazing away at random. When you reach the Merc you jump out of the jeep and get behind the Merc. If they want to shoot up their own car – their only means of ever getting out of here – let them. You'll be shooting back from behind the trunk. Got it?'

'Yes.' Brad licked his lips. 'You said something about plenty of diversion.'

'You, Moke,' Miller went on, turning to a soldier with a face which had a Mongolian cast. 'Saw where I got through the hedge across the road?'

'Yeah, I did.'

'You go into the field opposite with two automatic rifles and a ton of ammo. You huddle well down near the hole facing the entrance. At the right moment you start firing non-stop. Aim for the sandpile I've marked here on my map. The large half-round circle is the quarry at the back. That way, aiming for the sandpile, which probably has several men behind it, you won't hit Brad's jeep. Got it?'

'Piece of cake.'

'Moke, that's what it won't be.' Miller couldn't stop his temper breaking out. 'All of you, this is going to be tough. We'll kill them all, but it won't be easy. One of them is a woman.'

'Don't have to worry about her,' said Brad.

'I guess not.' Miller paused. 'She's the one who threw the grenade that could have blown you into the sky. Now, Alan, while I move up this side of the quarry you go up the other side, take out the machine-gunner.'

Alan walked a few paces back along the road, stared up at the side Miller would tackle. He studied it before he came back and spoke.

'Should be OK. If it's grassy like your side. A silent approach is needed to catch a machine-gunner off guard.'

'So you follow Moke through to the other side of the hedge, crawl through the high grass until you reach a point where you can cross over to the base of the slope. That's it. I will climb to the summit, then I can look down and see all of them. Should be a massacre. Timing is vital. So first we synchronize watches . . .'

When they had completed that task he gave each man precise timing to the minute. Some of the timings varied.

For example, Moke would let Alan get across and up on his slope before he started firing through the entrance.

'You'd all better drink some water before we start . . .'

He took bottles from the first jeep, handed them round. He was careful to take the bottles back. No attack force should be lumbered with anything except the weapons they'd use.

Miller again checked his watch while Brad, rather reluctantly, climbed behind the wheel of his jeep. Stu joined him. Alan and Moke cut across the road and vanished through the hole in the hedge, started crawling through the grass quickly.

Miller, his Magnum tucked inside his belt, picked up his automatic rifle, checked the action, loaded up. Then he began his climb up the slope, his long legs taking large and careful strides. Below him he heard Brad start revving up.

The tension was growing inside the quarry. Tweed glanced at his watch without letting his two companions see him do it. There were a lot of hours left while the blowtorch sun roasted them. It was a question of stamina.

Looking down, he'd seen Lisa behind the sandpile frequently talking to Newman. He almost wished Paula had stayed behind the sandpile to calm Lisa down. He glanced at Paula and she winked at him. Then the blank expression came back on to her face. She was leaning back against the bunker-like cave, showing no signs that she was in any hurry for something to happen.

'This reminds me,' Lisa was saying, 'of when I was hiding in the basement area with that tramp. Keeping so quiet while Barton and Panko spoke to him.'

'That was in Bedford Square,' Newman commented. 'Rather a long way from here.'

'But at least I'm here with you. I was thinking of when

403

I'd been hit by Delgado at Reefers Wharf and was rushed to the clinic. Lying in bed I felt so frustrated because I couldn't speak.'

'But you did speak. You gave us the clues about getting to Hamburg. Which were vital.'

Keep her talking, he thought. It will keep her mind off the heat, the present situation.

'Then,' he recalled, 'you had a really tough time when you were grabbed by Delgado in Flensburg. But you saved yourself.'

'I'm glad I choked him with those handcuffs,' she said with satisfaction. 'Some people would be haunted by that kind of experience. I won't be. It was a case of him or me – and I was determined it wouldn't be me. Like Bedford Square. If Barton had come down those steps I was going to snatch the bottle from the tramp, hold it by the neck, smash it and shove it in his rotten face.'

'Well, I doubt that we'll see them again.'

The light aircraft with Barton at the controls and Panko next to him was now flying some distance away from the quarry. It was a deliberate manoeuvre on Barton's part.

'Where hell is blue Mercedes?' Panko asked.

'We'll just have to hope it reappears on the road it was on, keeping our distance well clear of that road.'

Barton was as puzzled as Panko. Earlier the Mercedes had at one moment been driving along the road, then it had vanished. The disappearing act had happened while Barton was flying the aircraft further away from the road to avoid being spotted.

When he had turned the plane round the car had gone. Barton had not seen the quarry and couldn't imagine where the car had gone. If it was hiding from them he couldn't see where it could have hidden. There were no convenient barns it might have slipped inside. No buildings of any sort as far as they could see. He took the plane to a greater altitude.

'We tell Thunder?' Panko suggested.

'Oh, that would be really smart. We phone a powerful man like that and say sorry, we've lost it. He'd give us a medal, I don't think.'

'Phone Oskar?'

'Oh, sure. Phone Oskar, a man who bites your head off when you don't get something right. Any more brilliant ideas, Panko? If you have, keep them to yourself.'

'Try to help . . .'

'Panko, I'll tell you how to help. Sit still. Keep your friggin' trap shut.'

Moke had darted through the hole in the hedge after Alan, had crawled through the deep grass, was now opposite the entrance. He held back opening fire while Alan, crawling almost at the speed of a rabbit, reached a hole facing the bottom of the slope below where Harry crouched in his cave. Alan rushed across the road, paused at the foot of the slope, looked up, saw nothing, began to ascend the slope, keeping below the rim, an automatic rifle in his right hand.

While this happened Brad, with Stu beside him, was revving up like mad. He nodded to Stu to warn him. Stu raised his automatic rifle, nursed a grenade in his lap, gripped well above his knees.

Miller was halfway up the slope on his side of the quarry, crouching low. He wanted to reach the summit while the jeep careered round the interior of the amphitheatre, keeping the enemies' heads down. He held his automatic rifle in his left hand – he was left-handed. He heard the jeep take off, wished he could see it, but dared not risk giving away his position.

By now Moke was blazing away, sending a hail of

bullets at the sandpile on the left. He paused just before the jeep appeared, swung inside the quarry. Then he resumed his relentless firing. Moke thought the operation was going well.

In Tweed's cave, Paula, hearing the jeep starting to rev up, suddenly stood up, began climbing the sand slope above her before Tweed could stop her, before he could say a word.

Her ascent was swift. In her right hand she held the last grenade. Marler and Butler, stationed on the far side, saw her wriggling figure, fighting its way higher and higher. Both men were paralysed with fear for her. She was totally exposed.

'You crazy cow,' Marler said aloud, appalled, certain she wouldn't survive.

Tweed stared up, terror-stricken for the first time in his life. He had never felt more helpless, more affectionate, even thought of going up after her. Nield, also looking up, sensed what was in his mind.

'Stay where you bloody well are,' he snapped. 'Marler put us here. So here we stay.'

As he spoke he had grabbed Tweed by the arm, to imprison him in the cave. Tweed nearly hit him to gain his freedom, then realized the sense of what Nield had said so ferociously. He continued watching, unable to take his eyes off her.

Paula made a last spurt, arrived at the rim, hauled herself over, breathless but out of sight of the quarry. She looked down. She looked up. Then she saw him. A tall, massively built man with white hair. He was higher up, about thirty feet away.

She had rolled over to get clear of the rim. Now she stood up, took the pin out of the grenade, hoisted her arm, as she had once done playing netball at school. Something caused

Miller to look round. He saw her, saw the grenade leave her hand, come hurtling towards him. He flung himself down, rolled away from her like a top spinning, felt the ground slope beneath his body, continued the roll. The grenade landed the other side of the slope, detonated. Shrapnel burst into the air. A sliver hit him in the chest. His flak jacket saved him, but he felt a bruised rib where the sliver had ricocheted off him, tearing a second hole in his camouflage jacket. Who cared about a bruised rib?

He stood up, pulled the Magnum .375 out of his belt, went back. Paula was looking up. His head and body appeared, no more than thirty feet from her. That was when she remembered she'd left her shoulder bag in the cave – with her Browning automatic inside it.

He aimed the Magnum at her point-blank.

The muzzle looked to her like the mouth of a cannon.

She froze, braced herself.

His eyes, staring into hers, weren't human.

He pulled the trigger.

Nothing happened. The firing mechanism had jammed.

'You'll get yours later, honey.'

He started hurrying up the hill towards the summit. He could have used the automatic rifle to finish her off. But the bitch had delayed him. His timetable had gone all to hell. He could hear constant shooting in the quarry below, the jeep screaming on its wheels.

Behind their sandpile Lisa and Newman had seen nothing of the near-tragedy above them. The jeep had swung in through the entrance like a torpedo. Stu was firing non-stop with his rifle, spraying gunfire round the walls of the quarry. Firing at random. Brad aimed the jeep for the blue Merc parked below the summit of the quarry.

407

Newman crouched by the inner end of the sandpile. He had the stock of his rifle jammed into his shoulder. Bullets from Moke's fusillade were hammering into the far side of the sandpile. The sand was so dense none of them penetrated to where Lisa crouched.

Newman aimed his rifle at the jeep's driver. In his cave, Marler had the driver's head in his crosshairs. Inside his cave, Tweed was standing up, Walther gripped in both hands, aiming at the driver's chest. All three men fired at the same moment.

Newman's bullet hit the driver in the chest. Marler's bullet slammed into his head. Tweed's bullet tore through his throat. Brad collapsed, fell sideways on top of Stu. The rifle Stu had been firing left his hands, fell out of the jeep. Stu fought to take control. He heaved against Brad's corpse, saw to his horror that Brad's foot was jammed down hard against the accelerator.

The jeep went wild, began zigzagging across the floor of the quarry at top speed. Stu couldn't reach the wheel. Then it headed straight for the blue Merc. Tweed held his breath. If their car was smashed up they would be marooned in the middle of nowhere. If they survived and started walking, the sun would scorch them to cinders.

The jeep continued its mad zizagging. Almost making a tour of the amphitheatre. Then it zigzagged back towards their Mercedes. At the last moment it changed direction, skimming past the car, speeding now towards the rear wall of the sand quarry. Stu, hanging on to the windscreen, was horrified to see the quarry wall rushing towards them. The front half of the jeep slammed into the wall with tremendous impact. It stopped with the bonnet and the front seats buried deep inside the wall. Sand cascaded down on it. The motionless vehicle looked as though it had been sandblasted.

They were all staring at the phenomenon when Miller reached the summit. He was holding his automatic rifle ready for firing. From his dominant position he could look down and see all his enemies. He saw Tweed, decided to make him his first target. *Kill the leader and the rest lose their nerve.* He took careful aim.

Only Marler was not completely distracted by the weird end of the jeep. Out of the corner of his eye he spotted movement at the summit. A giant of a man with white hair, his rifle aimed across the other side of the quarry. He raised his Armalite, had the giant's chest in his cross-hairs, pressed the trigger. The bullet hit Miller in the chest. His flak jacket took the shock, largely absorbed it. The impact made Miller stagger, really bruised his ribs. He still gripped his rifle. The blow would have made most men fall down. He took two paces forward to the edge of the quarry, aimed again at Tweed.

Marler blinked.

Flak jacket, he said to himself.

He raised the Armalite slightly. In the cross-hairs he saw the giant's face. He squeezed the trigger. The bullet crushed the lower half of the face, blew it away. Miller fell forward over the edge, dropped head first a hundred feet. His body thudded on the quarry floor, lay still.

Harry was still alert. Moke was still firing through the entrance from the field opposite. Harry laid down a hail of fire on the road, then swiftly raised it a fraction. Moke saw what was coming, jumped up to run, took a volley of bullets, dropped. Suddenly there was total silence. Unlike the others, Harry had counted casualties. Five men had come to kill them. Two had been obliterated in the jeep, now half buried inside the cliff. Marler had shot the giant who had appeared on the summit. Harry himself had shot the man in the field who had fired non-stop through the entrance. That made four. Where was the fifth man?

While Miller had rushed up his slope to the summit after his failed attempt to kill Paula, Alan had been making his way up the far side more cautiously. There were rocks and some stones scattered in the grass. Alan wasn't sure of the precise position of the machine-gunner, so had been careful so far.

Harry was still very alert. In the heavy silence he heard the rattle of a stone falling behind him. Holding his Uzi at the ready, he stood up, facing the other way. Alan was yards away from him, standing up to get a better view, his rifle pointed at the figure which had suddenly risen up. Harry gave him a short burst. Alan, already dead, toppled over backwards, rolled down the slope to the bottom, lay motionless.

Paula's head and shoulders appeared over the rim of the quarry. She called down and her words echoed all round the amphitheatre.

'Hello, all of you. Is it safe to come down?' she enquired cheerfully.

Tweed felt relief surge through his whole body.

410

38

They were driving along country lanes with Newman behind the wheel. Behind him Tweed was checking the map, navigating. Paula would have given anything for a shower. Her body was bathed all over in perspiration. She looked back at Lisa, smiled and worked her fingers over her damp hand.

'Me too,' said Lisa. 'But one day we're bound to reach civilization.'

'Let it be today . . .'

Before they had left the quarry Tweed and Marler had checked all the bodies. It had proved to be a formality. They'd had no alternative but to leave them where they lay. Ahead of them Harry was riding his motorcycle, hardly in sight. When they had parked the Mercedes under the cliff Harry had hidden his machine behind the car.

'Next stop, Travemünde,' Tweed remarked. 'I'll guide you, Bob, so we bypass Lübeck.'

'And then we have to sit by the river at the café described by Mrs France – with large glasses of water,' said Lisa.

'Will it be Mrs France who comes to meet us?' asked Marler.

'No,' Tweed replied. 'She said Rondel would be here . . .'

They had been travelling some distance, had crossed over the autobahn beyond Bad Bramstedt, were again in

411

lonely countryside, when Tweed suggested to Newman that he pull off the road onto the grass verge.

'I need to stretch my legs,' he explained. 'Care to join me for a walk, Paula?'

'I'd love to. I'm going to get cramp if I sit still much longer . . .'

Newman parked the car and everyone got out, stretched, walked back and forth near the car – except for Tweed and Paula. She suspected he wanted to get her on her own because he had something he wanted to talk about. They had just started out when Harry came hurtling back on his machine. He pulled up.

'We're just going for a walk,' Tweed explained.

'You'll be OK the way you're going. I've covered miles and there's nothing. Hardly any traffic, either. Now I'm off to check no one's creeping up on us behind the car . . .'

'In this mysterious business,' Tweed began, 'no one is what they seem to be.'

'Most encouraging. Who do you think set those murderous thugs on us? Oskar Vernon?' Harry asked.

'Could be. More likely it emanated from Gavin Thunder – he immerses himself in detail. And I wonder if Danzer is still hiding out in that windmill near Sylt?'

'Why would he do that?' Paula interjected. 'Who might not be what they seem to be?'

'Mrs Gina France. I can't get it out of my head that I've seen her somewhere before,' Tweed mused.

'You did when she arrived at the Four Seasons. You'd seen her when we were leaving Rondel's mansion. She came out and gave me those beautiful hydrangeas,' Paula recalled.

'No. Before that. Earlier. I just can't place it.'

'Well, she did look different at the mansion. Plumper and muddle-headed. But that could have been the clothes she was wearing. That floral dress. The silly glasses she had on her nose, that floppy hat. She was transformed when she came to the hotel, even her personality. Clad in a flying suit and helmet, wearing huge glasses, her crisp way of speaking.'

'Weird,' said Tweed.

'But she explained,' Paula reminded him. 'She doesn't like Rondel – so she creates the impression of a disorganized mess when he's about. Doubt if he often visits the bank in Hamburg. I bet when she goes there she's in her career mode, as they say today. Stupid expression. Comes from America. Now, satisfied?'

'No. I have seen her before those two occasions you mentioned. The devil of it is I can't pinpoint where,' Tweed went on.

'I wonder where Oskar is at this moment? Waiting for us with a reception committee in Travemünde? And that light aircraft has come back. It's over there.'

'No reason to suppose it's the same one.'

'Yes, there is. It has a blue insignia on its tail. So did the light aircraft I saw flying when we were first approaching Tonder to spend the night there. It's sticking to us like glue. I suppose it couldn't have Barton and Panko on board,' Paula wondered.

'Rather unlikely. They're probably back in Tonder. If you remember, after the firefight in the maize field off the autobahn Harry spotted Barton and Panko climbing aboard the Land Rover Delgado escaped in. We know Delgado was in Flensburg – Lisa had that terrible ordeal with him. And where Delgado was I'm sure Barton and Panko were too. Not flying in some aircraft following us.'

Paula stopped, stood still, stamped her foot on the road. She was blazing.

'Every damned theory I come up with you shoot down.' She slapped his arm. 'What the hell's wrong with you?'

'I'm sorry, but I did have a shock when you shinned up the slope out of our cave. You seemed to be gone for ages.

And I heard a grenade explode. What happened up there?' Tweed asked.

'You don't want to know.'

'Yes, I do want to know,' he said quietly. 'So please do tell me.'

'It was a bit grim.' She paused. She could still see in her mind's eye the giant aiming his gun at her, the gun with a muzzle like the mouth of a cannon. So she told him everything. He stood still with her, listening, pursing his lips as he visualized the ordeal she had experienced. At the end of her description she broke, her body trembling, and tears appeared in her eyes. She threw her arms round him, hugged him. He hugged her back, stroked her hair. She was talking into his shoulder.

'I'm so sorry I blew my top. You're carrying most of the burden. I know you feel so responsible for us all. This whole thing is such a hellish ordeal for you I don't know how you bear it.'

He produced a handkerchief, lifted her chin, dabbed her eyes as he spoke gently.

'What you are experiencing is a reaction to the terrible business at the quarry. I'm getting a reaction too, but I mustn't show it to the others. They depend on me to sustain their morale.'

He was dabbing her face dry where tears had run down it and reached her chin. She stood quite still, her eyes on his, but the trembling had stopped. As he handed her the handkerchief to complete the job she leaned forward, gave him a kiss on his cheek, then backed away.

'Thank you,' she said in a normal voice. 'Thank you for being so understanding.'

At that moment Tweed's mobile began buzzing non-stop. He pulled a face, took it out of his pocket.

'Hello, who is this?'

'Monica. Thank heavens I've at long last got through to you. I've been trying for ages. I have important news.

414

I've been decoding messages sent over the Internet. They come from Seattle on the Pacific coast. Someone called Ponytail. I gather all the forces spread across the West, which are going to wreck everything, are in place. I don't know where. The important thing is they're expecting more coded messages telling them the exact local times to erupt. It's within the next two days at the latest. The new riots will be frightful. You have to stop Ponytail sending more messages.'

'How do you know he's in Seattle?'

'He slipped up once. He signs off a coded order "Ponytail". But in one message he was probably tired. He signed off "Seattle" instead.'

'You seem to have become an expert.'

'I just keep plugging away, surfing the net. I'm getting the hang of how he uses it. Someone else has taken over the phone so I can spend all my time on it. Howard is giving me all his support, running the place well during your absence.'

Howard was the SIS Director.

'When did you last eat?'

'Who needs to eat?'

'You do . . .'

Then the connection broke down. He put his mobile away and repeated what Monica had said to Paula. She now had complete control of herself.

'We can't do anything about Seattle, can we?'

'Not a thing. What we can do is to reach Travemünde as fast as we can. Let's get back to the car.'

Paula began to run. Tweed caught her up, gripped her by her arm.

'No running. Not in this heat. In case you haven't noticed it's getting hotter. We walk back. Don't say anything about Monica's news in the car.'

'You're right.'

*   *   *

At *Inselende*, on the island of Sylt, a fresh meeting of the four powerful men was taking place in a soundproof room. Thunder was chairing this meeting and his voice was fresh and dominant.

'I've been in touch with Seattle. Gentlemen, we're close to the climax of all our planning and endeavours.' He rather liked the way he had phrased that. 'I've been in touch with Seattle, as I've just said. Twelve hours from now the coded messages giving the times – local, of course – will be dispatched . . .'

'It was going to be later,' the Deputy Chancellor objected. 'We all need time to get home before the world goes up in flames.'

'Not quite correct,' Thunder said with a conciliatory smile. 'We need to be on our way home when everything blows up – that way it will give time for panic to take hold in the populations. But, more important, time for our respective governments to panic, to be desperate for strong leadership. *Our* leadership.'

'Makes sense,' the American Secretary of State agreed.

'So when do we leave this prison?' demanded the French Prime Minister.

'Within hours we fly from here in the helicopter to Hamburg. We are then on the spot to fly in our executive jets back to our home capitals when the moment is ripe.'

'You seem to have worked out this timetable rather well,' conceded the Deputy Chancellor. 'From Hamburg I can be back in Berlin in no time.'

'But not too early,' Thunder insisted. 'No one can predict how quickly the populations will become demoralized. And on that depends the cracking of the nerve of our governments.'

'It all depends on Seattle,' the American pointed out. 'So are you sure the vital messages will be sent out on time?'

'Seattle is secure,' Thunder said firmly. 'That is why I have refused to disclose the location of the building from where the messages will be dispatched. Now, if there are no more questions I suggest we adjourn to the living room and drink to success.'

He stood up as soon as he had said this. The last thing he wanted was any more discussion.

From the light aircraft Barton had suddenly seen the blue Merc driving steadily much further along the same road he had last seen it on. He had earlier kept his distance and hadn't seen it enter the quarry or the two jeeps which had arrived soon afterwards.

'There it is,' he burst out. 'Where the hell has it been?'

'We have it. Great,' replied Panko. 'Where it go now?'

'He's bypassing Lübeck.' Barton studied the map he had purchased in Flensburg. 'He's heading for Travemünde. Only place the road he's on leads to now.'

Barton pondered whether to call Thunder. He had given up Oskar as unobtainable. He decided he would call the Minister.

Thunder was relaxing in his suite. He was recovering from the arguing, coaxing, wearing down tactics he'd had to employ at the long meeting to bring the others round to his way of thinking. His mobile started buzzing. He swore, picked it up.

'Yes?'

'Barton here, sir. We are still in the air, tailing the Merc. Tweed is inside . . .'

'You are!'

Thunder was taken aback. He had enquired several times whether Miller's convoy had returned, which it should have done hours ago. He had been disturbed when told it had not been seen. Now Barton was telling him Tweed was still on the move. The news disturbed him greatly. They were so close to victory. Was there any chance of Tweed upsetting everything?

'Where is his car now?' Thunder barked.

'Bypassing Lübeck. He can only be heading for Travemünde.'

Lübeck? Travemünde? Thunder was appalled. It was amazing for Tweed to have travelled so far. Obviously heading for Travemünde for a reason. His voice was tense as he gave the order.

'You must eliminate Tweed and his team in Travemünde. You understand? Wipe them off the face of the earth.'

'Understood. But we have a problem. There is no airfield at Travemünde. I've checked on the map. We have to land at Lübeck and he'll be ahead of us . . .'

'Use your brain,' Thunder shouted. 'Contact the Lübeck control tower – you have to, anyway, before you can land. Tell them to have a car waiting for you. A VIP is aboard. Do it *now*! And keep in touch with me . . .'

He switched off, flung the mobile to the other end of the couch he was seated on. He emptied his glass of brandy, poured another large tot. Should he tell the others? No, he decided. They got upset so easily. He took another drink. He had a premonition. Something was going to upset the whole apple cart. Something called Tweed.

39

They had reached Travemünde, parking the car near the rail station. There were signs warning 'No parking', but Tweed had extracted from his wallet an old notice Kuhlmann had once given him. In German was printed the word 'Doctor'. It was used for undercover detectives who wanted to make sure their transport wouldn't be hauled away. He stuck it on the inside of the windscreen. Harry left his motorcycle chained to the rear bumper.

It was very quiet as they walked down a footpath and then they were in the riverside town. They passed an old and small red-brick police station which looked as though it had stood there since the Flood. The whole atmosphere of loneliness they had experienced driving along country roads changed as they reached the river front.

It was early holiday time. The rich people came at this time of the year, Tweed explained, before the masses swarmed in.

'Mustn't mix with the proles,' Newman said impishly.

Paula revelled in the animated activity as she walked with Tweed and Lisa. The river Trave was about half the width of the Thames at Westminster. Powerboats and larger luxury craft were moored beyond landing stages, ships costing a fortune. Tweed paused and divided up his team.

'Too many of us together would be conspicuous,' he explained. 'Harry and Pete, you check upriver until you

419

come to where the fishing boats are moored. We'll be in the café-restaurant I described to you in the car. Newman, you just float around, keeping your eyes open. I'll take Paula and Lisa to find the rendezvous, if we ever do.'

'I'm coming with you,' Marler said firmly. 'Hanging back a bit . . .'

The town wasn't packed but there were plenty of Germans wandering along in summer attire or sitting with drinks at tables. There was an air of jollification, of people enjoying themselves. The main street running parallel to the river was narrow and lined on both sides with shops and cafés and restaurants.

The buildings were small and mostly ancient, three or four storeys high. Several had white-painted picket fences and canopies over the area behind them where people sat drinking at tables. Tweed pointed across the river to a forested shore where two ferries carrying cars hustled back and forth.

'That's Priwall Island. I read once how during the end of the Second World War a British tank unit landed there and halfway across the island met a Soviet tank force coming from the opposite direction. The Russians tried to claim the whole island but the British tank commander was firm with his opposite Soviet commander. Ended in a compromise – we held this half of the island, the Russians the other. It's been developed a lot, as you can see – with those white blocks of flats.'

'I loved Tonder,' said Paula, 'but this is a lovely contrast. So much bustle and fun.'

'I think this is the place Mrs France described,' Tweed said. 'Where we should wait.'

There was an upmarket restaurant under cover and outside a wide spacious area with umbrellas over tables. It overlooked the river. Marler had caught them up, had heard what Tweed had said.

'Don't like you sitting here,' he said. 'Too exposed.

I suggest you sit across the road at those tables in the open.'

They crossed the road and sat outside the café he had suggested. They ordered large glasses of orange juice and plenty of water. Marler drank his quickly, stood up and looked at the open entrance next door where a staircase of stone steps led upward. He was still carrying his long tennis-like hold-all which contained his Armalite.

'Think I'll explore a bit. Back soon.'

'Look at that thing gliding past,' Paula called out.

An immense white wall, six decks high, was sliding past on their side of the river. Lifeboats were slung over the side high up. The white wall continued sailing past up-river as though it would never end. It loomed over the town, dwarfing it.

'Probably a car ferry coming in from Sweden,' said Tweed. 'It docks further up the Trave at a place called Scandinavienkai. The train going back to Lübeck stops at a long platform so passengers can go on to Hamburg or Rostock.'

Newman had appeared and he had heard what Tweed had just said. He pulled a sour face.

'Don't mention Rostock. Remember the Cold War days when you sent me in behind the Iron Curtain?'

'Yes. That wasn't pleasant for you . . .'

Marler, still carrying his hold-all, was quietly mounting the stone steps which were dusty, clearly little used. He came to the landing, listened, heard nothing, turned the handle of an ancient wooden door. It creaked open and he was inside a wooden-floored room with several wooden chairs and no other furniture. He walked across to the window, heaved it up. It groaned but the sound was muffled by the giant ferry's siren sounding non-stop.

He pulled up one of the chairs to the window, sat slowly on it, testing its strength. Then he opened his hold-all and extracted his Armalite. Looking down, he could see the three others perched under their umbrella. He also had a clear view across to the river.

'I think I'm going in search of a loo,' Lisa said, getting up from the table. 'Shouldn't be long.'

'I made use of the facilities behind the quarry just before we left,' remarked Paula. 'I'd just stood up, made myself decent, when Newman appears. I told him "There's no privacy round here". The devil grinned, said "No, but there is a makeshift privy". I could have killed him. Now he's gone off again – and so has Lisa. Isn't it nice to be able to relax here? I wonder when someone's coming to meet us?'

The light aircraft had landed at Lübeck airport, south of the town and port. Barton completed the formalities for both the plane and the hired Audi waiting for them. Once they left the airport he moved like the wind.

Ignoring all speed limits, he raced to Travemünde. He was lucky not to meet any patrol cars. Parking the car in a slot which had just become vacant on the front, he looked round and almost jerked away in the opposite direction. But the pro who had taught him years before had constantly warned.

'When stalking a target you have in view, never move quickly. People notice sudden movements faster than they hear unexpected sounds.'

'What is it?' asked Panko.

He was about to look where Barton had gazed but his partner grabbed his arm, holding it hard. His grip was so firm Panko was about to protest when Barton spoke.

'Keep still. We've hit pay dirt. Tweed and his dolly are sitting under an umbrella on the pavement. We walk normally back the way we've come.'

'Why we do that?'

'Because I bloody well say so . . .'

Barton himself had to stop himself hurrying. By the time they came back in the unusual way that had occurred to him, Tweed might have gone. Driving into Travemünde he had seen further back along the front a powerboat with a sign on it in German. He knew enough of the language to read the sign which had said 'For Hire'.

He smiled as they walked up to the lone seaman perched on the gunwale of his boat. The seaman didn't return the smile. He didn't like the look of either of them, despite the fact that they had bought summer clothes while in Flensburg.

'How much?' Barton asked, hoping the seaman spoke English.

'For what?' asked the seaman, looking at the river.

'Hire of your boat for two or three hours.' The seaman named a sum which nearly made Barton fall over. If it was a question of haggling, the seaman was starting at an amazing price. Barton looked again at the boat and his mouth watered. The control cabin was elevated near the prow, all the windows open. Barton again recalled what he had been told by Thunder.

'That's the price of buying this boat, not hiring it,' he said mildly. 'Could we look it over?'

'You're thinking of buying?'

The seaman's attitude was changing. He was less aggressive, a greedy look had come into his eyes.

'Welcome aboard. Is that not what you say in Britain?'

'We do.'

The seaman gestured for them to join him. They walked over the gangplank, followed him down into a saloon. Curtains were closed over the windows, presumably to ward off the heat. As the seaman was turning round to face them Barton struck him a hard blow on the side of the neck. The seaman reeled. Barton grabbed his long hair, jerked his head forward, then shoved it back against the wooden panelling with all his force. He fell and didn't move again.

423

'You kill him,' gasped Panko.

'Let's get this thing moving.' Barton took an automatic rifle out of a well-worn hold-all he had been carrying in his left hand. 'Control cabin.'

'What we do with him?'

Panko asked the question as Barton was hurrying back up the steps, disappearing into the control cabin. Panko ran after him.

'You know how boat works?' he asked anxiously.

'I've fooled around with stuff like this on the Norfolk Broads. Go down on the landing stage, untie the mooring rope off the bollard, come back aboard, haul the gangplank on to the deck. Get moving, for God's sake.'

Barton started up the engine. It had a powerful purr. He liked it. Panko had released the mooring rope, run back on board, hauled the gangplank in. He slipped down into the saloon, felt the inert seaman's pulse. There wasn't a flicker. He ran back to the control cabin. Barton was easing the boat away from the landing stage, heading out for the open river. Panko appeared.

'What we do with man you hit? He dead.'

'There's always the river.'

'What is plan?'

'You watch how I handle this. Watch carefully. You only have a handgun. I need to be free to pick off Tweed and his girl with my rifle. They'll never expect an attack to come from the river. Watch what I do, I said.'

'OK. How long it take?'

'To kill Tweed? Five minutes from now.'

On Berg Island, way out in the Baltic, Milo Slavic sat in his study, smoking one of his many small cigars. He looked at his modest watch, then his eyes revolved to Victor Rondel, standing by the sheet of glass from floor to ceiling at the narrow end of the oblong room.

'Time you went to meet Tweed,' he said quietly.

'A bit early.' Rondel checked his Rolex. 'We have to keep to the timetable to pick up tourist passengers.'

'There will be a lot of tourists today.' Milo spoke in an even quieter voice, spacing out his words. 'Because of the hot weather.'

'I guess I'll be on my way . . .'

'And Victor,' Milo called out as Rondel reached the door. 'If Tweed has his whole team with him, bring them with you.'

'I intended to . . .'

Opening another door at the end of a long, wide corridor, Rondel stepped out onto a footpath leading down to the coast far below. Long ago Milo had had his castle built near the summit. There was an elevator built into the rock but the athletic Rondel began to skip down the steep curving path. A goat might have hesitated to follow him but he raced down.

At the bottom a three-deck steamer was waiting for him, its engines throbbing away. He ran across the gangplank and gave the order to the captain who was waiting for him.

'Go! We are late.'

In his study Milo checked the time. Unusually, Rondel was cutting it pretty fine. Milo stubbed his cigar, then picked up from behind the pile of books on his desk a silver-plated automatic.

'You will soon be here, Mr Tweed.'

Tweed had ordered three more glasses of orange juice as he relaxed beneath the umbrella. A welcome relief from the burning rays of the sun.

'I wonder where Lord Barford is now,' Paula mused. 'And where he really fits into the picture.'

'That sheet of typed paper which flew out of Thunder's

case was pretty explicit. What I'm wondering about is the identity of Mr Blue, M. Bleu as the French call him, or Herr Blau. A strange assassin who kills without anyone hiring him or paying him.'

'Doesn't make sense,' Paula commented.

'It's beginning to give me an idea. Don't ask what – I'm still working on it.'

'It's so relaxing.' She stretched out her legs. 'I could stay here for ever.'

She glanced at Tweed. He was sitting upright, very still as he gazed at the river. She followed his gaze and gasped. A powerboat with a high bridge was cruising slowly along-side the waterfront. One small man she recognized – Panko – was holding the wheel. The other man – Barton – was holding a rifle aimed towards them. Tweed grabbed hold of her, dropped to the ground, hauling her with him.

She was still watching with her chin on the ground when she heard the sound of four shots fired in rapid succession. Then she stared in amazement. Another sliding white wall, six decks high, appeared from the left, its siren screaming non-stop. Its massive prow struck the powerboat, sliced through it, sailed over it, crushing it to pieces as it con-tinued its forward glide. Went on and on, as huge as a skyscraper laid on its side.

Tweed helped her to her feet. She looked at the window behind them. High up, way above where their heads had been, were four star-shaped holes in the large window.

'What is that monster ship?' Paula croaked.

'Ferry from Helsinki, Finland. Once those things are on the move they can't be stopped for quite a while – due to their momentum and incredible size.'

Marler appeared, after secreting his Armalite inside his hold-all. He had scrambled down the stone steps.

'Saw Barton in my cross-hairs. Saw out of the corner of my eye that leviathan of a ship on top of him. He saw it too. Made him jerk his rifle too high. Crazy fool was sailing down the wrong side of the Trave. Heading out for the Baltic you use the far lane. Coming in, the near lane, as the ferry did.'

People who had been seated across the road under the canopy had stood up, rushed forward to the river's edge, staring down. One woman was screaming her head off.

'I think,' said Tweed, standing up, 'we'd better get away from here before that orange juice arrives. Look at the ghouls, hoping for bodies in the Trave.'

'I've looked,' Paula and Marler said at the same moment.

'We'll go towards the Baltic,' Tweed decided and started walking. 'Whoever's meeting us should come that way – if anyone ever does. Here's Lisa. Don't say anything to her about the incident.'

'And here's Rondel, running like mad,' Paula said as they entered a narrow part of the street. 'Lord, he can move.'

'And don't say anything to him,' Tweed whispered to Paula.

Lisa was walking behind them with Marler. Paula stopped.

'What about Harry and Pete?'

'Coming up behind us,' Marler called out. 'And there's Newman, strolling along behind our host.'

Rondel jerked to a halt, gave Paula a warm smile, put his arms round her, kissed her on both cheeks. Then he spoke to Tweed.

'Sorry I'm late. Had to push my way through a load of passengers waiting for the steamer to Berg Island . . .'

'Passengers?' queried Paula.

'Tell you all about them later. It's not too far to walk. Thank heaven, in this heat. Plenty of refreshments on board. You'll enjoy your trip . . .' As usual he was talking non-stop, smiling at the same time. '. . . Baltic's like a mill-pond. Not much of a breeze, but there's air-conditioning in the saloon. We'll have that to ourselves. Can't mix with the proles, can we? The steamer has powerful engines, moves fast, gets there quickly. And there it is. Wasn't so far, was it?' He was holding Paula's arm. 'It is waiting for us. Captain can't move off without me – no matter how long he has to wait . . .'

The steamer was quite large, had two funnels and three decks. It was painted white and had five flags hanging limply. Not even the hint of a breeze.

'Why five different flags?' Paula asked.

'Germany, Sweden, Norway, Denmark and Finland. I'll explain why when we're comfortable in the saloon. Let me escort you on board.'

He still had hold of her arm as they crossed a wide railed gangplank onto the deck. The crowd of passengers above them were peering down, probably wondering who the honoured guests were. Rondel opened a door and Paula walked into a luxurious saloon, empty except for a white-coated waiter.

The others followed her, the gangplank was hauled on board, mooring ropes removed, the steamer began to move up the outer reaches of the Trave. As Rondel was releasing her arm she glanced up at him. His skin was tanned darker than it had been in Hamburg. He wore a smart white jacket and trousers and a sailor's peaked cap. She thought he looked extraordinarily handsome.

She had a shock after the steamer left the quay and moved closer to the Baltic. Going over to a window she looked out at the last of Travemünde, at a tall white block of a hotel, the Maritim. Standing on the shore was a tall plump man wearing a straw hat. Oskar Vernon. He had a satisfied expression on his brown face. That was when she began to worry.

40

Thunder, in his suite in *Inselende*, on the island of Sylt, was becoming angry. He had tried four times to call Barton without getting any response. In desperation he called Oskar on his mobile.

'Is that Oskar?'

'Yes.'

'What is your surname?'

'Oskar Vernon, for God's sake. I can recognize your voice so why can't you recognize mine?'

'All right, all right. Has anything happened to Tweed? I can't contact Barton.'

'You sound worried. Quite unnecessary. I saw him go aboard a ship with his whole team. The ship is sailing to an island far out in the Baltic. It will be his last voyage.'

'Are you sure?'

'No, I'm not sure.' Oskar paused, to let Thunder sweat. 'I am absolutely certain, positive. The world will never see him again. He will simply disappear.'

'You mean he will be dead?'

'How many ways do I have to explain it? He will be dead – *kaput*, as the Germans say. I can phrase it in French and Spanish, if you like.'

'That won't be necessary . . .'

Thunder closed the conversation. He wished that Oskar would show him more respect. But he felt like celebrating. He poured himself another large tot of brandy.

                              ★   ★   ★

Inside the saloon aboard the steamer Paula was sitting on
a leather sofa with its back to the beautiful panelled wall.
She sat close to Tweed and they were on their own. As
Tweed would have instructed, his team was spread out in
the large saloon.

A distance away Lisa was talking animatedly to Nield.
He seemed to hang on her every word. Newman was
chatting to Butler and Rondel at the far end of the saloon.
Marler, typically, sat by himself close to the door, gazing
round, apparently idly.

'I saw Oskar on the quayside as we were leaving,' Paula
said in a low voice. 'He looked very pleased with himself,
as though everything was going according to plan. As I
was turning away he even gave the steamer a little wave
of his hand. I didn't like that.'

'Well, at least we know where he is. And he's not on the
ship,' Tweed replied reassuringly.

Paula lapsed into silence. She had an awful feeling that
they were trapped. She found it difficult to keep still. Getting up, she stared out of a window. Rondel joined her.

'When do we see Berg Island?' she enquired.

'Soon after we can no longer see the German shore. It
is very distant now.'

'Can we see any shore from the island?'

'No. Perhaps I should explain to Tweed and yourself
how Milo came to buy the island.'

He guided her back to the sofa where Tweed was sitting,
placed himself between them. On tables there were the
remains of sandwiches, coffee pots and cups, buckets of
ice containing champagne bottles. Paula had eaten a few
sandwiches and had drunk only water.

'Many years ago,' Rondel began, 'Berg Island was dis-
puted, that is, its ownership, by Germany, Sweden, Denmark, Finland and even Norway. The trouble was, it is so

                              430

far out it wasn't near the coastal waters of any of those nations. They just didn't want one of the others to have it. Milo heard about the dispute, visited each capital, put a plan to them. He suggested paying each of them just enough to make them feel agreeable. The island would pass into his hands. At their request, he agreed tourists could visit Berg – but only about a quarter of the island. And they would have to board the steamer at Travemünde. He even paid for the steamer – to give him more control. Hence the tourists who came with us.'

'How long does the agreement last?' asked Tweed.

'Until the end of next month. Then no more tourists and Berg is ours for ever.'

'Milo is clever,' Tweed commented. 'Do any shipping routes pass near here?'

'None.'

Rondel stood up, smiled down at Paula, asked her to come with him.

'Why?' she wanted to know.

'To see the island. Look out of the window. Germany is gone, can't be seen. Follow me.'

Tweed, although not invited, accompanied them. Rondel led them out into the enclosed corridor outside the saloon, walked a short way, turned into a passage crossing to the port side. He gestured towards a large window, stood back.

Paula gazed in awe. Less than half a mile away a mountain seemed to rise out of the placid sea. It was unexpectedly green and near the summit was perched a massive castle. Beside it and rising higher than the summit was a large square chimney-like structure of stone. As they came closer she saw palm trees and huge cacti. Nearby were large cones of glass.

'It looks like a tropical paradise,' she said dreamily. 'But how do tropical things survive the winter?'

'Milo's idea. Those cones of perspex have heaters inside

431

them. When the temperature drops the guards lift the cones and place them over the palms and cacti. Then we turn on the heaters.'

'The guards?' she queried, looking at him.

'Vandals occasionally try to come ashore. The guards have loaded rifles, fire over their heads.'

'Where do you get guards willing to live such a lonely life?'

'They're Slovaks. They know just enough English for us to give them orders. I'd better go – we'll soon be landing.'

'Paula,' Tweed said quietly when they were alone. 'You must always stay by my side from now on. Always.'

'This island worries you?'

'Just a precaution . . .'

When the steamer had berthed at a quay they had to wait as the tourists were escorted ashore. In several languages they heard Rondel giving them instructions. They must keep to the paths marked with arrows. On no account must they wander into areas marked *Verboten*.

He led them off the steamer up a flight of steps that ended at the face of the mountain wall, rising sheer up above them. Paula looked up and felt a twinge of vertigo. With a flourish Rondel showed them wide double doors let into the base of the cliff. He pressed four figures in a combination box. She watched carefully. 3591. The doors opened and revealed an elevator the size of a cargo lift. All the walls were covered with mirrors, the floor had a deep pile carpet. It reminded her of the elevator in a five-star hotel. They all went inside and had plenty of room. The doors closed, the elevator began a slow ascent.

When the doors opened they walked into a spacious living room. Rondel guided them to another door, knocked on it, opened it and they walked into a long oblong study.

At the far end the wall was a sheet of glass with a panoramic view across the intense blue of the empty Baltic. Behind a desk within yards of the window sat Milo Slavic. He rose to his feet.

'Mr Tweed, welcome to Berg Island. You and I must talk. Do you mind if we go outside now?'

'I would like to do that. But may I bring Paula, my assistant, with me?'

'Miss Grey will also be welcome. If you will follow me.' He turned round just before they left the study. 'Blondel, please entertain our guests.'

Blondel. Paula saw a flash of annoyance cross the Frenchman's face. He quickly suppressed it and bowed his assent.

'This is it,' Paula said to herself.

Milo Slavic, heavier built than Tweed, seemed taller standing up. He wore a smart pale linen jacket and trousers, buttoned up at a high collar which circled his neck. It reminded Paula of pictures she had seen of commissars.

Leaving the study by another door, which clicked locked when he closed it, he guided them along a wide corridor with large rooms on either side and windows which allowed you to see inside. He paused before one window and, looking beyond it, Paula saw a huge room. Inside, girls in white smocks sat in front of computers.

'My decoding room,' Milo explained. 'They constantly surf – horrible word – the foul Internet, searching for coded messages, which they decode and bring to me. We are on the edge of a catastrophic disaster across the West unless we act quickly. I gathered from our earlier conversation that you don't agree with powerful dictatorships – of the kind that Iron Fist Thunder plans for the key countries in the West.'

'No, I don't.'

'A lot of sensible people feel we need more discipline – in schools, in the medical systems, on the streets. I agree. Thunder is exploiting this feeling to seize total power. It is all about *power*. It has to be stopped and I have worked night and day to establish a weapon which will destroy the insidious Internet. Come with me, both of you.'

He walked further down the corridor, stopped at a closed door on the other side. It was made of steel and had a combination box like the one at the bottom of the elevator, but much larger. He looked at Tweed, at Paula.

'Watch me carefully. Memorize the code.'

Paula repeated it to herself inside her head as Milo slowly pressed numbers. 8925751. Taking out a notepad she wrote it down. Milo raised his thick bushy eyebrows. She showed him the pad. She had recorded the code backwards.

'Very clever,' he said with a smile.

The door opened automatically. He immediately pressed a red button set into the door jamb, only visible with the door open.

'When we really operate the system loud buzzers go off in the coding room. The staff immediately evacuate so they do not suffer from what happens to the screens. But by pressing that red button I have turned off the buzzers. Let me show you . . .'

It was a small room, occupied only by a strange circular machine with three levers projecting from it. The door had closed behind them. They walked over to the machine.

'Watch again carefully. But before I forget, here is a duplicate key to gain access in here.'

He handed it to Tweed, who held it in his hand. He asked a question.

'Why do I need this?'

'In case something happens to me.'

Milo had spoken the words calmly, as though it was something which didn't really concern him. But the words chilled Paula. She studied his large, granite-like lined face. It reminded her of something. Then she remembered. It reminded her of pictures she had seen of Old Testament prophets.

'But where do you use this key?' Tweed asked.

'I am about to demonstrate.' He gazed at Tweed. 'Come closer, both of you.' He walked the few paces to the circular machine. 'Again, watch carefully. The sequence is important.'

Instead of pulling down the first lever on the left, as Paula expected, he pulled down the lever on the extreme right, then the lever on the extreme left. The lever in the centre was the only one with a red handle. He told them to look up as he carefully pulled the centre lever only halfway down.

Paula looked up. She saw for the first time a huge glass dome above the ceiling. Looking through it, she could see the chimney-like structure she'd noticed as they'd approached the island on the steamer. A thick steel pole emerged from the chimney's top, extended itself higher, stopped. At the top of the pole was an incredible array of dishes, facing in different directions. Each dish had a complex of wires protruding from it.

'Now look here, please,' Milo said.

He pointed to the central lever, which remained at right angles to the floor.

'When I pull that lever right down, the system operates and every Internet system in the West is destroyed. Also many further east. Have you understood?'

'Yes. It is quite clear how it is set in motion,' Tweed assured him.

Milo was returning the levers to their original positions. Paula, looking up again, saw the pole and its dishes slide down out of sight inside the chimney. She looked at Milo, who had closed the machine's door, had locked it, pocketed the key. Tweed, still holding the duplicate key in the palm of his hand, looked at it.

'You really want me to keep this?'

'I insist.' He took hold of Tweed's arm, squeezed it warmly. 'You are one of the very few people I can trust. I have had you thoroughly investigated for several years. Now, let us go into the garden and enjoy a little chat, the three of us.'

He had just closed the outer steel door, after pressing the concealed red button again, when Lisa appeared. Milo took her by the arm.

'You will join us. We go for a short walk. How are they getting on in my study?'

'Enjoying themselves. Rondel keeps telling jokes and has us all in stitches.' She paused. 'Oh, Harry Butler said he needed some fresh air. He went outside.'

Ah, Tweed thought, there is something in the atmosphere Harry doesn't like. He's positioning himself so he can intervene if necessary. I wonder why?

41

At the end of the corridor Milo opened a door and they stepped out into the open. Paula gasped. The curving pathway ahead led through a jungle of exotic plants, each with a perspex cone close to it. The pathway Milo led them along crossed the spine of the summit. On each side, beyond a railing, the land dropped away down to the sea. She looked first to her right. What she saw gave her a shock. She couldn't believe it.

She could see the quay, tiny it was so far down, the quay where the steamer had berthed. There was no steamer. It had gone. Milo was ahead with Tweed by his side. Lisa was behind them, in front of Paula. She decided she had to warn Tweed.

'Milo,' she called out. 'The steamer has gone. We were returning to the mainland aboard it. What is happening?'

Milo stopped, turned round. He had a strange smile on his face. He looked at Tweed who had turned round to look at Paula.

'Paula is disconcerted. She thinks I'm keeping you on the island as prisoners. I can see it in her expression. But she hasn't looked the other way.'

Paula quickly looked down over the other railing. Again a slope sheered down. But instead of the shore plunging into the sea, which frothed gently against the island, she saw a long wide platform extending a long way to the east,

437

a platform of concrete. At the end was a large private jet, a Gulfstream.

'That is how you will leave Berg Island,' Milo called out to her. 'If Tweed wishes to return direct to Hamburg the Gulfstream will take you all there. Blondel uses it a lot. You feel better now, Paula? You again have confidence in me?'

'Of course. It was just that . . .' She felt confused. '. . . As we came in the steamer . . .'

'I understand your surprise. I assume the tourists found it too hot down there and were happy to return early . . .'

Tweed was still looking back when Lisa gave a little dance of joy. She waved her arms, lifted them up towards the clear blue sky. Tweed continued staring at her and she stopped dancing and waving her arms. They walked a short distance further and entered a large grove surrounded by palm trees. A semi-circular banquette ran half way round the grove. On a table were glasses covered with tissue paper, bottles, sandwiches in cartons. They sat down.

'Milo,' Tweed began, 'when you said the Internet will be destroyed by your highly advanced system surely it could be repaired – the Internet, I mean?'

'Not for years. The Internet is linked to the telephone system. The telephone system will also be wiped out – and that will take years to build again. You know that certain satellites orbiting the earth are also linked to the phone system. Those satellites also will be rendered useless. We will go back to how we were in the pre-1900 era. That will be a good thing.'

'Why?'

'You are so busy I doubt you've had the time to trawl – better word than "surf" – the Internet. We know Thunder is using it – Thunder and his friends – to send coded orders to hundreds of brigands waiting to send our world up in flames. Soon it would be used by terrorists to plot their campaigns of murder and mayhem. Then, not to mention

438

the explicit sexual programmes which appear on it, it has become the lifeline for paedophiles to communicate with each other. The Internet is *evil* – and is it a good thing that nations can communicate with each other other in seconds? I think not. It will lead to wars.'

'You make a powerful case against it.' Tweed looked at Lisa. 'Now what do you think, Mrs France?'

'I think . . .'

Lisa stopped speaking, looked embarrassed, at a loss for how to reply, flushed deeply. She sat staring at Tweed.

'He's found out our secret,' Milo said and chuckled. 'I should have guessed this would happen. Paula?'

'I'm all at sea, don't know what's happening.'

'Then I'll bring you ashore,' said Tweed. 'When we first met her at the mansion outside Hamburg she had disguised herself with clothes much too large for her, a huge straw hat under which she hid her glorious red hair. When she came to see us in my room at Tonder she used a different disguise. I'm sure her flaming red mane was rolled up, tied back behind her head, hidden under a black wig. She wore glasses suitable for a headmistress. She had tinted contact lenses to change the colour of her eyes. Maybe she's had acting experience.'

'I have,' Lisa said quietly, 'at a drama school when I was living in London. Milo suggested the idea. I always pack flying kit in my case, hoping an opportunity to fly will crop up. When I left your room, Newman went back to his and I slipped in to mine, changed my clothes. How did you spot me, Tweed?'

'Your body language,' he said.

'Lisa,' said Milo, 'is my daughter. For years I was so busy building up the Zurcher Kredit I never thought of marriage. Then I met a brilliant German woman whose mind – as well as appearance – entranced me. We married quickly. Helga was born first, her intellect very limited.

Lisa who came later is also the result of that marriage. My wife died suddenly a number of years ago.'

'Milo,' Lisa said quietly, 'thought I could assess you better if you did not know who I really was. Few people do.'

'When do you propose to operate your system?' Tweed asked after glancing at his watch.

'I understand from messages from Seattle we have decoded we have two or three days.'

'Then I have grim news for you. The latest messages one of my staff in London decoded warned that the timing for chaos was imminent. Two or three days? We may have only two or three *hours* left.'

Milo jumped up, startled, his expression full of anxiety. He suggested that they hurry back to his study.

'You know there is a meeting on Sylt taking place?' Milo asked as they walked rapidly back.

'I do know all about that. Thunder and three other powerful men.'

'I have made arrangements about Sylt.'

'What arrangements?' Tweed asked.

'We can discuss those later. Those four villains.'

'Didn't you know there is a fifth man, as yet unidentified?'

As they continued hurrying along the path back to the castle, Tweed explained tersely the scene he had witnessed while hiding inside the windmill.

'So there is definitely a fifth man,' he concluded.

'Oh, my God!' Milo clapped a hand to his forehead. 'Then we are all in great danger.'

42

They went back into the castle along the corridor and Milo, who had been hurrying, slowed down. He had a large body with small feet and now he walked in his normal manner, padding forward with slow deliberate steps. He reminded Paula of a tiger stalking its prey. Something different about his mood too. She began to feel tense and wondered why.

'That's the laboratory where the scientists work,' he said.

She looked through the windows. Inside the large room were a number of men in white coats. On metal-topped tables were various pieces of advanced equipment she didn't recognize.

'Don't forget to press the red button,' Milo warned as they passed the steel door, 'unless it's an emergency. Then the girls need to get away from their screens damn quick.'

Behind their host Tweed looked at his watch. He was hoping Milo would operate his extraordinary system soon. They were running out of time. They entered the oblong study and a babble of voices greeted them. Rondel was performing as usual, making Paula laugh as he walked placing one foot in front of the other without losing his balance.

'We have things to discuss,' Milo said in a grim voice.

'All joy ceases from now on, ladies and gentlemen,' Rondel called out. 'Serious business is afoot . . .'

'Please keep quiet, Blondel,' Milo said severely. 'This is no laughing matter.'

'Everyone stand to attention,' Rondel called out.

Milo ignored him, sat behind his desk which was fairly close to the vast picture window at the other end of the study. Paula noticed Milo's desk was piled high with a muddle of books. She froze. Milo had put a cigar in his mouth and picked up a silver-plated automatic. Milo swivelled his eyes, sensing she was watching him.

'No call for alarm, my dear.'

He aimed the automatic at the far wall. He pressed the trigger. A small flame spurted up from the top of the muzzle. He moved it round the tip of his cigar, began puffing it. He dropped the 'automatic' back into the muddle of books, looked at her.

'It is just a lighter. My late wife had it designed for me in London. It is one of my most precious possessions.'

'It's so original,' Paula said.

'And this is so original,' Rondel burst out, as though he wished to hold the stage. He was pointing at the huge picture window comprising the end wall. 'You thought it was ordinary glass?'

'Yes, I did,'

'Milo had it made in the Czech Republic to his own specification. It's quite thin glass but very strong. If I threw a paperweight through it all you would see would be the exact hole, the shape of the paperweight. So repairing it would be simple – using the same type of glass.'

'I thought it had great clarity.'

'We have serious matters to discuss immediately,' interjected Milo. 'Tweed has told me the final messages informing the bandits when to wreck major cities will be sent out within hours.'

'Really?'

There was a sceptical note in the way Rondel spoke.

'You don't believe it, then?' Milo suggested.

'I do believe you have shown him the system you designed inside the chimney. The *diabolical* system.'

'Diabolical?' Tweed enquired.

Everyone, including Tweed, was now seated on the banquette that ran under the wall at the far end of the room, the wall opposite the special window. They had been ushered to the banquette by Rondel when they re-entered the study. In front of the banquette was a long table. On it were Meissen gold-rimmed plates with gold knives, forks and spoons. Each plate contained mouth-watering food. There were various glasses, buckets of ice with bottles of champagne, bottles of chilled white wine, wicker baskets with bottles of red wine resting at an angle, carafes of water.

'Diabolical,' Rondel repeated. 'He probably told you it was a system designed to destroy the Internet. He didn't, I am sure, tell you it is something different. Milo thinks the world has become a rotten place. The system inside the locked room is equipped with long-distance missiles. One is aimed at London, another at Paris, another at Berlin, and a fourth is aimed at Amsterdam. Each missile contains a huge quantity of poison gas.'

Paula stared at the place next to her which was unoccupied. Obviously meant for Harry Butler. She felt chilled by what Rondel had told them. She looked at Milo. He was sitting hunched behind his desk, his large body very still, his eyes gazing straight ahead at the blank wall opposite him. Oh, my God, she thought. We've got it all wrong.

43

Outside the study in the open air Harry stood leaning against the end wall. Beyond it was the special window, which he was not able to see. Below a rail which he rested his hands on the mountain wall fell sheer to the Baltic far below. At his feet was the hold-all containing the Uzi.

Harry had been bored by the conversation. He preferred action, or words concerned with what they would do next. He could hear nothing from inside the soundproofed study and was glad of it.

Harry had never suffered from even a hint of vertigo. So he looked down the precipitous drop frequently, watching the thin white line of surf breaking gently at the base of the cliff. A faint breeze had blown up. He thought the vertical drop was impressive.

Earlier he had worried when he saw the quay they had berthed at was empty. The steamer had gone. Later he saw at the far end of the castle Tweed and Paula emerging along the footpath with their host and Lisa.

He had seen both Tweed and Paula in turn glance down at the empty quay and then continue to walk away. As Tweed must have seen the empty quay and appeared to be enjoying himself, Harry stopped worrying. There must be some other quay on the north side he couldn't see, some other ship to take them home.

The sun was still very hot and he soaked it up. At times his eyes closed and he was almost asleep, standing up.

*　　*　　*

Milo took another puff at his cigar. He was still gazing at the far wall. He tipped ash into a crystal ashtray, took another puff. The silence inside the room was dreadful. It was as though no one dared to be the next to speak.

Paula glanced at Tweed. He sat very still, his eyes half closed. In her agitation she wanted to nudge him, to make him pay more attention, to speak, to say something, anything. She looked at Milo. He also sat very still except for the movement of one hand to tap ash from his cigar. How could they have made the fatal mistake of trusting this weird man? She remembered seeing Oskar on the Travemünde shore, how he had given a small wave which had seemed so final. Goodbye, for ever. Oskar had known the truth.

She switched her gaze to Rondel. He stood with his arms folded. His tall trim figure, his handsome face, were silhouetted against the huge picture window. Why didn't *he* say something?

Then she had another frightening thought. The key Milo had given to Tweed. A duplicate? It was a fake key that would never open that ghastly door. Milo was intelligent, highly intelligent, and wily. He had lulled any suspicions Tweed might have harboured.

It all added up as her thoughts raced through her mind. A rotten world that had to be destroyed. That had been the gist of what Milo had said to Tweed's face. Alone on this grim rock, Milo had brooded on the state of the world, had decided it no longer deserved to exist. Yes, it all made sense.

'Poison gas?' Milo said suddenly in a quiet voice.

'Worse, I suspect,' Rondel said savagely. 'Some of your scientists have been experimenting with bubonic plague. I wondered why they were ever engaged on such a project.

446

Now I see it all, too late. Some, maybe all, the missiles will be filled with bubonic plague.'

Paula's mind reeled with horror. Milo still sat calmly smoking his cigar. The sheer callousness of the hunched man appalled her. He must be the most evil man in the world, she thought. When the missiles fell, aircraft would take off to escape doom – carrying with them the plague to America, the Far East and God knew where else. She felt she couldn't move. Maybe that was why Tweed was sitting so motionless. The same terrible thoughts had been running through his mind.

Then she remembered the Slovak guards they had seen with rifles. They would be under the command of Milo. Maybe he spoke their language fluently. He had said he came from Slovenia. That was not very far from Slovakia. Milo Slavic. A very Balkan name. Apparently none of his missiles were aimed at the Balkan region. Then Milo, who had smoked half his cigar, spoke, the words spaced out more than usual, as though his mind had left the realm of sanity.

'Blondel is very good at telling amusing fairy tales.'

'Of course he would say that,' Rondel shouted. 'He has fooled all of us. Even his own daughter, Lisa.'

Paula turned her head slightly, looked for the first time at Lisa. She also sat very still, her gaze blank as she looked at Milo. She's in a state of shock, Paula decided. No wonder. She saw Lisa lick her lips briefly as she stared at her father.

Suddenly, it seemed to Paula that she was watching a nightmare tableau. Everyone so still. So little talk. And no one moving a muscle. She recalled her reaction when, at the quarry, the white-haired giant had aimed the gun at her, the gun with a mouth like a cannon. She had frozen then as she was frozen still now.

'One of them is wrong,' said Tweed, speaking for the first time. 'The question is, which one?'

'You can decide that for yourself,' Milo replied blandly.

Too bland, Paula observed. He sat behind his desk like a man in total command of the situation. An attitude that frightened Paula even more. A man out of his mind *would* react like that. Up here on this mountain he thinks he's a god on Olympus, she realized. You can't argue with insanity.

'Blondel always was clever at persuading people round to his way of thinking,' Milo observed, still gazing at the blank wall opposite him.

'Rondel, not Blondel,' the tall figure said in a controlled tone of voice.

'It is his blond hair,' Milo explained, as though discussing a minor detail.

'I am puzzled,' Tweed said in a calm voice.

'By what?' asked Rondel.

'How missiles could be fired from such a device as we have here. There was no sign of such a system when it was elevated.'

'Elevated?' Now Rondel sounded puzzled. 'You don't mean Milo elevated it while you were in the locked room?'

'Yes. I'm not an expert on missiles. Far from it. But the complex of dishes we saw did suggest to me some kind of radio and electronic system. But missiles? Never.'

Paula was looking at Milo, still smoking the last of his cigar. He had a faint, almost quizzical, smile on his face. He stubbed out his cigar butt.

Rondel waved both hands in a confused gesture, as if to say I don't see where you're going. Then his right hand had whipped out an automatic from under his arm. He levelled it at Lisa.

'Everyone except Milo stand up. Now! Or I'll shoot Lisa. And place your hands at the back of your necks. Lisa has five seconds to live.'

They all stood up quickly. They placed their hands behind their necks. Newman had thought of reaching for his revolver, but the automatic Rondel was gripping in both hands was a .32 Browning. A gun like the one Paula carried inside her shoulder bag. The magazine had a capacity to hold nine rounds. More than enough to kill them all. A bullet for each of them. On top of that, his professional eye noted the way Rondel held the weapon. He could use it swiftly, swinging it from one target to another as he pressed the trigger.

'How is Mr Blue, or M. Bleu if you prefer it? Or Herr Blau as you are known in Germany?' Tweed asked Rondel.

Surprise, followed by astonishment, flickered in Rondel's eyes. He looked taken aback, but still the Browning remained steady, aimed at Lisa. He spoke to Milo out of the corner of his mouth.

'Old man, you sit still,' he sneered insultingly. He spoke to Tweed, still staring at Lisa. 'What the hell are you talking about?'

'You are Blue, Bleu and Blau. I took the trouble to phone my assistant in London, asked her to get my friend, security chief at Heathrow, to check passenger manifests. Computers enable him to do that amazingly quickly. He came up with flights for M. Blon. That was audacious . . .' He had nearly said 'arrogant', but decided it would be too provocative with Rondel now living off his nerves. '—First on a flight to Washington, a week before Jason Schulz, aide to the American Secretary of State was murdered. Second, M. Blon was flying to Paris five days before Louis Lospin, aide to the PM of France was murdered. Third, M. Blon is off again flying to Berlin from Hamburg a day before Kruger, aide to the Deputy Chancellor of Germany was murdered. Killing Jeremy Mordaunt can't have posed any problems – lure him down to Alfriston, near where you have a house, and he is murdered inside the tunnel. Why?'

'You've been a busy little bee,' Rondel sneered again.

'Why were they a danger to you?'

'Because they carried confidential and compromising messages to their chiefs. I decided the time came when they knew too much. And their chiefs were nervous.'

'So we had a unique case of an assassin who hired himself.'

'That's rather a good way of putting it,' Rondel agreed, with a hint of hideous pride.

'But at least you got a lot of the money needed to finance the murderous bandits who would create chaos. Not all of it.'

'What the hell are you talking about?' Rondel demanded.

'Some money had to be sent, otherwise you would have become suspicious. It was sent from a deserved quarter.'

'What quarter?'

'An accountant friend of mine . . .' He was careful not to name Keith Kent. '. . . Burrowing into the Zurcher Kredit statements found Gavin Thunder had a secret and substantial deposit. To evade tax, no doubt. His money was sent.'

'Who by?'

'Irrelevant.'

'By me,' Lisa said quietly. 'I cleaned out his account.'

'You did *what*?'

Rondel's hands gripped the Browning just a little tighter. For an awful moment Tweed thought he was going to press the trigger.

'Clever little lady,' Rondel sneered.

'And also,' Tweed continued, 'I'm convinced you are the fifth man.'

Tweed was desperately keeping Rondel talking. In the faint hope that something would happen to make him drop the gun. Anything, he prayed, although his brain told him a diversion was hardly on the cards.

'The fifth man?' Rondel queried.

'Yes.'

450

Tweed then recalled the scene he had witnessed at the windmill near Sylt – when the FBI man had been told by a civilian that the fifth man had not arrived.

'The fifth member of the Elite Club,' he concluded.

Rondel's expression changed in a way that startled, disturbed Paula. He grinned, one side of his mouth twisted down. There was no mirth in the satanic grin. Only arrogance and triumph. For brief seconds he held the Browning with only his right hand, using the left hand to flick back the lapel of his jacket. Pinned to it was the Elite Club's symbol, the letter 'E' reversed so it had a Greek look.

Then he was again gripping the Browning with both hands, and again it was aimed point-blank at Lisa. Newman had been calculating whether he could rush at Rondel. Reluctantly he decided it would be committing suicide to no purpose. The distance between where he stood and Rondel, standing in front of the picture window, was too great. Everyone would end up dead.

'We know what you plan for the Western world,' Tweed informed Rondel. His brain was running out of subjects to talk about which would hold Rondel's interest. 'I have Thunder's outline of the plan in my pocket. It is even initialled GT. Gavin Thunder.'

'I don't believe you,' Rondel snapped. 'You're just talking for the sake of talking. Hoping for something – something which will not occur.'

'I can show you the document if you will permit me to take it out of my breast pocket. Slowly.'

'*Very* slowly,' Rondel ordered him. 'Any trick and Lisa will have departed this world with one bullet.'

Tweed moved his hand in slow motion. He pulled the corner of the folded sheet out inch by inch. Rondel's eyes were watching him but kept switching to the others. Tweed pulled the sheet clear of his pocket. He screwed it up into a ball and lobbed the ball of paper on to Milo's desk.

'Let Milo read it and then give it to you,' suggested Tweed.

'Yes, read it, Milo,' Rondel agreed. 'You always said what a master planner I was.'

'And a lot of it came from your brain, I suspect,' Tweed added, playing on Rondel's vanity.

'Oh, it did. The other members of the Elite Club made a few alterations but they were only minor changes. Basically, it *is* my plan. Go on, read it, Milo.'

The hunched figure put a fresh cigar in his mouth. Then, moving slowly, he unscrewed the paper, smoothed it out, began reading it, far more slowly than he normally absorbed a document. He picked up his lighter fashioned in the shape of an automatic. He finished reading it and nodded his head.

'Truly, it is brilliant. It should do the job, I'm sure. I congratulate you.'

Paula felt sick. They had got it wrong again. They were in this together. Of course they were. They were partners in the gigantic crime which was about to be committed against the world. Milo raised the lighter close to the tip of his cigar. In a lightning movement that Paula hardly saw he turned the lighter so the muzzle pointed at Rondel, pulled the trigger. Four bullets from the muzzle were embedded in Rondel's chest.

Rondel threw up both arms, dropping the Browning, fell back against the picture window. His body crashed straight through the glass, disappeared. Left behind in the special glass was a perfect silhouette of Victor Rondel, arms upraised. Paula thought it the most macabre epitaph she had ever seen.

Only Harry saw the final end. He heard the glass crack and a body flew out into space. He watched as it dropped down the side of the mountain, turning in the air like a cartwheel.

He watched as it reached the Baltic far below. The body hit the surface head first, sank below the surface, left behind a white circle of surf, which quickly vanished. The water closed over where Rondel had plunged into the calm sea.

Although the place was well soundproofed, Harry thought he had heard the crack of four shots. With the Uzi in his hands he burst into the study. Tweed shouted at the top of his voice.

'OK, Harry. It's OK. OK.'

Milo was still holding the silver-plated automatic so Tweed was scared stiff Harry would open fire on him. He had shouted in time. Harry lowered the muzzle of the Uzi, laid it on a nearby table. Looking round at everyone he made a typical remark.

'Whoever went out of that window has gone for a very big dive.'

'I have two automatics,' Milo explained. 'One the lighter my wife gave me as a present. I decided secretly to have a replica made which looked exactly like my lighter, but was a real gun. I thought it might come in useful one day.'

'It did today,' said Tweed. 'Isn't it time you put your system into action?'

'I'm sure you're right. Please come with me. Paula also. I invite the rest of you to have a drink, something to eat . . .'

44

Standing outside the steel door, Milo asked Paula to check that he pressed the right sequence of digits in the combination box to open the door. Up to that point she had been astounded at the glacial calm Milo had displayed during the whole ordeal. Now she realized he had hidden the inevitable tension he had experienced.

She watched him and he pressed the correct digits. As he opened the heavy door he looked at the red button but did not press it. Putting his hand in his pocket, he turned to her.

'You might like to see the end of the Internet. Stand well clear of the door into the computer room. The staff in there will rush out at top speed. Here they come.'

The alarm had gone off inside the room. About twenty girls in white coats left their computers, jumped up, ran for the door which Paula had opened for them. They kept on running down the corridor and disappeared. Looking into the room, Paula thought it looked strange – all those screens still working and no one left in the room.

'Put on these dark glasses and insert these earplugs,' Milo told her.

She was doing so when Tweed and Milo went inside, closed the door behind them. She checked her watch. From her previous experience she guessed it would take no more than five minutes for the system to emerge from the top of the chimney.

She imagined Milo opening the door of the circular machine, then pulling down the extreme right lever and the one on the left. The system would appear as the two men watched, looking up at the glass dome. Again, she imagined a pause before Milo pulled the red-handled lever down to its fullest extent. Later, Tweed told her Milo had not paused.

She was staring into the computer room, after closing the door, seeing it darkly through her glassess. She checked her watch again. Nothing had happened. Had Rondel sabotaged the sytem? He might well have done so, if he knew how.

Hell broke loose. She blinked even though wearing the dark glasses. The screens had gone mad. It was worse than the 'glitch' they had witnessed at Park Crescent, so long ago, it seemed to her. Much larger missiles seemed to be shooting at all angles across the screens. Some screens had blacked out altogether. Then she saw them fracturing, spilling whatever they were made of onto the floor. Even with plugs protecting her ears she could hear the most devilish screaming sounds. It was chaos, wiping out across the West a system people had worshipped, had indulged in perverse practices.

She thought of Monica, saw a phone on the wall, picked it up in the hope of calling Monica. The phone was dead, had also been destroyed.

At Park Crescent, Monica, sitting in front of her screen, warned by her previous experience, had fled from the room as the sound mounted to fresh crescendoes. She had slammed the door shut behind her.

Paula continued to stare into the room as more screens were shattered. In some cases the material they were made of stayed in place. These screens were fractured and showed instead a complex series of spider's webs. Someone touched her arm and she jumped. It was Tweed's hand. He gestured for her to return to the study as Milo came out behind him. When they re-entered the study everyone, including Harry, was seated at the banquette, eating and drinking as though they had starved for days. Milo went back to his desk, stubbed his smoking cigar, lit another.

'It's all over,' said Paula as she sank into her seat.

'Not quite,' Milo told her. 'I am waiting to hear from Danzer. He is close to the island of Sylt.'

Had Tweed been able to observe Danzer, standing behind a tree in a wood immediately above where the Sikorsky helicopter had landed, transporting its four VIPs from Hamburg Airport to Sylt, he would have been impressed. Danzer had waited patiently for several days while the meetings took place inside *Inselende*. He looked straight down on the grounded chopper, seen through a haze of brambles.

He had catnapped when he could, but for hours he had watched, checking the routine of American guards protecting the machine. As he had hoped, at night, after exercising great vigilance, the guards had got fed up, had become sloppy. Instead of patrolling round the machine they sat together in a hollow some distance away, playing cards.

Danzer had also noticed that a mechanic came just before dark to check the machine. He had further noticed that the mechanic took a flask from his pocket before boarding the chopper, gulped some of its contents, then climbed the staircase, which remained lowered. An appalling breach of security.

It was on the third night, or so Danzer thought – he was beginning to lose track of time – when the mechanic was staggering when he arrived. Clearly he had indulged his liking for the flask earlier. Danzer decided it was now or never. He had picked up his satchel, clambered down the slope, coming up behind the mechanic who had stopped to take another gulp from his flask. Bourbon, Danzer guessed. He tapped the mechanic hard on the back of his head with a leather-covered sap. The mechanic had sagged to the ground.

Checking his pulse, Danzer was relieved to feel it chugging steadily. He picked up the flask the mechanic had dropped, poured a small quantity down the front of his victim's boiler suit.

He next picked up the clipboard the mechanic had carried under his arm. Once an inspection was completed the mechanic had ticked the box alongside the date, confirming he had checked the machine. A fat pencil, attached to the clipboard, hung loose. There was just enough light left for Danzer to tick the clipboard in the way the mechanic always did.

With a last glance towards the hollow, where he could hear the guards singing, Danzer, carrying his satchel, climbed aboard. He then worked quickly, knowing he would be trapped if a guard appeared.

From his satchel he lifted out carefully a long black box with wires protruding. Lying down, he placed the box in what he hoped was an invisible position at the front of the control cabin. He elevated the small aerial, took a deep breath, pressed the button which activated the device. A small red light, out of sight almost, came on.

Standing up, he grasped the now empty satchel, peered out, ran silently down the telescopic staircase. He walked quickly back up the hill where he had waited for so long. Slipping inside the trees, he glanced back, startled to see the mechanic sitting up, rubbing the back of his head with his hand.

With luck he'd associate the pain with a hangover. Danzer saw him stagger to his feet, pick up his clipboard. He looked up at the staircase, fumbled with a torch, shone the beam on his clipboard. He obviously couldn't recall whether he had maintained the chopper. He peered closely at the clipboard. Apparently satisfied that the tick showed he'd done the job, he stumbled back away from the machine.

Danzer sighed with relief, made his way across to a more distant hilltop closer to Denmark. Inside the copse at its summit he extracted a pair of binoculars from the capacious pockets of his dark jacket, looped them round his neck, leant against a tree and closed his eyes.

Raucous voices woke him the following morning. It was broad daylight and a lot was happening. He saw a large trolley packed with luggage driven to the foot of the chopper's staircase. Soldiers carried it aboard.

Minutes later a black stretch limousine arrived, stopped at the staircase. Uniformed military officers opened the doors. By now Danzer had the binoculars pressed to his eyes. He checked the passengers aboard one by one.

First Gavin Thunder, thinking this was the last time he would agree to fly by helicopter. Followed by the American Secretary of State, then the Deputy Chancellor of Germany and the French PM. Danzer saw all their faces.

He had picked up the small red box with three buttons along its top. Two white, one blue. He raised the aerial as the staircase withdrew inside the machine. Then, to Danzer's horror, he saw an American soldier holding a rifle climbing up the hill towards him. Danzer froze. Movement attracts attention. The soldier stopped behind a bush and Danzer realized he was answering a call of nature.

Above the fuselage of the Sikorsky the main rotor and the tail rotor began to whirl slowly, then more rapidly. The pilot began to lift his machine carrying its valuable cargo off the ground. A squad of soldiers on the ground stood to attention, saluted.

The machine was about two hundred feet up when Danzer pressed the blue button of his radio device. The chopper exploded. Pieces of the rotors, of the fuselage, were hurled into the sky. The machine crumbled, fell heavily to the ground, lay there like a scrapyard. Danzer had expected fire but for seconds there was a terrible silence. Then the fuel tank detonated. Great orange flames flared up an incredible height, followed by black smoke.

Danzer shoved the master control box into his satchel, ran through the wood to where his old Volvo was parked. The engine started immediately and he began the long drive to the north, into Denmark and across Jutland.

45

They were leaving Berg Island. Stepping out of the elevator, the one with the shaft which ascended vertically through rock, Lisa led the way with Nield by her side. She turned right, away from the path leading to the quay where the steamer berthed. The footpath wended its way round the base of the mountain wall to the north side of the island. It was a long walk to where the Gulfstream aircraft waited on the runway.

The others followed in couples. The last two, trailing behind the rest, were Tweed and Milo. Ahead of them Harry had glanced briefly at where Rondel had plunged into the sea. No sign of anything. Rondel had come into the world, had gone out of it.

'For a long time,' Milo said to Tweed, 'I regarded Blondel as my eventual successor, almost as a son. Now, one day, it will be Lisa who takes over the Zurcher Kredit.'

'I'd say she's more than capable of doing that,' Tweed remarked.

'My late wife, her mother, was a brilliant woman. Rarely is an offspring blessed with the intellectual gifts of her mother. In this case it happened.'

'And in the meantime . . .'

'I must call Danzer,' Milo interrupted. He took out his mobile phone, then smiled. 'What am I doing? All mobile systems have also been destroyed. No bad thing. People so often used them for useless chatter.'

He hurled the mobile into the sea, watched as it vanished under the surface.

'And in the meantime,' Tweed began again, 'what will you do?'

'Devote myself to checking all the records in my different branches. With the aid of Lisa. I'd taken the precaution of duplicating the details on card-index systems, as we used to do. The computers will be useless from now on.'

'So we go back to the year 1900, a more peaceful world.'

'Yes. And I *am* Rhinoceros. Doubtless you had guessed that.'

'I wasn't sure,' Tweed said. 'The conversation we had in the garden of the mansion near Blankenese made me more sure.'

'The name "Rhinoceros", which certain powerful international people call me, originates with the Frankenheim Dynasty I inherited from that last childless head. He had plaques of the head of a rhinoceros fitted to the walls inside the main banking halls. Perhaps childishly, I never disclaimed the name. It continued the Frankenheim Dynasty under a new banner when I seized control of the Zurcher Kredit Bank.'

'There is a curious telescopic electronic system at Eagle's Nest in Sussex.'

'I dealt with that. I sent Danzer to that house when Rondel was here. Danzer, an engineer, told me when he returned that the system to neutralize mine wouldn't have worked, but he dismantled it.'

'This struggle has been quite a saga,' Tweed commented.

'With unfortunate casualties. I will tell you now I was the one who first hired the late Mark Wendover, poor chap.'

'Why?'

'To infiltrate him inside your team.'

'To spy on me?' Tweed asked with a smile.

462

'To confirm finally to me that you were a man of complete integrity. Which he did – before a villain ended his life.'

'Oskar Vernon?' Tweed asked in a strange tone of voice.

'No. We must go back to Gavin Thunder, a ruthless man with an insatiable appetite for power. Dictatorial power.'

'So Mark Wendover reported back to you where I was. And then Lisa took over reporting my movements to you?'

'Correct. She did a wonderful job. For most of the time I knew where you were – as you made your odyssey to find out the truth. Which you did admirably and with great courage.'

'Only part of my job. And Trent is an assumed name for Lisa?' Tweed asked.

'No. When she decided she wanted to be educated in Britain, she changed her surname. Inspired by a classic mystery novel, *Trent's Last Case* by E.C. Bentley.'

'And how did you come to choose Wendover?' Tweed mused.

'My contacts in the States told me he had left the CIA because he disliked some of their methods. He then established the most effective agency in America. Mark Wendover also had a great reputation for *honesty*, a rare virtue in this troubled world. Incidentally, the Gulfstream can fly you anywhere. Hamburg? London?'

'I'd appreciate it if the pilot would fly us to Hamburg. We can then catch a commercial flight to Heathrow.'

'I'll let him know.' Milo reached a hand towards his pocket and then laughed. 'It will take all of us a little while to learn to live without those wretched mobile phones. But the pilot and air crew are waiting and you simply give them your instructions.'

'What about the hired rioters who are waiting in large numbers all over the place to create chaos?'

'They will go on waiting until they get tired and disperse. The man in Seattle, called Ponytail, I understand, will have fled from his Internet screen, leaving behind the messages which will never be sent.'

They had walked a long way along the edge of the runway with the sea quietly splashing beyond. Now they were close to the large Gulfstream. At the foot of the staircase Lisa stood, like an air stewardess, her flaming red hair cascading down her back, ushering the team aboard. Nield stood beside her, arms folded.

Before they reached the aircraft Tweed paused and Milo halted with him. They looked at each other.

'It has been an honour to know you,' said Tweed.

'It is customary where I come from for friends to give each other a bear hug when they part. But I know Englishmen do not like it.'

'To hell with British reserve,' Tweed told him.

Milo grasped Tweed, gave him an affectionate bear hug. As they parted Tweed saw he had tears in his eyes. Beneath his impassive manner Milo had the warmest human feelings. He dabbed quickly at his eyes, stuffed the handkerchief out of sight. Tweed hugged Lisa before he boarded, grasping her with both arms.

'Take care of yourself, Lisa.'

'Sorry I lied about having an English father.'

'I will take you out for the finest meal London can provide.'

He hurried up the staircase. He did not trust his emotions sufficiently to look back. The pilot was already revving up the engines as he sat in the seat waiting for him next to Paula. The plane was airborne when Tweed looked back at the other passengers.

'Where on earth is Pete Nield?' he asked.

'He's staying for a while,' Paula explained. 'Lisa wants him to go with her to Stockholm. Sometimes, Tweed, you really are not very observant when it comes to human relationships.'

'Oh.' Tweed remained silent as the aircraft took off smoothly, then began to climb. 'I'd better tell the pilot I want him to take us to Hamburg Airport.'

'He already knows. While you were climbing the staircase Milo signalled to him with his hands, forming a letter H. And the pilot immediately confirmed over the tannoy that, as instructed, he was flying us to Hamburg Airport.'

'Oh,' said Tweed.

As the plane flew towards the German coast Paula stared fixedly out of her window. She could see the castle on top of the mountain, the grove where they had sat talking, surrounded by palm trees and huge cacti. She felt she was leaving something behind she would miss.

Epilogue

As Tweed, followed by the rest of his team, entered his office at Park Crescent, he saw two folded newspapers on his desk. Monica rushed forward to remove one of them. He sat down in his familiar seat behind his desk, glad to be home. Then he unfolded the newspaper. The headlines shrieked at him.

AIR DISASTER

Four World Statesmen Die As Helicopter Crashes
Gavin Thunder Among Casualties
Tragedy On German Island Of Sylt

WORLD COMMUNICATIONS

No Internet. No Phones

'So Danzer planted a bomb. Wiped out the top villains,' he said as he passed the newspaper to Paula.

'Who is Danzer?' Monica asked.

'Just someone we heard about while we were abroad. I see your screen has disappeared.'

'It started again – the missiles, the terrible noise. I fled from the room. When I came back it was still going on so I pulled the plug. I took a taxi to a firm where I know people. Couldn't use the phone. It's dead as a dodo. My friends had experienced the same thing. It's not coming back – the Internet. Don't know about the phone. So I got George from downstairs to take the computer away, to dump it. When he came back he said the dump was piled high with computers.'

'I'm glad you got out in time. I was worried about you.'

'You knew?'

'I'd heard rumours. Incidentally, Buchanan called me in Hamburg. He found the real Mrs Mordaunt had been called away to a fake emergency. He also told me they had rounded up the refugees Marler saw in Dorset – they found them scattered across Dartmoor. Now can I see that newspaper you snatched off my desk?'

'Prepare yourself for a shock.'

She brought him the other newspaper. She handed it to him, opened at an inside page. He stared at the headline, dazed, then slowly read the brief text underneath it.

LORD BARFORD COMMITS SUICIDE

The distinguished Brigadier, Lord Barford, was found dead in his room at the Four Seasons Hotel, Hamburg. He was found holding in his right hand the revolver which had fired the fatal shot. No note has been found to explain why he took his life.

'There's an express letter from him,' Monica said quietly. 'It's addressed to you but, in your absence, I took the liberty of opening it. Here it is.'

Tweed, normally a swift reader, read it slowly three times. He looked out of the window as though trying to see something. He stood up, walked across to Paula's desk, handed it to her, returned to his own desk, again stared into the distance. She read it as carefully as Tweed had.

My dear Tweed – By the time you read this you will

probably have heard of my decision. Why did I do it? Because after a long and reasonably honourable career, I made an appalling mistake. Gavin Thunder, who hopes to be Prime Minister, and probably will be after what is going to happen, persuaded me to accept the post of Supreme Governor of a Britain divided into six military areas. On reflection, I realized that, although I thought some change was needed in our way of life, what he proposed – and what I agreed to – was a crime. I decided I could only make amends for my ghastly error of judgement by removing myself from this fragile world. I remember gratefully your friendship in the past. Goodbye.

The letter was signed 'Bernard Barford'. Paula folded up the sheet and looked at Tweed.

'This is awful. Poor man. I don't know what to say.'

'It was his only way out,' Tweed said, so quietly that she only just caught the words. 'He was an honourable man. I shall go to the memorial service, if there is one.'

The letter was passed round to everyone. Afterwards there was a silence in the room that no one seemed inclined to disturb. The intercom Monica had just installed buzzed. She answered it, frowned, looked at Tweed.

'There's someone downstairs who won't give a name.'

'Tweed here. Ah, it's you. By all means, come up. George will show you the way.'

Tweed looked round the room. *This will stun them*, he thought. He spoke quickly.

'When our visitor arrives do not be alarmed. You are all in for a surprise.'

The door was opened by George, who stood back to let someone walk in. Everyone, except Tweed and Monica, stared in disbelief as the visitor entered.

Oskar Vernon was smiling, as always. He wore a bright

469

green shirt, a pale lemon suit and a wild white tie decorated with clusters of lemons. In his hand he carried a straw hat.

'Meet Oskar,' Tweed said, 'a man who helped me greatly all through the saga we have experienced.'

'I don't understand,' said Paula.

'I can appreciate Paula's confusion,' Oskar commented. He looked at Tweed, who had gestured for him to sit down. 'Maybe you had better explain.'

'Oskar,' Tweed began, 'has kept me closely informed about the enemy's movements as often as he could. Knowing his underworld contacts, I suggested he used his reputation to infiltrate the enemy organization . . .'

'Some reputation,' snapped Marler, leaning against the wall.

'It has taken Oskar years,' Tweed went on, 'to build up a reputation among the police, the security services and the underworld as being a mastermind behind every kind of villainy. Except he isn't a villain. He detests all the people he has had to impress.'

'I hate their guts,' Oskar remarked. 'So I revel in first fooling them, then destroying them. I arranged for rumours to be spread about my criminal activities long ago, but they could never prove anything. I mean the police. Because I am innocent.'

'Anything else you did to help us?' Tweed enquired.

'Well . . .' Oskar straightened his tie. '. . . I did try to kill off those two paragons of virtue, Barton and Panko. In the middle of the night at Tonder airfield I placed a bomb inside their aircraft. But they must have discovered it since they took off safely. On the other hand, I did shoot dead two men of the Special Reserve in the third jeep, coming up behind them in my black Audi – incidentally, just before they were going to kill me.'

'That was a great help,' Tweed commented. 'Otherwise we'd have had seven instead of five enemies to deal with at the sand quarry. Also, Oskar phoned me when I was alone in my room, gave me news of the enemy's latest plans. Without him we may not have survived.'

'One thing puzzles me,' said Paula. 'While I was in Lisa's room someone phoned and said they were Oskar.'

'Not me.' Oskar looked perplexed. 'Anything else strange that happened about the same time?'

'There was a man vacuuming the floor outside. He didn't look like staff and disappeared soon afterwards.'

'Ah!' Oskar beamed. 'That would be Thunder's idea to discredit Lisa, make you suspicious of her. The fake servant would use his mobile to tell whoever phoned that you were in her room.'

'We'd better take you out to dinner for starters,' Paula suggested. 'After all you've done for us.'

'Thank you so much,' Oskar replied. 'But I must decline your kind invitation.' He beamed. 'It would ruin my reputation to be seen with such law-abiding citizens! I must slip away now. It has been a pleasure to work for you.' He stood up. 'Bless you all . . .'

'Well, I'll be damned,' said Newman when Oskar had left.

'I did tell you, Paula,' Tweed remarked with a smile.

'Told me what?'

'That no one was what they seemed to be.'